What's a ghostbuster who believes in ghosts to do?

Oozing slime that changes colors like a chameleon. A demonic pig that levitates. Waking up every night at the precise moment Ronald DeFeo, Jr. slaughtered his entire family. Ordinarily parapsychologist Stephen Kaplan would have a field day with the Lutz family's horrific story. But this case was different. The facts just wouldn't fit together.

From the moment George Lutz first phoned him, Stephen Kaplan kept a detailed diary of the entire investigation. Follow him day-by-day and step-by-step as he chases down the witnesses, digs up the dirt, battles rival ghostbusters, convinces talk-show host Joel Martin to interrogate DeFeo's lawyer, bombards a reluctant media with the facts (which they ignore), and finally attends a hilarious Halloween party at the "horror house" where he and Roxanne personally get to meet "Jody the Demon Pig."

"Dr. Kaplan—the first ghostbuster to label the Amityville Horror case a hoax (February 1976)—defends the public's right to know the real truth behind paranormal claims."
—Max Toth, author of *Pyramid Power*

"A dramatic story of persistent and intelligent detective work."
—NAPRA Review

"The investigation is always engaging with its description of the strange occurrences and its uncovering of what was behind them."
—The Small Press Book Review

"The diary takes us step-by-step through the entire Amityville phenomenon. Kaplan leaves no stone unturned—and throws quite a few stones himself."
—The Houston Tribune

The **Amityville** **HORROR** Conspiracy

by
Stephen Kaplan, Ph.D.
and
Roxanne Salch Kaplan

Belfrey Books
A Division of Toad Hall, Inc.

book design by Jennifer Zehren, Montgomery Media, Inc.
book layout by Michael Kurland
Belfry Books logo designed by Lisa Wray Mazzanti

Library of Congress Catalog Card Number: 95-079154
ISBN: 0-9637498-0-3

First printing: October 31, 1995

Second printing: February 1998

Belfry Books
a division of TOAD HALL, Inc.
RR2, Box 16–B
Laceyville, PA 18623

Dedication

To my parents, the late Shirley Karron Kaplan and Sol Kaplan: My mother's love of truth and my father's genius for pursuit and scholarliness taught me to never give up my dreams,

Dr. Edmund Cohen, my dearest friend for the past 30 years, who helped me to survive and graduate CCNY and encouraged all my unusual work and efforts throughout; my wife, "Rocky," my co–author and mother of our two gifted children, who has endured my classic eccentric behavior for 17 years and continues to share my life and my passion for truth.

— Dr. Stephen Kaplan

To my wonderful parents, Eleanor Ziehl Salch and the late Edward J. Salch. Your love and total dedication has always been my inspiration. Dad, I miss you. And to my beautiful, brilliant and loving daughters, Jennifer Anne Kaplan and Victoria Lynne Kaplan. May you always have truth and beauty in your lives.

— Roxanne Salch Kaplan

Acknowledgements

We would like to thank the following individuals for helping us to keep our story alive for all these years: F. Lee Bailey ("Lie Detector"); Ed Baxter (San Francisco); Mohammed Bazzi (*Newsday* and *Queens Tribune*); Prof. David Benfield; Dr. Bernard Boal; Bill Boggs ("Midday"); Peter Boyle (WRC); Bob Braun (Cincinnati); Dr. Philip Bresnick; Ed Bush (Dallas); Craig Butcher (NBC—Delaware); Doug Cameron (Miami); Alan Christian (WBAL—Baltimore); Barbara Clark; Dr. Edmund Cohen; Gwen Cohen; Allan Courtney (WINZ—Miami); Cristina (Miami); Richard and Janice Diana; Charles DiDonato (Grand Spectacle); Corey Dietz (Dayton and Toledo); George Dobbins ("People Are Talking"—San Francisco); Myron "Mickey" Donoth; Mike Douglas; Brian Dow (WTIC/CT); Sandy Feldman (UFT); Dr. Lorenzo Fitzig; the late Curtis and Maggie Fuller (FATE Magazine); John Gambling (WRKO); John Gambling Jr. (WOR); Pat and Joy Garrison; the late Dr. Bentley Glass; Bob Grant (WOR); Alan Handelman (North Carolina); Hong (Hot Shots 30–Minute Photo); Carole Kane; Warren Kaplan; Brian Kent Kaplan; Stacy Erin Kaplan; the late Shirley Karron Kaplan; the late Sol Kaplan; Jennifer Anne Kaplan; Victoria Lynne Kaplan; Kelly Kerr (WTWN); Stephen King, author (Bangor, Maine); Stephen King, radio broadcaster (Chicago, Illinois); Jim Knusch; Michael Kurland; Jim LaBarbara (WLW—Cincinnati); Don Lane (Australia); Dr. Uri Lavy; Elise LeVaillant; Rochelle Kaplan Lowenthal; Robert Lowenthal; Kenny Lukasik; and Chris Martin.

Also: Ron McArthur (WNBF—Spokane); the late Tiny Markle (CT); Terry Moyer ("Morning Exchange"—Cleveland); the late Long John Nebel (WMCA); Jim Owen (WKHQ); Prof. J.J. Papike; Anne Pinzow; Dr. Seymour Pollack; Peter Raabe (Alberta); Jenny Randles (U.K.); Ralph Rice; Carol Salch Risner; Charles Risner; the late Dar Robinson (world's greatest stuntman); Nancy Rosanoff; Charlie Rose; Elena Saiz; the late Edward J. Salch; Eleanor Ziehl Salch; Donald E. Salch; Steven T. Salch; Harold R. Salch; Joe Sena;

Acknowledgements

Rajah Sharma; Tom Snyder; Mike Spindell (WNWS—Miami); Bob Stevens; Dr. Steven Swerdlin; Stacy Taylor (WING—Dayton); Lee Tracey (New Orleans and California); Charley Tuna (Los Angeles); Prof. Benyada Varma; Julia Walker (Pres., the Bobby Vinton Fan Club); Mike Warren (WTIC—Hartford). Joan Winston; Craig Worthing (Boca Raton); Perry Wright (WFNT—Flint, Michigan); and Dr. and Mrs. Sidney Zuckerman.

The following organizations also contributed invaluable assistance in our quest: New York City Board of Education, Forest Hills Adult Division; all the libraries who invited me to lecture, including Centereach, Smithtown, Northport, Lawrence, Franklin Lakes, Monroe, Peekskill, Baldwin, Patchogue, Medford, Flushing, and Donnell; University of Virginia; Arcadia Univ., Nova Scotia; past and present members of the Parapsychology Institute of America; AAPHR; Copley News Service (currently Wireless Flash); Bantam Books (since 1988); *N.Y. Daily News; Newsday; American Teacher* (May '85); AFT; NYSUT; AFL-CIO; *Three Village Herald; N.Y. Sunday News Magazine;* Queensborough Community College; Counter Point Magazine (Mar.'83), Wyoming, PA; Statesman (SUNY at Stony Brook); *Port Jefferson Record; Long Island Press;* Suffolk Life; Three Village School District, Ward Melville High School, Plainview; the Spiritual and Psychic Convention (1978); St. Francis College; CHOM, CHUM and CBC—Canada; WCAU, Philadelphia; "Morning Exchange," Cleveland (1980-1987); "Kelly and Co.," Detroit; *Queens Tribune; The Torch* (St. John's U.); "To Tell the Truth" Goodson/Todman Productions; N.Y. *Teacher Magazine; MacClean Magazine;* "Buffalo A.M." (ABC-TV); "Live At Five," Cleveland; William Howard Taft High School, Bronx, N.Y.; City College of N.Y. Downtown and Uptown (1958-1970); SUNY at Stony Brook Alumni Organization.; the staff of Mather Memorial Hospital, Port Jefferson, N.Y., (July, 1976) for saving Stephen's life; and the historic Caroline Church, Setauket, N.Y., where we were married.

Very special thanks to: Joel Martin—writer, radio and TV personality, scholar, media advisor and long-time friend, who helped us to see all sides of the issue while always maintaining his professionalism and integrity, no matter what the costs.

Max Toth—parapsychologist and psychic researcher, whose friendship and brilliant advice helped us to complete our research.

Regina Shanley—writer, lecturer, godmother and dearest friend, who remained loyal to the cause and devoted many hours to this project.

The Amityville Horror Conspiracy

Sharon Jarvis—our literary agent and long-time supporter, who liked the manuscript from the very beginning and helped to keep it alive, and to her associate Anne Pinzow, for her continued support and assistance.

John Krysko—our metaphysical expert and good friend, whose visualization and grounding techniques kept us from going off the deep end during the many, long and difficult years.

If we have left anyone out, or misspelled anyone's name, please forgive us; it has been a long time. We thank all of you and hope you continue to support us.

—Roxanne and Stephen Kaplan

Contents

Preface

Part I—The Case

Chapter 1

Chapter 2

Chapter 3

Chapter 4

Chapter 5

Part II—The Book

Chapter 6

Chapter 7

The Amityville Horror Conspiracy

The **Amityville**

HORROR Conspiracy

An early publicity shot of Dr. Stephen Kaplan.

Joel Martin interviews Dr. Stephen Kaplan outside the Amityville "Horror" House.

Preface

The Amityville Horror has been labeled by Stephen Kaplan as "the greatest haunted house hoax in America." This book is unique, for here is a firm believer in ghosts and haunted houses, a scholar, a pioneering psychic researcher, who has proof that this tale is not true, and has dedicated himself to telling his side of the story. But I'm getting ahead of myself....

The Amityville Horror story really began on a November night in 1974, when six members of the Ronald DeFeo family were found murdered in their home. I remember that night well, for I was there as a reporter—one of the first called to the scene. I received a phone call from United Press International shortly after 7:00 p.m., November 13, telling me there had been a mass murder at 112 Ocean Avenue, Amityville, Long Island. Five minutes later I was on my way there....

Ocean Avenue is a comfortable, tree-lined suburban street, with large, neatly kept homes and manicured lawns. The scene, however, is eerie. As we get as close to 112 Ocean Avenue as the police will allow, we are met by a bevy of police cars and the coroner's van. Soon, reporters from other media gather. This is being called the worst mass murder Long Island has known in years.

It is so warm this night that you don't need a coat, even though it is November. The scene and the mood, however, are far more chilling. It is deadly quiet. Reporters from virtually every TV station in the New York area watch. Police stand silently by. Neighbors huddle in horror as, one by one, the members of the DeFeo family are carried out. Each one. Two adults. Four children. Each in a body bag. Each placed in the coroner's van.

The silence is broken once...the horror of the sight intensifies... the body of one of the dead children falls from the body bag before it can be placed into the coroner's van. A collective gasp.

The Amityville Horror Conspiracy

A short while later the reporters begin questioning the official police spokesman. Are there suspects? Who could have done such a thing? Is there a clue? No answers from the spokesman. And the neighbors, visibly shaken, stand there numb. Just a few hours ago the DeFeos were as alive as we are this night. Now they are dead. How were they killed? By whom? Why? And where is the sole surviving son, Ronald DeFeo, Jr.? How did he escape the slaughter? Is he safe? Is he a suspect? I am not getting any answers.

I begin wandering a few feet from the DeFeo house...the murder site. I ask some of the neighbors if they had heard or seen anything. A man stares at me. Tears in his eyes, he turns and walks away. A group of children. "Ronnie did it. Ronnie did it." I listen.

I am recognized because of my talk show on WBAB, a Long Island radio station. A teenager tells me to speak to the old lady a couple of doors away. I walk away from the other reporters, their cameras and lights. I am introduced to the old woman.

"What happened, ma'am?" I ask quietly. "Did you hear or see anything?" I strike an answer!

"Yes, I heard the DeFeo's dog bark. Well, not so much bark as bay. Like a hound dog howling at the moon."

What time?" I ask.

"Three in the morning, or a little after."

"Did you hear any gunshots?" (We've been told the family was shot to death.)

"No," she says. Only her recollection that the dog was crying. It woke her up, she says. Three or three-fifteen a.m. I want to go on with more questions, but other reporters with their cameras and microphones discover I have found someone on the block who is willing to talk. I leave for other parts of the neighborhood.

I speak to more kids, more cops I know. This is the suburbs of New York City. Long Island. Amityville. I know where I am. It's my territory. The guys from city TV stations, they're only thirty miles from the city, but they might as well be on the moon. That's okay. I watch and question. I listen and learn. I go to the nearest phone and file my story to UPI. I cannot accuse Ronnie DeFeo, Jr. of killing his family, although every kid in the neighborhood tells me it's so; but I do tell UPI in my story that, according to the dog's crying, I place the time of death at about three or three-fifteen a.m. Next day that is how I heard it reported everywhere. On radio, TV, in newspapers. Later, in the book and the film, the county coroner was credited with fixing the time of death. Three or three-fifteen. I did not get credit. Which is quite all right with me. It was one very disquieting night. Who thinks of getting credit?

Eventually I go home. Three million Long Islanders will go back to business as usual, I guess. And they do. Almost. My cat dies in my arms that night. I do not know to this day what the connection is. Probably none. But...disquieting.

The months go by. The scene changes. Ronald DeFeo, Jr. is convicted of murder. He is sentenced to multiple life sentences. Is the story over? It seemed so at the time. I never dreamed that the grisly November night would become the subject of an internationally disputed story—a story alleging a multitude of psychic happenings in the Amityville house where once the DeFeo family lived—and died.

Enter Mr. Stephen Kaplan. Parapsychologist. We have done verbal battle on the air before. He has heard that the Lutz family, who lived in the DeFeo house between December 1975 and January 1976, have claimed they were terrorized by psychic forces in the house. Haunted. Possessed. His research concludes it is not true.

A hoax? These fantastic claims of the supernatural? The walls oozing slime? The flies covering windows in the wintertime? Doors torn off their hinges by psychic forces? A demon pig? None of it true, says Stephen Kaplan. He is not buying any of it.

You find, in fact, that you cannot buy Stephen Kaplan. He will not suppress the truth. Like David fighting a mighty Goliath, he takes them all on. He will talk to anyone who will listen. Yes, he believes in ghosts. Yes, psychic phenomena do occur. But no, he does not believe it ever happened in the Lutz house in Amityville.

Who will listen? Not many. People love a good ghost story. They want to believe. And who wants to hear a story of an unhaunted house? Kaplan approaches me, since I do a talk show about psychic phenomena. Do I want to touch it? In March, 1976, I agree to let Kaplan tell us why he suspects the house on Ocean Avenue is not haunted. He does, and so begins his long and lonely journey against the publishers, the TV networks, the newspaper syndicates, the talk shows, other parapsychologists, and the Lutzes, to name but a few.

Meanwhile, the story becomes a best-selling book: *The Amityville Horror: A True Story.* Kaplan does not stop fighting. It is not true, he says. It is a hoax, he says. (The film does not call itself a true story.) An intriguing battle. The Amityville Horror becomes a multi-million-dollar story. Book sales. Movie rights. Lawsuits. Counter-lawsuits.

But the truth will out. Stephen Kaplan's long battle to expose his research to the public does not stop. It is told here, in this book, in detail. His work and the work of his associate, Roxanne Salch. A psychic Watergate. They are like the Woodward and Bernstein of the psychic field.

It is not the field Kaplan disputes; it is the Lutz's story of the Amityville Horror that he disputes. The 100–million–dollar grosser. The defrauding of the public. And the real reason behind the story.

On my WBAB talk show, I have interviewed virtually every principal involved in this story. Pro and con. I have heard them all. No, I do not believe it. But it's not that simple. How was such a magnificent hoax created? By whom? How was it allowed to continue? My radio programs have become part of important testimony in several court cases involving the Amityville Horror.

But it is not my story. I simply report and interview. It is Stephen Kaplan's story, and he stakes his reputation on his version. He told it first to me in 1976. Then he told it before school groups, at public meetings, on radio shows around the country—anywhere he could get people to listen. He told it on network television in 1979. Are more people listening? Yes. Should all of us who wanted to believe there was an Amityville Horror know how this hoax was created? And why? Of course. The story was purported to be true. It was not.

Stephen Kaplan stood alone to tell the American public that. Read his compelling story; it is provocative, often strange and bizarre. Once you read it you will know the truth. Then many ghosts will rest, especially the spirits of the murdered DeFeo family. And I think you will agree with me that the true story is every bit as eerie as the alleged story of ghosts and demons at 112 Ocean Avenue.

Joel Martin

Formerly with WBAB Radio, Mr. Martin is now host of "The Joel Martin Show" for Viacom TV, and co–author of three successful books: *We Don't Die*, *We Are Not Forgotten*, and *Our Children Forever.*

part I

THE CASE

1

How I Became Involved
in the Case

Sunday night, Feb. 15, 1976

Today I was interviewed by *Newsday*, the largest circulation news-paper on Long Island. They wanted my opinion of the "haunted" house at 112 Ocean Avenue, Amityville. It is widely known that I have been researching ghosts on Long Island for several years. The article will appear in tomorrow's edition of the paper. I'd told the reporter that I can't give an opinion of a case unless I personally investigate it; and that in true ghost cases there could be some danger involved, so the investigating should be left to professional researchers. He will put this in his article.

Monday, Feb. 16, 1976

The phone is ringing. I answer, and it is George Lutz, the current owner of the DeFeo house in Amityville. He has read today's *Newsday* article and would like me to make an investigation of the house.

"I'm afraid—really afraid," he says. "We've called the Psychical Research Foundation in Durham, North Carolina, and the American Society for Psychical Research in Manhattan to investigate, too. We've got to find out what's happening in that house."

After questioning George at length, I agree to take a group from my organization—the Parapsychology Institute of America—to inves-tigate the house. I ask when he will be able to meet with us there.

"I'm not going back to that house," he says. "I just can't face it again, not yet." I tell him we will need a letter of authorization from him if he won't be there. He says okay. "How much will this investiga-tion cost me?" he asks. I tell him it won't cost a cent. We're a research organization, we don't charge for our work. We agree to meet at Zum

The Amityville Horror Conspiracy

Zum's, a restaurant in nearby Smithhaven Mall, next Friday—February 20, where he will give me the letter. My investigation will begin on Saturday night. Before we hang up, I tell him that I will do all I can to discover what is going on at 112 Ocean Avenue. I also assure him that, if it is a hoax, I will not hesitate to expose it.

I am skeptical as I think over my conversation with Lutz. But I begin planning the investigation. We'll take two teams of eight researchers along, made up of parapsychologists, psychics, photographers, and a few others. We'll take tape recorders, cameras and debugging equipment. We know what to do—we've made dozens of similar investigations over the years. We'll have to stay up all night, so one team will work from 9 p.m. to 2 a.m.; the second team will relieve them from 2 a.m. to 6 a.m.

Thursday, Feb. 19, 1976

9:45 p.m. The teams are ready. The *Long Island Press* had an article about our project in today's edition. All we need now is the letter of authorization from Lutz tomorrow, and we'll be in business.

The phone rings. It's George Lutz, telling me to forget about the investigation! I ask why. He says he and his family don't want any more publicity. He says maybe in a few weeks I can make my investigation, but not yet. I am left with a strong feeling that something's not quite kosher. If Lutz is so afraid, why would he cancel the very thing that could help solve the problem? He's had so much publicity already, what difference would it make? I call the *Long Island Press* and tell them what happened. On Friday, February 20, they run an article headlined, "Ghost Hunter Smells A Hoax." Four days later my hunch is proved correct.

Tuesday, Feb. 24, 1976

I'm watching the 10 o'clock evening news on Channel 5. They're showing a group of people holding a seance at 112 Ocean Avenue—George Lutz's house! Three alleged psychic researchers—among them Ed and Lorraine Warren. And two mediums. Holding a seance in front of an audience of millions! Trying to contact the psychic powers in the house. By now I'm nearly certain that the whole thing is a hoax. Lutz obviously lied to me about not wanting publicity. Why? Right off the bat I can think of two good reasons: A: If it is a hoax, which I strongly suspect, I had told him that I would expose it; and B: I made it plain to him that my services can't be bought. No wonder he dropped me.

But he hasn't heard the end of me. I decide to do some investigating of my own. I don't know it yet, but I'm about to begin one of the most complex investigations of my career.

In the years that follow I will be asked over and over why I spend so much time, energy and manpower to make the results of my research known to the general public. "After all," they will say, "did it hurt anyone?" I always say yes. I am a parapsychologist. I have actually seen ghosts and know beyond a doubt that they exist. I also know this is a very easy area to pull off a hoax. People love ghost stories. But each time a hoax occurs, it takes away the credibility of legitimate researchers. And the Amityville hoax has hurt in another way: it cheated the public of millions of dollars. The story is interesting, no doubt about it. But people believed they were buying a true story; the subtitle says so. This is out and out fraud—and they are using my field to carry it out.

A third factor—which I only discovered after I began my investigation—made me work even harder to get my story known. The fact is, George and Kathy Lutz's story is only one part of the Amityville hoax. The rest of the story is just as bizarre and twice as interesting.

I have found enough evidence to point to a conspiracy between the Lutzes, Ronald DeFeo, Jr., and several other key people; a magnificent effort to get DeFeo—who was convicted of murdering his parents, sisters and brothers—out of prison by claiming he was possessed by psychic forces at 112 Ocean Avenue.

This is a story that *must* be told.

2

The Mass Murder

Wednesday, Feb. 25, 1976

It is drizzling tonight, with a brutal chill that goes right through you. I watch the cars streak by on Queens Boulevard from inside the rain-smeared picture windows of the diner in Elmhurst.

My first Parapsychology class of the semester at the Adult Center in Bryant High School, Long Island City, has just concluded (rather successfully, I think contentedly to myself) and I am having coffee and cake with three of my staff who had driven in from Suffolk to assist me and to hear the lecture. Chelsea has been with me since the beginning of the summer of '74—he was a student in my C.E.D. class at SUNY at Stony Brook on "The History and Philosophy of Witchcraft and Satanism." When the university subsequently excised the course, along with my other one on parapsychology, it was Chelsea who helped me to set up the August lecture series for the public at my own home in South Setauket. The university had cancelled my courses based on their ridiculous claim that there was "no interest" in the topics. My August lecture series, offered free to the general public, covered a broad range of parapsychology and the occult—ghosts, vampires, witchcraft, Satanism, possession, UFOs, etc. My large living room and connecting den were packed to the walls with people of all ages from all walks of life, and I had to open up new sections of the series in order to accommodate the overflow. No interest, indeed!

Grace was one of the participants in that lecture series, as was Roxanne Salch. When the August lectures ended, these two ladies, along with Chelsea and a few other people from the series signed up for my parapsychology course at the Adult Center of Ward Melville High School in the Three Village School District. When I decided to open up my Parapsychology Institute of America to dues–paying members in October 1974, Chelsea, Grace and Roxanne were the first three to join. They had, from that time to the present, become invaluable to me as researchers, consultants and good friends. They were also the key people who worked with me on my first book (privately published) and hung in there with me through all of the unbelievable hardships we encountered. The story of the making of that book is one which should, in itself, be told sometime, but suffice it to say that they gave countless numbers of hours of their time and effort to help me through a project which unfortunately yielded much less financially than was put into it. Ironically, we received the first one hundred copies of that book on the very same night that George Lutz called to cancel our investigation of his home.

The four of us now sat sipping our coffee and discussing George Lutz and the "seance" we had witnessed last night on Channel 5. We all agreed that the whole thing just didn't add up. Chelsea put down a forkful of cherry-cheesecake and folded his hands under his chin.

"You know, Steve, it just doesn't make sense for the guy to allow that whole production number on TV, when he had cancelled our investigation specifically for the reason that he wanted absolutely no publicity at all!"

This was the thing that bothered all of us. Why was George playing games? Was the whole thing really a hoax? And to what end? What motive could he possibly have for inventing this haunted house story? I was determined to find out. With my staff I would find out everything there was to know about this case, from the very beginning. I thought back to that morning in November 1974 when I had first heard the name of Ronald DeFeo, Jr....

Thursday, Nov. 14, 1974

My '69 Chevy Impala stalled for the third time that morning as I sat in the bumper-to-bumper traffic on Long Island's "longest parking lot in the world"—the Long Island Expressway. Sighing, and wishing I had bought that new battery which I had been putting off for a while now, I got it started again and flipped on the radio to my favorite all-news station. I had been so tired last night that I had fallen asleep before listening to the 11:00 p.m. news as was my usual habit.

For four years now this drive had been my morning and evening daily ritual as I commuted to and from my job in Jackson Heights,

The Amityville Horror Conspiracy

Queens, where I work for the New York City Board of Education as a Communication Skills specialist. It was already 7:45 and here I was again, stuck in this foul-smelling sea of cars, all moving like one monstrously huge tortoise at 5 MPH. Groggily I reached for the radio to turn up the volume and keep myself alert.

The newscaster went on about Richard Nixon's hospitalization for a bad leg and how three doctors had been ordered by Judge Sirica to determine whether Nixon would be able to fly out from California to testify at the trials of his former White House aides in the Watergate cover-up.

Having long ago become oversaturated with the whole Watergate affair, I found my attention beginning to drift. Suddenly I snapped back to attention. The announcer was relating a tragedy that had occurred yesterday in Amityville, Long Island: a man, his wife, and four of their children had been found shot to death in their beds at their South Shore home. The discovery was made by the only surviving member of the family, Ronald DeFeo, Jr.

Back at home that evening, I settled down to read about the tragedy in *Newsday*, Long Island's largest newspaper. The headlines read: "SIX IN AMITYVILLE FAMILY SLAIN, EACH IN BED, ONE BULLET IN BACK." The story read something like this:

The killings were reported shortly after 6:00 p.m. by the family's oldest (and only surviving) son, 23–year–old Ronald. Suffolk County police identified the victims as Ronald DeFeo, Sr., 43, a car sales manager; his wife Louise, 42; their two daughters, Dawn, 18 and Allison, 13; and two of their sons, Mark, 11 and John, 9.

Ronald Jr. told police he had arrived home at 112 Ocean Avenue shortly after 6:00 p.m. on November 13 and found the front door locked. He managed to crawl through an open window and discovered his parents' bodies. He then ran from the house and drove to Henry's Bar at 180 Merrick Road, screaming that his parents were dead and asking for help. Three friends and another man from the bar, John Altieri, drove back to the house with Ronald. Altieri, alone, went through the front door and up the circular staircase to the second floor where he discovered Mr. and Mrs. DeFeo dead on their bed. DeFeo, Sr. was shot in the center of his back. Louise was covered to the neck with blankets and he could not see her wound. Altieri then crossed the hall and found the two little boys. John, 9, wore pajamas and was covered with blood; 11–year–old Mark lay in another bed clad only in shorts and shot in the center of the back. Altieri did not open the door to 13–year–old Allison's room or climb to the third floor to 18–year–old Dawn's bedroom. Both lay dead in their beds, also. Instead he ran downstairs to his three acquaintances. Ronald remained in the driveway in a "hysterical" state. Police were called, and both Suffolk County police and Amityville Village police arrived.

DeFeo was questioned at the Fourth Precinct station in Happauge. He stated he had not been home on Tuesday night, nor had he gone to work in Brooklyn at the Brigante-Karl car dealership, owned by his maternal grandfather and where his father was sales manager.

Along with the article in *Newsday* is a photograph of the house. It is dark–shingled with white shutters. A sign at the driveway entrance shows the name given to their home by the DeFeos—it reads "High Hopes." The house is described as well equipped, with a large in-ground swimming pool and a completely finished basement. The first floor consists of a living room, kitchen and an enclosed sun-porch, with the carpeted circular stairway leading to the second and third floors.

Neighbors, quoted in an article from *The New York Times* of that same day, express shock and disbelief: "This is one of the last places where you'd expect this to happen" says one. "Allison was so quiet, so sweet" says a 12–year–old girl friend and classmate of Allison's. Others confide that the only prior "crime" in their neighborhood has been vandalism of some small boats docked nearby.

Laying aside the papers and settling down into bed, I am sad-dened and shocked by the story, but much too exhausted and involved with my own hectic life to dwell on it for long.

Friday, Nov. 15, 1974

Newsday story headlines: "DeFEO SON IS ACCUSED—$200,000 in Insurance Was Apparent Motive For Murders."

Today's papers tell this shocking new development in the case: Ronald DeFeo, Jr., 23, was charged last night with murdering his father, mother, two sisters and two brothers as they slept. It is being called the largest multiple murder on Long Island in more than a decade. The family was insured for a total of $200,000, and Ronald, Jr., as only surviving member, would have been the beneficiary.

Police sources claim that DeFeo had drugged his family's dinner so they would not awaken as he moved from bedroom to bedroom shooting each one with a rifle. A police spokesman told how Ronald

9

used the rifle, then drove to New York City and dumped it in a sewer (The weapon has been recovered). Ronald then returned to Long Island and spent part of the afternoon shooting heroin with a girlfriend before returning home to "discover" the bodies. The murders are believed to have taken place in the early morning hours of Wednesday, November 13. Mr. and Mrs. DeFeo were each shot twice in the back; the two boys were each shot once in the head. Autopsies have not yet been completed. The DeFeo's watchdog, a sheepdog named Shaggy, has been taken to the Babylon Town Dog Shelter. Neighbors have reported hearing Shaggy barking and howling at approximately 3:15 a.m. on Wednesday. [I first heard this estimated time of death as I listened to Joel Martin on WBAB radio of Babylon. He had been the first on the scene to interview the woman who remembered the time of the dog's howling.]

Neighbors described Mr. and Mrs. DeFeo as "devoted parents willing to do anything for their children." They were a religious family and attended St. Martin of Tours R.C. Church in Amityville. Grace Fagan, 18, Dawn DeFeo's best friend, said that Ronald "...loved that family too much" to have killed them. "He loved those kids... He could never do it," she said. However, other friends and neighbors felt differently about the matter. They described Ronald as a "trouble-maker" who did not get along with his family. He was a known heroin addict and patronized the local bars quite frequently. "Butch," as Ronald, Jr. was known, had been thrown out of schools in the past, once arrested on grand larceny, and was a high school dropout. One neighbor described him as "wild and undisciplined," another as "noisy." Patrons at Henry's Bar said DeFeo felt rejected and left out by his family. They described his physical appearance as "5 feet, 7 inches, 155 pounds, neat, clean, well-dressed, with many girlfriends."

Police confirmed that "Butch" is on probation for stealing an outboard motor and also related this strange story of an incident allegedly occurring to Ronald on November 1. It seems that on that day, as Ronald reported to police, at 2:40 p.m. as he drove to the bank to deposit $17,900 worth of cash and certified checks for his grandfather's auto dealership, a shotgun-wielding assailant held him up at a traffic light in Brooklyn, escaping with all of the cash and checks.

As I read of this incident and also of the alleged rumors that the DeFeo family had "mob connections," I had to wonder whether

Ronald had taken his grandfather's money to pay off an underworld debt that was hanging over his head. Was it money he owed for his drug habit, or for some other, more nefarious reason? In either case, it could be the same motive that led him to plotting to get the $200,000 insurance money by killing his family. Twisted reasoning, yes, but in Ronald's tortured mind it might have made sense.

Saturday, Nov. 16, 1974

Gray clouds scuttle past my bedroom window, throwing long shadows on the beige-colored walls across from me. It is the dreary type of November day on Long Island when you can't tell whether it will rain or snow, or maybe just blow over altogether.

I am stretched out full length on my bed with my cassette tape recorder, taping ideas for the book I plan to write about my parapsychological research. Downstairs my three–year–old son Brian is ringing a bell as he rides his tricycle through the living room, crashing into walls along the way. Seven–month–old Stacy is screaming for her bottle, which her mother is preparing in the kitchen. Distracted, and unable to concentrate, I put down the microphone and go downstairs to get the *Newsday* from the mailbox.

Telling Brian to keep the noise down to a roar, I take my paper back upstairs and open to an inner page. The headline there catches my eye immediately: "A REMORSELESS DeFEO CONFESSES TO SLAYING 6." The story then went on to tell how Ronald had confessed to the murders after more than twenty-four hours of interrogation. He was quoted as saying, "I took the rifle and ammunition from my room, then I shot my brother Mark like this." Standing before police interrogators, DeFeo then calmly acted out the shooting. The article also related an incident which had occurred several weeks ago, in which DeFeo had fired a pistol outside "The Intrepid" bar in East Massapequa in an attempt to intimidate the owner into rehiring DeFeo's girlfriend, who had been fired. At the time Ronald told the owner that his father was "big in the Mafia." Other neighborhood rumors told of Ronald DeFeo, Sr.'s alleged boasts of organized crime connections.

The article stated that DeFeo was arraigned yesterday on one charge of second-degree murder for the killing of his brother Mark. Police state he has confessed to murdering the entire family. DeFeo's lawyer, Leonard Symons of Mineola, requested of District Court

The Amityville Horror Conspiracy

Judge Donald L. Auperin that his client be allowed to submit to psychiatric examinations to determine his ability to stand trial. DeFeo is being held without bail and the felony hearing has been scheduled for November 18.

The earlier report that the rifle had been dumped in a New York City sewer turned out to be false. Yesterday police scuba divers recovered a Marlin rifle in the water off the Amityville Village dock at Ocean Avenue and Richmond Avenue. It is the same make and caliber as the murder weapon and a ballistics test will be made to determine if it is indeed such.

The New York Times article for today went into detail about DeFeo's arrest in September 1973 on the grand larceny charge. DeFeo and a friend had stolen an outboard motor worth $1,750. DeFeo was originally charged with grand larceny but was sentenced to one year's probation for petty larceny on December 14, 1973. In April 1974 a girlfriend of DeFeo notified the police that he was using drugs. A probation officer, discovering needle tracks in DeFeo's arms, ordered a urine analysis which showed traces of quinine, a substance commonly used to dilute heroin. Quoting the *Times* article, "On May 29, Judge Harry E. Seidell gave probation officers the right to check Mr. DeFeo for drugs. He was later checked three times and tests were negative, according to Mr. Benjamin." DeFeo's family would not admit to their son's being on drugs; however, Mr. Benjamin (of Suffolk County's Babylon Probation Office) stated that DeFeo's attitude had improved while on probation. Mr. Leonard Symons, the attorney who represented DeFeo in last fall's larceny case, also represented him today in the request for a psychiatric examination.

Sunday, Nov. 17, 1974

The New York Times reports that the police in Brooklyn now believe that Ronald, with the help of an accomplice, was the one who stole $17,900 from his grandfather's business.

This news does not exactly come as a shock to anyone. As a detective sergeant is quoted as saying, "I would say it's all pretty minor stuff compared with what he's being held for out in Suffolk County."

As I play-wrestle with my son and our golden and white collie, Nova, in the den that afternoon, the friends and relatives of the DeFeo family gaze mournfully at six dark wood coffins in Boyd Funeral Home in Deer Park. All six—each one propped on a satiny pillow—lay amidst mountains of floral displays. The sweet, cloying smell drives many of them to escape outside, where it is, once again, gray and drizzling.

Monday, Nov. 18, 1974

I read about yesterday's wake in *Newsday* as I take my lunch break. In the same article is a new revelation—it seems that all of the bodies were found face down *with their arms stretched above their heads*. Suffolk County's chief deputy medical examiner, Dr. Howard C. Adelman, has no explanation for this. It strikes me as very bizarre, indeed, almost reminiscent of the ritualistic ceremonies of certain cults that I talk about in my "Witchcraft and Satanism" lectures.

The DeFeos were buried today at St. Charles Cemetery in Pinelawn after a funeral mass at St. Martin of Tours Church in Amityville.

Tuesday, Nov. 19, 1974

The papers tell of the funeral, attended by 1,000 friends, relatives and village residents. As the services were held, a Suffolk County grand jury in Riverhead handed up an indictment charging the only surviving family member, 23–year–old Ronald DeFeo, Jr. with six counts of murder in the second degree. DeFeo is being represented by "attorneys hired by DeFeo's maternal grandfather, Michael Brigante." I wonder how Ronald's grandfather could still be willing to help him after Ronald had confessed to killing so many of Mr. Brigante's loved ones. Perhaps he doesn't believe in Ronald's guilt.

Wednesday, Nov. 20, 1974

My confusion about the attorney was justified. Mr. Symons, the lawyer hired by Michael Brigante, has called County Court Judge Frank L. Gates in Riverhead to notify him that he has withdrawn from the case. (Symon's bid to have DeFeo examined by psychiatrists has been denied.) Symons is associated with Mineola attorney Richard Hartmann, who represents the Nassau and Suffolk Patrolmans' Benevolent Associations, and it has been rumored that this is the reason why Symons and Hartmann have dropped the case. However, Hartmann claims that he has been told by Michael Brigante that another lawyer has been hired.

The plot thickens. Suffolk district attorney's trial bureau chief, John L. Buonora, says that "his office understood that Babylon lawyer Lester P. Lipkind had been asked to take the case, but had not decided whether he would appear or not."

The Amityville Horror Conspiracy

Judge Gates has put off the arraignment until today, when both Lipkind and Symons are supposed to show up in court to determine who will take DeFeo's case. But there is yet a third lawyer up for the job: Lipkind claims that a DeFeo relative has told him that the case will be handled by a lawyer who regularly represents family members but is currently out of town.

*　　　　　*　　　　　*

The winter of 1974-75 passed by very quickly for me as I became more and more involved in psychic research cases with my fast-growing Parapsychology Institute of America. The papers had lost interest, for the time being anyway, in the DeFeo case, as the court process is slow and rather uneventful. Articles about DeFeo now were small and sporadic. I did learn, however, that *none* of the three lawyers previously mentioned ended up defending DeFeo. When none of them showed up in court to accept the case, the court appointed defense lawyer William Weber for the task. I could not have known at this time just what an important role Mr. Weber was to play in the snowballing effect begun by Ronald's horrendous crime.

The murder trial of Ronald DeFeo, Jr. was not to go to the jury until November 1975. The year that intervened was probably the most hectic one of my life. I still commuted to and from Queens and worked at a full-time job during the day, which meant I had to be up at 5:30 a.m. on weekdays and didn't arrive home until 5:30 p.m. or later, depending on weather and traffic conditions. Two evenings a week I taught parapsychology at different adult centers.

Once a month I held a business meeting of the Parapsychology Institute of America at my home. Membership was to reach thirty members during this time. Once or twice a month the PIA would sponsor lectures for the public, also held at my home, on a donation basis or for a nominal fee. We hardly ever broke even. In late December I saw my first "ghost" at a home in Holbrook. I had experienced psychic happenings many times before, but this was my first visual perception of an apparition. In January 1975 five members of my staff and I barely escaped being annihilated by a group of Satan worshippers in Mastic Beach who had set up my group to be sacrificed. Luckily we were warned in time by a frightened initiate of the coven. After this incident, which made us realize that kooks and crazies are not only in the big cities but scattered throughout our suburbs too, we developed better safety precautions for future investigations.

I became deeply involved in the writing of my book, which was eternally fraught with every setback that could happen. This was particularly true in the summer, when I was on vacation from work and could devote more of my own time. Roxanne, Grace, Chelsea and other volunteers from my organization were at my house constantly sorting, editing, transcribing, proofreading, etc. It was a scorching summer; we must have consumed gallons of iced tea and lemonade as we pored over that manuscript together.

In September 1975, after a New York City teachers' strike which lasted for about a week, I returned to work in Queens while my volunteers and friends drudged on with the book. On October 30 the PIA had its first Halloween costume party, an informal but successful gathering. I had long ago forgotten about Ronald DeFeo, Jr. until one busy day in November when I picked up a copy of *Newsday*....

Monday, Nov. 17, 1975

I am swamped in paperwork, and I should be getting to sleep soon so I can get up at 5:30 a.m. I toss the whole mess into a corner and settle down with the newspapers instead. *Newsday*'s headline reads: "SUMMATIONS STARTING IN DeFEO CASE." Ronald DeFeo, Jr.'s murder trial is expected to go to jury by mid-week. Defense lawyer William Weber is trying to establish that robbery was not the motive for his client's acts. DeFeo has admitted killing his family but "denied that he took any money or jewelry from a box in his parents' bedroom." Weber's defense for his client has been insanity.

Harold Zolan, a Massapequa Park psychiatrist, testified that Ronald had told him that large sums of money were kept in the master bedroom. John Kramer, a cellmate of DeFeo's in the Suffolk County jail, testified that "DeFeo had told him that he would feign insanity and fool the jury and, when he was released from a mental institution, DeFeo would collect insurance money from his relatives' deaths and recover money and jewelry he allegedly took from a box in his parents' room and later buried."

Weber intends to dispute this by showing that the DeFeos' safe deposit box in the Amityville bank held all of the money and jewels, not the box in the house, which had been found empty after the murders.

The Amityville Horror Conspiracy

Tuesday, Nov. 18, 1975

Newsday: "I COULDN'T CARE LESS, DEFEO SAYS." At the close of yesterday's trial proceedings, Ronald is quoted as saying, "I couldn't care less what happens to me or the rest of my life."

The final witness for the prosecution had been 22–year veteran New York City police officer Borton Borkin, a friend of Ronald DeFeo, Sr., who knew him and his son for seventeen years. Borkin testified about the last time he saw father and son together: Friday, November 8, 1974 at the family's car dealership in Brooklyn. According to Borkin, DeFeo shouted at his son, "There's a devil on my back and I have to get that devil off my back," apparently referring to the fake robbery in which Ronald allegedly stole the company's payroll. Ronald Jr. answered, "I'll kill you, you fat *!x*!x" and then sped off in his car. Borkin earlier testified that he had seen Ronald at the car dealership with a bruised lip on November 13, 1974, the day the bodies of his family were discovered.

Weber introduced evidence showing that his client had been rejected for military service in 1971 for psychiatric reasons. DeFeo denies charges made by the prosecution that his family paid $5,000 to keep him out of the service. Gerard B. Sullivan, the prosecutor, refuted this by stating the records show the reason for rejection was habitual drug use.

DeFeo denies ever talking to any inmates or guards at the prison about feigning insanity or about stealing money and jewelry. He expressed only love for his deceased family and claimed never to have felt hatred toward any of them.

I read all of this while eating supper before rushing off to teach at Ward Melville.

Wednesday, Nov. 19, 1975

I am lecturing tonight for a PTA group in the area. I feel as though I am on a merry-go-round with hardly a chance to breathe. I skim the latest murder article quite briefly.

Weber, in his final summation, says DeFeo "exploded in a wild, raging storm of psychotic pressures the night he calmly, methodically and systematically killed his father, mother, two brothers and two sisters." He cited testimony by defense psychiatrist Daniel Schwartz in stating that Ronald was clearly insane. He asked for a verdict of not guilty because of insanity.

Quotes from prosecutor Sullivan: [DeFeo] "callously, calmly and coldly planned the executions of his family, carried them out and then went about carefully taking the murder rifle and the used cartridges and his blood-stained clothing and hiding them in an obscure Brooklyn storm drain to cover up his role in the murders." Sullivan stated the motive as being the "hundreds of thousands of dollars" kept in the strongbox in the parents' bedroom.

Once again, the mix-up with the lawyers plays a part in the case: Weber charges that on November 13, 1974 a relative of DeFeo's who is also a lawyer, Richard Wyssling, went looking for Ronald but was put off by police, thereby denying Ronald his right to a lawyer. On this basis, Weber asked the jury to discount all police testimony.

Sullivan is asking for a verdict of six counts of murder in the second degree.

Thursday, Nov. 20, 1975

The jury deliberated until 10:30 last night and continues on today.

Friday, Nov. 21, 1975

There was still no verdict as of last night, with one holdout on the jury still not convinced of DeFeo's guilt. The jury re-read testimony in which an aunt of DeFeo's, visiting him at the jail, had asked him if he had killed his family. The aunt claimed Ronald's reply was, "You'll never hear me say that."

The jury also went over DeFeo's testimony that although he had heard the dog, Shaggy, barking that night, he had not heard the first shots fired in the killings.

Saturday, Nov. 22, 1975

Newsday: "DEFEO GUILTY OF FAMILY MURDER—Jury Reported Convinced By Defendant's Own Testimony and His Statements To Police."

The guilty verdict came at about noon yesterday, after seven weeks of the trial, the longest criminal trial ever held in Suffolk County.

Yesterday morning the jury had asked to review the testimony of Homicide Squad Detective Dennis Rafferty who said, "And then I asked him why he did it, and he told me 'I don't know why; once I started it went so fast, it all went so fast I just couldn't stop.'"

The Amityville Horror Conspiracy

DeFeo stood silently and without emotion as the verdict was read. Weber is considering handling the mandatory appeal but will talk first with DeFeo's relatives.

The jury's decision was largely affected by police testimony of how Ronald had drawn detailed maps of where to find the murder rifle and the pillowcase with the bloody clothes and used cartridges. An unidentified juror is quoted as saying, "That was a major sign of guilt. He knew what he was doing."

State Supreme Court Justice Thomas M. Stark has ordered DeFeo held in maximum security without bail until sentencing on December 4.

As I glance over my appointment book for next week's schedule, I notice that today is the twelve–year anniversary of President John F. Kennedy's death by an assassin's bullets. Ironic timing. Also, DeFeo's sentencing yesterday came exactly one year and one day after the murder of his family. It makes me wonder if the month of November cultivates a ripe time for violent crimes with guns. But then, in our chaotic times, any month is ripe with potential victims.

Friday, Dec. 5, 1975

Newsday reported today that Ronald DeFeo, Jr. was sentenced to six consecutive twenty-five–year to life prison terms. State Supreme Court Justice Stark called the killings the "most heinous and abhorrent crimes."

Although Stark asked that the terms be served consecutively, the law permits them to be served concurrently if charges stem from one continuous act, as they do in DeFeo's case. Having already served one year in prison, DeFeo could be eligible for parole in nineteen years. Stark is quoted as saying, "I am of the belief that [DeFeo] is a real danger to society in that he may kill again, and the law provides for certain sentences to insure the community's safety."

DeFeo, now 24, stood impassively until asked by Stark if he had anything to say. DeFeo's statement was, "I'm going to appeal this sentence and conviction. *I'll bet I'll be back here in one year.*"

*   *   *

Waving to my three friends as they drive off from the diner's parking lot in Grace's sleek, black car, I settle into the seat of my Chevy and prepare for the fifty–mile drive back to Suffolk. I should be home in time to catch five hours of sleep before it's time for me to get up and drive back to Queens for work.

The Lutzes Go Public—
February 1976

Saturday, Feb. 28, 1976, [9:30 A.M.]

I am sitting at the desk in my den trying to organize my thoughts about the Lutz case. Spread in front of me are the articles from *Newsday* and the *Long Island Press* which have been published over the last two weeks. Opening my red journal/notebook, I begin to jot down notes pertinent to each date. It was exactly two weeks ago today that *Newsday* first informed its readers of the possibility that the "DeFeo" house was haunted:

Saturday, Feb. 14, 1976

It is Valentine's Day, the weather clear and in the mid-40s. Patty Hearst's trial for bank robbery is in all the headlines. Opening my *Newsday* to the table of contents, I scan the column headed "The Island." There are three subtitles under this heading: the first reads, "Detergent Ban Successful" and directs you to page 4 to read about the fifth anniversary of Suffolk County's ban on detergents and how it has decreased the suds in our water supply. The second reads, "Layoff by the Numbers"; it concerns Suffolk officials attempts to avoid a massive layoff of county workers this year. This story is also found on page 4.

It is the third subtitle which catches my eye: "Bad Vibes—The house is a luxurious, three-story colonial near the water in Amityville, and the Lutz family paid $40,000 for it. But they moved out in ten days after feeling strange vibrations and detecting other weird phenomena. It's the DeFeo house, where six persons were shot to death in 1974. Page 6."

Turning to page 6, I see a photograph of a screen storm-door, ripped and hanging off its hinges at the entrance to the house. The

The Amityville Horror Conspiracy

headline proclaims "DeFeo Home Abandoned; Buyer Calls It Haunted." The pertinent items are as follow: George and Kathleen Lutz bought the former DeFeo house on December 23, 1975 and moved in a few days later. *Within ten days* they moved out, leaving furniture behind and telling friends and neighbors that the house was haunted. Neighbors say they have not seen the Lutzes for about a month.

Kathleen had gone to the Suffolk district attorney's office to get a blueprint of the house, allegedly telling sources there and also other acquaintances that she and her family had seen human shapes in the house, had heard strange sounds and vibrations, and that the power would fail for unexplained reasons. The Lutzes are both in their 30s and have two sons and a daughter. George works for William H. Parry, Inc. at 600 Jericho Turnpike in Syosset.

Jerry Solfvin, a research associate at the Psychical Research Foundation in Durham, North Carolina confirmed that the Lutzes had talked with the Foundation but would not reveal whether or not his group would be conducting any scientific investigations of the phenomena. The following passages are quoted directly from *Newsday*, for, as we shall see later, they will become extremely relevant to the case:

"One friend of Lutz said that the family left the house because *they had used up all their money buying it and could not afford to repair the heating system*, which failed when they moved in. But the friend would not deny that Lutz had talked about strange happenings in the house.

"Shortly *after they moved out*, according to a neighbor who asked not to be identified, Lutz, a land surveyor, came back to the house with a priest, carrying a large cross. They walked around the house and spent a couple of hours inside. 'I don't know what they were doing,' the neighbor said. Associates said that Lutz is a Methodist, and his wife a Catholic.

"Last month, according to sources, the Lutzes, frightened, convinced Sgt. Pat Cammarato of the Amityville Police Department to come to the house, for which they paid $40,000, and check their story. Cammarato did so, and later told other law enforcement officials of feeling strange vibrations, sources said. He then researched the history of the house, which is about 80 years old, and found that a tragedy had happened to every family that had lived there, according to sources. Cammarato could not be reached for comment last night.

"According to agents at Conklin Realty in Massapequa Park, who sold the house to the Lutzes, the family knew of the killings. 'They said it didn't bother them. They liked the house and they took it', one agent said.

"The Lutzes are reported to be skiing in Vermont and unavailable for comment."

Sunday, Feb. 15, 1976

Roxanne Salch has come to my house to work on the files of the Parapsychology Institute of America. She is our secretary. She is also returning my cassette tapes and my notes from the book which we have finally completed. The covers are being made up at the printer's and we should have the first copies back any day now.

Roxanne is just finishing up the filing when I get the call from *Newsday*, asking for my opinion of the Lutz case. They have written articles about me in the past (as a matter of fact, just as recently as two days ago, Friday, the 13th, when I talked about superstitions), and often use me as a consultant on matters of the occult.

Monday, Feb. 16, 1976

Today's *Newsday* article is entitled "The Curious Haunt the DeFeo House." The local people, intrigued by the idea of a haunted house, and especially one with such an infamous history, have responded to Saturday's article by milling around the house hoping to see ghosts. Amityville police were kept busy shooing the curiosity–seekers away from the property. I was quoted in a small paragraph which said, "Stephen Kaplan, head of the Parapsychology Institute of America, an occult research organization in Setauket, who does believe in ghosts and hopes to investigate the house, warned that amateur ghost hunters 'should not mix into these things because they don't know how to handle a hostile spirit. Those butting in could be adversely affected, perhaps transferring the apparition from the DeFeo house to their own. Let the exorcists work in exorcism and keep the neophyte out,' Kaplan said."

That night, George Lutz calls me at my PIA business number, having read the *Newsday* article. He says he would like me to investigate the house.

I begin to ask questions. What actually happened to him and his family? George, who asks that I call him by his nickname Lee, says that he simply can't describe the psychic phenomena. But there are demons there. He even knows their names!

The Amityville Horror Conspiracy

"What are the names?" I ask. Lee won't tell me. He claims they'll appear if he as much as mentions their names out loud.

"Who told you that?" I ask.

"I read it in a book," says Lee. I ask him for the title, but he can't remember—he's read so many books since they bought the house. Books on demonology, witchcraft, Satanism, ghosts, psychic phenomena—the list went on and on. And all in just a few short weeks, or so George claims.

"I took a crash course in the occult, I guess you could say," Lee says. "I wanted to understand what was happening to me. Up until this happened, Kathy and I knew nothing about the occult at all; I don't think I had ever read even one book on the subject."

I press him about the demons and he answers by reciting "facts" he has learned about demons and Satan worship. In a discussion about witchcraft, Lee mentions Ray Buckland, a prominent witch in the area who ran the Witchcraft Museum in Bayshore before moving to New England.

"Oh, you've heard of Ray Buckland?" I respond.

"Sure, I knew Ray," replies Lee. "We had some interesting conversations about witchcraft when he ran the museum."

I am getting more suspicious by the minute. Didn't George just tell me he knew nothing of the occult up until the past two months? Ray Buckland had been gone from New York for a year or two now. That would mean George had discussed "the craft," as it is called, with one of the most knowledgeable witches in the country long before he bought the house; actually even before he married Kathy, as George had told me they were married last summer (1975) and that the three children are Kathy's by a previous marriage.

In spite of my skepticism, I agree to take a group from my organization out to the house. But I tell George that he must at least give me the times that the phenomena seem to occur most often.

"The demons come out between eleven p.m. and three a.m.," Lee admits.

During the course of the conversation Lee and I discuss the DeFeo murders. I am curious why he and his wife, newlyweds just starting life together, and with three children, would choose a home where six people were brutally murdered.

"Oh, we knew all about Ronnie," Lee explains, "but it didn't bother us that we were buying the house where his family was killed. We liked the house, and we're not superstitious about things like that."

Lee continues discussing the murder case, always referring to DeFeo as "Ronnie." I find it somewhat unusual that he should refer to a mass murderer by his nickname but rationalize it by thinking that he could have picked up the habit from living in the neighborhood where everyone knew "Ronnie."

However, something is just not right here. He is discussing DeFeo in such an intimate manner that I almost get the feeling that George knows him personally. In fact, his tone of voice and even his comments sound somewhat sympathetic towards "Ronnie."

Toward the end of our conversation I suddenly recall that the Lutzes were supposed to be "skiing in Vermont."

"Oh, that was just a cover", says Lee, "we didn't want to be inundated with phone calls. Actually, we're staying with relatives in Nassau County and we don't want the publicity."

Lee gives me his office number at William H. Parry, Inc. so I can contact him when I have discussed the case with my members. We set a tentative date for the investigation for Saturday, the 21st, and I will meet him at Zum Zum's on Friday, the 20th to get the letter of authorization since George will not be going into the house with us.

Again, I assure George that we will do our best to discover the truth, and whatever that truth is we will report it to the public—be it legitimate phenomena, misinterpretation, or an out and out hoax.

Tuesday, Feb. 17, 1976

I have called my members and organized two separate teams to investigate the Lutzes' house. Each group consists of eight researchers composed of two psychics, a photographer, an electronics expert to detect any rigged devices, and four other parapsychologists or researchers. Team A will stay in the house from 9:00 p.m. until 2:00 a.m., while Team B sits in cars in the driveway to observe anything unusual that may happen outside the house. At 2:00 a.m. the teams will exchange places and Team B will remain in the house until 6:00 a.m. We also have a professional magician scheduled to come along to detect any tricks that may be able to fool us; after all, we are trained in psychical research, not in "how to pull the wool over one's eyes."

The Amityville Horror Conspiracy

My research staff is composed of many diverse types of people; we have teachers, nurses, electricians, telephone company repairmen, artists, photographers and housewives. All have had to rearrange their schedules quite extensively to be able to stay overnight at the Lutz house. The professionals who work Saturday nights have had to get someone to cover for them, and the housewives have had to explain to their husbands and families why they won't be home till Sunday morning. But we are a well-organized group by this time and have established a good working rapport since we began in 1974.

Roxanne will accompany me on Friday to the Smithhaven Mall to meet George Lutz at Zum Zum's restaurant. Once we get his letter of authorization we will be all set. I was quite surprised today to read another article in *Newsday* about the Lutz family: "DeFeo House: Legal Twist." Surprised because George had given me the distinct impression that they were trying to *avoid* the press. However, according to this article, the Lutzes had held a press conference yesterday—the same day George had called me!

And where was this conference held? In the Patchogue office of William Weber, Ronald DeFeo' s defense lawyer!

This was either the biggest coincidence of all time (that Lutz would just happen to choose the same lawyer who represented DeFeo) or there was more to this story than meets the eye. I remembered my impression of last night that George seemed to know of "Ronnie" on an intimate basis and this seemed to tie in directly with this quote from William Weber: "Based on certain facts related to us by the new owners, George and Kathleen Lutz, and certain physical evidence brought to our attention...we are considering a motion for a new trial." Weber did not elaborate, except to say that DeFeo would be visited at the Clinton Correction facility in upstate Dannemora, where he is serving his sentence.

Weber and the Lutzes were working together to get a new trial for DeFeo! What legal grounds did they plan to use? How did Weber and Lutz meet? And when? Does Lutz know DeFeo, and, if so, for how long? All of these questions went through my mind but few were answered by the article. They did, however, have several quotes about the Lutzes' experiences: "The new owners *denied having seen human shapes in the house,* but said a psychic phenomenon—a 'very strong force'—made them move out 28 days after they moved in." This statement threw me for a loop. The original article on the 14th had said the Lutzes moved out within *10* days.

More quotes: "There were no 'flying objects,' nor were there 'wailing noises' or 'moving couches.' But there were, Lutz said, psychic phenomena he could not describe that persuaded him and his family to move out suddenly 'because of concern for our own personal safety as a family.'"

Lutz did not mention a word about the demons he had told me about in such great detail. He did deny that his family had reported "seeing human shapes in the house, of hearing strange sounds, or experiencing unexplained power failures. Lutz also denied having had a priest—carrying a large cross—accompany him to the house one day, or asking Amityville police Sgt. Pat Cammaroto to check the house for vibrations, as neighbors had said. Cammarato also denied that yesterday."

I couldn't help but wonder, if George had seen no human shapes, heard no strange sounds, etc., then just what had they experienced? If he had seen or heard demons, why not mention it? After all, he had called the press conference. Why do that and then withhold information? I suppose he could be afraid to talk about it, but then why face the press at all? I was not buying any of this.

The article did state that George and Kathy, both 29, had met Weber about three weeks ago "through mutual friends" and that he and Burton (his law partner) are now "providing them legal advice." He did not say where he met them nor did he name the friends. The Lutzes were married July 4, 1975 and George owns a surveying company in Jamaica and Syosset founded by his grandfather, William Parry, who died February 9. George is a former Marine, former air traffic control trainee, and holds two associate degrees (in what, they do not say). He and Kathy bought the house for $80,000 and half was held in escrow by the title company "because of an unspecified problem with the DeFeo family estate."

Contradictory to the February 14th article, this one states that the Lutzes moved into the house on *December 18*—the prior article said they bought the house on *December 23* and moved in a few days later. To quote today's *Newsday* once more, "On December 18, Lutz said, they moved in, and were at that time nonbelievers in psychic phenomena. They moved out *January 14*, taking with them, he said, only three changes of clothes. Since then, he said, they have been living

The Amityville Horror Conspiracy

with a relative [he would not say where], and have returned to the house twice." (The continuation of the article, which began on page 3, is headed, "A Dream House Became a Nightmare.")

The following passage also interested me: "But Lutz refused to answer questions on whether the Catholic Church had been contacted, whether the family had felt vibrations and whether he had turned over a gun to the Amityville police because of the 'strong force.'" Why would George turn over a gun to the police—if, indeed, he had actually done so? He had not denied the rumor, merely refused to comment on it.

My suspicions are growing rapidly. There are too many contradictions in the different versions of the story. George did not want publicity, yet he had called a press conference. Lutz was now linked to DeFeo via William Weber, who would somehow attempt to use the Lutzes' story to exonerate a mass murderer. My gut instinct is telling me that "something is rotten in Denmark." But I have already told George I would investigate the house, and so I shall attempt to proceed with an open mind.

Wednesday, Feb. 18, 1976

As I prepare for the investigation on Saturday, another 22-year–old son is smothering his mother with a pillow in Roslyn Heights, Long Island. On Monday night, Leroy Ludeker allegedly killed his 55-year–old mother, Anna, with a blow to the neck after a long–running feud involving Ludeker's plans to get married. Once again, the son told police he had "discovered" his mother's body; once again the police suspected the son after finding no evidence of forced entry to their home. The similarity to the DeFeo case is unmistakable; I silently hope this is not the beginning of a trend toward settling family strife by matricide/patricide.

This evening I received a call from the *Long Island Press*; they, too, wanted my opinion on the Lutz case. Since the Lutzes had gone public with their press conference on Monday, I saw no harm in mentioning the fact that my staff and I would soon be investigating the house. Of course, I was cautious not to mention what day we would be going there, as I did not want our investigation to attract hoards of curiosity-seekers. I was also called by a network T.V. news program in Manhattan. They wanted me to go on the air to talk about the "haunted house." I told them I had not yet investigated the house, and therefore it would not be ethical to discuss it. Incredibly, they tried to "bribe" me into saying, on the air, that it was haunted, and in turn they would make me a "national star"! I told them no, thank you; I was already a "star" and I would not con the public for anyone.

Thursday, Feb. 19, 1976

The *Long Island Press* printed their article with the heading: "GHOST HUNT—Expert To Probe 'Forces' in DeFeo House." Other than rehashing the same information about the Lutzes and the DeFeo case, they basically stated that "Long Island's leading ghost-hunter has agreed to investigate the house."

My organization is sponsoring a public lecture this evening at my home, and afterwards my staff will meet to coordinate our plans for Saturday's investigation.

9:00 P.M. The lecture has just ended and Chelsea is coming in the front door with a huge carton. It is the first one hundred copies of my book! My members congregate in the den to get their autographed copies and to get down to the business at hand...the Lutz case.

9:45 P.M. My office phone rings as we are celebrating the book printing with coffee and cake. Excusing myself, I go to the desk and pick up the receiver. It is George Lutz. He sounds rather annoyed.

"You told the press you would be investigating!" he says. "I told you we didn't want any publicity."

"Yes, George, but you failed to tell me about the press conference you held on that very same day. I didn't feel I was giving away any secrets and, in case you didn't notice, I took special care not to mention the date." I could not believe the audacity of this man! "Since you are not going to be there, I have some apprehension that people may misunderstand when they see a large group of people entering a vacant house. The police may think we are intruders attempting to break in. We are merely covering all bases by making it public knowledge that we will be investigating at some unspecified date."

This did not pacify George. "Well, I told you we didn't want any publicity, and you told the press anyway. I'm going to have to postpone your investigation for at least a couple of weeks."

I interrupted his lengthy diatribe on how I had seemingly betrayed his trust.

"George, how much are we charging you for this investigation?" I asked.

"Why...nothing," he answered, confused.

The Amityville Horror Conspiracy

"That's right. We're not charging you a single penny, George. And we do have other cases to investigate. Yours is not the only one. So it doesn't really matter to me whether we investigate your home or not. We are a public service organization; we do not 'ambulance chase' or 'ghost chase.' You came to us for our help. We are quite willing to spend our time and money to help you if you are sincere, but we must always reserve the right to tell the public the true results of our investigation."

George backed down a little with his verbal assault. "Well, I guess you're right, but we're really tired of this whole thing. We only gave that press conference to clear up the exaggerated rumors about our story. I think I'll wait until the publicity has died down some before having you investigate. Cancel your plans for this weekend and I'll call you in about two weeks."

"Fine, George," I said. "Our egos will still be intact whether you call or not. We'll be here if you need us"

Wishing him and his family good luck, I hung up the phone and went to tell my staff that this weekend was off. They were rather annoyed that they had changed their weekend plans for nothing and, like myself, could not understand George Lutz's rather strange position on publicity. In my opinion, the Lutzes' press conference had started more rumors than it had cleared up.

After discussing the situation at length, my staff and I decided that, should Lutz decide to call back again, we would not accept the case after all. None of us liked the Weber connection between Lutz and DeFeo; it was possible that George was even a friend of "Ronnie's." My group had been set up often enough in the past to be suspicious of people who changed their stories every day.

To end my involvement in the case once and for all, I called the *Long Island Press* and told them the investigation was off, elaborating on my suspicions of a set-up to reporter Thomas Condon.

Friday, Feb. 20, 1976

Mr. Condon's *Long Island Press* article reads: "GHOST HUNTER SMELLS A HOAX." The article has immense relevance to the future of this case.

"The possibility that reports of supernatural goings-on at the Amityville house where six members of the DeFeo family were slaughtered in 1974, might be sparked by more down-to-earth motives was suggested yesterday by a noted ghost-hunter.

"According to Dr. Stephen Kaplan, director of the Parapsychology Institute of America, headquartered in South Setauket, there is also the possibility that the entire story of 'strange forces' inside the home at 112 Ocean Avenue may just be a hoax to get a new trial for Ronald DeFeo, the convicted mass murderer who is now serving a 150 years to life sentence.

"Dr. Kaplan, who became interested in the Amityville 'haunted house' story earlier this week, told the Press yesterday that he is less interested in the entire matter now.

"The occult researcher said he suspects that the house's present owners—George and Kathy Lutz—are really friends of DeFeo, convicted last year of murdering his family of six. The Lutzes abandoned the house after living there only 28 days, claiming it was besieged by 'strange forces.'

"Kaplan initially had shown interest in seeking out the suspected supernatural forces, but recanted yesterday. 'If he [Lutz] does not invite me to the house, then I would have to believe the possibility that a hoax was being presented,' he said.

"Lutz, who works at William Parry, Inc., surveyors in Syosset, could not be reached for comment.

"'I'm bowing out,' Kaplan said at his Setauket home. 'I don't like the set up.'

"Kaplan is a former teacher of parapsychology at the State University at Stony Brook.

"When asked whether DeFeo and Lutz are friends, Kaplan replied: 'He [Lutz] sounds like a friend of DeFeo. He refers to him [DeFeo] as Ron or Ronny, and you don't normally talk of a mass murderer so casually.'

"Kaplan also implied that DeFeo himself may have devised the idea to gain a new trial. 'I believe that if I was serving 150 years in prison I would think of getting out somehow, too,' Kaplan said.

"Kaplan now teaches an adult education course in parapsychology in the Three Village school district in the Stony Brook-Setauket area.

"'I'm only interested in serious research,' Kaplan said. He explained that his early interest in the strange case was because in the past two years about 85 percent of the ten to fifteen reported instances of mysterious happenings all came from places on the south shore within one mile of the waterfront. The Lutz house is on the south shore and on the waterfront."

The Amityville Horror Conspiracy

The last paragraph, relating the correlation between my cases and a location near the waterfront is true. It is a correlation which I have noticed recently but have no explanation for at this time. I plan to attempt to determine whether or not it has any significance.

But the Lutz house will not figure in my statistics for that theory. I have totally washed my hands of the entire Lutz/DeFeo matter. With the publication of the article today, February 20, 1976, I am now officially on record as believing the Amityville haunting to be a hoax.

Tuesday, Feb. 24, 1976

Changing into the clothes I will wear for tonight's class at Ward Melville, I flip on the T.V. in my bedroom to catch some of the day's events. Finding nothing of interest on the network news shows, I turn to Channel 5, a local New York station based in Manhattan.

"...and don't forget to tune in tonight, folks, to our Ten O'clock News. We'll be taking you on a tour of the famous haunted house in Amityville! Don't miss it!"

I cannot believe my ears. George Lutz, the man who was so dead-set against any more publicity that he would rather cancel an investigation than risk more coverage—this same George Lutz is now allowing millions of viewers to "tour" his home on television?! I must get home from class in time to see this.

At class I tell my members—Chelsea, Grace, Roxanne and a few others—that I will not be joining them for coffee and cake at Chucky's diner tonight, as is our usual custom after class on Tuesdays. When I tell them the reason, they also are anxious to see the news segment. Since class ends at 9:30 and my home is closest to the school, I invite all of them to watch it in my den.

Rushing in my front door out of the rain at 10:05 with my entourage in tow, I hurry to the T.V. and turn to Channel 5. They are still giving the headline news and will not get to the features until later. We all cluster around the small striped couch in my den to wait.

Soon Channel 5's Marvin Scott was introduced and they started the taped segment. Scott stood in front of the dark facade of the Amityville house, introducing the story to viewers who may or may not be familiar with it by now. The scene then changed and we were seeing the interior of the house. A group of individuals was seated around a table conducting a seance. They were introduced as Lorraine Warren, a clairvoyant; her husband, Ed, a demonologist; psychics Mary

Pascarella and Mrs. Alberta Riley; and George Kekoris of the Psychical Research Foundation in Durham, North Carolina. Outside of the seance circle were Jerry Solfvin, also of the Psychic Research Foundation in Durham, Marvin Scott and the camera crew.

The three women began to moan about "negative forces" which they sensed in the house. Channel 5's cameras followed them up the circular staircase to the bedrooms where the six DeFeos had met their tragic deaths. Mary Pascarella clutched at her throat and rolled her eyes back in her head, claiming an "evil black shadow" was enveloping her. Lorraine Warren stated that the force was "demonic, nothing human, from the bowels of the earth." Mrs. Riley just gasped, eyes tightly closed and in a "trance." Ed Warren said that the house harbored a demonic spirit which could only be removed by an exorcist.

My members were laughing hysterically! It was a three-ring circus! My group had been well trained in scientific investigative procedures for researching an alleged haunting and were also quite familiar with the numerous types of quacks and phonies in the field. This so-called "seance" had incorporated most of the classical stereotypes of fraudulent spiritualism: demonic forces, evil spirits, black shadows, moaning trances, etc.

I was very surprised that members of the Psychical Research Foundation in Durham would be present at such a farce! The PRF is one of the most respected parapsychological research organizations in the world. It is an independent group which branched off from the original ESP department at Duke University founded by J.B. Rhine, the "father of parapsychology" whose staff developed the original ESP testing cards (Zener cards) back in the early 1930s. Many people still refer to the PRF as "Duke University's ESP lab," but in actuality the university closed their parapsychology department when J.B. Rhine retired many years ago. The modern PRF is headquartered in a small cottage which they rent from the Duke campus.

I decide to call the PRF as soon as possible to see if they can shed any light on this bizarre case. This latest episode has only served to confirm my suspicions that there is a definite motive behind the Lutzes' public claims of a haunting in Amityville.

4

My Investigation Begins

Saturday, Feb. 28, 1976

I was able to reach the Psychic Research Foundation on Thursday night and had spoken with Gerald Solfvin, one of the PRF's two investigators who was present at the Channel 5 seance. He was about to lock up the office there, and didn't have much time for conversation, but did tell me that he was rather annoyed by the Lutz case.

"It was a circus there," said Jerry. "There were so many people roaming around the house that there was no way we could conduct a scientific investigation. When the Lutzes originally called us in to investigate, they did not tell us they would be bringing in a camera crew on the very same night."

Jerry went on to say that the PRF had originally assigned George Kekoris to investigate the case for them because he was the field investigator located closest to Amityville. "I went along only because I happened to be in New York that day," said Jerry. "We have no official conclusions on the case because we were not given the proper atmosphere in which to conduct an investigation, and George Kekoris has not yet turned in his report on his interview with the Lutzes."

I had thanked Jerry for his time and promised to keep in touch. Now, after looking over all of my notes and clippings this morning, I decide to have a look at this infamous haunted house for myself. I call Roxanne Salch and ask if she will accompany me on a drive out to Amityville.

I pick up Roxanne at her home in Centereach and the drive from there to Amityville takes about 45 minutes. Amityville is a quaint, picturesque town located right on the Suffolk side of the Suffolk-Nassau border. The main street is lined with small shops, bars and gas stations.

Not knowing how to find Ocean Avenue, we stop at one of the gas stations and ask the attendant for directions.

"Oh, another one looking for the haunted house, huh?" The young man leans up against the car and grins at us. "We got people from miles around lookin' for that place. You don't really believe in that ghost stuff, do ya?"

Handing him my business card, I briefly explain who I am and why we are interested. He points back in the direction from which we have just come and directs us to turn left at the pizza parlor.

Following his instructions, we turn onto a quiet, tree-lined street: Ocean Avenue. The homes all appear to be upper-middle class, with two to three stories, and neatly manicured front lawns. About two blocks down, on the left-hand side, we get our first view of 112 Ocean Avenue.

We park the car across the street on the corner, and as we get out to have a closer look, we realize that we are not the only ones who have come to view the house on this unseasonably warm, sunny February afternoon. There are several cars parked on the side street and a group of about a dozen young people are clustered near the driveway of the house. In addition to this, cars which pass the house slow down to about 5 MPH as the passengers point, chatter excitedly among themselves and take snapshots out the windows.

The Lutz/DeFeo house looks almost exactly as it did in the papers: dark and boarded up. There are "No Trespassing" signs plastered all over the boards, put there "by order of the Amityville Police Dept." Our only surprise is that the main entrance to the house does not face Ocean Avenue but, instead, faces the driveway, which intersects with the street at a right angle. The DeFeo's sign, "High Hopes," is no longer there, but the post from which it hung has a small figure of a squirrel on top. There is a white, circular object on the front lawn, which, I am told by a local youngster, is what remains of the fountain which was once surrounded by religious statues when the DeFeos were alive.

Facing the house from Ocean Avenue, we see an enclosed sun porch, the roof of which reaches to the two second–story windows. Above these are the two attic windows, each shaped like a quarter section of a wheel with spokes dividing it into six panes. The local boy tells us that these oddly shaped windows look out from what was once Ronald DeFeo, Jr.'s bedroom.

The Amityville Horror Conspiracy

Wary of the police signs, but wanting to glimpse the back yard, we venture down the length of the driveway, stopping first at the main entrance. The metal storm door is just as it was pictured in the *Newsday* article on the 14th—hanging askew from its hinges, the metal ripped and the glass smashed and scattered over the brick-lined steps. The inner door is not damaged; it is made of heavy wood and painted white like the shutters. At the end of the driveway is the garage with a dog house in front of it, the heavy chain still attached. To the left of the garage is a large, in-ground swimming pool surrounded by a chain-link fence. Almost out of view behind the pool and the garage is the Amityville River. Such a pity that all of this should be going to waste.

Going back to the car, I take out my cassette recorder to tape some of my impressions. The neighborhood youngsters, seeing me with the microphone, gather around to find out what's going on, and I decide to question them about the house. None of them remember ever seeing the Lutzes during the time they lived there; the Lutz family doesn't seem to have had any contact with the neighbors at all. But most of the kids remember "Ronnie." They were all afraid of him. They characterize him as a drug addict, a thief, a heavy drinker and an all-around troublemaker with a nasty temper. The children had all steered clear of Ronnie, and none were surprised when he was arrested.

One brown-haired boy of about fourteen remembers passing the house sometime during the past Christmas holiday and glancing in the windows of the enclosed porch where there were no curtains hanging. This would have been the period in which the Lutzes were living there (for how long depends on which version of the story you believe) and yet the boy glimpsed nothing but stacks and piles of unpacked cartons, most with the cords still tied securely around them. Of course, all of this is just hearsay, but interesting nonetheless. Perhaps the Lutzes had never unpacked because they knew they would not be staying for very long.

I am about to head back home when Roxanne suddenly has an idea. "Since we haven't accomplished very much here," she says, "why not go to the Amityville Police Department and interview Sgt. Pat Cammaroto."

I thought it was a great idea; Cammaroto was the officer whom *Newsday* had originally claimed had come to the Lutz house to investigate the "vibrations."

It is a simple matter to get directions to the police department from the young people we had been talking to. We park in front of the red-brick building and go up to the officer at the front desk. He is a tall, muscular-looking man with an unruly shock of thick, black hair. When we tell him of our purpose in being there, he shakes his head and sighs.

"You know, we've been chasing people away from that house for two weeks now," he complains. "We don't appreciate having to use all those man-hours on babysitting a vacant house when we have more important things to take care of."

We ask him if he had met the Lutzes.

"Oh, sure, I remember the guy. He came in here one day to turn in a hand gun. Strange character."

I remember reading something about a gun in the newspaper, and my curiosity is sparked. "George Lutz turned over a gun to the police?" I asked. "For what purpose?"

"Well, he came in here one evening, shortly after they had moved in, put the gun up on the desk, and asked us to hold it for him. When we asked why, he said that he *had an impulse to shoot his wife and kids!* I thought, 'this guy must be some kind of loonie, and he just stood there, telling us how the 'strange forces' and 'vibrations' in his house were telling him to kill. We asked him if he had a permit for the gun, and he said yes, he was an ex–Marine and that's why he had the gun. We agreed to keep it for him, but then the next day he comes back asking for his gun! He did have a permit, and since he hadn't committed any crime, we gave it back to him. Look, you can ask Sgt. Cammaroto, he was here that day, too. I'll go see if he's busy."

After waiting about ten minutes, we are shown in to Sgt. Pat Cammaroto's small office. The sergeant greets us with a strong handshake and a big, friendly smile. He is medium height, broad-shouldered, with partially greying hair, and appears to be in his late 40s to early 50s. I hand him one of my business cards.

"Dr. Stephen Kaplan. Yes, I remember the name. You're the one who's calling the case a hoax, right? Perhaps you can help me to straighten out this whole thing."

Sgt. Cammaroto motions for us to sit down, as he settles into the swivel chair behind his desk, leaning back with a styrofoam cup of coffee in his hand. The sergeant is very upset with the statements that have been attributed to him by the press.

The Amityville Horror Conspiracy

"I have been discussing with my lawyer whether or not to sue *Newsday*. They've made me the laughing stock of the neighborhood, saying that I 'felt the vibrations.' I never felt any vibrations because I *never set foot on that property the whole time the Lutzes lived there!* As a matter of fact, I have not been near that house since the night of the murders, a night I prefer to forget. That was the only tragedy that I know about; I've lived here for a long time and I know nothing about any other tragedies occurring to anyone in that house."

The black-haired officer knocks on the door to give us two cups of coffee. I thank him and turn back to Sgt. Cammaroto. "Do you remember the incident with George Lutz and the gun?" I ask.

"Oh, you've heard about that already? Yeah, that's true. He came in here with his gun saying he had an impulse to kill his family. I thought maybe the whole DeFeo thing was beginning to get to him... you know, living in the same house where it happened."

"But then he picked it up the very next day?" asks Roxanne.

"Yes, that was the strangest part of it. If he was so nervous about having the gun around that he would surrender it to the police, then why pick it up again so soon?"

The very same thing that I was wondering. I ask the sergeant if he knows anything about the history of the house.

"Just that it was built around the turn of the century. The house that stood on that site before this one was built was moved to another piece of property just around the corner from the DeFeo house. It's still standing, too; it's a much smaller house than DeFeo's, and I believe an elderly male descendant of the original family lives in it. But I have never heard of any tragedy occurring in either house until the DeFeo murders."

When I ask the sergeant about the discrepancy in *Newsday*'s reports of the price the Lutzes paid for the house (one said $40,000, the other $80,000) he says the correct price had to be $80,000. *Newsday* had corrected their figure after the initial article. Actually, the house is worth over $100,000, according to Cammaroto. He also says that when Lutz had come to turn in the gun he had complained about noises in the pipes.

"What old house doesn't have noises in the pipes, especially when you first move in?" Says Cammaroto. "I don't see anything occult about that at all."

Sgt. Cammaroto says he is glad to see that at least one person is trying to expose the Lutz story as a hoax. He says he would appreciate it greatly if I would discourage the press from mentioning his name anymore.

"I've been on the force for thirty years now and I plan to retire soon. Until then, I just want to do my job in peace and quiet. I don't need to be involved in this nonsense and neither does this town. It's been like a circus at that house!"

He isn't the first person to have called it a circus; I recall Jerry Solfvin's comment. Assuring the sergeant I will talk to the press, we get up to leave. He shakes hands heartily with both of us and we thank him for his time and hospitality.

Before dropping Roxanne off in Centereach, I decide to make one more stop—*Newsday*'s offices in Ronkonkoma. We speak with Neill Rosenfeld, the young reporter who had written the article of February 16 in which I was quoted. He does not know whether or not *Newsday* will be printing any more articles on the case but takes notes on my suggestions on his computer key-punch machine. He says they are sorry that Sgt. Cammaroto had been misquoted and promises they will not connect him with the case in the future.

I get home just as my children are being put to bed. After kissing each of them goodnight, I go downstairs to my desk phone and call Joel Martin of WBAB radio in Babylon. Joel runs the talk show there and I have been doing shows with him on a regular basis since 1974.

He likes my idea to do a show on the Amityville case, and we set the taping date for Saturday, March 6.

Wednesday, March 3, 1976

A reporter from the *Long Island Press* will be observing my parapsychology class at Bryant Adult Center in Queens tonight. They plan to do a feature article for this Sunday's paper.

Saturday, March 6, 1976

I've just returned home from taping the Joel Martin Show. This time I took my twin sister, Rochelle, and a few of my members along to observe how a radio show is done. Joel and I spoke about my involvement in the Amityville case and why I think it's a hoax. I also explained to him the reason for my initial interest in the case—because it was on the south shore near the water, like such a large percentage of my other cases—and made comparisons to the famous "Seaford Case" of the 1950s.

Seaford is a town in Nassau County, near the Suffolk-Nassau border and on the South Shore, only about three miles away from Amityville. The case was popularized in William Roll's book, *The Poltergeist*, and concerned a house where objects would levitate and fly across the room. Allegedly this phenomena had been observed by many witnesses, including the police.

Before I had concluded that the Lutz case was a hoax, I had been interested in similarities between the two cases: the families were about the same size, in the same age bracket, the towns were in close proximity, the police were supposed to be involved, etc. The show will not air until Sunday, March 28.

Sunday, March 7, 1976

The *Long Island Press* article by H.L. Klein is titled: "HE'S THE MAN TO SEE IF YOU'VE SEEN A GHOST," subtitle, "Dr. Stephen Kaplan Gives His All to Parapsychology." It describes me as "A City College graduate with degrees in sociology, education, liberal arts, communications and a healthy sprinkling of public relations...." Klein also calls me "a pleasant, cherubic man with a ready smile." I don't mind the pleasant part, but am I really seen as "cherubic"? I have been gaining weight lately, but it is rather unsettling to me. (At least he didn't say fat!)

All else aside, it is quite a good article and covers most of what I lectured on that night: ESP, auras, and ghosts. I dealt strictly with my legitimate ghost cases; the Amityville case is *not* mentioned because I did not choose to waste the class' time, or mine, on a hoax.

This is the third article the *Press* has printed about me in a period of two and a half weeks. I am glad that the last one has associated me with something more worthwhile than Amityville.

Sunday, March 28, 1976

Just finished listening to the "Joel Martin Show" which aired the tape we did on Amityville. I'm glad I had this chance to inform the public of the facts so they can now draw their own conclusions.

I have not been able to avoid discussing the Amityville case in my classes—the students know of my involvement and want to hear about it. Of course, never having been in the house, I cannot give them 100% assurance that there are no ghosts there. But, based on Lutz's actions, the discrepancies in the different stories, Sgt. Cammaroto's testimony, the observations of Jerry Solfvin, and my own conversations with Lutz, most of my students independently conclude, as I did, that it is a hoax.

Monday, March 29, 1976

Today I received a call from Sgt. Pat Cammaroto, thanking me for relating his side of the story on WBAB. I am quite honored that this busy man would take the time to personally call me. I assure him that I will continue to cooperate with the Amityville police in any way I can. He said he hoped to be able to return the favor some day.

Thursday, April 8, 1976

Grace and Chelsea will be lecturing for the public tonight at the monthly lecture sponsored by the PIA. The topic is astrology, and they are both very good at it, Grace having studied the topic for twenty years.

We are having a brief business meeting among the members before the lecture, and Roxanne has just handed me an article she took from the April 6 edition of *The Star*, one of those weekly tabloids. My eyes fill with incredulity as they take in a photo of the Amityville house next to the headline "Psychics Fight Evil Force in House Where Six Died." Here we go again, I think to myself.

The article, written by Paul Dougherty, is a recounting of the night of the Channel 5 seance, although they seem to have gotten the date wrong (not unusual for a "supermarket tabloid"; they are not generally known for accuracy). The Lutz/DeFeo home is now referred to as "the 'horror house' in Amityville". My members and I go over each statement to compare it with what we already know:

> **1:** "Ex-marine and self-proclaimed skeptic George Lutz bought the house a year (after the DeFeo murders), despite the dark rumors already circulating about it."

What dark rumors"? The murders were a historical fact, and none of the local people we interviewed, including Sgt. Cammaroto, had heard any "ghost" rumors prior to the Lutzes' story.

> **2:** "Lutz told of furniture levitating and hurtling across the room..."

Didn't the Lutzes say during their press conference of February 16 that there had been no "flying objects" or "moving couches"? What does he call levitating and hurtling furniture?

The Amityville Horror Conspiracy

3: "...A 250-pound back door ripped from its hinges by an unseen force..."

Roxanne and I had seen the doors with our own eyes in February; only the light, metal storm door had been ripped from its hinges (presumably by the strong gale-force winds from the Amityville River; Sgt. Cammaroto had told us that a recent storm had ripped many storm doors off their hinges. I myself had lost a storm door to the winds this winter). The main, heavy wooden door was still securely in place, as were the large double doors in the back which lead out to the back porch and the pool.

4: "...his pretty wife's face changing before his eyes into that of a horrible old woman."

This was a new one, and quite comical to my members.

5: "A priest, a Doctor of Canon Law, was called in. He told the Lutz family that an awful force possessed the house, that exorcism would be useless, and that they should flee for their lives."

In the February 16 press conference, Lutz denied having had a priest accompany him to the house. Get your story straight, George! Even if the story, attributed to a neighbor by *Newsday* on February 14, about Lutz coming back to the house with a priest is true, the timing is off. According to the neighbor, the incident involving the priest took place shortly after the Lutzes moved out, which would make it pretty much impossible for them to take the advice of the priest to "flee for their lives" when they had already moved out of the house.

6: "He [Lutz] won't even go back to the house for his clothes, furniture, $3,000 tool kit and the $20,000 cabin cruiser.... 'George won't go within four blocks of the place' a close friend said. 'He is mortally and dreadfully afraid.'"

Quote from *Newsday*, February 17: "They [Lutzes] moved out January 14, taking with them, [Lutz] said, only three changes of clothes. Since then, he said, they have been living with a relative (he would not say where), and *have returned to the house only twice.*" The word "they" seems to indicate *more than one* of the Lutzes returned to the house *twice*—and not one of them left carrying any of their belongings on those return visits? Most important, why would George risk his own safety, and that of *at least* one other member of his family, to return twice to a house of which he is "mortally afraid"? Especially if they did not even leave with any of their precious possessions!

The rest of the article deals with the seance night. Much to my surprise, it claims that representatives of *The Star* were also present, and that they arrived at about 5:30 p.m. just as two men were leaving. The two men were Dr. Alex Tanous and Dr. Karlis Osis of the American Society for Psychical Research. Once again I am shocked that a prestigious psychical research group is being connected with this case. The ASPR has been around for as long, or longer, than the Psychical Research Foundation. Tanous is quoted as having encountered a "powerful negative force," "possibly diabolical." The PRF's George Kekoris supposedly had chattering teeth and a pounding heart, but shrugged it off by saying, "I'd had a lot of coffee." Channel 5's cameraman, Steve Petropolis, also allegedly had a pounding heart, with numbness and shortness of breath.

Lorraine Warren and the two other psychics once again told of demonic or evil forces. One interesting quote states, "A semi-hysterical party atmosphere began to seep through the house...." This seems to go along with Jerry Solfvin's description of a "circus" atmosphere. None of the demons would materialize for observers, and Mrs. Warren explained this away by claiming "It's not going to declare itself to all of these people."

The seance ended at 5:45 a.m. Lorraine Warren concluded by saying, "But make no mistake. The force is still here. Nobody could possibly live in this house until something is done."

I am very annoyed that this travesty of a haunted house story is continuing to be sold to the public—and this time in a *national* newspaper.

The audience is beginning to arrive for the astrology lecture, and I see my son Brian in pajamas and bare feet, hiding conspicuously on the staircase observing us grownups through the railing. I scold him, kiss him, and send him back up to bed, knowing that in a few minutes he will probably try to sneak down again. But it is time to introduce the speakers, so I return to the lecture area.

Saturday, April 10, 1976

Sun streams through the windshield of my Impala as I drive west on the Long Island Expressway, headed for WBAB in Babylon. I am going to tape another Joel Martin Show, this one to be on the topic of Theoparapsychology (relating events in the Bible to parapsychological occurrences). The green sign looming up in front of me proclaims, "AMITYVILLE—RTE. 110 SOUTH." Ironically, this is the same exit I must take to get to WBAB, but I will turn from 110 onto Route 109 before I reach Amityville.

The Amityville Horror Conspiracy

The exit for "109—Babylon" approaches quickly, but on a sudden impulse I bypass it and continue south on Route 110. Two of my members who have accompanied me on the trip begin to complain. "You missed the exit!" says one.

"I can't really explain it," I reply, "but I have a very strong hunch that if we go to the Amityville house right now we will be able to get inside. Don't ask me why, but I'm certain of it."

Both of my associates protest, scoffing at my "hunch" and assuring me that there is no possible way we could get into a locked, vacant house that is regularly patrolled by police. But I must see this through and, besides, we are two hours early for the Joel Martin Show.

Arriving at 112 Ocean Avenue, we see a man standing by the main entrance. I park the car and the three of us walk up to him.

"Hi," I greet the man, "is Lee around?"

"No," he replies, "I'm just handling the auction for him; we're selling the furniture. Are you a friend of Lee's?"

"Sure," I bluff. "I've spoken to Lee. Any chance we could take a look inside the house?"

"Well, sure, if you're a friend of Lee's. See if you're interested in any of the furniture; some of it belonged to the DeFeos, you know."

Leaving one of my members outside to chat with the auctioneer, two of us go into the house. The associate who accompanies me is an archaeologist; he will briefly examine the structure of the house to determine whether underground streams could have caused the vibrations.

Knowing that we will only have time for a preliminary investigation, we immediately climb to the third floor and examine the rooms there. Seeing and sensing nothing out of the ordinary, we descend to the second floor and go through each bedroom. Though nearly empty now, the house seems warm and pleasant. We encounter no "cold spots" or other sensations indicative of a haunted house. Being myself a "sensitive" (one who can sense a positive or negative atmosphere, as opposed to a psychic who can "pick up" specific details, such as names, events, etc.), I have been in a number of homes in which I could sense hostility or negativity. Such is not the case here; I find the house very comfortable to be in, as does my associate.

Returning to the first floor, we go through the living room, enclosed porch, dining room (which looks out through glass doors to the back porch and the swimming pool), kitchen and the narrow hallway with a small bathroom at the end. Another door in the hallway leads to the basement, and we proceed down the narrow wooden stairs. Directly ahead of us is a large open space with a tiled floor. Paneled walls separate this area from a room on the left, which is finished but empty, perhaps used as a playroom.

To the right, we walk around the wall of the stairwell and examine a small storage closet built under the stairs. There are a few scattered objects on the shelves, but for the most part, everything has been cleaned out. At the end of the closet is a pipe well, partially hidden by wooden shelving, in which the concrete walls and floor have been painted red—it is merely a narrow space which allows access to the plumbing which supplies water to the rooms above. On the far right hand side of the basement is the boiler room, which still has its original concrete walls and floor.

My associate can make no conclusions on the theory of underground streams as he has not come prepared with equipment. But we both agree it is one of the most pleasant homes we have been in; certainly the most comfortable of all our "haunted" cases.

Joining our colleague outside, we thank the auctioneer for his time and ask if he has experienced any "vibrations" in the house. He tells us that he and the movers have spent many hours in the house and have found it very pleasant, with nothing unusual. During our conversation, the auctioneer, who claims to be a friend of George Lutz, mentions that George is writing a book about the house! Somehow this does not surprise me.

Rebirth, Resolve and Pursuit

Friday, May 14, 1976

Long John Nebel is a very popular radio talk-show host in New York. I have been listening to him for many years and his show helped to stimulate my interest in strange phenomena. Long John has interviewed almost everyone who was anyone in the field, from the legitimate researchers to the people claiming to be from another planet.

Tonight, Long John and his wife Candy Jones are interviewing Ed and Lorraine Warren, who are talking about their awful experiences in the Amityville "horror house." Listening to the program in my home, I am appalled to hear that the story has spread once again. I learn that the Warrens are from Monroe, Connecticut. This strikes another question in my mind: Why would the Lutzes turn down the various legitimate researchers in the L.I./N.Y. City area and then bring in people from as far away as Connecticut? The show angers me enough to phone the program during the call-in portion.

What follows is a debate between the Warrens and myself, pro and con the Amityville case as a legitimate haunted house. The Warrens stick to their claims and reiterate their opinions about evil forces and demons.

Hanging up the phone at the end of the debate, I have the uneasy feeling that the Warrens do not intend to let this story drop. The infamous house seems destined to receive much media exposure.

Thursday, June 17, 1976

Tonight I gave a public lecture, sponsored by the P.I.A., on "Ghostology." It was a discussion of my legitimate cases of apparitions (ghosts), but the audience asked to hear about the Amityville house.

It is the most well-known haunting on Long Island now and the public wants to know the truth: Is it or isn't it? They are thrilled to hear the inside story from someone who has been inside the house and is familiar with all the principals of the case.

Although I regret having to cut time from my talk about the actual cases, I do recognize my responsibility to inform the public of the truth. The P.I.A. is a public service organization dedicated to just such a purpose, and I will tell anyone who asks that the Amityville case is a hoax.

Sunday, June 20, 1976

It is Father's Day but I must spend my evening with the P.I.A. on a research case. A young woman in Dix Hills has experienced various psychic phenomena and came to us for help some months ago. Since then we have been working with her to try and help her understand her experiences. She now feels that a spirit is trying to communicate with her. The P.I.A. will conduct a seance tonight under rigid control conditions to attempt to contact this spirit.

11:15 P.M. We have been at the seance table for hours and nothing has happened, other than a few people sensing cold drafts in an otherwise hot, humid room. The tape recorder has been on through the session and we have been taking readings of temperature and humidity. There has been no significant change in either. We have previously "debugged" the room with electronic equipment to be certain there were no devices being used for trickery. Everyone is tired and stiff from clasping hands for so long. We break for coffee.

11:45 P.M. We return for a second session. Our host (we'll call her Barbara) sits at the head of the dining room table, eyes closed and silent. I sit to Barbara's left and she clasps my hand tightly. Outside of the actual circle we have impartial observers and our own photographer, using regular infra-red film.

12:05 A.M. Everything is so quiet you could hear a pin drop. Nothing has occurred. Suddenly, the silence is broken by a long, ear-splitting, unearthly scream and we all nearly jump out of our seats. The scream comes from Barbara, but does not sound human. Gently, I calm her down and ask what happened. She claims the scream came from a female spirit, who was chased off the end of a cliff and fell to the rocks below, her bones breaking through her skin. Barbara is sobbing and quite shaken; the rest of us have been quite unnerved.

The Amityville Horror Conspiracy

After gaining her composure, Barbara says that another spirit wishes to communicate—it claims to be a rabbi. Wishing to see some physical proof of his existence, I challenge the "Rabbi" to do something physical to me.

"I don't mean just a tap on the shoulder, or a wind in my face," I say with "macho" abandon. "'Do something to me that is *so impressive* that I will be convinced of your existence."

The "Rabbi" gives a frightening laugh. "You are a very stupid man to challenge me so," he sneers. "You will get your proof soon, but not tonight."

Tonight I scoff at this as a cop–out, but I am to look back on his words sooner than I know.

Friday, July 2, 1976

It is a scorching, humid July morning. I have been feeling slightly under the weather all week. I think I must have twisted my arm playing softball with the local league—it occasionally feels stiff and sore. And it certainly didn't help any when I was moving furniture around yesterday. I had gone to Brooklyn to pick up a used bedroom set that my mother-in-law was donating for my daughter's bedroom, and I had lugged the heavy pieces into and out of an elevator and then onto a U-Haul-it trailer.

All in all, it has been one very rough year for me. I have been taking diet pills prescribed by a new Oriental doctor recommended to me by a friend in an attempt to shed the extra pounds I have put on. At 5'10" and 215 lbs., I am feeling very sluggish. The tension in my family life has been building also. My wife and I have not gotten along well since we were married in 1970, but lately we have been fighting more than ever. I am reluctant to separate because of the young ages of our children, but I find the situation quite intolerable. I am torn between my children and my peace of mind. I feel that my first book has not been a success for more than financial reasons—I need a ghostwriter to help organize my thoughts into a more readable form. Just last week a writer acquaintance has offered to help me write a second book. This afternoon Roxanne will be coming over to help transcribe the tapes of my various cases.

After dropping off my wife and children at the supermarket to do the grocery shopping, I pick up Roxanne at her home in Centereach. We return to my house and begin the tedious business of transcribing one of the tapes. I will help Roxanne with this work until I get the phone call to pick up my family at the store.

Ten minutes into the transcribing I begin to have some difficulty breathing and I am sweating profusely. I stretch out on the floor with my notebook where it seems a little cooler. But it doesn't help. Ten minutes later I am nauseous and beginning to have stabbing pains in my chest. Since I am not one to give in to pain, and not wanting to frighten Roxanne who is only 22–years–old, I excuse myself and go to the bedroom to lie down for awhile. Instead of letting up, the pain gets increasingly worse. I am getting frightened. My throat feels dry and parched and I feel unable to go downstairs for a drink. Trying to sound normal, I call downstairs for Roxanne to bring me a glass of juice.

Being a young, single girl, Roxanne is somewhat suspicious of being summoned upstairs to the bedroom of a married man. Realizing she has not taken me seriously, I drop all pretense of normality and call for the juice in a strangled voice. This time she gets the point—something is wrong. She immediately pours a glass of juice and brings it upstairs.

At this point I must let Roxanne herself describe what followed, as my own memory of it is somewhat fuzzy:

"When I reached the bedroom and saw the look on Steve's face, I knew something was seriously wrong. He was white as a sheet and clutching at his chest, sprawled across the bed with his knees drawn up. When I asked him what was wrong, he said that he felt as though a blade had been plunged into his chest. He was unable to drink much of the juice I had brought him but asked for a cold cloth. I ran to the bathroom and returned with the cloth, placing it on his forehead which was clammy and drenched with sweat.

"The pain did not let up. Steve thought he may be having an allergic reaction to the diet pills and told me to call the Oriental doctor for advice. This excuse for a doctor made an outlandish reply: 'Tell him to stop taking the pills.' I replied that this would not help us with our present situation. It was then that he mentioned the possibility of a heart attack and said, 'Maybe you should take him to a hospital.'

"To me there was no maybe about it—this could be a life or death situation. I told Steve we must either call an ambulance or drive to Mather Memorial Hospital in Port Jefferson Station. He protested, 'No, no, I'll be all right,' even as he gritted his teeth in pain. I was insistent. Although I was terrified and had never been in a situation like this before, I knew I had to act fast. 'You're going whether you like it or not!' I yelled. 'Or do you just want to lie there and suffer?'

"This seemed to shock Steve back into reality. 'Okay,' he said. 'Let's take the car. Can you drive?' He had known me for two years and for all that time I had been driving to and from his classes, lectures and cases—the shock must have caused him to forget. I assured Steve that I could drive. Privately I was somewhat nervous because I had never driven his particular car before.

"Steve managed to get down the stairs and out the front door, insisting he didn't need any help. Walking like a hunchback, he managed to get into the passenger side of the car, as I quickly acquainted myself with the dashboard and turned on the ignition. Thank God it was an automatic transmission; I had never driven a stick-shift before and I did not relish learning at a time like this. I backed down the driveway and sped out towards Nesconset Highway. I vaguely remembered that the hospital was somewhere off Route 112, which I thought intersected with the Nesconset. Steve said he would be able to direct me from there.

"Honking the horn and speeding through stop signs and red lights we were getting very close to the hospital when we suddenly approached the railroad crossing. The gates were down and a train was passing. Cars were stopped in front of us and in back of us and we were trapped in the middle. Steve pounded the dashboard with his fist in extreme pain and anguish. 'Hurry!' he moaned. ' I know I must get there soon.' But I could not drive through the train as I had the stop signs and red lights. Oh please God, we both thought to ourselves, let it be a short train! Luckily it was and we arrived at the emergency entrance a few minutes later. Steve insisted on walking in rather than waiting for a stretcher! I was amazed that he was still able to function so rationally."

*   *   *

I was 35 years old and I had just suffered a major heart attack—or to put it in medical terms, an anterior myocardial infarction. I was to be in the cardiac unit of intensive care for six days, and altogether in the hospital for 3 weeks. I had never shown any sign of a heart condition in the past and had always thought of myself as a "gorilla"—

strong and nearly immortal. These illusions were shattered as quickly as my health and it would be some time before I would recover from the mental as well as physical shock.

I am not a superstitious person, but lying there in the ICU with so many tubes and monitors connected to me that I felt like Frankenstein's monster, I could only sleep or think—and I could not help but recall my foolish challenge to the spirit at the seance to do something really impressive to me.

Sunday, July 18, 1976

Today is my 17th day in Mather Memorial Hospital. The Bicentennial celebration has come and gone as I fought for my life in the ICU. I have been in this semi-private room since July 8th and my condition is listed as "stabilized." The doctors have given me permission to walk from my bed to the bathroom and I maneuver those few yards as if they were 10 miles. I am allowed to leave my room only in a wheelchair, which is pushed by a nurse or one of my visitors.

The nurses have been wonderful to me, in spite of the fact that I am not exactly a "model patient" to deal with. I have told them all about the P.I.A. and my psychic research, in fact, I even had Roxanne distribute the flyers for our summer lecture series throughout my entire ward. (I sometimes helped as she rolled me up and down the aisles in my wheelchair.)

Lunch time is now in progress and one of my favorite nurses comes in carrying the magazine section of the *New York Sunday News*. "Weren't you involved in this Amityville thing?" she asks. "Here's a story about it in today's paper."

I look up from my meal at the paper she holds open in front of me. There is a full–page, eerily distorted picture of the Amityville house facing the text on the opposite page which is titled, "Life In A Haunted House—The ghosts in the $80,000 house In Amityville were too much even for an ex-Marine and his family."

Snatching the paper from the hands of my startled nurse, I push away my half-eaten lunch and begin to quickly read the article. The more I read, the more agitated I become, mouthing comments of disbelief aloud. My nurse is sorry she ever showed me the story, for she knows that I am not supposed to get excited.

"Calm down!" she admonishes. "Do you want to give yourself another heart attack over a stupid newspaper story?"

The Amityville Horror Conspiracy

She is right. Getting control of my emotions, I finish the article in relative quiet. A few minutes later, Roxanne comes in to visit me and I immediately hold up the story in front of her. She has not seen it yet and is also incredulous as she reads it. Once again Lutz's story has mutated and grown. Roxanne helps me to take notes on the startling new events revealed by author Paul Hoffman's version:

1: The Catholic priest, now described as a "cleric in the chancery of the Rockville Center diocese," is said to have blessed the house shortly after the Lutzes moved in, warning them not to use a particular second-floor bedroom. The Lutzes took his advice, placed holy water in the room and used it as a sewing room, later learning that it was Ronald DeFeo Jr.'s former bedroom.

This disagrees with what I was told—that Ronald's bedroom was on the third floor.

2: "Lee became impulsive about building roaring fires in the living room fireplace..." And who wouldn't, when the heating system had failed shortly after they moved in?

3: Kathy and Lee had arguments "for no apparent reason."
What couple doesn't? They also changed their policy of not hitting the children, raising welts on the boys' bottoms with a wooden spoon. Sounds to me like the Lutzes got a little carried away with old-fashioned corporal punishment.

4: "The in-laws spent a whole evening sitting and glaring at each other..." This is occult? Kathy's aunt, a normally placid ex-nun, came to visit and, according to Lee, 'sat there and cut me down for three hours.'" Perhaps she just doesn't like Lee. "When Kathy's sister-in-law visited, she reverted to childhood, spending all her time with the children in the third-floor playroom." Roxanne says that many young women her age enjoy being with children and prefer their company to that of certain adults. This does not mean that they are reverting.

5: Once again we have the report of "strange noises," but the Lutzes admit that "every new house has strange noises." The fact that they were not able to account for the source does not mean it had to be supernatural.

6: Some new phenomena which we have not heard of before: doors and windows mysteriously opened or shut, black stains appeared on bathroom fixtures, trickles of red ran from keyholes, a smell of decaying bodies in the playroom, clusters of flies (in winter) on the playroom window. Lee claims the second-floor bathroom had an odor "like a whore's perfume from Paris."

How would you know, Lee?

7: "Night after night, Lee was snapped wide awake at 3:15—the hour of the murders." This is very interesting. I know that the exact time of 3:15 was picked up by the media from Joel Martin's interview of the neighbor, in which she stated that was the time she heard the DeFeo dog barking. The actual coroner's report stated only that the murders occurred in the "early morning hours," as that was as close as they were able to pinpoint it.

8: Kathy felt the comforting hand of a woman clasp hers and "knew, instinctively, that it was Louise DeFeo's."

9: Throughout the Christmas holidays the Lutzes remained baffled by what was happening, but they weren't afraid...yet. They stayed home on the night of Dec. 31 to welcome the New Year and Lee's 29th birthday. Then on Jan. 6, Epiphany, or "Little Christmas," as Kathy calls it, they took down the holiday decorations. After that..."havoc."

It is a fact that Lee turned over his gun to the Amityville Police only a few days after moving in. How could he not be afraid until Jan. 6th? Wouldn't it be a most fearful occurrence if one had the urge to shoot his entire family?

10: On the night of Jan. 10th, Lee claims to have felt a compulsion to flee the house. He had trouble awakening Kathy, and as he watched, "she turned into a 90-year-old woman." Her hair became old and dirty, creases and crow's feet formed on her face, water drooled from her mouth and drenched the sheets. She did not return to normal for several hours.

Perhaps Kathy was dreaming of the overdue bills.

11: The next night, Lee observed Kathy "sliding across the bed, as if by levitation." Lee had the impression of a cloven–hoofed animal climbing up on the bed.

12: On Jan. 12th, Lutz allegedly called the priest, who promised to talk to the bishop. Lee then told his story to a woman in his office who claimed to have psychic powers. "Roz" and her friend "Bill" came to the house and Lutz felt a turbulence "like an elephant rolling over in its sleep" when the couple arrived.

"Bill examined the house and explained that it was haunted by the spirits of those who had died in their sleep and didn't know they were dead." This statement sounds like a cliché from every old book on spiritualism ever written. Following the couple's instructions, Lee and Kathy went to each room, opened a window, and prayed, "God bless this house. God bless this room. This is our house. Whoever you are, get out!"

13: It didn't seem to work. Kathy observed "red, beady eyes" at the living room window six feet above ground level.

14: On Tues., Jan. 13th, Lee opened a window in each room, recited the Lord's Prayer in each corner, and once again told the spirits to, "Get Out!" Afterwards their son Danny suffered a slight cut (which Kathy treated) when an aluminum storm window which he was closing fell on his hands. Lee took this as a sign that the spirits were rebuking him. He states that he was so furious, "I could have killed." He compares this rage to what Ronald DeFeo must have felt.

15: This same Tuesday night, the Lutzes also claim to have had: even louder noises, beds sliding across the floor and a Bible that flipped over by itself. Three doors were found open the next morning: the front door (supposedly double-latched), the locked basement door, and the garbage shed doors (which had been nailed shut). The priest advises them to get out before sundown and they all flee to Kathy's mother's house in West Babylon that very afternoon, Jan. 14th.

16: The next few paragraphs of the article deal with outsiders' reactions: neighbors do not believe the house is haunted, nor does Sgt. Pat Cammaroto; and attorney William Weber is called a "doubter." Yet Weber is considering making a motion for a new trial for DeFeo on the grounds he was possessed by the force in the house when he killed his family. Quite a daring motion for a "doubter."

17: The Lutzes repeat two statements which agree with what Lee told me on the phone in February: First, that they took a "crash course" in the occult after they fled the house (including astrology, mysticism, mediums, psychics and parapsychologists). Second, Lee claims the house is possessed by a number of spirits, "some of whose names I won't pronounce, since merely to mention their names will bring them here." This is just what he told me except that he now calls them "spirits," rather than "demons." Lee says that Kathy and he will not go back to fight the house because "it knows us too well."

*　　　　*　　　　*

I am angered and upset by these new additions to the Lutzes' story. Just what is George trying to pull? Is this what the auctioneer meant when he said George was writing a book, or is this just the preview of what's to come?

Trying to analyze this new version, I tend to trace it all back to George's apparent preoccupation with demons, combined with a morbid obsession with the DeFeo murders. The demonlike traits include: George's compulsion about building fires; Kathy turning into a haglike creature; the cloven-hoofed animal; the red, beady eyes; and efforts to fight it with holy water, Christian prayers and a Bible. Then we have the obvious psychological connections to the mass murder: fear of Ronald's (alleged) bedroom; trickles of red (blood?) running from keyholes; the smell of decaying bodies (and the flies); Lee awakening at 3:15; Kathy sensing Louise DeFeo's spirit; spirits who "died in their sleep and do not know they are dead"; and Lee's impulses to kill (especially to shoot his wife and family, as Ronald did).

Throw in a handful of what George has read in his occult books about haunted houses, mix well, and you get the whole, half-baked fairy tale.

I believe that Lee and Kathy were more spooked by the idea of living in a house where such violence took place then they want to admit. The *house* did not possess Ronald and in turn the Lutzes; instead, Ronald's crime became an obsession in the minds of the Lutzes—the more they thought about the murders, especially late at night, the more their imaginations worked overtime. However, it is quite possible that this was not the start of it all—perhaps the Lutzes moved in with a plan to help DeFeo, if indeed they knew him. If not, then how did they meet up with Weber? In either case, the Amityville haunting is mutually beneficial to Weber and the Lutzes—Weber uses it for his appeal, the Lutzes make money on a book.

I must try to put a stop to this right now. The public is being misled and lied to and it could tarnish the reputation of legitimate cases of hauntings. I will not have Lutz use and abuse my field for his own personal gain. I make a solemn vow to myself: If I recover from this heart attack and survive to continue in my parapsychological research, I will dedicate myself to informing the public of the truth. The truth about Amityville and the truth about any other hoaxes or deceitful practices in this field.

Roxanne has become a close confidant, and I tell her of my vow. She agrees to help me compose a letter to the editor of the *New York Sunday News Magazine,* denouncing the case as a hoax. However, I am becoming too weak and drowsy to dictate anything intelligent; I have been pumped full of pain killers and other medications. Groggily, I tell Roxanne to compose the letter herself this evening and sign my name to it. She promises to have it in the mail by morning. It is the last thing I remember as I slip into unconsciousness.

Thursday, July 22, 1976

I was released from the hospital early this afternoon, just in time for tonight's lecture at my home. It is the first in a series of summer

The Amityville Horror Conspiracy

lectures sponsored by the P.I.A. entitled, "Are You Psychic?" and tonight's speaker is Dr. Max Toth, author of *Pyramid Power*. Max is a thrilling lecturer, and I am so happy to be home and able to attend it. It is still very difficult for me to sit up for long periods of time, and I'm hoping I'll be able to go through with my own scheduled lecture one week from tonight. Friends have advised me to cancel it or get a replacement, but it is very important for me to have that goal to look forward to. Most of all, I am just happy to be alive.

Thursday, July 29, 1976

My lecture on "Ghostology, Haunted Houses and Seances" was a big success. Not being able to stand for such a long time, I had purchased a tall stool which I sat on throughout the lecture. Twenty-two people were in attendance, a large crowd for summer-vacation time. A reporter from *The Three Village Herald*, a local paper which is covering our entire series, was present.

With my new-found determination to expose the Amityville hoax, I did not wait for the audience to question me. I myself brought up the topic and gave the audience all the straight-forward facts that I knew. Some were shocked and indignant that they had been fooled into believing. Many had thought that newspaper articles were more thoroughly researched before being printed. They felt they had trusted the media and were betrayed by them. And almost all of my listeners were disappointed—they had *wanted* to believe in the Amityville ghosts.

Exhaustion racks my body now, but I am mentally content. I settle down to sleep on the Castro convertible in my living room—I am not yet allowed to climb the short flight of stairs to my bedroom because of the strain to my heart.

Wednesday, August 4, 1976

The Three Village Herald article came out today entitled, "Investigator Uncovers Ghosts and Hoaxes." The following paragraphs referred to Amityville: "One of Kaplan's most recent cases involved the house at 112 Ocean Avenue, Amityville, where Ronald DeFeo Jr. murdered all six members of his family in November, 1974. After some preliminary investigations, including extensive interviews with neighbors, he decided that the reported 'strange forces' within the house were a hoax, and withdrew from the case. Kaplan feels they may have evolved from a plan by new owners George and Karen [sic]

Lutz, who he suspects are friends of the convicted murderer, to win a new trial for DeFeo, currently serving a 150 years to life sentence. Kaplan is distressed at the attention being given to Lutz's story by the media, and called a recent *Daily News* article authored in collaboration with Lutz, 'creative writing.'"

For a local paper, I feel the article is very well written. *The Three Village Herald* has always treated me fairly and I have never known them to distort or manipulate fact as some of the major publications do.

I am feeling a little stronger and tomorrow, I will visit my cardiologist for the first time since being released from the hospital.

Monday, August 9, 1976

My mother arrived from Florida today and we are sitting in the kitchen having coffee (that is, Mom is having coffee—my doctor forbids me to drink it). She is saying that she, "sure picked a fine time to visit!"—we are in the midst of a storm called "Hurricane Belle." The lights went out an hour ago and the glow from our candles casts weird, looming shapes on the wall. As the wind screams and strains against the house outside, Mom and I discuss my health. The doctor does not want me to return to work until November (I am due back in September), but how shall I support my family? According to my wife, who manages the money, we have no savings, huge debts and my children "will starve." The doctor has advised me to move closer to my job because the commuting is too dangerous to my condition. But my wife does not want to sell the house and move.

The hurricane outside is mild compared to the moral dilemma raging inside me.

Sunday, August 22, 1976

On Friday, I put our house on the market, despite strong protests from my wife. I have not fought this hard to recover to end up dying on the Long Island Expressway. The real estate agent will be bringing a couple by to look at the house today. But I have a few hours yet to myself to settle down with the Sunday papers. Halfway through the *N.Y. Sunday News Magazine,* I come across the letters to the editor. Surprise, surprise! They have finally printed my letter (or mine and Roxanne's, since she composed it). Under a topic called simply "Haunted House," there are three letters: the first from two young men from New Jersey who want to spend a night in the Amityville house to get proof of the "unseen forces"; the second is mine, and the third from a lady in Queens who got "chills" from the story and claims she had a "weird experience" 30 years ago.

My letter reads as follows:

> Setauket, N.Y.: The Parapsychology Institute of America has investigated the Amityville house and we found no phenomena of any kind. It is our belief that a hoax is being perpetrated on the public and we feel you are helping to spread this science fiction. I hope that in the future you will see that Mr. Hoffman thoroughly checks out his facts before submitting such an article.
>
> Dr. Stephen Kaplan
Executive Director

Short, and to the point. I do hope this will at least make some of the believers reconsider the facts.

Monday, September 6, 1976

This morning Roxanne and I took our staff photographer, Jim Knusch, out to Amityville and to Bayshore to get photographs of two allegedly haunted houses. The one in Bayshore is a huge, rambling old house which was once part of an old estate. Its owner had reported hearing strange noises in the house, and he wanted it explained because he planned to turn the place into a school for emotionally disturbed boys. We had conducted a brief investigation in which many of my staff had heard the strange sounds also (like a ball being bounced off the walls) in a totally empty room. However, for some reason unknown to us, the owner has not contacted us to set up a date for further investigation.

The second house, of course, was the notorious Lutz/DeFeo home in Amityville. It is still vacant and "No Parking" signs have been added to the "No Trespassing" signs. We shot photos from the sidewalk only. I may use some of these pictures for the book I had begun working on before my heart attack, if the project ever gets off the ground. My potential "ghostwriter" lives too far from me for us to get together often enough and I will have less time and energy when I return to work this Wednesday. Yes, I will be commuting, against doctor's orders. I feel I have no choice, as we have not been able to sell the house or find an apartment in Queens.

Photo by Jim Knusch

Dr. Kaplan in front of the house during the vacant period after the Lutzes "fled." Note the sign post where the DeFeo's "High Hopes" sign once hung.

Photo by Jim Knusch

Note the original wooden door is still intact in the main entrance of the house, which faces the driveway rather than Ocean Avenue. The combination garage/boathouse is in the background.

The Amityville Horror Conspiracy

The famous windows of Ronald DeFeo's bedroom. Note the original panes of glass are still intact.

Sunday, November 7, 1976

Newsday ran a small article today under the heading, "Updating the News." After a brief summary of the history of the Amityville house, there are some quotes from attorney William Weber. The Lutz family now lives in California, having signed the house over to a bank and moved in March. Weber says there will soon be a "major announcement" about an application for a new trial for DeFeo. The Lutzes' experience will play "just a small part" in the motion. Neighbors of the Amityville house are quoted as saying that there are not many sightseers stopping by to stare at the house any more.

This is the first time I have seen anything in print about Amityville since August when my letter was published in the *N.Y. Sunday News* (the story seems to be dying down, thank God). But I did see something about William Weber in September—it seems he had been arrested on charges of illegal possession of a gun. Police claimed to have stopped his car on a routine traffic check and discovered a 32-cal. Smith and Wesson revolver on the floor. At the time I read the article the hearing was going on and Weber was being defended by his partner, Bernard Burton. A conviction on gun-possession would mean automatic disbarment for Weber. I have not heard anything more about the case since then.

Saturday, November 13, 1976

A reporter named Joe from a men's magazine in Manhattan came to my home to interview me today. He was doing research on an article he planned to write about Amityville concerning what he called, "The Lutz/DeFeo Connection." Joe was trying to find the link that would explain how and when and if the two men met. He told me a somewhat disturbing story about William Weber. He had gone to interview Weber for his story and, according to Joe, Weber showed him 8 x 10 color glossies of the murdered DeFeos' bodies. The photos were those taken by the police and were grossly livid and detailed. Joe was repulsed when Weber smugly offered to sell him any or all of these photos for a huge sum of money. In spite of the fact that the magazine Joe works for is of a type that may have some readers who would take a perverse pleasure in seeing the photos, he turned Weber down politely but emphatically.

Since Joe wanted to photograph the Amityville house but did not have a car, I offered to drive him there. It was dusk when we arrived and the street seemed quiet and peaceful, with not a soul in sight. Quite different from past months when it had been in the spotlight. As Joe took a few shots from each angle, I told him about all the phone calls I had received this past summer from teenagers who wanted to investigate "the ghost house." Why, young men had even had the nerve to phone and tell me that they were planning to "break in and spend the night," and could I give them any professional tips on what to look for. In that case I phoned Sgt. Cammaroto of the Amityville Police to inform him and his colleagues of the date these boys had planned to break in. The officers were very appreciative of the information.

As I drove Joe to the Amityville train station, I wondered why Weber was trying to sell the murder photos, if indeed Joe's story was accurate. It certainly does not seem to be an ethical practice for a defense lawyer to sell evidence of his client's atrocities.

Friday, November 19, 1976

Following my lecture for the P.I.A. this evening on ghosts, I and my members were interviewed by feature writer John Pascal of *Newsday* about the Amityville case. We supplied him with more of the inside information than we have previously related to reporters, as he told us that his article would be a full–length feature in the Sunday magazine section. He does not know yet when it will be published,

The Amityville Horror Conspiracy

and it must first be approved by his editor, but if it comes out it will be the first full-length article to present the Amityville case as a hoax.

Wednesday, December 1, 1976

His article was never published and when I called *Newsday* they told me it would not be coming out in the near future. They did not give me a reason. This evening I did a radio talk-show via phone for Alan Handelman's program on WRQR in North Carolina. The show will be aired this Sunday. We discussed the Amityville hoax and how I became involved in the case. My position is beginning to become known in distant states as well as New York.

Sunday, December 5, 1976

Ronald DeFeo is in the news once again. The "Ideas" section of today's *Newsday* has an article by August Franza entitled, "Murder Too Foul for Words." Franza is head of the English department at Miller Place High School and has been writing a novel based on the DeFeo murders. He had called me during the summer to discuss the case with me, but he is basically not interested in the Lutz part of the story, only the murders. In fact, he does not even make mention of the Lutzes' ghost story in his article; it is a psychological examination of the phenomena of killing one's entire family.

Franza notes that the English language does not have a word to describe this act because it is a modern problem. He suggests the word, "familicide" be used. The topic of "familicide" has renewed interest once again since a case took place last week in Montvale, N.J.: Harry de La Roche, Jr., an 18–year-old home on Thanksgiving holiday from a military college, allegedly shot to death his father, mother and two brothers (ages 12 and 15).

According to Franza, there have been eleven cases of "familicide" within the last 5 years: four in New Jersey, three on Long Island, one in upper N.Y. State, one in Pennsylvania, one in New Orleans and one in Detroit. Franza attributes this to increasing tension and upheavals in the nuclear family.

An interesting note about DeFeo: Franza states that Ronnie made an attempt on his father's life in 1973. He drove a loaded shotgun into his father's chest and pulled the trigger, but the gun didn't go off. DeFeo Sr. saw this as a miracle and an indication that God was watching over him. This only seemed to increase Ronnie's hatred for his father.

The article is intelligent and thought-provoking and I am glad that Franza had the good sense not to mention the Lutz story.

Sunday, January 16, 1977

I made a decision today. I cannot continue to commute to my job in Queens from Suffolk County. While my health is slowly improving, the strain of the trip is more than I can bear. My wife does not want to give up the house; she discouraged the few prospective buyers we had and then took the house off the market a few months ago. She is adamant about not moving to Queens and suggests that I rent an apartment for myself. She does not seem to understand that we are grossly in debt and could not possibly afford to keep up two homes. I feel that she cares more about her house than about my life. Therefore, we have discussed our feelings toward one another and decided to legally separate. There is no love in the relationship and staying togeth-er for the children's sake no longer seems reasonable or fair. She will call a lawyer and I will register with an apartment hunting agency.

Wednesday, February 2, 1977

Last night we signed the separation papers and today I moved into a cramped basement apartment in Elmhurst, Queens. It is one mile from my job and if I walk there and back each day, it will ful-fill the daily exercise requirements recommended by my cardiolo-gist. I am torn between feelings of relief and loneliness. Already I miss my children and they are too young to really understand why Daddy had to move.

My organization will now hold meetings at a member's house in West Babylon as we can no longer use my home in South Setauket, and the Suffolk members do not want to travel to Queens. I am hav-ing a new business phone installed at my apartment, and our public lectures have been postponed until we find a new place to hold them.

Monday, February 28, 1977

My energy level is much higher since I gave up commuting. I am now able to devote more time to lecturing and researching. Tonight I lectured on "Haunted Houses and Ghosts" for the Northport Public Library. The room was filled with an over-capacity crowd of more than 100 people, and I devoted a large portion of my talk to exposing the Amityville case as a hoax. Quite a few people came up to me after the

The Amityville Horror Conspiracy

lecture to congratulate me on my efforts to promote the truth. It makes me feel good to know that my honesty is appreciated by the public.

Wednesday, March 9, 1977

Max Toth, my friend and the author of *Pyramid Power*, just dropped by to visit. He had called earlier to tell me that he had something he knew I'd be interested in seeing. When he arrived and handed me the April copy of *Good Housekeeping* magazine, I looked up (Max is 6'4") at him rather strangely until I examined the cover more closely. Next to the photo of a smiling, blond, blue-eyed baby and beneath the picture of a patchwork quilt design, is the following lead-in for a story inside: "So you don't believe in haunted houses? Now you will!"

Max did not have to tell me what the story was about; I knew even before I turned to the table of contents and read, "119—Our Dream House Was Haunted, Paul Hoffman." With a groan, I turned to page 119 where I saw a ghostly, black and white sketch of the Amityville house. Beneath the main title is the teaser, "Lee and Kathy Lutz were delighted with their new home—in spite of its tragic history. Then strange and bizarre things began to happen."

Basically, this version of the Paul Hoffman article is the same as the one printed in the *N.Y. Sunday News*. Many paragraphs match word for word, although in some cases the phrasing has been edited. However, there are quite a few important changes that have been made in this version. Max and I have noted the following discrepancies:

1: Included in the belongings the Lutzes left behind at the house are two boats. Previously only one boat had been mentioned.

2: When the priest warns the Lutzes not to use a certain bedroom, they do not specify which floor it was on. In the *News* article, the "second-floor bedroom" was specified, and later identified as having been Ronald DeFeo Jr.'s bedroom. As I have previously mentioned, I had been informed that Ronald's room was on the third floor. Hoffman and the Lutzes must have discovered their error and "moved" the evil to another floor! This version still claims that the Lutzes evil "sewing room" was once Ronald DeFeo Jr's bedroom. Don't the Lutzes even know which floor their sewing room was on?

3: Whereas the *News* article had the Lutzes developing a "thing" about not leaving the house, this version states that although they did make up excuses not to go out, and did procrastinate, they eventually went out. Lee went to the office to prepare the payroll, and he and Kathy went out to attend one class of a home-improvement course they'd signed up for. They even attended the wedding of Kathy's brother, although Hoffman states that they were late and delayed the ceremony.

None of these items were mentioned in the *News*, and though they may not seem like a great deal of activity, one must remember that this all occurred within a 28 day (or less) period.

4: In the *Good Housekeeping* article, Lee and Kathy are no longer "yelling and swearing" at the kids, but merely "yelling." They have also deleted all reference to beating them with wooden spoons and raising welts on their bottoms. The Lutzes must have realized that those actions made them appear to be crazed or violent.

5: Where the *News* article had stated that "few of their visitors could be induced to return," this one merely says, "Few visitors returned." There is a big difference between the two. The first one implies that no amount of coaxing could convince frightened visitors to return to the Lutzes' house; the second simply says that few paid the Lutzes a second visit. Once again, we must remember that it was only less than a month that the Lutzes lived there, and it does not seem unusual that a visitor would not have a chance to visit the Lutzes twice during that period.

6: Lee's amusing comment about the odor in the bathroom, "like a whore's perfume from Paris," has been changed to an odor "like a cheap perfume." I assume *Good Housekeeping's* editors did not find Lee's original comment wholesome enough for their magazine.

7: Two completely new sentences have been added. I quote, "One night, five-year-old Missy asked, 'Do angels talk?' It was the first indication that the children were aware of the mysterious phenomena."

Does it seem unusual in a Christian household shortly after Christmas for a little girl to ask a question about angels? She most likely had helped to hang angels on the Christmas tree and listened to carols about angels. Has the normal childhood curiosity and wonder of Christmas now been deemed occult or mysterious?

8: This time, when Kathy turns into an old hag, she has water drooling from her mouth, but no longer do we read that the sheets became "sopping." Another detail which must have been judged to be too gross for housewives.

9: Once again, a new paragraph is added just after Lee recites the Lord's Prayer to exorcise the spirits, and just before Danny is injured: "In the bathroom, the perfume scent was stronger than ever. In Missy's room, the rocking chair started swaying of its own accord. And as soon as he started the ritual, Kathy began to suffer from a severe headache."

The Amityville Horror Conspiracy

Since Lee has just gone from room to room opening a window in each, it is likely that a winter breeze from an open window could start a child's rocker swaying. And Kathy could certainly develop a headache with George stomping around the house, opening windows and screaming for the spirits to, "Get out!" It is interesting to note that both new additions to the story have mentioned the five-year-old child, Missy. Are the Lutzes now attempting to use their daughter to back up their story?

10: This time, after Lee feels the killing rage that DeFeo must have felt, he then looks at Kathy's crucifix on the wall and immediately realizes that, "his rage would serve no purpose."

This is another obvious attempt to make Lee seem more sane, and even more religious.

11: After Lee sees the Bible flip over, he and Kathy lie awake, "frozen in total terror" and "clutching each other for safety." The News article did not include this and in fact, did not even mention that Kathy was awake when Lee saw the Bible move.

12: In the *News* story, when the doors on the garbage shed are found open, it is stated that some of the doors had been nailed shut. This version says, "including the one that had been nailed shut."

13: When the Lutzes call back the priest on the morning of the last day, he tells them to, "Get out of there...." In the *News* version he had stated, "Get out of there before the sun goes down." Some one must have realized how corny this sounds.

14: All comments skeptical of the Lutzes' story have been eliminated in the G.H. article. Gone are the statements of neighbors who were quoted in the News as not believing the house to be haunted and who thought it was all, "a bunch of lies." Gone is any reference to Sgt. Pat Cammaroto. Gone is any reference to William Weber and his motion for a new trial for DeFeo on grounds of possession.

They have taken out what little information was left to give the public a view of the other side of the story.

15: In place of these omissions, *Good Housekeeping* has substituted more about the Lutzes and their "crash course" in the occult. They include here a paragraph which really upsets me:

With [the Lutzes] consent, a group from the Psychical Research Foundation associated with Duke University in Durham, N.C., conducted a seance in the house—one that was filmed by TV cameras. Because of what one participant called the "sideshow" atmosphere, it was not particularly successful. Only two of the participants reported feeling psychic sensations.

With Max listening on the amplifier, I immediately call Jerry Solfvin at the P.R.F. in Durham. Luckily, Jerry is in to answer the phone. He has not yet seen the *Good Housekeeping* article so I read the paragraph concerning the P.R.F. and ask for his comments.

"That's wrong, we did not conduct the seance," says Jerry. "It was conducted by the people brought in by Channel 5—the Warrens and their group. George Kekoris sat in on the circle, but I was merely an outside observer. Most of the time I was attempting to investigate the house on my own, but it was such a circus there that it was impossible."

"Do you realize, Jerry," I ask, "that the Lutzes are using the good reputation of the P.R.F. and Duke University to add credence to their story? And this time it's in a national magazine!"

Jerry is not pleased at all by this prospect; in fact, he says he is quite fed up with the whole case. George Kekoris never did turn in his report on his interview with the Lutzes, and Jerry says that Kekoris is no longer a representative of the P.R.F. As far as Jerry is concerned, their involvement with the Amityville house was inconclusive and they have severed all connections to the case.

After thanking Jerry and hanging up the phone, I show Max to the door and bid him goodnight. It will take me hours to calm down. I am incensed by this new article! Millions of people in the country will read this copy of *Good Housekeeping* and believe the Lutzes' story. They will believe because they equate the magazine with Mom and apple pie. It is wholesome and All–American, a trusted institution. I scan the listing of "Articles and Features"; it includes items such as, "Would You Like To See *Your* Baby in *Good Housekeeping*?"; "The Dogs in Our Life"; "Letters to Amy Carter"; "Look Who Won Our Benji Contest"; "My Life in the Peace Corps," by "Miss Lillian" Carter; and last but not least, Paul Hoffman's story. Babies, dogs, patriotism, and the Amityville Haunting: Why, they have as much as given it the *Good Housekeeping* Seal of Approval! As the heading on the title page proclaims," *Good Housekeeping*—The Magazine America Lives By." How many people in this country follow that credo? How many believe that whatever they read here must be true? The *Good Housekeeping* editors and their publishers, The Hearst Corporation (chaired by Randolf Hearst, father of Patty Hearst) have done a grave disservice to their loyal readers by betraying the public trust. They have published the article with no regard to the fact that there was another side to the story.

The Amityville Horror Conspiracy

Angrily I pick up the phone and dial information. After getting the Manhattan number from the operator, I call *Good Housekeeping* and ask for the features editor. A young woman picks up and identifies herself as the associate editor for features. She listens patiently to my story and explains that the staff was not aware that the Amityville story was in any way disputed.

"Mr. Hoffman's credentials were quite impressive," she says. "We did not see any reason to question his story. But since you seem to have a legitimate complaint, and evidence to back it up, I suggest you write a letter to our features editor. We will be glad to print it as the other side of the story."

The woman then tells me something that gets me more upset than before: The Amityville story will soon be coming out as a book published by Prentice Hall. And C.B.S. has already bought the rights to turn the book into a television movie!

Thanking the associate editor for her time, I hang up and sit down at my desk to dash off a letter to the editor of *Good Housekeeping*, outlining my reasons for declaring the case a hoax. I will mail it in the morning on my way to work.

Thursday, March 10, 1977

As soon as I returned home from work this afternoon, I made a call to Prentice Hall and asked to speak to someone connected with the Amityville book. I was transferred to an editor named Tam Mossman. After explaining who I was, I asked Mr. Mossman if he knew that the story he was printing was untrue. I said that the Lutzes had changed their story so many times as to constitute out-and-out lying.

Mossman said that he's a friend of the author, a man named Jay Anson, and that Jay merely wrote the book from tapes recorded by the Lutzes. The Lutzes described their experiences and Anson transcribed the tapes into book form. Mossman claimed that he and the people at Prentice Hall have listened to the original tapes and have no reason to doubt the sincerity of the Lutzes. He confirmed the fact that CBS-TV had already purchased the movie rights, and that the book will come out early this fall. Mossman did not seem interested in any of my reasons for why the book should not be published as nonfiction, so I asked to at least be allowed to examine an advance copy of the book. He told me that the book was just coming out in galley-form at the present time, but "that he would arrange to have a copy of the galleys sent to me as soon as they are ready."

*   *   *

I never did receive the galleys from Prentice Hall, and much to my chagrin, *Good Housekeeping* did not publish my letter. One thing that I couldn't help but wonder was what happened to author Paul Hoffman? He had carried the Lutzes' story this far, so why was he now being replaced by Jay Anson? I was not to learn the answer to this for quite some time.

In the months that followed, the Amityville house was purchased by a family named Cromarty. They moved in sometime in April, and when I learned of this through a small article in the newspaper, I mailed a letter to 112 Ocean Avenue. In the letter, I warned the Cromartys about the new book which was soon to be released, and asked if they were aware of the *Good Housekeeping* article. I told them that they could expect many curiosity–seekers at their home when this book was published.

Some time later my letter was returned to me stamped: NO SUCH ADDRESS. This was very puzzling—112 Ocean Ave. is such an infamous address that it did not seem possible that an error had been made. I decided to deliver the letter in person the next time I was in the area.

By summertime, Roxanne and I had begun dating and she was with me on the day I decided to visit Amityville. It was a sweltering July day in that summer of '77; the summer that brought us the big Blackout in the N.Y. Metropolitan area, a nine-day heat wave where temperatures rose to 104 degrees, and the notorious "Son-of-Sam" killer.

I had planned to just put the letter in the mailbox but instead decided to knock on the door and introduce myself. Roxanne and I were invited inside by a woman who introduced herself as a temporary maid for the Cromartys. She and her husband were helping to prepare a wedding reception for the Cromartys' daughter, who was getting married that day. In fact, the family ha already left for the ceremony; the maid and her husband were the only ones in the house.

The maid told us that the reason my letter must have been returned was that the Cromartys had changed the house number. They were already being harassed by sightseers, many of whom had traveled long distances just to see the house after reading the *Good Housekeeping* article.

The Amityville Horror Conspiracy

The house itself was in beautiful condition; the Cromartys had gone all out to renovate and refurnish it. The maid had the dining room table all set for the wedding guests and it looked exquisite. We could see the pool gleaming brightly in the sun through the open double doors in the back, as we stood in the lobby speaking with the maid. She told us that she had also been the maid to the DeFeos and had known them quite intimately; in fact, she still corresponded with "Butch" in prison. She said that Butch liked being where he was and had no intentions of trying to get paroled. She also mentioned that Butch had told her, when she asked him for the truth about the murders, that someday the whole truth would come out. The maid seemed to know more than she was willing or able to talk about.

We did discuss the murders though, and the maid seemed to be as puzzled as we were as to how Butch had managed to shoot each victim without awakening the others. During the trial, the coroner's test results had shown that the victims were not drugged during dinner as was previously assumed. They found no traces of drugs whatsoever. Reading between the lines of the maid's conversation, I got the impression that she felt that Butch had had an accomplice. This brought to mind an article I had read during the trial which brought up the possibility that the older sister, Dawn, had participated in the murders and then Ronald had killed her.

The maid said that the Cromartys were familiar with my name, as were the relatives of Louise DeFeo. She said that the DeFeo relatives had been pleased that I had attempted to expose the hoax because they felt the whole ghost story was an insult to Louise's memory. The Cromartys had experienced nothing supernatural in the house and were disgusted by the disruption of the enjoyment of their new home by tourists. They were already aware of the upcoming book by Jay Anson, in fact, they had requested and received a copy of the galleys from Prentice Hall. I privately wondered how they had succeeded in obtaining the galleys when I had failed.

The Cromartys were attempting to prevent the book from being released and had threatened to sue. They claim it constitutes an invasion of privacy, as it will undoubtedly cause their home to be besieged by the curious.

I told the maid to offer my assistance to the Cromartys, if they should need any help in proving the story to be a hoax. Roxanne and

I left the house determined to get an advance copy of the book. The next day I called Tam Mossman at Prentice Hall and asked why I had not received the galleys as I was promised in March, whereas the Cromartys had. He claimed it was merely an oversight and said he would send me an advance copy of the book which was just being printed up for a September release.

The book arrived at my home in mid-August. It was a hardcover edition consisting of 201 pages and entitled: *The Amityville Horror— A True Story.*

part II

THE BOOK

A Publishing Horror

Tuesday, August 16, 1977

My landlady just came downstairs with my mail, including a brown package from Prentice-Hall. Pulling open the staples, I slide the contents of the package out onto my desk. It is a hardcover book with a dust-jacket, the background color navy-blue. Two large drawings of houseflies seem to buzz above the words: Jay Anson: *The Amityville Horror—A True Story.* One leg of the letter "H" in "Horror" extends down, ending in an arrowlike point resembling a devil's tail. On the back cover is a photograph of the Lutz house as it appeared in February of '76. Beneath this are two quotes from *Newsday* articles, one from the *New York Daily News,* and one from the preface by the Reverend John Nicola.

Opening the book I turn past two title pages each containing a black and white drawing of the house. On the next page is the copyright information: Copyright 1977 by Jay Anson, George Lee Lutz, and Kathleen Lutz. On the facing page is a four-line statement: "The names of several individuals mentioned in this book have been changed to protect their privacy. However, all facts and events, as far as we have been able to verify them, are strictly accurate."

Beginning this evening, I will examine this book from cover to cover, compiling extensive notes on why *The Amityville Horror* is not "strictly accurate."

*   *   *

Accuracy in this book can not even be maintained from pages 2 through page 5. In the Prologue on page 2 it is stated, "They [the Lutzes] moved in on December 23." Turning to Chapter 1, beginning

The Amityville Horror Conspiracy

on page 5, we read the following: "Dec. 18, 1975—George and Kathy Lutz moved into 112 Ocean Avenue on Dec. 18. Twenty-eight days later, they fled in terror." On the front sleeve of the dust-jacket, the Dec. 18th date is repeated, but on the back cover of the book the quote from *Newsday* Feb. 14, 1976 reads, "Amityville: On Dec. 23, George and Kathleen Lutz bought the house and a few days later they moved in."

Interesting also is the fact that this quote omits pertinent data. The book jacket continues to quote *Newsday* with the following sentence, "Within...days, they moved out...." Looking back at the original article, we see that the actual sentence read, "Within 10 days, they moved out..."

What we have here is three different dates for when the Lutzes moved into the house: Dec. 18th, Dec. 23rd, or a few days after Dec. 23rd—all three taken from Anson's book and each contradicting the others. If the Lutzes can not even correctly remember the date they moved into the house, how are we expected to trust their account of what follows? Also, they were very careful to omit the mention of them leaving within 10 days, as it contradicts their present claim of being there 28 days.

The Amityville Horror is written in diary form, with a chronicling of events for each day beginning with Dec. 18, 1975 and climaxing on Jan. 14 or 15, 1976. Once again the book contradicts itself with dates—page 185 has the Lutzes fleeing the house at 7:00 a.m. on Jan. 14, 1976; but the chapter that follows (25) is headed Jan. 15th and quotes George saying to the priest, "We couldn't get out until this morning." So we are now unsure as to when the Lutzes moved in and when they moved out!

The Roman Catholic priest in the story has taken on the role of a major character in Anson's version. He is no longer just a priest who blessed the house and counseled the Lutzes. Father Frank Mancuso, as he is called now, experiences strange phenomena in the Lutzes' house, in his car, and where he lives at the rectory in North Merrick. It is incredible to me that none of this was mentioned in any of the articles during the past one-and-a-half years! Certainly if all of this were true the Lutzes would have come out with the information long before now, as it would certainly lend credence to their story.

Let's take a look at how the role of the priest has evolved. In the original *Newsday* article of Feb. 14, 1976, a neighbor says that Lutz walked around the house with a priest carrying a large cross shortly after the Lutzes moved out. In *The Star* article of April 6, 1976, the priest is contacted while the Lutzes still live there and he tells them the house is possessed and that they should flee for their lives. In the two Paul Hoffman versions of the story (*N.Y. Sunday News,* July 18, 1976 and *Good Housekeeping,* April 1977), Lutz calls in the priest to bless the house after being urged by a friend who has just learned about the history of the house. The priest tells them not to use a certain bedroom and later promises to talk to the Bishop on the Lutzes' behalf.

In the Anson version, Lutz had previously arranged for the priest to come bless the house on Dec. 18th, the day they move in. "Truth" has never had so many different versions! Nor is this an isolated incident; numerous occurrences in the Lutzes' story have evolved through many different versions.

Father "Mancuso" has a strange foreboding about going to the Lutzes' home before he even arrives. He gets there at 1:30 p.m. and begins his ritual of blessing. With the first flick of holy water, Mancuso is shocked by a terrible, disembodied voice which says, "Get out!"

Sound familiar? And well it should. In Hoffman's versions it was George Lutz who uttered the words, "Get out!" as he was blessing the house himself! Is George's role now being played by an invisible spirit?

On the evening of this same day, Dec. 18th, we have the good Father driving his blue Vega home from his mother's house in Queens. On the Van Wyck Expressway the car is mysteriously forced onto the right shoulder and then the hood flies open and smashes back against the windshield. A hinge tears loose, the right door flies open and the car finally stalls.

The hood smashing into the windshield is a phenomenon indeed! Anyone who is familiar with the Chevy Vega knows that the hood opens in the opposite direction, away from the windshield. It would be a physical impossibility for the Vega hood to smash the windshield.

On page 23 of *The Amityville Horror,* George laments over the situation he has gotten himself into: "a second marriage with three children, a new home with a big mortgage. The taxes in Amityville were three times higher than in Deer Park. Did he really need that new speedboat? How the hell was he going to pay for all of this? The construction business was lousy on Long Island... If they aren't building houses and buying property who the hell needs a land surveyor?" It sounds like George needed an economic miracle to bail himself out of this one. Perhaps an occult miracle? This appears to me to be the primary reason why George would have to abandon his dream house—and he had already realized his situation on this second night in the house.

George's mood gets progressively worse as the days roll on; he yells at the children, does not shower or shave, and gripes about the lack of heat.

I do not see this as occult at all. The man had an enormous financial burden weighing heavily on his mind. And as for his obsession with the lack of heat and building fires in the fireplace, we already know from prior sources that the heating system broke down in the house shortly after the Lutzes moved in. Anson's book, however, implies that it was not mechanical failure that caused the heat loss. We know better.

The flies enter the story on Dec. 22. Kathy and George discover "hundreds of buzzing flies" clinging to the inside of a window in the sewing room. George opens the other window, chases some outside and kills the rest. Once again we read about the black stains on the bathroom fixtures, but this time only the toilets are stained.

On the morning of the 23rd, George awakens at 3:15 a.m. (as he has every night thus far) and goes downstairs to find, "the two hundred and fifty pound wooden front door wrenched wide open, hanging from one hinge!" The doorknob and brass lock plate were twisted and bent from the inside and a locksmith was needed to repair them.

Kathy relates these mysterious events: Five-year-old Missy hums a strange tune and asks if angels can talk. Seven and nine-year-old Chris and Danny have a fistfight. As I have noted before, a child's interest in angels at Christmas time hardly seems occult, and two brothers fighting is a very normal occurrence.

Back to Father Mancuso. On Dec. 23rd he comes down with the flu with a temperature of 103-104 degrees. His head swims with images of "evil" in the Lutzes' sewing room. In past versions of the Lutz story, we have been told that the priest had called to warn the Lutzes about a certain room. But we were never informed that the Father was suffering from the effects of a high fever at the time. This would certainly influence his judgement, if not cause hallucinations.

On Dec. 24th, Father Mancuso, unable to reach the Lutzes by telephone, calls a friend in the Nassau County Police Dept. There is no explanation of what Mancuso tells the police, but on the next page a Sergeant Al Gionfriddo of the Amityville Police Dept. is parked in front of the Lutz home observing George at the boathouse. He radios in to "Cammaroto," telling him to call North Merrick back and say that the Lutzes are home. How is it possible for Father Mancuso to call the Nassau Police and have his call returned by the Amityville Police? Amityville is not even in Nassau; it is under the jurisdiction of the Suffolk County Police. And having personally interviewed Sgt. Cammaroto, I know that he was never involved in any interaction with the Lutz family. I am shocked that the Lutzes would continue to use Cammaroto's name while knowing how strongly he objects to this.

At 3:15 on Dec. 25th, George awakens once again and comforts Kathy who has just had a nightmare about Louise DeFeo's killing. He then goes out to check the boathouse, as he has done every night he's been living in the house. It has become an obsession with George, along with stoking the fireplace. Note that the words "obsession" and "compulsion" are used quite frequently in relation to George. Walking under a full moon, he looks up at the house to Missy's bedroom and sees his daughter staring at him. Directly behind Missy, George is shocked to see the face of a pig, with little, glaring red eyes! When he checks Missy's room, she is fast asleep in bed but her rocking chair is rocking back and forth. Later that day Missy tells her brothers and then Kathy that she has a friend named "Jodie," who's a pig that only Missy can see. This seems to me like a normal child's imaginary playmate.

In chapter eight, Kathy feels that her two sons have changed since moving to the house because they are answering her back. She claims that Danny and Chris never questioned her requests before now. Are we expected to believe that 7– and 9-year-old boys have never questioned their mother's authority, that they had previously blindly obeyed every thing she told them to do? If so, then Kathy must be raising a new species of child, for I have never heard of a child that did not once question his parents' authority.

Anson leads us to believe that it was a mysterious occurrence when George did not make love to Kathy for nine days after they moved into the house. Of course, he also tells us that George did not shower or shave for those nine days. I believe there is a definite correlation between the two.

The Amityville Horror Conspiracy

When a small neighbor boy named Bobby refuses to play upstairs with the Lutz boys, George and Kathy wonder, "What's wrong with the house that makes everybody so uncomfortable?" The answer is that some people are uneasy being in a house where a mass murder was committed. Especially a small boy who had lived in the neighborhood when the DeFeos were murdered and may remember that night with horror. Bobby may even have played with the DeFeo boys. Is it any wonder that the boy would be nervous about now playing in that same house?

In Chapter 10, the mythical Sgt. Al Gionfriddo of the Amityville Police Dept. pays a visit to Father Mancuso at the priest's request. The Father asks Gionfriddo to tell him about the DeFeo murders. Gionfriddo, supposedly on duty that tragic night, explains that Ronald drugged the family at dinner and then shot them. As I have mentioned before, this was only a theory ventured in early media reports; it was later shown by the coroner's tests that the DeFeos had not been drugged. Anson obviously took this information from early newspaper accounts, never bothering to check further where he would have learned about the coroner's results.

On the next page, Gionfriddo says that the police found out about the murder after Ronald told the bartender at "The Witches' Brew." Once again, sloppy research. If Anson is going to invent characters to tell about the real life murders, he should at least get his facts straight! The bar to which Ronald ran that night was called simply "Henry's Bar." Perhaps Anson or the Lutzes felt that the word "witch" would add a more demonic flavor to their story.

By a strange"coincidence," Gionfriddo drives past "The Witches' Brew" on his way home and observes George Lutz entering the bar. Gionfriddo does a double-take because he thinks he has just seen Ronald DeFeo. The bartender also is taken by George's supposed resemblance to Ronnie. This is pure nonsense. I have seen pictures of both DeFeo and Lutz. DeFeo is thin, swarthy-skinned, with dark hair. George Lutz is husky, has a pale, cherubic face and dirty-blond hair. The only similarity is that both were bearded and had mustaches; by this token every bearded, mustachioed young man would resemble Ronald DeFeo Jr.

Another "strange phenomenon"—George catches a glimpse of Ronald DeFeo's face in a small, hidden "red room" in the basement.

I had seen this "red room" when I was in the house in March of '76. It could hardly be called a room. It is merely a tiny area behind the shelving in the closet under the basement stairs. Two people would barely be able to fit into the area between the cement walls; I believe it is an access to the plumbing for the upstairs rooms.

When George stumbles over a large ceramic lion in his living room and falls into the logs by the fireplace, Kathy sees the injury on his ankle as "teethmarks." My impression is that they are both beginning to spook themselves with all this discussion of the DeFeo murders.

By the end of Chapter 11, Father Mancuso has developed bleeding palms. In the following chapter he compares his affliction to "stigmata," marks resembling Christ's wounds, which to quote Anson's book, are"said to be supernaturally impressed on the bodies of holy people." This is such a rare occurrence in Catholicism that those individuals so afflicted are usually designated as Saints. Quite a miracle that the same priest who blessed the Lutzes' home would turn out to be one of these rare individuals. It is also the first case I know of where the person developed stigmata because he visited a suburban home! When a doctor examined Mancuso's affliction, he said it "could be anything from an allergy to an attack of anxiety." This seems likely, and Mancuso was still suffering from the flu at the time. Another small detail that disturbs me is that Father Mancuso prays at his own private altar in his room. According to my Catholic consultants, no priest has his own altar and especially not within his living quarters.

When Kathy and George stare into the fireplace on New Year's Eve, they believe they see a demonic, horned and hooded figure burned into the bricks, with half of its face blown away, "as if hit with a shotgun blast at close range." This to me is another indication of the Lutzes' growing obsession with the DeFeo murders. They read into the vague, smoke shape whatever was on their minds, as one would in a psychiatrist's "ink blot" test.

On New Year's Day, George and Kathy glimpse "beady, red eyes" outside their living room window. Running outside, they find a line of footprints in the snow, "left by cloven hooves—like those of an enormous pig." The following morning the footprints are still visible in the snow and the garage door is torn off its hinges. Kathy feels unseen hands gripping her in the bedroom, and George hears a strange tale about the "red room" from the bartender at "The Witches' Brew."

The Amityville Horror Conspiracy

The man once tended bar at a DeFeo party, discovered the hidden space, and subsequently had nightmares about dogs and pigs being killed in there for a blood ritual.

Seeing the size of that "room," anyone would know that if blood cultists ever conducted evil ceremonies in there, they would either have to be smaller than "Tatoo" on "Fantasy Island" or be conducting the ceremony on their knees. None of these events had been mentioned in the Hoffman or *Newsday* versions of the Lutzes' story, and I can hardly believe the extent to which this book is stretching credibility.

It gets worse. Following a mass said for the Lutzes by Father Mancuso at the Sacred Heart Church in North Merrick, the priest returns to his apartment to find it filled with the odor of human excrement. The horrible smell then permeates the entire Rectory, driving the other priests into the adjacent school and extremely upsetting the Pastor. On Jan. 3, Lutz goes to the Amityville Police Dept. and brings Detective Sergeant Pat Cammaroto home with him to see the cloven footprints, "still visible in the frozen snow." Cammaroto observes the footprints and then is taken to see the "red room." When he leaves he thinks to himself that he had "a creepy feeling" and felt "strong vibrations" in the house.

I must once again stress this point: Sgt. Pat Cammaroto told me that he was never on the property at 112 Ocean Avenue for the entire time the Lutzes lived there! How then could he examine the footprints of Jodie the demon pig, look at the "red room" and feel any vibrations? It is an outrage that Anson and the Lutzes have used an actual, respectable person to support something that is an out-and-out lie!

Also on Jan. 3rd, Father Mancuso's Pastor picks an argument with him and glares at the Father with hatred, all for no apparent reason. The Pastor is full of jealousy and sarcasm for his former friend. If this were true it would be a shocking and nearly unheard of way for a Roman Catholic Pastor to act. I feel it is another tasteless display of Anson's imagination.

Meanwhile, back at the Lutzes', the ceramic lion which George had placed upstairs suddenly reappears in the living room. A case of teleportation? Or, more likely, hallucination? One evening George hears a marching band parading around on the first floor. When he gets there, of course, the room is empty. He then returns to the bedroom to find Kathy floating two feet above the bed and drifting towards the window! So now we have levitation added to the story.

At the end of Chapter 16, George hears the marching band once again, only this time "every piece of furniture had been moved. The rug had been rolled back." Remember the Lutzes' press conference in February of '76? That's when they said there had been no moving furniture. You can't have it both ways, George.

On Jan. 6th, Father Mancuso discusses the Lutz situation with the Chancellors of the Rockville Centre diocese. "Father Ryan" goes into an explanation of possession and then, wonder of wonders, parapsychology! He and "Father Nuncio" advise Mancuso to tell the Lutzes to call in Duke University. Father Ryan mentions "Dr. Rhine, who works at Duke University in Durham, N.C." Misinformation once again; the Durham organization is no longer with Duke and J.B. Rhine retired 15 or 20 years ago. In any case, it is quite unusual for the Catholic Church to be advising parishioners to call in parapsychologists.

On the night of Jan. 6th, Kathy Lutz levitates once again, this time only one foot above George. After yanking Kathy back by the hair, George turns on the light, looks at her and sees a ninety-year-old woman, the same toothless hag from the Paul Hoffman articles. By the time Kathy got to the mirror though, she saw only deep lines in her cheeks. These lines could have been the type of creases one sometimes gets on the skin from lying in a certain position on the sheets.

So far there has been no mention of the red liquid trickling from keyholes that had been such a major part of the Hoffman versions. However, in Chapter 20 we have a new color substance: green, gelatinous slime oozes from the walls and settles in Jello-like puddles on the floor. Kathy accuses the children of having made the mess and they, of course, deny it. Kathy suspects them anyway, but George would rather choose to believe that the green Jello is a demonic occurrence. But then, this is George's first experience at being a father.

The incident in which Danny's hand is crushed by the window has been completely changed from the Hoffman versions. In the latter, Danny is helping to close the sewing room window after George's exorcism rite; in Anson's story, Danny is closing the window in his parent's bedroom because there is a violent rainstorm outside. In Hoffman's version, the aluminum storm window falls on the boy's two hands; in Anson's it is the heavy wooden frame window which traps his right hand. In Hoffman's story, Danny is treated for a slight cut by his mother downstairs; in Anson's version, Danny's fingers are "flattened from the cuticle

The Amityville Horror Conspiracy

to the second knuckle" and George rushes him to Brunswick Hospital Center where an intern securely bandages the hand.

It is certainly no mystery that a window could close on a child's hand when there are hurricane-force winds raging outside. But it is quite unbelievable that the Lutzes are not capable of giving an accurate account of what room the incident occurred in, what type of window it was, how many of Danny's hands were trapped, how bad the injury was, and whether it was treated at home or in a hospital!

On the evening of Jan. 11th, George has a nightmare in which he sees himself torn in two. He screams aloud, "I'm coming unglued!" I would tend to agree with George here.

Immediately following this incident, Missy calls her father to her bedroom to meet "Jodie." George sees the little red eyes at the window and when Kathy walks in and sees the eyes also, she goes wild and smashes the window with a chair. George supposedly hears an animal cry in pain and then squeal as it runs away. This "Jodie the Pig" is becoming such a major character in the story and yet he was never mentioned by the Lutzes before this book. Perhaps they decided to cash in on the huge success of "Miss Piggy" of Muppet fame.

On Jan. 12th, Father Mancuso goes to the Bishop of the Rockville Centre diocese to seek advice. The Bishop's secretary offers Mancuso tea to warm him after he comes in from the cold. Mancuso's meeting with the Bishop is brief; the Bishop says he has assigned another cleric to the case and that Mancuso should dissociate himself from it. He also tells Mancuso, "You've become obsessed with the idea that demonic influence is involved." The Bishop advises the Father to see a psychiatrist. For the life of me I cannot understand why Anson has included this dialogue. It is certainly not supportive of Father Mancuso's reliability; in fact it would seem to discredit him.

On the evening of the 12th, George screams in his sleep in two strange languages. I suppose we are now expected to believe that he is "speaking in tongues."

When the Lutzes try to flee the house on Jan. 13th, their van will not start and then a hurricane-force storm strikes. The Lutzes are forced back into their house, where the telephone and the electricity are both out. George discovers more green slime (shades of "The Blob"!) oozing from the door of the sewing room and slithering down the staircase. The heat in the house goes up to 90 degrees, then drops to 60 degrees. Harry the dog throws up. Kathy walks in her sleep. Beds slide across the floor, dresser drawers open and close. George hears voices and the marching band again downstairs, but he cannot move out of bed. He screams but no sound comes out of his mouth. The marching band is getting closer, closer! It is coming up the stairs, and now doors are slamming back and forth. And yet Harry the dog hears nothing! George thinks,"Either that dog is drugged or I'm the one who's going mad!" Touché, George! Since we know that the dog has not been drugged, we must accept your only other rational explanation. After all, four other people are sleeping in that same house, two in the same room, and with all that racket not one of them has awakened!

There is a flash of lightning—BOOM! George lies panting, waiting for something to happen. And who is it that shows up? Boris Karloff? Larry Talbot? Bela Lugosi? Noooooooooo! It's good ole Jodie D. Pig, doing the Mexican Hat Dance on George's stomach!

The very next sentence reads, "George must have passed out from fright, because the next thing he remembers was the sight of Danny and Chris standing beside his bed." They were telling George to wake up. I do not believe that George passed out. He was already asleep and having a nightmare. He had all the classical ingredients of a nightmare—the inability to move in a frightening situation, the soundless scream, etc.

Danny and Chris tell George there is a faceless monster in their room. George rushes into the hall and sees a "gigantic figure in white" on the stairs. It is by this time 7:00 a.m. on Jan. 14th and the Lutz family flees the house in their van, which is now working perfectly.

In the meantime, Father Mancuso makes plans to visit his cousin in California. Later he receives a call from Lutz and as they are talking, Mancuso begins to see blotches on his palm. He quickly hangs up on George and begs the demon to "let me alone. I promise I won't talk to him again." A priest who makes a deal with a demon to save his own skin (no pun intended) in exchange for deserting his parishioners? Bull!

You would think now that the Lutzes have fled the house forever that the horror would be over, right? Wrong! The first night at Kathy's mother's house, both George and Kathy levitate and float around the room. And the green slime has somehow followed them to East Babylon, only this time it's greenish-black and slithering up the stairs! The last line is the kicker: "Whatever he had thought they left forever

The Amityville Horror Conspiracy

back at 112 Ocean Avenue was following them—wherever the Lutzes fled." This sounds like an obvious lead-in for a sequel. God (or Jodie) only knows what the new book will be called: "Travels With My Slime," or perhaps "Jodie, Come Home"?

There is an epilogue to the book which describes the Channel 5 seance, tells of Father Frank Mancuso's recovery from pneumonia (who even knew he had it?) and transfer from the parish, and ends with a few lines about the Lutzes. The epilogue is followed by an afterword by Jay Anson. It is his brief attempt to compare the Lutzes' story with classic occult phenomena. Anson stresses that the Lutzes truthfully recounted their adventure on tape, from which he then transcribed it into book form. He tells us there is too much corroboration by independent witnesses to suspect the Lutzes of fakery, namely Father Mancuso and the local police.

But this is not so! Eliminate any police corroboration, for I have interviewed Cammaroto, and we know that the only interaction between Lutz and the police was when he complained of vibrations and turned in his gun! Eliminate any testimony from the priest, because he did not witness any of the occurrences which happened to the Lutzes in their house. So who do we have left as witnesses? George, Kathy and the children, ages 5, 7 and 9. Children that age are very impressionable and are likely to see whatever Mommy and Daddy say they see.

I plan to question some of the individuals mentioned in this book, and I believe I shall begin with Mr. Jay Anson.

7

Fighting for the Truth

Tuesday, Sept. 6, 1977

Three weeks have passed since I received my copy of *The Amityville Horror*. I have been calling various people involved in the story ever since. Now I sit on the old black–and–white plaid couch in my tiny living room trying to sort through my notes. Tomorrow morning I will be returning to my teaching job after the long summer vacation so I will not have as much free time to do my research.

The first person I called was Jay Anson of Roslyn, Long Island. Mr. Anson had a very pleasant voice and said that he had heard of me and my reputation as a ghost investigator. I asked him if he realized that the book was inaccurate, that it contained many claims which were contrary to what I had uncovered in my investigation. In an apologetic voice, Mr. Anson told me that he is just a reporter, telling the Lutzes' story and putting it in order for them. He said that he had not even met with the Lutzes face–to–face but merely transcribed their story from the tapes which they sent to him from California. Anson said that if anything on the tapes was untrue, it was strictly the Lutzes' responsibility.

"But don't you realize that you're pushing a lie?" I asked.

Anson responded by saying that he did not feel he was doing anything wrong. "The Lutzes are nice people," he said, "and I have no reason to believe that they would lie to me."

I then told Anson of my own experiences with the case, and how Lutz's story had gone through so many different versions.

"Well, obviously there are some inconsistencies," Anson replied, "but it's too late to change them now. I never meant to upset anyone by writing this book."

The Amityville Horror Conspiracy

I questioned him further about the inconsistencies concerning specific dates in the book. Anson admitted to using some literary license when he arranged the events related by the Lutzes into a chronological order. My feeling is that if you are reporting a true story, and you say that certain events occurred on a specific day, you should pinpoint that date as accurately as possible. Naturally it may not be possible to remember exact dates for all of the events, but an attempt at accuracy should be made. Anson gave me the impression that he took a list of all the strange occurrences, and divided the list up equally to distribute some to each date.

I then asked Anson if he was prepared to tell the public that there were many untruths in the book, or, in Anson's words, much "literary license." Of course he replied that he was not in a position to do that. Anson certainly did not intend to rock the boat now when he stood to make a small fortune from the book and the movie rights. I suppose I cannot really blame him for that. But when does "literary license" become a lie? Does a reporter who is relating a "true" story have a responsibility to check thoroughly into all the evidence, pro and con, concerning his topic? I feel he does.

When I confronted Anson with the knowledge that I knew that Sgt. Cammaroto had never been on the Lutzes' property to view the cloven hoofprints, he merely repeated his same tried–and–true litany: "I only reported what the Lutzes told me."

"Jay," I asked him, "if I told you I had just come from Mars on a flying saucer, wouldn't you have a responsibility to verify my claim before writing it under the subtitle of 'true story'?"

"Look," he said. "I was called in to write the book by Tam Mossman of Prentice Hall. It's not like I was a friend of the Lutzes or something. I had never even heard of them before I got the assignment. But Tam is a friend of mine and, if he said the Lutzes were O.K., I trusted his judgement."

I had come to a dead end with Anson and so I thanked him for his time and said goodbye. He had, at least, been very sympathetic and polite to me and I respected him for this.

A quick phone call to the Amityville Police Department was enough to reassure me that none of the events involving police officers in the case were true. There is no such person as Sgt. Al Gionfriddo, and even if the name was an alias there is no officer in the Amityville

Police Department who did any of the things in the book ascribed to Gionfriddo. In fact, the officers at the precinct were quite shocked to learn what had been written about them in *The Amityville Horror.*

Alan Levy is the Director of the Vanderbilt Planetarium in Centerport, Long Island, and I had heard him speak on the Joel Martin show several times. I called Mr. Levy to determine whether or not there had actually been a full moon on Dec. 25th, when George Lutz had claimed to see Jodie the Pig in Missy's bedroom window. Mr. Levy told me that less than a quarter of the moon was visible that night. I suppose Jay Anson would call this literary license. However, seeing Jodie in the light of a full moon, and being able to see him with less than a quarter of the moon's light are two different situations entirely. Visibility would have been very poor that night, making it quite difficult to observe anything in the second–story window from the back yard.

The next place I called was the office of the Bishop of the Rockville Centre Diocese on Long Island. The bishop who had been in charge when the Lutzes lived in Amityville had since died, but the former bishop's secretary was now working for the new bishop. This secretary would have to have been the same man who saw Father Mancuso into the office and offered him tea to warm him up. Yet the secretary assured me that no such event had ever taken place! No priest from Sacred Heart Church or any other church had come to the Bishop to seek advice on the Amityville case. The secretary was most emphatic that he had never chatted with or offered tea to any such person, and in fact he never even drinks tea and so never offered it to anyone! The Church was just beginning to get word of their mention in Anson's book and they were not happy with it at all.

I also called the pastor of the Sacred Heart Church itself. He was furious about the book! Although he had not been the pastor at the time of the alleged happenings, he was familiar with Anson's claims and had questioned all of the priests in the Rectory quite thoroughly. There had never been any stench permeating the Rectory and driving the priests out of their rooms! There had been a priest at Sacred Heart who had counseled the Lutzes, but as far as this pastor could ascertain, none of the other events attributed to "Father Mancuso" were true. He was also quite shocked by the scene in which the former pastor berates Father Mancuso. All the priests at Sacred Heart assured him that the former pastor had been a kind and gentle soul who had never behaved in such a shocking manner.

Another individual who was not exactly happy to learn of his inclusion in the book was Channel 5's Marvin Scott. He did not even know that he had been mentioned until I called to interview him. I read to Marvin the paragraph where Anson claims that Scott came out of the sewing room saying that he had experienced a momentary chill. Marvin denied that he had ever felt anything strange in the house and asked me, "Do you think I should sue?" I assured him that he should, as they were using his good name to perpetuate a hoax. I also questioned Marvin about the comment that cameraman Steve Petropolis had experienced heart palpitations and shortness of breath. Marvin said that Steve was feeling slightly ill that night but he doesn't think it had anything to do with ghosts. None of them had eaten properly and the seance went on into the wee hours of the morning. They all left feeling exhausted.

Jerry Solfvin was also upset to learn that his organization had once more been used to support the story. We spoke about the book during a long phone conversation but what it all boiled down to was that there was nothing he could do about it.

Remembering that Dr. Karlis Osis and Alex Tanous of the American Society for Psychical Research had been at the Amityville house on the same day as the Channel 5 seance, I decided to give them a call. I had tried calling Dr. Osis once before when they were mentioned in *The Star* article in April of 1976. At that time he had been extremely uncooperative, saying only that he and Tanous had been there for about an hour on that day and he had no further comment.

"But surely you can tell me, Karlis, as one professional to another, whether or not you found anything there," I said. "After all, we are both working in the same field on the same case, and I'm not asking you to reveal any trade secrets."

"No comment," Karlis had repeated.

This time when I phoned the A.S.P.R. in Manhattan my call was answered by Alex Tanous himself. Alex was also reluctant to talk, repeating often that he was under contract to Karlis. But I kept pressuring him, telling him that by remaining silent the A.S.P.R. was in effect supporting the story.

Finally Alex said, "Look, Steve, I'll tell you what happened, but if you ever repeat the story to anyone I will deny having said it and I will never work with you again."

Since I had never worked with Alex in the past and had no plans of working with him in the future, this did not faze me in the least. Alex said that he and Karlis had spoken to the Lutzes for a while and then Alex had asked George for a sample of his handwriting. Alex wanted to analyze George's handwriting to get an impression of his personality. George handed Alex a sample of his signature, which just happened to be on the bottom of a contract for a book! So, in February, 1976, before any psychic researchers had been called in to investigate the house, the Lutzes had already contracted to have a book written about the haunting! When Alex and Karlis realized this, they left rather hastily, feeling that something was rotten in Denmark.

Alex did not recall the name of the publisher on the book contract, but he did know that it was not Prentice Hall. Somewhere along the line the Lutzes had switched publishers. Putting myself into a hypothetical situation, I asked myself this question: If I were so terrified by all the things that George claims happened in that house, so petrified that I had to flee for my family's safety leaving behind all belongings, what would be the first action I would take after escaping? My answer would be to immediately call in experts in the occult to see if I could discover the cause of the horror and see if it could be eliminated. This was not George's first action, though. First, he contracted to have a book written and then called in the experts to verify his story. Sounds a little backwards to me.

I told Alex that if he would be willing to tell this story to the public, it would certainly help to put a dent in Lutz's story. Alex repeated that he would deny ever having told me any such thing. What Alex didn't know was that I had two friends listening to the conversation on amplifier to witness that it did take place.

So much for cooperation from colleagues in the field.

Next I called Brunswick Hospital Center in Amityville to check on whether a Danny Lutz had ever been treated in the emergency room during December or January of 1975–1976. There is absolutely no record of anyone by that name having been treated in the emergency room during that period. So much for the story about George's mad rush to the hospital to have poor Danny's crushed hand bandaged.

The Amityville Horror Conspiracy

I did give Tam Mossman another call once I had uncovered all of this data. He was quite uninterested in what I had discovered. After all, this is the book he is trying to promote. All I represent to Mr. Mossman and Prentice Hall is potential trouble for the sales of the book. It would not look good for a book promoted as "A True Story" to be refuted in public.

The two people I would like to interview most are George and Kathy Lutz. Perhaps Joel Martin of WBAB could get them as guests so we can have an on–the–air debate. I will call him tomorrow.

Thursday, Sept. 8, 1977

Newsday published a brief article today about *The Amityville Horror.* The article is entitled, "A Treasure Haunt," referring to the fact that the book is becoming a big money–maker. It has already earned six figures in a paperback sale and will be turned into a CBS–TV movie. To quote the first paragraph, "It used to be that a haunted house was just a haunted house, but now, with the help of the right medium, an allegedly haunted house can turn into a pot of gold." It goes on to say that Prentice Hall will be sending the Lutzes to 10 major cities to discuss their experiences on radio and TV talk shows as part of a major advertising and promotion campaign. Jay Anson, who is described as a TV writer, is quoted as saying, "You believe or you don't believe, I leave it up to the reader. This is what these people say happened to them."

The article also mentions the fact that the present occupants of the house are quite happy with it and have not been bothered by any ghosts.

I have spoken to Joel Martin about doing a show with the Lutzes and he is going to let me know if he can arrange it.

Friday, Sept. 23, 1977

This evening I taped a Joel Martin Show which will be aired on WBAB radio on October 2. The Lutzes were not there; they refused to do the show, claiming they would not come back to an area so close to their former house. However, I have it from a good source that the Lutzes will not return to Long Island for legal reasons—their former creditors are still after them.

Instead, the Lutzes were represented by Ed and Lorraine Warren, the demonologist and his clairvoyant wife from Monroe, Connecticut. A reporter named Don Longo from *The Amityville Record* was also present and will be writing an article about the show for that paper.

Joel Martin introduced the Warrens and read from their promotional material that they teach non–credit courses in Demonology at Southern Connecticut State College in New Haven. I was introduced as the first parapsychologist called into the case who was now here to debunk it. The Warrens seemed to be giving off nearly visible waves of hostility towards me. As the debate progressed and became more heated, Ed Warren became so angry that his face grew bright red. Lorraine stated most emphatically that everything the Lutzes had claimed in *The Amityville Horror* had actually happened. She said that they have spoken to the priest and he corroborates Lutz's story.

I respond by pointing out that the priest had been very ill at the time and in any case had never witnessed any of the events which happened to the Lutzes in their home.

"Are you saying that a priest would lie?!" exclaimed Mrs. Warren in a high voice.

"No. I'm merely stating that he was not a witness to the phenomena," I said.

"Are you attacking a judge of the Catholic Church?" Lorraine asked in a shocked voice.

I explained that this was not a personal "attack" against anyone. I was merely attempting to portray the facts and dispel the erroneous notion that anyone but the Lutzes had witnessed the phenomena at 112 Ocean Avenue.

That's when Ed took over the verbal onslaught from his wife. Turning his back to me, he said to Joel, "Look, Joel, this man is an extremely vindictive individual who is trying to get back at George Lutz because he wasn't allowed into the house to conduct his investigation!"

I was stunned by this accusation. Joel asked, "Is this true, Dr. Kaplan?"

"It most certainly is not," I calmly replied. "Mr. Lutz was the one who called me to ask for help. When he cancelled it meant nothing more to my organization than saving the time and money it would have cost us to investigate."

"That's not what George claims," said Lorraine. "George says that Kaplan called the Lutzes and begged to be allowed in to investigate."

Joel was doing a great job of moderating this vicious debate which would have become little more than a scream-fest with a less experienced interviewer. "Mrs. Warren, please force yourself to address your opponent as Dr. Kaplan or at least Mr. Kaplan," he said. "I realize you are angry, but calling him 'Kaplan' is really not right, especially since he refers to you as Mrs. Warren." Joel's request went unheeded. Both Lorraine and Ed continued to refer to me as "Kaplan," and to accuse me of being motivated by revenge and jealousy.

"Lorraine's statement that George never called me is not true," I said. "There are many witnesses who were present when I received the calls from George. And I certainly never 'begged' him to be allowed to investigate! In fact, I made it quite clear to George that it really didn't matter to us one way or the other if he called back to reschedule the investigation."

I went on to elaborate on the many claims in Anson's book and to explain why they could not be verified or in some cases how they could be totally refuted. When I said that I did not believe that Kathy had ever levitated two feet off the bed, Ed Warren nearly rose to his feet in anger.

"You call yourself a parapsychologist and you've never heard of levitation?!" he yelled.

"I did not say that I never heard of levitation," I replied, "but merely that I had never seen anyone with the ability to levitate two feet in the air."

"Have you ever seen a 350-lb. refrigerator levitate two feet off the ground?" Ed asked.

"No, Ed, I can't say that I have. Have you?" I asked.

"I most certainly have," he replied. "My wife and I both saw it float during one of our haunted house cases."

Frankly I found this statement a little hard to believe. The Warrens went on to describe how the evil entity from the Amityville house had followed them home to their bedroom in Connecticut and then proceeded to levitate their own bed! Lorraine explained that this incident would be included in their next book.

During the commercial break, Joel questioned the Warrens about this new book. They said that it was to be published by Prentice Hall, the same publishers who did *The Amityville Horror*. Ed and Lorraine also showed Joel a copy of a book they had written a couple of years ago about their demonic cases, with illustrations by Ed himself. It looked as though they'd more than likely paid to have it published by a subsidy press.

Mrs. Warren summed up their position by saying that the Lutzes had become friends of theirs and that she would personally attest to their credibility.

I concluded my argument by telling the public that George Lutz had needed an economic miracle to bail himself out of debt and so had manufactured one. I pointed out that with the publication of *The Amityville Horror*, Lutz is no longer destitute but in fact on his way to becoming quite well-off. Lastly, I stressed once again that the Lutzes were the only witnesses to their own alleged phenomena.

I must make it clear that while I have nothing personally against the Warrens, I will not back off from any challenge to my integrity and I will expose anyone who attempts to lie to the public. This may not make me very popular in some circles, but popularity is not my main concern.

Sunday, Oct. 9, 1977

The Amityville Horror is quickly becoming a best-seller nationwide. Prentice Hall's grand publicity campaign has certainly paid off. Millions of readers have accepted the book as a true story; those who are not quite sure are reading it anyway. There is no way to circulate my side of the story as widely as Anson's—I am only one man fighting a multi-million dollar media blitz. But I shall not give up.

I've been reading today's *New York Times*. A column called "Interview" has an interview with Jay Anson entitled, "A Real-Life Horror Story" by Lawrence Van Gelder. It reviews and summarizes the book and also explains how Anson got the job of author.

Jay Anson has spent the last 15 years working at Professional Films as a writer of documentaries about movie-making. In March of 1976 Jay's friend Tam Mossman of Prentice Hall brought the Lutzes to meet Jay and tell their story. The rest, as they say, is history.

Van Gelder asks Anson if anything odd had happened to him since he began writing the book. His answer reads like pure Hollywood hype.

"'Leave it no,' he said, noting he had had a heart attack not long ago. 'Blame it on my smoking, my idiot life style. I'm not going to blame it on this.'"

Mr. Anson, if you didn't intend to blame your heart attack on your involvement with the story, why bring it up in the context of that question? It makes people wonder, that's why.

Anson goes on to relate other bizarre events which happened to people who had come in contact with the manuscript. Tam Mossman had a fire in his car while driving to work with the manuscript. A friend and his son nearly drowned in their car but the manuscript was the only thing that remained dry in the trunk. Another friend died in a fire the same night she received the first two chapters, but the manuscript was found unburned.

I suspect that some or all of these incidents are about as accurate as Jodie the Pig's little dance under the full moon. But they do sell books and newspapers.

I am infuriated with *The New York Times,* supposedly the bastion of respectability among newspapers. I throw down the paper and call up Mr. Van Gelder.

"How can you support this hoax?" I ask. "Have you checked out any of the facts?"

"We are familiar with Mr. Anson," Van Gelder replies, "and his reputation is totally reliable."

I attempt to tell Van Gelder the facts about the case but he seems annoyed and disinterested. Not only does he refuse to print a retraction, but he refuses to print even a letter from me giving my side of the story!

Their motto, "All the News That's Fit to Print," should be changed to read, "All the News We Feel Like Printing." My idealistic ideas about freedom of the press have been shot to hell. Remember in the movies when the hero runs to the *New York Times* to expose the Truth? Like Al Pacino in "Serpico" or Robert Redford in "Three Days of the Condor"? Well, it's only in the movies folks, only in the movies. The Truth doesn't stand a chance in real-life when it's up against that all powerful motive called, "Making a Buck."

Monday, Oct. 10, 1977

I am not satisfied with Van Gelder's refusal to print my letter. After all, he is merely a staff writer. I'll give it one more shot and go straight to the top.

The editor of *The New York Times* sounds polite but rather noncommittal toward my phone call. He tells me to write the letter and mail it to him and they will look it over and try to be fair.

My letter will be in the mail this evening but I shall not hold my breath waiting to see it in print.

Media Plugs and Pans

Friday, November 4, 1977

Reviews of *The Amityville Horror* have been coming out fast and furious. In my hands I now hold an ad which I tore from *The New York Times Book Review,* Sunday section, some time ago. It is a quarter of a page, with two huge flies looming ominously around the print. The catch-line reads, "More frightening than *The Exorcist* and *Audrey Rose* because it actually happened!"

The New York Times never printed my letter, and recently I found out why. According to several New York papers, *The New York Times* has bought the syndication rights for *The Amityville Horror* to be sold to over 400 other newspapers! How would it have looked to their prospective buyers if the *Times* had printed an article saying, "Leading parapsychologist calls book a hoax."?!

The ad from the Book Review section quotes some of the great reviews *The Amityville Horror* has received. One is a quote from Robert Kirsch of the *Los Angeles Times.* It reads, "The scariest true story I have read in years... What has come out of that nightmare is a fascinating and frightening book." The other two quotes are from *Newsday* and *Publishers Weekly,* both glowing with praise. A friend recently told me that *Newsday* and the *Los Angeles Times* are both owned by the same conglomerate. Well, *Newsday* has already failed to print my expose as told to John Pascal, but I might as well try the *Los Angeles Times.* I call the editor of the paper in L.A.

"How can your reviewer recommend this story when it's pure nonsense?" I ask. I go through all of my reasons for calling the case a hoax. I ask the editor to retract or at least reassess their endorsement of this book. I am cut off in mid-sentence.

The Amityville Horror Conspiracy

"We most certainly will not retract a word of it," Mr. Editor snorts. Before I have a chance to reply I am listening to a dial-tone.

I am still stewing over this incident when a strange coincidence occurs. I get a phone call from *The San Francisco Chronicle* in California. They have heard me briefly mention the Amityville hoax on a San Francisco radio station at Halloween–time and they would like to hear my story!

Finally those Halloween–time shows have paid off. For a few years now I have been doing radio talk shows via phone for stations all over the country, with a large percentage of them done at Halloween. This past Halloween was the most incredible one of all. I did literally dozens of shows in a period of a few days; as soon as I would put down the phone at the end of one interview, it would ring immediately and another station would ask me to do a show. The radio stations were scattered all over the country and one of them had happened to be in San Francisco.

The *Chronicle* reporter spoke with me for well over an hour and I told him most of the details of the case. I mentioned all of the key people involved, including those who would take umbrage to my story. The reporter said he would be contacting some of these people to get their reactions to my comments.

The article should be published on Monday and the reporter has promised to mail me a copy.

Thursday, Nov. 10, 1977

I received the article from The *San Francisco Chronicle* today. It is dated Mon., Nov. 7th and is titled, "Disagreement Over the Lutzes' Story." I shall quote excerpts from the article below:

"*The Amityville Horror* is certainly an unusual story, but a check by *The Chronicle* indicates there is at least disagreement over the facts within it.

"For instance there is Stephen Kaplan, director of the Parapsychology Institute of America in Elmhurst, Queens, N.Y., who goes so far as to call the story a hoax.

"...[Kaplan] compared the book to Clifford Irving's fake biography of Howard Hughes."

(The article goes on to quote "Kaplan's detractors," Tam Mossman and Lorraine Warren, who question my credentials.)

"An additional point of contention between Kaplan and Warren is whether he conducted an on-site investigation of the Amityville house. Warren said that Kaplan is 'just mad because Lutz wouldn't let him in the house. He seems extremely vindictive that he was not permitted to investigate.'"

"Kaplan claims that *The Amityville Horror* was created by George Lutz. 'He created a mythology and tried to pass it off as reality,' Kaplan said.

"'We have to feel he lacks credibility,' Kaplan said. 'There wasn't one bit of primary or secondary evidence... We only have George Lutz' word.' [I elaborate on George's apparent motives: the financial burden of the house, the I.R.S. auditing his business, and trying to impress his new wife.] So far Kaplan is alone in taking issue with the book.

"'Most of the people in this field [parapsychology] know this is a hoax. Thank goodness, I can afford the privilege of being moral. I blew the whistle on this case.

"'I treat this field in a very serious manner. I don't like people putting the public on.'

"Kaplan suggested that the reason no one else is trying to shoot down the book is that others go in looking for ghosts and do their best to find them.

"As to clairvoyant Warren's questioning whether Kaplan was ever in the house, Kaplan says:

"'I was inside the house (in February). It was warm. It was not haunted. There were no demons.'"

It feels so good to know that finally someone had the guts to print my version. And to think a west-coast paper should beat out the major Long Island paper, *Newsday*, not to mention New York City papers, in exposing a Long Island–based hoax!

Thursday, Nov. 17, 1977

It has taken *Newsday* little more than a week since the *San Francisco Chronicle*'s article to realize that they were being out-scooped. Today's *Newsday* has a two-and-a-half page article entitled, "Fact or Fiction." It is the cover story for Part II of the paper, and it includes large photos of the house, the book, and the Lutzes.

Newsday had their reporters try to contact every principal person involved in the case. They were unable to contact the Lutzes through Prentice Hall, despite repeated requests. The Catholic Diocese of Rockville Centre denied that any of the events described in the book involving clergy had ever happened. The Amityville Police

The Amityville Horror Conspiracy

Department likewise denied that their officers had ever seen or been asked to check for strange phenomena at the Lutz home. Neighbors, former and current residents of the house, and the village historical society denied that any strange events had ever happened in the house before or after the Lutzes lived there. Two national psychic research groups (the A.S.P.R. and the P.R.F.) said they decided not to investigate because of the commercialism and the lack of observable data.

The next excerpt I will quote directly: "Tam Mossman, the book's editor at Prentice Hall, said that he and the author agreed to change names *and facts* (italics mine) because his firm might otherwise incur a libel suit or other action."

How can one change facts in a "true story? Isn't the word "fact" in itself synonymous with the truth? The way I see it, if you change a fact, it is no longer a fact. Therefore Mossman is admitting that, at least in part, the Lutzes' account has been fictionalized.

The *Newsday* article goes on to point out various inaccuracies in the book. Neighbors who live in the houses on either side of the former Lutz home say that they never had their blinds drawn on the windows facing the Lutz house when the family moved in, as the book claims. In fact, neither of them even have blinds on those windows. One of these neighbors has a dog whom he describes as very alert, and the dog never noticed anything occurring at the Lutzes'. The man who bought the Lutzes' previous home in Deer Park says that he and his wife visited the Lutzes in Amityville about two weeks after the Lutzes had moved in. Mrs. Lutz gave them the grand tour of the place and she seemed content and in high spirits.

Let's take a closer look at this revelation. Two weeks after the Lutzes moved in would be January first, if we accept the Dec. 18th version of when they moved in. By that time, according to Anson's book, the following phenomena had already occurred: noises, lack of heat, the beating of the children with strap and spoon, the ghost embracing Kathy, black in the toilets, awful smells, hundreds of flies, the front wooden door ripped off its hinges, Missy acting strange, the boys fistfighting, the crucifix hanging upside down, Father Mancuso's illness, trouble with the phones, George not bathing and being obsessed with the fireplace, windows opening, Kathy's nightmares about the DeFeos, George seeing the face of DeFeo in the red room, the ceramic lion biting George and moving toward Kathy, the IRS auditing

George's books, Father Mancuso's stigmata, and the demon's face in the fireplace. *WHEWWW!*

I ask you: if you had been through all of this in just two weeks, would you now be pleasantly conducting a tour for friends through your lovely new home? NOOOOO! You would most likely be on the verge of a nervous collapse!

The *Newsday* reporters also tell about being shown the "red room" by the Cromartys. They describe it as an area that "allows access to piping along that side of the wall that would otherwise be unreachable." They confirm what I already had discovered about the night George saw Jodie at the window under the full moon—actually the moon was in its last *quarter*, giving off only eleven per cent of a full moon's light. Sgt. Cammaroto again says that he was never on the property during the Lutzes' stay.

The true identity of Jodie D. Pig has now been revealed. Are you ready folks? Jodie is really "Evinrude," a Siamese cat! Evinrude's owner, Mrs. Ireland who lives in the house next to the former Lutz home, says that a Siamese cat's eyes will glow red in the dark. Also that Evinrude has a habit of climbing up to the windows of the Lutz home and looking in. Mrs. Cromarty confirmed that she has seen the cat looking in from the window ledge and was quite startled the first time she saw those glowing red eyes.

About those garbled and interrupted telephone calls between the Lutzes and Father Mancuso—the New York Telephone Co. never received any complaints from the Lutzes about the problem. It seems more than strange to me that the Lutzes would not have at least checked with the company to find out if the phone was malfunctioning. The Lutzes also never checked with any outside sources to determine the origin of the "green slime."

The Cromartys showed *Newsday* reporters the fireplace where George and Kathy claim to have seen the hooded demon. The fireplace has not been used since the Lutzes left. The reporters did see a white pattern burned into the gray cinder block, but they describe it as similar to those in most other fireplaces.

Seth Purdy, Jr., curator of the Amityville Historical Society says that the Lutzes did not come to him seeking information on the house until Jan. 25, 1976, a month later than the date claimed in the book. This would have been 11 days after the Lutzes had fled for their lives.

The Amityville Horror Conspiracy

By that time they were already working on writing the book. The Society never gave the Lutzes any information about Shinnecock Indians housing insane and dying persons on that property, and Purdy in fact points out that the Shinnecocks have always lived far east of Amityville. The Massapequa Indians would have been the only ones inhabiting Amityville. Purdy also says the information about John Ketcham, the devil worshipper, was never obtained from the Society. Purdy concludes by calling the Lutz version of the incident, "completely erroneous." The simple fact of the matter is that the Amityville Historical Society has *no information at all about that parcel of land!*

Father Frank Mancuso has also been unmasked. He is the Rev. Ralph J. Pecoraro who does serve in a legal capacity for the church. Pecoraro helped to annul Kathy Lutz's first marriage and instructed George in Catholicism, and also admits to knowing Anson and Nicola (who wrote the preface). In an interview with *Newsday* Pecoraro denied that he had ever gone to the Lutz home as "Father Mancuso" had. Lutz did telephone Pecoraro complaining of psychic phenomena, and Pecoraro referred Lutz to his local Amityville parish, St. Martin of Tours. The pastor and priests at St. Martin of Tours said the Lutzes had never called them nor attended mass there.

The Rockville Centre Diocese told *Newsday* just what they had told me: no priest ever met with the Bishop (then-Bishop Walter P. Kellenberg) concerning the Lutzes, nor did the diocese ever take any action in the case.

When *Newsday* reporters contacted Anson, he claimed that he had attempted to verify pertinent data through the Bishop's office and the historical society, but "could not reach people at either place." Come on, Jay! Anyone else who has cared enough to try to reach either source has had no trouble whatsoever. Anson also flatly states that he did not contact Cammaroto. Why not? Wouldn't he want to talk to the only outside witness who had allegedly seen Jodie the Pig's hoofprints? As for Sgt. Al Gionfriddo, Anson now claims this is an alias for a county policeman, not an Amityville Village policeman as stated in the book.

Anson is quite open about the fact that he has used "a little literary license," particularly in the reconstruction of the vicious quarrel between Mancuso and his pastor. But Tam Mossman is even more revealing: "the necessity was—and the author and I agreed on this—

was to change the circumstances so that, *yes, the book is not strictly true.*" He goes on to say that facts were changed to protect Prentice Hall from being sued by individuals in the story. But this explanation is irrelevant. What is relevant is that Mossman and Anson knowingly took a book which was, in Mossman's own words, "not strictly true," and sold it to the public labeled as "A True Story."

Newsday also has a secondary article with the subtitle, "Horror Seems to Sell," which tells of the book's financial success. It confirms that *The New York Times*' syndicate division has bought serialization rights for over 400 papers. An illustrated English magazine called *Woman* has also purchased serialization rights. The hoax is now becoming an international one.

The Lutzes in the meantime are busy making personal appearances in Baltimore, Boston, Washington, Philadelphia, Cleveland, Milwaukee and Chicago. With such extensive publicity, they can afford to reach millions more people with their hoax than I can with my truth. At least the *Newsday* article will reach the local residents where it all began.

I must mention here, however, that *Newsday* can not be given all the credit for tracking down most of these facts. A few nights ago, Joel Martin did a show for WBAB in which he interviewed an investigative reporter named Rick Moran and Moran's two associates. They had discussed Father Ralph Pecoraro on the air, the first time the name had ever been revealed to the public. A lot of the other revelations made in the *Newsday* article had already been revealed by Moran on the Martin show. Moran is also a field representative for the PRF and had done quite a thorough job of checking out certain allegations in the book.

I strongly suspect that the *Newsday* staff had paid close attention to the Joel Martin Show that night and then followed through on the information with their own interviews. Of course, they had also pumped me for information at various times on the premise of considering an article about my exposure of the case. More than a year ago they could have published John Pascal's extensive interview with myself and my members. But the book was not in existence then. Now, as a bestseller, *The Amityville Horror* is a commercial draw and this expose by *Newsday* can sell more papers. And that, my friends, is the bottom line.

The Amityville Horror Conspiracy

Monday, Nov. 21, 1977

Flipping through the *Daily News* on my lunch hour, I suddenly stop cold at page 35. The headline there reads, "Jodie, the pig-demon. What did it want with 5–year–old Missy?" The serialization of *The Amityville Horror* has begun. As a matter of fact, I must have missed the first installment in yesterday's paper—I was vacationing for the weekend in Tarrytown, N.Y., home of the Sleepy Hollow/Headless Horseman legend.

This excerpt is labeled, "Second of a series" and includes a photo of the house plus side-by-side photographs of Ronald DeFeo and George Lutz, the supposed look-alikes. I must admit that if one was to look quickly at the photographs they would seem quite similar in appearance. In these fuzzy black–and–white pictures, George's hair appears darker than its actual dirty-blond color. Complexion and skin color cannot be distinguished at all, so the major differences there do not show; and by placing George at a further distance from the camera than the close-up of Ronald, the large discrepancy in weight is equalized. However, if one takes the time to examine the photos more closely, it is still quite apparent that the facial features are totally different.

Tuesday, December 6, 1977

I am watching a television program on one of the major networks when a commercial comes on for the *National Enquirer*, the weekly tabloid scandal-sheet. Normally, I would use this time to get a snack from the kitchen, but I am stopped dead in my tracks when I see Jay Anson's book on screen.

The announcer barks out the following: "Now it can be told. The chilling untold story behind this bestselling book, *The Amityville Horror*. Only the *National Enquirer* has it. (The camera zooms in on the paper's front page where huge banner headlines shout, "THE AMITYVILLE HORROR.") As Kathleen Lutz tells for the first time (picture of Kathy) how it felt to spend twenty eight days of terror in this cursed house (picture of house). Don't miss this gripping story (picture of article). And why childhood friends say daredevil Evel Knieval was a big crybaby (picture of Evel). It's all in the *National Enquirer*. At your check-out counter now. (We see a cashier in a supermarket wearing a button which reads, "'The Untold Story.") Get the real untold story. Like me. In the *National Enquirer*. It reaches 17 million people. More than any other paper in America."

Seventeen million people. The thought makes me so nauseous that I decide to skip my TV snack. Instead I turn off the television and walk to the corner to Tony's Candy Store to buy the *Enquirer*. I do not enjoy paying money for this drivel, but as the major debunker of this case, I must be informed as to what the public will be reading. And seventeen million people is a very large public indeed.

The paper, as usual, is dated a week ahead of time: Dec. 13, 1977. The entire front headline reads, "Housewife Reveals Story Behind the Best Selling Book... THE AMITYVILLE HORROR... A Suburban Dream House Ruled by Evil Spirits." On page 28 is a picture of George and Kathy holding the book, and the title, "Exclusive: Wife Tells Chilling Story Behind Our 28 Days of Horror in House Terrorized by Evil Spirits." The byline is "by Kathleen Lutz" and the prologue tells that never before has Kathy Lutz revealed her true feelings about the story...until now. Once again, I feel I must detail the changes that plague this story.

In Jay Anson's book, the only one who had actually seen Kathy turn into an old hag was George. By the time Kathy got to the bathroom mirror, there had been nothing left but the deep lines in her cheeks. To quote directly from the book, "The ancient crone George had seen was gone, her hair was upset, but it was *blonde* again. Her lips were *not drooling* any longer, *nor was she wrinkled*. But deep, ugly lines ran up and down her cheeks."

In Kathy's *Enquirer* version, she did not run to the bathroom mirror to see why George was frightened but instead immediately looked into the mirrored wall of the bedroom. And what she saw was, "a disgusting-looking 90-year-old hag! My hair was white and scraggly. Ugly creases and crow's feet scarred my face. I drooled all over my shriveled up, dried skin."

What can I say? Each description is in direct contradiction to the other. Then comes the matter of the slime. We all remember the green slime, right? Well now we have not only green, but also *black* slime! And now it hardens, too! "From some unknown source, thick green slime oozed out of the ceiling while black slime dripped out of the keyholes of doors in several rooms. It hardened quickly and couldn't be washed or scraped off."

If we think back to Anson's book, the green slime oozed down to the floor into gelatinous puddles, which then had to be slopped up with rags and placed into buckets from which it was *poured* into the river. This is quite different from hardening to such an extent that it could not even be *scraped* off!

This slimy substance has gone through more changes than almost anything else in the Amityville story. In Paul Hoffman's versions, it was a red, bloodlike substance dripping from keyholes. In Anson's it changed to *green*, oozing Jello. And now with the *Enquirer*, we have black slime which hardens. They need a color-coordinator to keep it straight!

Another new twist is that Kathy is now claiming that she *also* heard the marching band. In Anson's book, George was the only one who ever heard that particular phenomenon.

Below the main article is a smaller one which tells how Kathy Lutz's story was checked by a stress-evaluator which measures the emotional reactions in the voice. But the man who conducted the test is the same one who tests many of the *Enquirer*'s subjects. He is paid by the *Enquirer* to validate their stories. This seems like quite a conflict of interests to me. When the boss is paying you to confirm a person's story as true, you're not about to endanger your job by saying otherwise.

I will call the editor of the *Enquirer* tomorrow to see if he will print the true story of the hoax.

Wednesday, Dec. 7, 1977

This morning I taped a program for "To Tell the Truth," the Goodson-Todman game show. On this show they centered on my vampire research—vampires seem to be very popular this season. This past September an excellent play opened Off-Broadway called "The Passion of Dracula," to which I was the technical consultant on vampirism, and tonight Roxanne and I will be guests of the premiere of a new Broadway play called "Dracula," starring Frank Langella.

This afternoon, however, I will take a break from vampires to continue my parapsychological research of *The Amityville Horror*. I put in a call to Lantana, Florida, home of the *National Enquirer*, and ask for the editor, Iain Calder. After being switched through several secretaries, I am finally connected with Mr. Calder.

I tell my story to Iain and ask him how he could print this story which has been continually exposed as a hoax. He claims to know nothing about any opposition to the credibility of the Lutzes' story.

"We have a whole list of respectable, credible witnesses for this story," says Mr. Calder.

"Fine," I answer. "Name one of those credible witnesses."

"Well," Calder hedges, "If you send me a stamped, self-addressed envelope I'll mail you the entire list. Then we'll discuss your point of view further."

Although I suspect that Mr. Calder is merely being patronizing, I agree to write for the list. After hanging up I sit down to compose a letter, including a summary of my exposé of the case. I will mail the letter tonight on my way to see "Dracula."

Friday, Dec. 23, 1977

Today *Newsday* ran an article entitled, "Horror House Is Haunted, But Not by Ghosts." It tells the story of how the Cromartys have been harassed by curiosity-seekers since *The Amityville Horror* was published.

The Cromartys have filed a $1.1 million suit in State Supreme Court, Riverhead, against Prentice Hall, the publisher of the book; the author, Jay Anson, and the former owners of the house, George and Kathleen Lutz. The Cromartys are also seeking to have the subtitle of the book, "A True Story," dropped from further printings.

Mr. Cromarty relates that although there had been some harassment after the *Good Housekeeping* article appeared, things had quieted down afterward, Now, he says, since Anson's book came out, they never have a moment's peace. Trespassers included an artist who set up his easel on the lawn; a teenager blowing taps on a bugle at 4 A.M.; goats brought to graze on the lawn; and two elderly women who parked in the driveway, gestured obscenely and refused to move. The Amityville Police confirm that they are called to the house nearly every day to chase off trespassers. Thirty of those have been arrested this year.

The Cromartys have even changed the house number so that 112 Ocean Avenue technically no longer exists. But this has not stopped the steady parade of people from as far away as California. Cromarty says, "The book is fiction. We want them to admit that it is not a true story. They said it was a true story because who would buy the book if it was fiction?"

Another interesting point brought out in the article is that the Lutzes are suing *Good Housekeeping* for invasion of privacy. They claim that the story entitled, "Our Dream House Was Haunted" was written without their knowledge or consent. Seems to me there's been a falling-out among thieves. I will be interested in hearing the outcome of this suit, as well as the Cromartys' suit.

The Amityville Horror Conspiracy

Thursday, Jan. 12, 1978

I received a letter today from Iain Calder, editor of the *Enquirer*. It contains no list of witnesses, credible or otherwise. I shall reproduce the letter in full:

Jan. 10, 1978
Dr. Stephen Kaplan
Executive Director
Parapsychology Institute of America
Elmhurst, Queens, New York 11373
Dear Dr. Kaplan:

Thank you for your recent letter and for your interest in *The Enquirer*. I appreciate your taking the time and effort to detail your views on our recent article on *The Amityville Horror*. I found them sincere, and I am sure you feel very strongly about them.

I would like to assure you that all of our stories are carefully researched and fully documented. We interviewed many reputable people for this story. We feel justified in having published it.

Once again, thank you for writing.
Yours sincerely,
Iain W. Calder
President

If this is Mr. Calder's idea of a joke, I am not very amused. I did not write to express interest in the *Enquirer*, I wrote to him because he promised to mail me the list of witnesses. This letter once again states that there are "many reputable people" but so far he has not named even one!

I will try once more. This time I will write to Iain and make it very clear that I am merely requesting that which he promised me: a list of names of the people who verified this story.

Monday, Jan. 23, 1978

Snow still covers the ground from last Friday's blizzard, though it is now the uniform gray color that is typical on the winter streets of New York. I have been in the process of moving out of my cramped basement apartment into a larger, sunny, first-floor apartment also in Elmhurst. As of today, about half of my belongings reside in each place as I have not yet been able to get a mover to transport the larger things. The snow has created a backlog of appointments for the moving companies.

Trudging home through the slush in my oversized rubber boots to my old apartment, I pick up my mail and go inside. The first letter I open is from Iain Calder. My blood begins to boil as I read the following:

Jan. 20, 1978
Dear Doctor Kaplan:
Thank you for your interest in the *Enquirer.*

I appreciate your taking the time and effort to inquire about our article entitled "The Amityville Horror."

As far as we are concerned, our involvement with this story ended with our publication of it. At the present time we have no plans of doing anything further on this subject.
Yours sincerely,
Iain W. Calder, President

I am furious! He has no credible witnesses; that was merely a bluff to get me off the phone. Iain probably never thought I would pursue the matter in writing.

The first two paragraphs of this letter are nearly identical to the first letter. It actually has the sound of a form letter. And this last paragraph is a total cop-out! What Iain is really saying is we will not justify our story and we will not print your rebuttal. Period. The End. It is an arrogant kiss-off from Mr. Calder. I have been dismissed.

In the past I have often gotten calls from *Enquirer* reporters requesting information on various aspects of the occult, and I was always quite cooperative in referring them to the proper organization or individual. But never again. From now on the *Enquirer* is *persona non grata.* And I will also tell the public about this whole incident with Calder.

This Friday I have a lecture scheduled for the "Spiritual and Psychic Awareness Weekend" at the Hotel Americana in Manhattan. My topic is an expose of the Amityville Horror, and I will use that opportunity to relate the Calder incident to the audience.

Friday, Jan. 27, 1978

My lecture this evening went very well. When the organizers of the Psychic Weekend had originally called me a couple of months ago, I had been most interested to learn that the Warrens had already been scheduled to do a lecture espousing the credibility of the Amityville Horror. I then scheduled myself to do a lecture debunking the case preceding the Warrens' on the same evening. This was the lecture I gave tonight.

The audience at my lecture was quite large in size and listened most attentively. After I had presented my evidence of the fraud, the majority of them believed that this was indeed a hoax. They were shocked and angry that the publishers and the media would push lies and distortions on an unsuspecting public. The question and answer period ran overtime and still there were people who came to me with questions outside the lecture room. Many of them praised my efforts to expose the truth against such great odds.

It is this kind of praise and public support which encourages me not to give up.

Friday, February 3, 1978

I am at home in my new apartment watching the WCBS-TV/Ch. 2 Six O'clock News. Yesterday reporter Dave Monsees started a series called "Hoaxes, Horrors and U.F.O.'s" and the audience had been promised a review of the Amityville Horror for tonight.

The segment comes on near the end of the hour-long news. Dave Monsees is standing in front of the Amityville house. After a brief introduction, the scene changes to George and Kathy Lutz relating the experience of her transformation into a hag. Monsees then explains that there is a private group called the "Psychical Research Institute" which has spent four months investigating the case and has come away with a conflicting story. We see Rick Moran (as I have explained previously, Rick is a field investigator for the Psychical Research Foundation) stating the following:

"What we found out was that 83 of the 103 reports of phenomenon in the house could be proven false. In our opinion, the book is a complete miscarriage of justice in that it makes the research community involved in this type of study look like a bunch of raving lunatics."

Monsees goes on to state that this opposition to the story has not affected sales of the book. Hardcover copies printed so far number 200,000 and a paperback version and a movie are yet to come. To quote Mr. Monsees:

"Millions stand to be made from the story, although none will go to the family that now lives at 112 Ocean Avenue. Barbara and Jim Cromarty moved in on April Fool's Day of last year, and they say the joke has been on them ever since—not from spirits, but from curiosity seekers."

We see the Cromartys sitting in their living room talking about their ordeal of harassment since the book came out. Then they take Monsees on a tour of the upper part of the house. They point out the hallway carpeting which has been there since they moved in, contradicting Lutz's claim in the book that he "got out of bed one night and padded across the cold, uncarpeted floor of the hallway and into the sewing room."

Cromarty also points out that in the book, the Lutzes put boards across certain doors to keep the evil spirits from getting out of the room by opening the doors out toward the hallway. In actuality, all the doors on the second and third floors open inward.

When Monsees goes to interview Jay Anson, he asks about this contradiction.

The conversation goes like this:

JAY ANSON, AUTHOR: That was part of the phenomena—that those doors did swing outward.

DAVE MONSEES: You're telling me that...

JAY ANSON: I've seen myself doors on a hinge like that swing the other way.

Monsees then goes to California to track down the Lutzes. The Lutzes claim that they first got involved in the book, "to counter what they called fabricated newspaper stories. Now they say the book they collaborated on *was hyped, some of the information distorted and exaggerated to make it sell.*" (Italics mine.)

We see Dave Monsees and George Lutz walking along a pier near the ocean. George makes the following statement:

"One of the things in the publicity is that we lived in 28 days of terror. *We didn't live 28 days of terror.* We didn't have anything like that. *We enjoyed living in that house up until the last week that we were there, actually...*we looked forward to living there. We had planned on staying there for quite a long time. We really—*to us it really was a dream house.*" (Again, Italics mine.)

Based on this interview, I must say that George Lutz himself is my best witness to the phoniness of this story! He has admitted that the book was distorted and exaggerated, and his on-camera statements totally shatter the main premise of the book—that the Lutzes lived in 28 days of terror! If George says that the Lutzes enjoyed the house up until the last week, that means that all of the phenomena which is supposed to have happened between Dec. 18, 1975 and Jan. 7, 1976—or between page 5 and page 138 of Jay Anson's book—is *not true!* This revelation comes right from the lips of Mr. George Lutz himself! Straight from the horse's mouth, one might say.

I can't help but wonder just what the big boys at Prentice Hall think about George's little performance tonight.

Tuesday, Feb. 7, 1978

This morning I did a live radio show with one of the major Manhattan talk–show hosts—Mr. Bob Grant. It is the first Manhattan radio program that has allowed me the opportunity to expose the Amityville Hoax in detail and at some length. Mr. Grant, normally famous for his gruff attitude with guests and callers, was extremely gracious and courteous with me. He even told his public on the air that he supports my position that the case is a hoax, and thinks that it is disgusting that these people can be allowed to con the public this way.

One of the things which helped win Mr. Grant over to my side was Prentice Hall's refusal to send anyone to the program to represent their side of the story in a debate. Bob said that it's the first time in all his years of doing radio that a publisher turned down a chance to plug their book on the air for free. That made him very suspicious.

There have been many hosts in the past who have agreed with my position but who didn't have the guts to say so on the air. For this reason, Mr. Grant has earned my respect and gratitude.

Monday, Feb. 13, 1978

Two things happened today which relate to the Amityville case.

First, I received a letter in the mail from a law firm representing *Good Housekeeping* magazine. Lipton, De Groot & Sugarman are defending *Good Housekeeping* in a lawsuit brought against them by the Lutzes based on last year's article. This is the invasion-of-privacy suit which I had read about in *Newsday*'s December article.

Mr. Sugarman heard my conversation with Bob Grant last Tuesday and was impressed by my knowledge of the subject. He would like me to consider being a witness for the defense. I can hardly believe the nerve of these people! Less than a year ago *Good Housekeeping* would not even print my letter to the editor denouncing the story; now they expect me to run to help them! I have no intentions of getting involved with this. However, I shall place the letter in my files in case I need a good laugh now and then.

The second thing that happened is that I picked up a copy of *People* magazine dated for today. The cover features Clint Eastwood and Sondra Locke, but in the upper left-hand corner I read the following: "Amityville Horror: its specter grips a second family." The table of contents for Pg. 28 reads, "Up Front—The latest horror in Amityville is a bestseller's legacy of recrimination and litigation—" followed by the magazine's other main features. The title of the article itself is, "The Amityville Horror Lives On—In A Snarl Of Lawsuits and Suspicions." There are six photos: One of Ronald DeFeo Jr.; one of Jay Anson; an eerie, dark photo of the house; an amusing shot of Barbara and Jim Cromarty crouching pretzel-style in the "red room"; Barbara's 19-year-old son, Dave, in his bedroom (formerly Ronald's bedroom); and George and Kathy Lutz, walking their dog Harry in California.

The article does not take sides but merely presents the viewpoints of the various participants. The Cromartys say that it's all lies, Jay Anson says that he'll leave it up to the reader to decide, and the Lutzes say that it's true, in spite of some inaccuracies in the book.

Thursday, Feb. 16, 1978

Today I did the television program "Midday Live" with host Bill Boggs for New York's WNEW-TV, Ch. 5. The radio show with Bob Grant seemed to stimulate some interest in my story and I was called by the producers of "Midday" a couple of days ago. They asked if I could debate *The Amityville Horror* on the air with Ed and Lorraine Warren. (Remember, Channel 5 was the station that originally called the Warrens into the case to do the on-camera seance for their news show in '76.)

Anxious for the chance to confront the Warrens in public, but wary of being outnumbered by them again, I asked "Midday" if I could bring along one other person to help support my side of the debate. They graciously agreed. I then called Mr. Rick Moran, the photo-journalist and investigator who had denounced the case on the Joel Martin Show and on CBS-TV News. Rick was excited by the offer but, unfortunately, was unable to get out of a prior commitment to appear on the show with me. However, he offered to send in his place his partner, Peter Jordan. I did not know very much about Mr. Jordan but I had heard him on the Joel Martin Show with Rick. Peter had helped Rick to expose many of the falsehoods in the book and had seemed fairly good at elaborating on those points on radio. So I agreed to have him come on the show with me.

The segment was a circus from beginning to end. The Warrens dodged my accusations by launching a full-scale attack on my personal integrity. Any time I would bring up a specific incident in the book and explain why it could not possibly be true, the Warrens instead of replying would come back at me with an attack on my academic credentials. As for Mr. Peter Jordan, my supposed ally, he just sat there in his chair as silent as a log. Unable to draw the Warrens into an intelligent debate on the specifics of the case, I became angry and hurled insulting remarks back at them. Poor Bill Boggs, exasperated by his attempts to moderate the "discussion," ran his hands through his hair and looked uncomfortable.

In the course of the discussion I did manage to describe some of the blatant contradictions in the book, while the Warrens merely made blanket statements of their trust in the Lutzes and their belief in the Lutzes' story. Ed also described his experience with a "demon" during the seance in the house. Peter Jordan opened his mouth once to make a rather non-committal statement.

As the segment neared the end, Mr. Boggs asked each of us to give a brief statement summarizing our positions. I stated that the Amityville Horror is and always has been a hoax. The Warrens said the story is absolutely true and that they had never felt such evil in a house in all of their thousands of cases. Peter Jordan shrank back in his chair and mumbled that he was "sitting on the fence" for now— or in other words, was undecided as to the truth or untruth of the story. I was in shock at Jordan's cop-out and furious with him, but did not get a chance to ask him why he had changed his position. He was out of the studio before I knew it.

When I got home, I called up Rick Moran. He did not understand Jordan's actions and was also furious with him. He felt that Jordan blew the opportunity to present to the public all of the data that the two of them had researched. I am angry because I specifically brought Jordan on the show to support my position against the Warrens and instead I ended up debating them two-against–one, as usual.

Friday, Feb. 17, 1978

Waiting in Tony's Candy Store for a cup of coffee, I wander over to the newspapers to browse. One bright blue headline on a yellow background immediately rivets my eye: "INSIDE THE HOUSE OF EVIL." It is the *National Examiner*, a clone-like rival of the Enquirer. The headline continues, "Book Bonus: True-Life Occult Best Seller. Jay Anson—*The Amityville Horror*—A True Story. First Chilling Installment Starts Page 2." The book's title is a copy of the actual book cover with the flies. Next to that is a black and white picture of the house; and below it, the same old pictures of George and Kathy Lutz taken by the *Newsday* photographer back when it all began in 1976. A small caption below the photos reads, "This husband and wife tell all."

Inside is Part I of a serialization of Anson's book. The introduction entices you to read this terrifying true story, pointing out that it was previously available only in the hardcover book. Now you can read it for just the cost of the *Examiner* (35¢)!

Keeper of the Flame

Friday, Feb. 24, 1978

Yesterday, I underwent a cardiac catheterization at New York University Medical Center in New York. My cardiologist, Dr. Bernard Boal of Booth Memorial Hospital in Queens, felt that it was necessary to determine the extent of the blockage in the three main arteries surrounding the heart. The so-called "procedure" (it seemed more like an operation to me) involved inserting a tube with a tiny camera at the end of it into my inner thigh and up through the blood vessels to the heart, and taking pictures of the insides of the arteries. I was given only a local anesthetic, as it was necessary for me to remain awake during the one and a half hour long procedure to tell the doctors when pain indicated that their probe was hitting the wrong areas. It was an extremely unpleasant ordeal to say the least, but worth it, I feel, to determine the severity of my condition. The restrictions placed on my physical activities following the heart attack in 1976 had begun to make me feel like a "cardiac cripple." I had to know whether I was going to live or die.

The results of the test were at the same time frightening and a relief. One of the major arteries had been rendered completely useless by the heart attack. A second one is partially clogged—a warning to me to be more careful of my diet. The third one, thank God, is clear. The good news is that new capillaries have begun to open up surrounding the scar tissue in the heart, enabling the blood to bypass the dead muscle.

It has given me new hope. With the proper discipline and determination, I have a chance to live a normal life.

Thursday, March 9, 1978

This morning I was a guest on the Long John Nebel radio talkshow in Manhattan. As I have mentioned before, my interest in strange phenomena was quite stimulated in the early years by Mr. Nebel's program. No topic was too "weird" to be discussed on his show. John Nebel has not lost his touch despite rapidly deteriorating health. His questions are probing and designed to get the most mileage from his guests. It is important, as the program lasts from midnight to 5:00 a.m., 5 nights a week.

It was quite a challenge but I was very capable of holding my own and in the course of the program I discussed many aspects of my research into strange phenomena, including my position on the Amityville Horror hoax.

Monday, March 20, 1978

It is the first day of the Easter vacation from my job. I am relaxing at my desk with the newspaper when the phone rings. It is my red "hot-line," my business number which is widely known to the public as a clearing center for information on strange phenomena. I pick up, expecting another request for a psychic to locate a lost pet or child. Instead, it is Mrs. Barbara Cromarty, current owner and occupant of the Amityville house.

Barbara explains that they did receive my letter to them which I left with the maid last year. "It's just that we've been so troubled by all the harassment that we haven't had a chance to call you," she says. "It's been awful. I really love this house but I don't know how much more of this we can stand. As you probably know, we're in the process of suing the publishers. We have heard about your exposé of the case and we would like to discuss it with you. Would it be convenient for you to come out to the house some night this week?"

I realize that the Cromartys are looking for ammunition to use in their lawsuit, but I am not adverse to that. We are basically on the same side, even if for different reasons. Besides, it is the perfect opportunity for me to interview them about their experiences in the house. We set the meeting for this coming Thursday evening.

I immediately begin to make a few phone calls to my members. Three people will accompany me to the house—Roxanne Salch, Dr. Max Toth, and Richard, a psychic who sometimes works with my group. Max will pick up Roxanne and myself in his car, and Richard will meet us at the house. We will bring cameras and tape recorders along but will not use either if the Cromartys object in any way. They are quite sensitive to that sort of thing right now.

The Amityville Horror Conspiracy

Max Toth, Joel Martin and Stephen Kaplan at an awards dinner.

Thursday, March 23, 1978

It is the third time I have been in the Amityville house; Roxanne's second. Max and Richard have never been inside before. All of us are quite comfortable sitting in the large armchairs or on the off-white, overstuffed couch in the spacious living room. Barbara and Jim Cromarty graciously offer us drinks as a big, friendly dog barks to be let outside. A teenage girl opens the front door to show the dog the light drizzle which is coming down out there. The dog quickly retreats to the warmth of the living room, nuzzling at Barbara's feet. Settled in this domestic tranquility, it is hard to believe that we are in the very house where such unholy terror was alleged to have happened to the Lutzes. Indeed, even the shadow of the DeFeos' tragic night seems to have been washed away by the Cromarty's love for and restoration of the house.

For some reason, there are not many "tourists" pestering the family tonight. Perhaps the rain is keeping them in. In any case, we are disturbed only by the sound of an occasional car slowing down outside to get a glimpse. From the sound of the stories the Cromartys relate to us, this is extremely mild in comparison. They often find people hanging from the window sills trying to look inside, or grabbing shingles from the house to keep as souvenirs, or screaming obscenities at them.

The Cromartys are quite cautious in their discussion with us. It seems they have been burned once too often by other so-called "para-psychologists" whom they had allowed into their home. Barbara and Jim request that we not take any pictures or recordings and we must respect their wishes, being guests in their home. They are worried about anything that could affect their current litigation.

Barbara and Jim can not stress enough that they have had absolutely no strange occurrences in the house. They do explain away one of the Lutzes' so-called phenomena—the windows which open and close themselves. All of the windows in the house work on the weights-and-pulleys system, and this being an old house, things do not always work as they should. The weights are sometimes not properly balanced, causing the windows to open or close "by themselves." It is a quite normal occurrence, mechanical and not supernatural in nature.

The heating system works quite well, says Barbara, and has since they moved in. There are no unnatural cold spots. No noises in the night (other than from the tourists outside); no green, black, or red slime. No monster pigs peering in the windows, though they do confirm the report that they observed Evinrude the cat looking in. The fireplace has only the normal carbon deposits burned onto the wall; it does not resemble a demon. No foul stenches; no gripping spirit hands. If it were not for the public harassment, this would be an ideal place to live.

The Cromartys are quite interested in hearing about my evidence of the hoax. They believe some of it could help them in their court case. Meanwhile, our psychic, Richard, decides to go into a trance to attempt to pick up any vibrations—positive or negative—in the house. He is "out" for a half-hour or so while Max, Roxanne and I continue our discussion with Jim and Barbara. Every so often they glance at Richard uneasily, observing his limp position, eyes closed and head back. I believe they are afraid that Richard will do something strange, what I'm not sure. But they are obviously not familiar with psychic trances, as we are from working so often with psychics. They seem relieved when Richard finally opens his eyes and smiles normally.

After several hours of discussion it is mutually decided that it is time for us to leave. Richard has sensed nothing evil in the house, and the rest of us—not actually psychic, but certainly sensitives—have found it warm and pleasant. Being veterans of many haunted house cases, we have experienced definite "bad vibes" in many but there is no feeling of that whatsoever in this house.

The Amityville Horror Conspiracy

The Cromartys assure me that they will contact me if they need my help in the trial. We thank them for their hospitality and get into our cars for the drive home. It has been a quiet but interesting evening.

Sunday, March 26, 1978

Excerpt from *The New York Times, Book Review* section, "Book Ends" column by Richard A. Lingeman, subtitle: "Amityville Horrors." (I come across this small item while reading the Sunday papers. It is two paragraphs long. The first summarizes the book, the second follows below.)

A reporter for *The Morning Call* of Allentown, Pa. has reported some rather strange doings connected with the book itself. Among the unexplained phenomena that the reporter, Pete Stevenson, describes in a three–part series in *The Morning Call:* A police officer portrayed in the book as investigating some cloven footprints in the snow told Mr. Stevenson the incident never occurred.

Another police officer mentioned in the book turns out to be nonexistent. The pastor of the local Roman Catholic Sacred Heart Church disputed the book's description of unusual occurrences involving a priest called Father Mancuso in the book. The Psychical Research Foundation of Durham, N.C., held seances at the house for a television station shortly after the haunted couple moved out, and it detected no signs of supernatural activity. Mr. Stevenson, of course, does not prove that the strange occurrences reported in the book did *not* take place, but there are inveterate cynics who will entertain the possibility.

How ironic that the *Times* should print this tiny mention of opposition to the book now. Of course, they have already finished unloading the syndicated story to hundreds of other papers, so I guess they feel it is safe now to suggest that one reporter has reason not to believe the story. And to pretend that they first heard of this opposition from this small newspaper in Pennsylvania.

Remember, the editor of *The New York Times* had all of the information contained in today's article plus much, much more as of Oct. 10, 1977, when I spoke to him on the phone. Plus, that phone call was followed up with my letter to him detailing the hoax, which he never saw fit to print.

Tuesday, April 18, 1978

This evening I lectured to a good–sized audience at the Flushing Library in Queens. The lecture was entitled, "The Amityville Horror—

Hoax or True Story?" It was received very well by the audience, in spite of a strange occurrence which interrupted my talk about halfway through. A group of young teenage boys had sneaked into the library and into the doorway at the back of the lecture room, where they proceeded to pelt my unsuspecting audience with small, hard rubber balls! Security was summoned to escort the pranksters out, and I never found out what had provoked the boys to choose my lecture group as a target.

Friday, April 21, 1978

I just received in the mail a copy of *The Journal–Courier*, a major Connecticut newspaper. It contains the results of an interview I gave to them on the phone last week. I had precipitated the interview myself, in an attempt to discredit Ed and Lorraine Warren, who are now travelling the country singing the praises of Anson's book. I had decided to hit them where they live, so to speak, by calling the largest newspaper in their area of Connecticut—The *Journal-Courier*. I told my story to a staff reporter named Donna Kopf, who then called the Warrens to get their side of the story.

The result is this article published on April 18th entitled, "Spirited Argument Could Be A Draw." In it, I charge that Ed and Lorraine Warren, two spiritualists from Monroe, Conn., are frauds and should resign from the profession. I am quoted as saying that I want to "exorcise this so-called demonologist (referring to Ed). I'm trying to educate the people in Connecticut to what is going on. If he is the only demonologist in the state, I think it's time they got a new one." I explain that the Warrens are misleading the public by perpetuating the lie of the Amityville Horror.

Ed Warren, in turn, calls me a "crackpot" and a "sick man." He states there is no foundation for my claims. In answer to my challenge that the Warrens and I both take lie-detector tests, after which the loser(s) will retire from the field, Lorraine replies, "My husband is not going to be challenged by any individual such as Steve Kaplan."

I also received in the mail today a letter from my cousin, Paula and her daughter Dawn from their home in Arizona. Dawn had heard all about this "true story," and knowing that it occurred in my area and that I research such phenomena, she wanted to know what I knew about it. This only brings home to me the realization of how far the lie has spread.

The Amityville Horror Conspiracy

I call Dawn to let her know the truth. Her reaction is a common one among the public: How can a lie be published in black-and-white as a true story?

Thursday, April 27, 1978

Last night I once again did a show on WMCA radio with Candy Jones—this time with one major, tragic difference. Candy's brilliant husband, Long John Nebel, finally and very recently succumbed to his long and agonizing battle with cancer. His widow is now attempting to push on with the show alone.

I received the call from the producers of the show only yesterday afternoon. A guest had cancelled out at the last minute and they were at their wit's end trying to find a replacement. Since I had been a frequent guest of Long John and Candy, they felt I would be excellent as a spontaneous guest and fairly begged me to agree. In spite of the late notice and my quite hectic schedule, my respect for Long John and my sympathy for his recent widow caused me to accept.

The topic of conversation was Parapsychology in general, and the other guest on the show was Milbourne Christopher, a professional magician notorious for publicly denouncing the entire field of parapsychology as nonsense and fraud. I did not know he was to be on the show until I arrived and was introduced to him. During the course of the program the topic of the Amityville Horror came up (I don't recall whether it was Candy or myself who initiated the topic), and I figured this would be a perfect opportunity for Mr. Christopher to seize upon this obviously fraudulent case and use it in his arguments to discredit the entire field. Much to my surprise however, Milbourne did not even join in the discussion until I pushed him for a comment, and then only to say that he had no opinion of the case one way or the other.

I do not understand why Christopher and other infamous debunkers of parapsychology, such as "The Amazing Randi" and Philip Klass, have not seized upon the Amityville Horror as a potent tool in their fight to discredit the field. For years they have wasted the public's time attacking legitimate, responsible researchers; but on the biggest, internationally known fraudulent case in history, they have all remained strangely silent.

Aside from all that, my appearance on this Candy Jones program turned out to be a tiring and frustrating experience for me. Candy launched an all-out verbal attack on my credentials, my experience, my cases, my book and my knowledge of the field. I was shocked. I could understand her being in a bad state of mind in light of the circumstances of John's death but, after all, I had agreed to do this spur-of-the-moment show as a favor to her! I defended myself quite admirably but at the same time sincerely resented having to defend myself at all. I had expected an intelligent discussion, not a personal attack.

At one point in the show, Candy thumbed through a stack of books on parapsychology (with the home listeners totally unaware that she was reading from books) and asked me questions such as, "Who was J.B. Rhine's medium in 1934 and what was the title of the chapter he wrote about the case?" When I would admit to not recalling the answer, she would read the information from the book, pretending of course that she knew it all along, and comment something like, "You call yourself a parapsychologist and you don't know about its history?!"

Needless to say, I will think twice before I ever agree to do another program for Candy Jones.

Saturday, April 29, 1978

I just received the May issue of *Fate Magazine*. It features an article entitled, "The Amityville Horror Hoax," written by Rick Moran and Peter Jordan (good old "sitting on the fence" Jordan). I had no idea that the article was going to be published until now, and I'm more than a little miffed that I was not approached to contribute my knowledge of the case to the exposé.

In spite of this, Moran and Jordan do make some important points in the article. They say that Anson's book "reads like a primer of paranormal occurrences, with every conceivable type of experience reported. Either this was the most incredible haunting case on record, we thought, or Anson's book was something less than 'A True Story.'" In other words, sure, some of these strange phenomena could occur or have already occurred at various times in history—but all to one family in less than a month?! It stretches credibility beyond the breaking point.

Moran and Jordan back up this observation by going back to the original newspaper and magazine reports predating Anson's book, all of which do not mention any of the more shocking phenomena in the book. They paraphrase George's remarks from an article they say appeared in the *Long Island Press* of January 1976. This must be a misprint; they had to mean *February* 17th, as the Lutzes did not go public until February.

The Amityville Horror Conspiracy

Just to make sure of this date, I take a little trip to the local library to check out the microfilm copies of the now–defunct *Long Island Press*. I am interested to read any *Press* article on this case which pre-dates Feb. 19th of 1976, the date when I was first mentioned as planning to investigate the house, and Feb. 20th, when I called it a hoax. Prior to those two articles, I had not read any *Press* articles about the Lutzes, as I was not in the habit of buying that paper.

After first ascertaining that there was no mention of the case on Jan. 17th, or any other day in January, I proceed to the February film. I find there not one, but two articles I had not read, dated Feb. 17 and Feb. 18, 1976.

The Feb. 17th article is titled, "Did 'supernatural force' play role in DeFeo murders?" It centers on William Weber's hopes to reopen DeFeo's case based on the Lutzes experiences. This quote is attributed to George Lutz during the interview: "What *didn't* happen were all the usual things associated with a haunted house. No objects flew around; there was no wailing." The Lutzes claim only that they felt a "strong force" and that they felt "threatened." They dispute "rumors of vibrations, power losses and an attempt at exorcism by a local priest."

The article from the following day, Feb. 18th, is called, "Ghosts Chased—Cop pours cold water on DeFeo 'haunted house' tale." It is briefer than the previous article, and is mainly a vehicle for Sgt. Pat Cammaroto to deny all reports that the police had investigated alleged supernatural phenomena at the Lutzes' home. Cammaroto states, "There was no documentation, and no official investigation in this area." He also emphatically denies ever having said that tragedy had struck every family who had lived in the house, a statement erroneously attributed to him in earlier media reports. Cammaroto says, "I have known the previous families who have lived there, but I know of no tragedy other than that of the DeFeos."

Once again, the article states that the Lutzes moved out because of "strange forces," and that Weber had called a press conference on the 16th to announce his plans to get an appeal for DeFeo because he may have been "possessed."

But back to Moran and Jordan's *Fate* article. They point out that even in the April 1977 Paul Hoffman article in *Good Housekeeping*, the Lutzes still made no mention of "a horned creature, a marching band or the extensive damage supposedly done to the house." It is significant that the Lutzes never reported any of this damage described in Anson's book to the Amityville Police, or to their insurance company. No repairman or locksmith in the Amityville area recalls having done any work on the house while the Lutzes lived there.

Moran and Jordan also claim to have witnessed the "mysterious" movements of the bedroom windows, and as the Cromartys had described to us, it is caused by counterweights in the window which are too heavy and move with any vibration. According to Moran and Jordan, "Father Mancuso" flatly denies ever having entered the Lutzes' home or hearing any demon voice telling him to "Get out!" Furthermore, a fellow clergyman who was with Mancuso on the Van Wyck Expressway the day the car allegedly went out of control says that the only thing that occurred was a flat tire, and that neither of the two men attributed the trouble to anything other than the car's general state of disrepair! The pastor of the Sacred Heart Church says the reports of a stench in the rectory are "pure and utter nonsense" and the priests who were living there at the time recall no stench and were never forced to leave the building.

In spite of official police department records and Sgt. Cammaroto's continued insistence that no policeman ever investigated anything at the Lutz home, Anson, in an interview with Jordan, continued to insist that Cammaroto had been there, seen a wrecked garage door and cloven hoofprints, and felt "strong vibrations" in the house.

An interview with Jerry Solfvin of the Psychical Research Foundation suggests a logical explanation why some participants during the Channel 5 seance may have felt "queasy" or experienced "palpitations": the room was small, hot and emotionally–charged, with more than twenty people crammed in—including the film crew using hot movie lights. Solfvin called the Lutzes' phenomena "far too 'subjective' to be measured reliably."

Moran and Jordan conclude their insightful article by stating that the book's subtitle, "A True Story," could not be further from the truth.

Sunday, June 11, 1978

It has been an exhausting weekend. Yesterday I investigated the case of an alleged haunted house in Bellport, L.I.; today I took my children on an outing to the beautiful Bayard Cutting Arboretum on the south shore of Long Island. After finally settling down into my bed in Queens with the *T.V. Guide*, I saw a listing for the David

The Amityville Horror Conspiracy

Susskind Show—the topic was hauntings, with guests including Jay Anson and Ed and Lorraine Warren. Tired as I was, I did watch and record the program. In the first half of the show, David had on a few people who had experienced strange occurrences in their homes (including one who wrote a book about it) and Jay Anson.

Jay spoke after two of the others had told their stories and explained that the Lutz story went beyond mere ghosts, because it was demonic in nature. He reiterated the story of the priest and his terrible suffering at the hands of these demonic forces. At one point Jay says that the Lutzes suffered, "a complete breakdown of personalities," and Susskind asks if he means that they had a nervous breakdown. Jay replies, "Not a nervous breakdown PER SE (emphasis mine), their personalities changed completely where they were fighting with one another where normally this was a very happy family of five."

Jay also claims that George Lutz had no belief or interest in the occult before moving to Amityville; that he never even read anything about it. This is a blatant contradiction to the original conversation I had with George where he told me he had met Ray Buckland and been to the Witchcraft Museum on Long Island a year or two prior to our conversation. (By February of '76 the Witchcraft Museum had already been closed and Buckland had moved to another state.)

Of course Jay stuck to his handy cop-out by stating "...in the book I leave it up to the reader, either you believe or you don't believe. I don't commit myself one way or the other...." I fail to see how people can make an intelligent choice when they've been fed lies and gross misinformation.

Noncommittal, Jay goes on to try to obliquely link every tragedy in his life to some type of Amityville curse: friends' car accidents, fatal fires, and his own (second) heart attack. After interweaving these tragic stories with the knowledge that all of these people had been given copies of *The Amityville Horror,* Jay then denies trying to link the events, saying "I don't try to make a link, but people try to make the links."

The Warrens appear in the second half of the program. They were involved in investigating the case of one of the other participants in the program, a man named Fred Moore who claims that his daughter's involvement with a Ouija board had caused his family to be tormented for 8 1/2 weeks until Lorraine came and "cleared the house." The rest of the show consisted of discussion of that case and a prolonged demonstration of the Ouija board by Lorraine. This took up so much time that the Warrens didn't get a chance to discuss Amityville.

Saturday, June 17, 1978

This afternoon I gave a free lecture to a fair-sized audience at the Donnell Library Center on West 53rd St. in Manhattan. It was called, "The Amityville Horror: Fact or Fiction." I got much the same reaction from the audience as I did in Flushing: outrage that fiction can be published under the category of non-fiction, and an eagerness to learn what really did happen in Amityville.

This common reaction tends to discount the theory held by much of the people in publishing and the media that the public doesn't want to hear truth, they merely want to be entertained. No one is interested in an *un*-haunted house, they say. I feel the public is done a grave injustice by this attitude, for public reaction cannot be accurately assessed when the public has been fed misinformation to react upon. Nearly everyone I have come in contact with in my lectures has found the truth even more fascinating than the fable.

Sunday, July 23, 1978

Amityville is about to go Hollywood—the story is about to be produced as a major motion picture. Today's *New York Times* (Lawrence Van Gelder's column) had an interview with a man named Elliot Geisinger, a resident of Sands Point, L.I.; who along with his partner Ronald Saland will be producing "The Amityville Horror" as their "first big feature." The two have previously been involved in producing documentaries about the making of movies, and one of their writers was none other than Jay Anson! Small world?

Strangely enough, this Long Island born-and-bred story will be filmed beginning late summer in Toms River, *New Jersey!* Perhaps they were worried about the reaction of Long Islanders to this continual perpetuation of a story that most locals now know as a hoax.

10

Only the Names Have Been Changed

Tuesday, August 1, 1978

Today I was a guest on the Bob Grant radio show on WOR. The topic, once again, was the Amityville hoax. The interesting thing about this is that prior to the show, Bob Grant had called Prentice Hall and told them that their book was to be challenged by me on the air. Would they care to send a representative of Prentice Hall or Jay Anson to defend their book? Once again, they were not interested. This surprised Bob. Here was a chance for them to get a lot of free publicity for the book and they were turning it down flat. Perhaps an interview over the telephone, Mr. Grant suggested, so that we can present the public with both sides of the story? No. They very curtly turned him down.

So I went on the program alone. Mr. Grant told his listeners that he was going to stand behind Dr. Kaplan's story as the truth. Why? Because never, in his long career as a broadcaster, had a publisher ever flatly turned down *two* offers to plug their book for free. It seemed so suspicious to Bob that he had to believe that they had something to hide, and he strongly stated that opinion on the air.

It felt good to have an ally.

Wednesday, August 2, 1978

I am browsing through the book store at Queens Center mall when a distorted vision of the Amityville house looms up in front of me. The image is blood–red and large flies swarm around it. Has the pressure of the investigation finally gotten to me? No. This screaming visage is part of a large cardboard publisher's display containing the brand new copies of *The Amityville Horror* in paperback. I knew that a paperback version was due out soon, but stumbling into it this way was a momentary shock.

Only the Names Have Been Changed

I pick up a copy of the book with its slick black cover; the raised, blood-red letters of the title blazing out at me with the "H" in "Horror" descending into a pointed, scarlet devil's tail. Similar to the hardcover, but more effective with the devil's tail in red. Disgustedly I start to place it back in the display but stop myself halfway there. It goes against my grain to purchase this book, but it would be a handy prop in my lectures about the hoax. Still, I do already have the hardcover, and why contribute even $2.50 to these scoundrels and liars?

I flip to the copyright page. The small print there claims that this Bantam edition is an exact replica of the original text. But what if it's not? A voice inside me says, they lied about 'A True Story,' why even trust their word about this?

Reluctantly, I take the book to the cashier and plunk down my $2.50 plus tax. Returning to my car in the parking garage, I toss the package on the seat and promptly forget about it as I maneuver the car down the circular, tunnellike exit ramps of the concrete monolithic garage.

All through dinner with Roxanne I think nothing of the small package tossed carelessly on the car seat. As we get into the car though, she pushes the bag aside and asks, "What's this?"

I explain as we drive to my apartment, almost embarrassed by my silly purchase. Roxanne, however, is fascinated. When we get inside, she promptly goes for my bookshelf and searches out the hardcover; then, with the two side–by-side, proceeds to turn the pages simultaneously and compare the two editions.

"Why are you doing that?" I ask her.

"Oh, I don't know," she replies," "I just thought I might notice some differences."

"You know, I had the same impression when I decided to buy it," I admit.

Before long Roxanne excitedly begins to point out passages to me. It seems that the two editions are not the same. They're not the same *at all.*

I supply Roxanne with a red pencil and a large pad. Hours later, she presents me with this astonishing list of inconsistencies (what an understatement!) between the Prentice Hall and the Bantam editions of *The Amityville Horror: A True Story:*

[Note: The Prentice Hall edition used for this comparison is the original 1st printing. Subsequent printings of the hardcover were changed and may match the Bantam paperback.]

The Amityville Horror Conspiracy

1: Page 15 hardcover (HC), pg. 21 paperback (PB): The description of Father Mancuso's duties has changed. In the HC he is, "a lawyer, a Judge of the Catholic Court, and a practicing psychotherapist." In the PB, he "handles clients in family counseling for his diocese." Also, the Sacred Heart Rectory has been changed to "the Long Island rectory" in the PB.

2: Page 16 HC, page 22 PB: The sentence, "Now he was in a high position in the diocese, with his own quarters at the Rectory in North Merrick." has been changed to, "Now he was very well regarded in the diocese, with his own quarters at the rectory in Long Island." I suspect that pressure from the Church is responsible for these changes concerning Father Mancuso.

3: Page 16 & 17 HC, page 23 PB: The sentence, "He seldom read the news when he picked up a paper, only 'Broomhilda' and 'Peanuts'" has been changed to, "He seldom read the news when he picked up a paper, only looking for items of special interest." Perhaps the publishers decided that a priest who ignored world matters and only read comics was not exactly the image they wanted to present.

Also on page 23 of the PB, an amazing occurrence takes place. In the HC, Father Mancuso's car is a blue Vega, but in the PB it has changed to a tan Ford! The purpose of this change would have been a puzzle were it not for the fact that I own a Chevy Vega. To explain it, I must first go ahead to page 26 of the PB (18 in the HC) where Father Mancuso is driving his car home when, "the...hood suddenly flew open, smashing back against the windshield."

This is a physical impossibility for a Vega, because the Vega hood opens in the opposite direction, away from the windshield! It seems when they fabricated this incident they were not familiar with Vegas and did not realize their faux-pas until some sharp-witted editor pointed it out! I never would have noticed the incident myself if not for my new familiarity with Vegas combined with Roxanne's comparison of the books.

4: Page 17 HC, page 24 & 25 PB: In the HC, Mancuso plans to have dinner with his mother at her "home in Queens." In the paperback she has a "house in Nassau" on pg. 24, but on pg. 25 the Father drives "off to Queens" to make his dinner-date with mother. Does Mancuso's mother's house levitate back and forth between Queens and Nassau?

5: Page 39 HC, page 55 PB: Mention of Mancuso's "Bishop" has been changed to his "Confessor."

6: Page 41 HC, page 58 PB: Again in relation to Father Mancuso, the phrase "cases on his court calendar" has changed to "items on his busy calendar"; and "patients in psychotherapy" have changed to "clients in counselling." Mancuso is losing rank fast.

7: Page 44 HC, page 62 PB: Mancuso is worried about the Lutzes and supposedly has not been able to reach them by phone. So, in the HC, "He called a friend in the Nassau County Police Department." In the PB this has changed to, "He dialed a number he normally used only for emergencies." This certainly eliminates the possibility of getting corroborative testimony about the incident from the police department.

8: Page 45 HC, page 65 PB: Oh, what a tangled web we weave...! Our good friend Sgt. Cammaroto is now being called "Zammataro." Good work guys, nobody will ever guess his true identity with that clever alias! As if that's not bad enough, the Sgt., who was with the Amityville Police in the HC, is now with the Suffolk County Police Dept. in the PB!

9: Page 69 HC, page 97 PB: Here again the name of the Sacred Heart Church is omitted in the PB. They must obviously fear reprisals from the diocese. Also the non-existent Sgt. Gionfriddo is with the Amityville Police in the HC but with the Suffolk County Police in the PB.

10: Page 80 HC, page 115 PB: In the HC, Father Mancuso had developed "red splotches" on his hands, but in the PB he has only "redness."

11: Page 82 HC, page 117 PB: In the HC, Mancuso prays for help "at his own altar in his room," because his palms have begun to "bleed." In the PB, he merely prays "in his own rooms," because his palms are "itching."

They must have realized that a Roman Catholic priest does not have his own altar in his room, so they changed it. But when they change his bleeding palms to itching palms, it sure makes one hell of a difference to the story!

12: Page 85 & 86 HC, page 123 PB: There are so many words omitted or changed here that it's hard to believe this is the same book! The hardcover tells about Father Mancuso's bleeding palms, compares them to the stigmata (wounds resembling Christ's said to afflict certain holy individuals), and talks again of Mancuso's "private altar." The PB tells only of blisters which had begun to fester (not bleed) and totally omits mention of an altar.

13: Page 92 & 93 HC, page 134 & 135 PB: Here, in the original version, Mancuso is reading his medical journals on psychotherapy when he notices reddish stains on the magazine and then sees that his palms are smeared with blood. In the Bantam edition, Mancuso is reading "subscription magazines," just to distract his mind when be notices a "slight discoloration" on the magazine and sees that his blisters look as if they are ready to burst.

The Amityville Horror Conspiracy

14: Page 136 PB: On this page of the paperback they have forgotten to omit the reference to bleeding palms, even though all previous references to blood have been omitted. They're not even consistent with their lies!

15: Page 103 HC, page 149 & 150 PB: All reference to Father Mancuso's bishop had been taken out up to this point, referring instead to his "superiors." But here they have forgotten to replace the word "bishop" so it becomes another incongruous element of this edition.

16: Page 109 HC, pg. 156 PB: In the original version, the horrible stench in the rectory has driven many other priests out of their rooms and into the school building, and the Pastor is so upset that he suggests that everyone burn incense to dispel the odor. In the new version, Father Mancuso fantasizes what might happen if the odor were to seep through the rectory—the other priests might be forced out to the school and the pastor might get upset! But none of this has actually happened; the smell has remained confined to Mancuso's room and he is merely worried about what could happen.

There is a world of difference between having the Pastor tell everyone in the rectory to burn incense to dispel a stench which has forced many of them to flee and having only Mancuso deciding alone to burn incense in his room! The important factor to remember here is that with the changing of this one paragraph, we have lost all possible witnesses who could have verified Mancuso's story—namely, the Pastor and all of the other priests. We now have only Mancuso's story that there ever was a stench.

17: Page 109 & 110 HC, page 157 PB: Sgt. Pat Cammaroto reenters the story here as Sgt. Lou Zammataro in the scene where he goes to check out the Lutz home and sees Jodie the Pig's hoof-prints in the snow. At least now they have a fictional name for a character in a fictional scene.

18: Page 110 HC, Page 158 PB: In the HC, the heavy smoke from all the burning incense in the rectory combines with the stench and succeeds in burning the eyes and lungs of anyone in the building. In the PB, only the visitors to Father Mancuso's room are affected by the smoke, as it is confined to his room only..

19: Page 111 & 112 HC, page 160 & 161 PB: This has got to be the mother-load of changes! There are more words changed or omitted on these two pages than there are words left intact! The awful scene, in which the pastor wages a vicious verbal assault on Father Mancuso, has been totally reversed so that, in the PB, it is Father Mancuso who verbally assaults the pastor!

It is now Mancuso who becomes disrespectful and rude to his Pastor because he is angry that the stink has picked only his room to invade. In the original version, this was not even the subject of the argument; instead, the Pastor was jealous of Father Mancuso because the Bishop assigned him more court cases. The incident has also been toned down a bit.

Where the Pastor was previously possessed with something that caused him to "glare with hatred" at the Father, this time Father Mancuso is merely possessed by "emotion." Is this supposed to be the same book? Which "true story" are we supposed to believe? When an incident can be this drastically changed, it is obvious to me that neither of the two versions ever happened.

20: Page 119 HC, page 172 PB: In the HC, Father Mancuso thinks to himself about the "demonic attack" he has been through and feels guilty that he has not done more to help the Lutzes through their own. "Why, by God," Mancuso thinks to himself, "the Pastor was right! I am a fake!"

In the PB he merely fears he will have a "debilitating attack" because of talking to George, and his thought is, "Why, by God, I'm not worthy!"

21: Page 120 HC, page 173 PB: In the HC, Mancuso calls and asks to see the Chancellor of the Rockville Center diocese to discuss the Lutzes' problem, and they give him an appointment for the next day. In the PB, Mancuso does not bother to call the Chancellor's office, but instead decides to just go to see them in the morning.

22: Page 177 PB: Up until now, the paperback has eliminated all mention of Father Mancuso being a psychotherapist, but on this page the Chancellor begins a question to Mancuso with the words, "In your capacity as a psychotherapist..."!

23: Page 145 HC, page 209 PB: Mancuso's "private altar" is now being called a "prie-dieu," which the dictionary defines as a small reading desk with a ledge for kneeling in prayer.

24: Page 145 HC, page 210 PB: In the HC, Father Nuncio from the Chancellor's office cautions Father Mancuso about visiting the Amityville house again and tells him to relay the message [for the Lutzes to move out of their house] by phone. In the PB, Father Mancuso informs Father Nuncio that he will not be returning to the house, and tells him that he will call the Lutzes instead.

25: Page 146 HC, page 211 PB: In the original version, Mancuso tells George that he should never again attempt to bless the house himself, that he should let a priest do it instead because a priest is "a direct intermediary between the Lord and the Devil...." George gets quite upset over the mention of the word

The Amityville Horror Conspiracy

"Devil" and Mancuso wishes he "could have bitten his tongue" for making the slip because he knows he is expressing his own personal fears, not those of the Church. In the PB, Mancuso never makes this slip of the tongue at all.

26: Page 166 HC, page 243 PB: In the HC, Mancuso has an appointment with the bishop to discuss the Lutz case. In the PB his appointment is with the bishop's secretary.

27: Page 195 HC, page 290 PB: In the Epilogue, it is mentioned that Father Mancuso has been transferred to another parish. The paperback omits this sentence which, appears in the HC: "And he still bears the scars of humiliation and fear of whatever he encountered there." Also, when they mention that George has sold his interest in his surveying business, they omit (in the PB) the line, "He finds it difficult to leave his family alone for too long a spell." Perhaps they decided that this line made George sound a little too paranoid.

*   *   *

This is the list of major changes. There are other, more minor changes, in the Bantam edition, but they are mostly just repetitions consistent with the changes Roxanne has listed.

I take the paperback and flip back to the copyright page to reread the statement there: "This low-priced Bantam Book has been completely reset in a type face designed for easy reading, and was printed from new plates. It contains the complete text of the original hardcover edition. *Not one word has been omitted.* "

Not *one* word has been omitted, *hundreds* of words have been omitted or changed. How can they blatantly lie to the public like this? This is not the original version of the book. I notice one other thing has been omitted on the facing page. The statement from the Prentice Hall version—"However, all facts and events, as far as we have been able to verify them, are strictly accurate."—has been completely eliminated. What's the matter, folks, are the facts somehow no longer "strictly accurate"?

This is a definite consumer rip-off. They can't possibly be allowed to get away with it; someone should sue. I believe I will call up the Consumer Frauds bureau tomorrow.

Thursday, Aug. 3, 1978

I just finished talking with the Consumer Frauds bureau and I discovered a shocking thing: the only thing I am entitled to do is to get my money back on the paperback. In order for an individual to sue Bantam for damages, the individual must be able to prove that he was hurt *financially* by the printing of that book.

"Is that the case with you, sir?" the woman asked me.

"Well, no," I replied, "But the lies in this book have hurt the field of parapsychology."

"But did you, personally, suffer financial damages due to the inaccuracies of the book?" she asked.

"No," I replied.

"Then you can't sue for damages."

"What about the fact that the public has been blatantly lied to when Bantam stated that this book is the same as the original, with not one word omitted?" I asked.

"Any individual who bought the book is entitled to return it for the amount of the purchase price," she stated.

"And that's it?" I was becoming frustrated. "You mean they can get away with omitting and changing hundreds of words and then saying that it's the original version?"

"I'm afraid so, sir," she impatiently explained. "Unless someone can prove that they suffered a financial loss due to this misrepresentation, then they can do nothing more than get their money back on the book."

I thanked her and hung up the phone, still incredulous of a system that could allow this to happen. Extremely agitated, I pick up a copy of today's *Newsday* so I can try to just read and relax. I am distressed to see in the headlines that a brilliant comedienne, Miss Totie Fields, has died. I had really enjoyed her performances on T.V. and admired the bravery of the woman. I scan the table of contents to locate the article on Miss Fields. Instead, I am distracted by another item: "'Horror' House Suit Loses—The residents of the house upon which the bestselling book 'The Amityville Horror' was based lost a $1.1 million damage suit which claimed that their existence has been made a horror by the curious who invade their property—Page 21."

Good God, I can't get away from this horror story. I was trying to forget about it for awhile, but I suppose now I'll have to read this article.

State Supreme Court Justice Douglas F. Young has dismissed the suit against Prentice Hall, Anson and the Lutzes, saying that the suit had no firm legal precedent and so "fails to set forth facts upon which any claim of liability...might be predicated." The Cromartys and their attorney, Michael Zissu, are disappointed but will appeal the decision. Mr. Zissu was shocked that the judge would not allow his request that the words "A True Story" be removed from the title in future printings.

The article closes by mentioning that the paperback edition of Anson's book has been released, and that the hardcover has sold more than 300,000 copies since it was released last Sept. This information comes from Anson's attorney, a Mr. Myron Saland. That name sounds very familiar.

Of course! The co-producer of the A.H. movie is named Ronald Saland. Coincidence? After all that has happened, I doubt it.

Monday, August 7, 1978

This evening I taped a "Joel Martin Show" in which I exposed to the public most of the inconsistencies between the two editions of the "A.H." It is a dynamite show, but it will not be aired until Sept. 4th because Mr. Martin is ahead on his tapings.

In a few days I will be leaving for a two-week vacation in New England and Canada. It will be great to get away and leave all this behind me.

Tuesday, Aug. 29, 1978

I spent most of last night waiting in the emergency room at Booth Memorial Hospital to be treated for two sprained ankles—a souvenir from my vacation. Most of the trip was fantastic but, on the second–to–last day, my close friend, Ed, who works for the government, invited Roxanne and I to double with him and his date—an instructor of women's history at Dartmouth College. They took us to a private lodge owned by Dartmouth, nestled in a ravine on Mt. Moosilauke in the White Mountain National Forest of New Hampshire.

It was a long ride from Dartmouth to the lodge and we arrived there Friday after dark, exhausted and ravenously hungry. We were promptly told that the kitchen was already closed and we could not get any food that night. There was no place to go out for food because we were in the middle of the wilderness. With grumbling stomachs we were shown to our rooms—small wooden cells, barren except for a narrow bunk bed and a dresser. As we passed the bulletin board, I noticed a sign proclaiming Saturday night "Ghost Story Night" in which contestants would compete to tell the best ghost story. Oh, brother. I go on vacation to get away from it all and even here I can't avoid the subject. Even at Dartmouth that morning someone I had been introduced to had insisted to me that the Amityville Horror was true.

We arose Saturday morning stiff from the cramped mattresses and wolfed down our breakfast. The lodge had been freezing all night (no heat, of course, because this was just one step above "roughing it" or camping outdoors) and the hot food tasted great. After breakfast, Ed suggested we "take a short walk" up the mountain trail. His lady friend had to teach a class at Dartmouth and we would be back before she was, he said. It sounded like a good idea, and the weather was gorgeous, though rain was expected towards evening. So we bought some bag lunches from the lodge and the three of us started on our way.

Four hours later we collapsed on the mountaintop. It had been a nightmare climb, sometimes climbing up vertical piles of jagged rock. Roxanne had threatened to quit after an hour, but Ed insisted that the mountaintop was "just around the bend" and I trusted him. So Roxanne trudged on with us, only because she didn't want to be left alone to find her way back to the lodge through the wilderness. We passed some very agile students who were jogging their way down and asked, "How far to the top?" "Oh, not far," was the answer and so on we went. At least Ed had hiking boots; Roxanne and I were wearing nylon-and-suede sneakers. The jagged rock-points jabbed into our hands and feet as we climbed. At one point we had to walk across two narrow logs which had been laid across the river as a bridge, with a mini-rapids rushing by beneath us.

"It can't be much further," Ed kept saying, "I think I can see the peak from here." But it was heavily wooded and there were many outcroppings that looked like the top until you got there and realized the "trail" kept going. By the time we finally got there, Roxanne was ready to kill Ed and I was considering helping her. Instead, we sat down to eat lunch. The view, at least, was quite spectacular, and I began to relax. My pleasure was not to last long. Five minutes later Ed crumpled his sandwich wrapper, jumped up and said, "O.K.! Time to start back!"

Roxanne and I looked at him as though he had just sprouted another head. "Back?" I said.

"No way!" said Roxanne.

"But my friend is expecting us; I told her I'd meet her at three, and it's already past that now! Besides, it looks like it's about to rain and that will make the rocks quite slippery, especially in the dark," he said. "We've got to make it back before dark or we're in trouble. We didn't even bring a flashlight! And she'll be furious with me!"

Of course we hadn't brought a flashlight; it had been 11:00 in the morning when we left the lodge for a "short walk"! As much as I hated the idea I convinced Roxanne that Ed was right—we had to start back right away.

The rain started fifteen minutes later. The water combined with the moss on the rocks to make them nearly impossible to get a foothold on, and we soon found that walking forward down those steep out-croppings was impossible. We had to turn around in some spots and climb down backwards while clinging to the rocks with all four limbs. Many times Roxanne (or "Rocky" as I had begun calling her) slipped and fell a few feet down, bruising and twisting her limbs. I tried to help her, but I wasn't doing so well myself, especially when I tried to keep up with Ed, who was nearly running he was so anxious about getting back.

About halfway down, Roxanne spotted a large, flat rock and lay down on it. "That's it!" she cried. "I'm not going a foot further. You can both leave me here to die if you want, but I just cannot go one more step!"

Ed mumbled something about being late and kept going. I stayed and tried to convince Roxanne to get up. I finally got through to her when I noted that it was getting darker and I wouldn't want to leave her alone in the dark with whatever was out there in the woods. I helped her to her feet and we went on. At every rough spot I stopped and turned back towards her to urge her on.

We were now only about a mile from the lodge. It was quite dark, but we had gotten past the worst of the rock cliffs and the path was starting to level off. I turned around to encourage Roxanne. "Don't worry Rocky," I yelled above the sound of the rain, "We're almost there. We're going to make it! We...AAAAAAAHHHH!!"

Pain shot through my legs as I landed in a small ravine a few yards below the path. Not looking where I was going as I turned around to talk to Roxanne I had stepped off the edge and done a backwards somer-sault down into the trench, landing with both legs twisted beneath me.

Ed heard the yell and came back to see what had happened. He and Roxanne tried to help me up but it felt like both ankles were bro-ken. I was in agony. Ed, always one to come prepared, took out a pocket knife equipped with a miniature saw and cut down a sturdy young tree. He then removed the branches and gave me the trunk to use as a staff. Holding onto it with one hand and Ed with the other, I was able to get to my feet despite acute pain.

Since Ed now had to help support me, poor Roxanne, who had been ready to die an hour earlier, was given both of our knapsacks to carry. It seemed we might be able to make it back.

But we had forgotten about the "bridge." We saw it as we turned the bend and I groaned—there was no way I could walk across the two logs. I finally got across by crawling an inch at a time on all fours, petrified that I would topple off into the white waters below.

About a quarter of a mile from the lodge, two more joggers passed us on the way back and we asked them to send back help. A few minutes later a strong young man arrived from the lodge with ace bandages and a helping hand.

We arrived just in time for dinner and an angry balling-out from Ed's lady, who demanded to know where the hell we were all this time!

The hospital was more than an hour's drive away and I was exhausted, so we decided not to go but to sleep at the lodge for the night and go home to New York on Sunday. They propped my legs up with pillows and ice bags and I slept on and off. I was a little better by morning, but by then all of Roxanne's muscles had stiffened up so badly that Ed had to lift her down from the top bunk. I'm surprised she didn't try to choke him to death while she had the chance.

And that is how I ended up in the emergency room back in Queens on Monday. Luckily, I had no broken bones. I just looked up Mt. Moosilauke in my road atlas and discovered that it is 4,810 ft. high. That is like four Empire State Buildings on top of each other. It is a miracle that I, a cardiac patient, and Roxanne, an asthmatic, were able to survive such an ordeal. Ed pointed out to me that if my heart had been able to endure Mt. Moosilauke, then I must certainly have made an amazing recovery from my heart attack two years ago. By the way, he did apologize and admit that he had had no idea that the mountain trail was anything more than a pleasant hour's hike.

But back to business. An hour ago I received a phone call from Barbara Cromarty. It seems she has just about had it with the vandals at the Amityville house and is considering selling the house. She wanted to know if I would be interested in buying it at the low price of $85,000.

The Amityville Horror Conspiracy

"Well, Barbara," I said, "I really don't think I can afford such a purchase right now, even at such a bargain. Anyway, what would I do with it? It's too big for just one man to live in and it's too far from my job." Half-jokingly I added, "However, it might come in handy as a ghost or vampire museum."

"I don't care what you do with it," she said. "I just want out. I haven't had a decent night's sleep since we moved here. I had such plans and we've already spent thousands remodeling. Jim and I have always loved the house but can't take this harassment from the kooks and crazies out there. It's gotten even worse since the paperback came out."

We talked awhile longer and then I thanked her for the offer, politely turned it down, and wished her luck in whatever she decided. She asked me to let her know if I hear about anyone who's interested in buying.

Picking up my log-crutch from Moosilauke, I get up from my bed and limp out to the kitchen for some orange juice, sneezing all the way. It seems I also came home from "vacation" with a nasty cold. I think it will be some time before I decide to get away from it all again.

Monday, Sept. 4, 1978

This is the evening that the program I did with the Joel Martin Show will air. I also did a live show this morning on the phone for Alan Christian of WBAL in Baltimore, on which I summarized the discrepancies between the two books and also passed along to the public Mrs. Cromarty's offer to anyone in the market for an infamous house.

Sunday, Sept. 17, 1978

Barbara and Jim Cromarty appear in living color on the cover of *Newsday*'s *Long Island Magazine* today, with images of *The Amityville Horror* floating above their heads. The headline reads, "Haunted By a Horror Story." Most of the article is just an interview with the Cromartys and three of their teenage children about the various harassments they have endured in the house. There is also a short description of some of the physical impossibilities of the Lutzes' story: there is no keyhole in the door where the green slime was supposed to have oozed out of the keyhole; the doors that were boarded up to keep them from opening out into the hall open instead into the rooms; the fact that it is physically impossible for George to have viewed the "entire cellar" from his position on the stairs because he would have had to have been seeing through walls. They also give the dimensions of the notorious "red room": 2' 4" wide; 3' 6" long; and 3' 6" high.

There is a smaller, accompanying article that has been included in the magazine with the article about the Cromartys. It is called, "Between the Covers, Some Changes" and—surprise, surprise—it chronicles the changes between the hardcover and the paperback. These include: the change of Mancuso's car from a blue Vega to a tan Ford, the fight with the Pastor, Mancuso's mother's house moving from Queens to Nassau, and the changes concerning Sgt. Cammaroto and Sgt. Gionfriddo.

Coming only thirteen days after the airing of my program for Joel Martin, it seems something more than a coincidence that a *Newsday* writer suddenly got the inspiration to read both books simultaneously and compare them. More likely, someone listened to the program, took notes, and then looked up the changes using the page numbers that I provided. I don't mind them informing the public about it, but I do resent the fact that Roxanne and I did all the work and received no credit in the article. I suppose it makes them seem a lot more clever if they uncovered the deception themselves.

All of that aside, I do give the *Newsday* reporter credit for noticing two discrepancies that we had missed. One is the book's claim that there were hurricane-force winds raging on the South Shore on Jan.10, 1976. *Newsday*'s check with the U.S. Weather Service showed that the winds recorded at Kennedy that day averaged 15.7 MPH, not the 74 MPH that would be the minimum to be considered hurricane force. Second, they noticed that the floor plans of the house were changed, reversing the position of the sewing room and Missy's bedroom.

Another interesting thing here is the comments of representatives of Bantam and Prentice Hall when they were called by *Newsday*. Bantam points out that, "the paperback is a word-for-word duplicate of the 14th printing of the Prentice Hall hardcover." That means that the staggering changes in the story were made by Prentice Hall. Still, Bantam retains responsibility because of their statement that their edition is an exact replica of the original version. Prentice Hall refused to explain why they had made changes, citing only the Cromarty's suit (which as we know was already dismissed) as their reason for refusing to discuss it.

This mini-article closes with a statement by Chief Ed Lowe of the Amityville Police Department: "'I never gave much credence to the story. All the while he [Lutz] lived there, he never called the police department. The only time he contacted us was after he moved out. Sgt. Cammaroto was never there while Lutz lived in the house.'" The major article closes with a statement by Jim Cromarty: "'What we've found out,' Jim said, 'is that you can write anything you want in a book.'"

A very sad-but-true commentary on the American publishing industry.

Friday, Oct. 6, 1978

I received a letter in the mail today from Scholastic Magazines, Inc., the company that owns the TAB book club which offers books for sale to teenagers through the classroom. I had paid them a little visit earlier this week to strongly protest the fact that they were offering "The Amityville Horror" to youngsters in their TAB magazine under the category of non-fiction. Being a reading specialist myself, I am often called upon to select material for my junior-high school students. It upset me greatly to see this travesty of a book being pushed on unsuspecting, trusting children with a promo that read something like this: "More shocking than *The Exorcist* and more frightening than *The Omen* because this story is TRUE!"

I had first phoned Scholastic to complain. They sounded a bit annoyed but told me that I should bring them proof that the story was misleading, and so I did. I met with three editors of TAB in their Manhattan office and brought with me all of the evidence I have collected over the years. The result of that meeting was this letter dated Oct. 4th:

> Dear Dr. Kaplan:
>
> Thank you for taking the time to come to our offices to discuss your criticisms of *The Amityville Horror* with Ms. MacEwen, Ms. Colligan and myself. We were all surprised and concerned at what appear to be discrepancies between the novel and what you feel actually took place. We share your interest in seeing that some attention is focused upon the matter so that unsuspecting purchasers are warned against believing what you as an expert feel cannot be.
>
> Unfortunately, as we explained, the damage is done, so far as our part is concerned. As we mentioned, the offer is out, orders have been filled and there is no opportunity for "retracting" what some may consider a misleading promotional description and what you feel is a potentially damaging book.

However, let me assure you, should we have an opportunity to correct this inaccuracy, whether by providing some disclaimer in the promotional materials or appended to the book itself, we shall do so.

Again, we thank you for your sincere interest and concern for TAB readers. Sincerely,

> Daniel B. Weiss, Editor
> Teen Age Book Club

Only the future will tell whether Scholastic keeps their word, but at least they were open to hearing my side of the story. Coming from such a large corporation this letter alone is quite an accomplishment.

And now I'm off to Broadway. Tomorrow is Roxanne's birthday and tonight I'm taking her to dinner at Mama Leone's and then to see the successful Broadway musical, "Annie."

part III

THE MOVIE

11

"Lights..., Camera..., Amityville!"

Friday, Oct. l3th, 1978

"The First National PARAPSYCHOLOGY PSYCHIC CONVEN-
TION," the posters proclaim. "Guest Lecturer: HANS HOLZER—
Scentific Proof of Life After Death. The Real Truth of the Amityville
Horror—the untold inside story!—presented by DR. STEPHEN
KAPLAN."

The signs are plastered everywhere in the lobby of the Stouffer's
Valley Forge Hotel in King of Prussia, Pennsylvania where Roxanne
and I have just arrived to participate in the three–day convention. In
the few short weeks since I was first asked to participate in the affair,
which is sponsored by the Association to Advance Parapsychology and
Healing Research, (AAPHR), I have become involved in the planning
and executing of the convention, as a personal advisor to Mrs. Penny
Raffa. Mrs. Raffa is the Executive Director of AAPHR, a group which
is dedicated to helping the public explore alternate methods of healing and also trying to scientifically prove or disprove various paranormal occurrences.

My lecture is scheduled for tomorrow at 6:00 p.m. and I will also
participate in the Open Panel Discussion on Sunday at 5:00 p.m.

Our friend Max Toth is also here. He will be lecturing on
"Pyramid Power," as well as acting as Master of Ceremonies for the
entire convention. He has brought with him a young acquaintance of
his named John Krysko, who is a psychic and a metaphysician and
who will lecture on something called "Crystal Healing."

Of course there are also many interesting individuals whom I
have not as yet had the pleasure of meeting. All in all, it should prove
to be a most fascinating weekend.

The Amityville Horror Conspiracy

Sunday, Oct. 15, 1978

Roxanne and I have stopped at a diner for coffee on our way back to New York. The convention was exciting and successful in terms of bringing people in the field together in a united front. Financially, it had its problems just as any convention of that magnitude is bound to have, but Mrs. Raffa, her husband Tom (founder of AAPHR), and all of their staff handled themselves like pros.

Hans Holzer proved to be the biggest disappointment to all concerned. Despite receiving a huge fee for his appearance, he remained aloof from the rest of us and refused to stay long enough to participate in the Panel Discussion. I had met Mr. Holzer once before briefly, at a television taping in Chicago, in addition to speaking to him on the phone a few times and corresponding with him via mail once. In Chicago I had asked him his opinion of *The Amityville Horror* and he had told me that he had originally been offered the opportunity to write the book for the Lutzes, but had turned it down because he knew the whole thing was a lot of nonsense and he didn't want to be involved in it.

My lecture on Amityville was well received although the audience was small in number. I enjoyed attending the other lectures and visiting the various booths set up by individual psychic readers, healers, and purveyors of holistic health. Roxanne and I became particularly friendly with John Krysko, who turns out to be not only a most gifted psychic but also a captivating lecturer and an all-around charming and charismatic individual. We exchanged addresses and phone numbers with John and plan to keep in touch with him both on a professional and a personal level.

It would be nice if a convention like this could become an annual event. Perhaps it will happen if the financial hurdles can be overcome.

Thursday, Oct. 26, 1978

I lectured this evening at Peninsula Public Library in Nassau County on the Amityville Horror. My audience was substantially larger than the one in Pennsylvania but then, it's getting closer to Halloween and this is a Long Island story.

The lecture went quite well with only one slightly weird incident. During the question-and-answer period, a man in the very back of the room raised his hand and was quite vocal in criticizing my investigation of the case, saying that I had no proof that the story didn't happen exactly the way the Lutzes said it did. As I debated the issue with him, I tried to see his face more clearly from across the room because he looked very familiar to me. I wasn't sure why until after the lecture when Roxanne, who had been sitting in the back of the room near this man, asked me if I had noticed that the individual in question was the spitting image of Jay Anson. By this time the man had left so we couldn't take a second look; but Roxanne was right, he had looked just like Jay. Well, Mr. Anson does live in Nassau County and he very well may have been interested in the topic of my lecture.

Monday, Dec. 4, 1978

A friend from Long Island mailed me a copy of an article that appeared in the Nov. 30th issue of *The Amityville Record* newspaper. It's called "'Horror' house not for sale." The paper had interviewed me on the phone a week or so ago and I told them about Mrs. Cromarty's offer to sell the house to me. However, the article starts off with this statement: "The owners of the infamous 'Amityville Horror' house on Ocean Ave. this week emphatically denied that they are offering their house for sale to various psychic researchers." They then went on to quote me as saying that I had been offered the house for sale by Mrs. Cromarty.

Mrs. Cromarty explains in the interview that she had been close to a nervous breakdown from curiousity seekers when she offered the house for sale several weeks ago, but that she has since taken a vacation to regain her sanity and subsequently has taken the house off the market. "'We're ready to stay and fight it out,'" she says. But she also expresses concern about what might happen when the movie of "The Amityville Horror" is released this spring.

Friday, Jan. 5, 1979

Newsday has an article today entitled, "Amityville House Is For Sale Again." The tresspassers and crowds plaguing the Cromartys got worse during the Christmas holidays when people were on vacation. Michael Zissu, attorney for the Cromartys says that they had decided to sell the house some time ago but had trouble finding a broker. Now they just want to unload the house before the movie, which is due for release in July, comes out and attracts even more kooks and crazies.

I don't think they ever took the house off the market in the first place. Mrs. Cromarty probably just told that to *The Amityville Record* to

The Amityville Horror Conspiracy

avoid being overwhelmed by people claiming to be interested in purchasing the house but really only interested in getting inside for a first-hand look.

Thursday, Feb. 22, 1979

The Cromartys are still having trouble trying to sell their infamous house. Today's *Daily News* quotes a Mr. E.L. Budde, the realty man who is handling the sale as saying, "The house went on the market about four months ago, but so far we haven't had many real buyers. Some wanted to be shown the house, but not for the purpose of buying. We even tried to sell it to the movie company making the picture...but they had already built a replica for the filming in New Jersey."

Once people hear about the history of the house, they want nothing to do with it. If it were not for its infamous reputation, the house would be a steal for $100,000. with its bayfront location, pool, boat house and 14 rooms. The way things stand though, the Cromartys may still be the owners in July when the movie comes out.

Wednesday, April 4, 1979

I just picked up a copy of *The Star*, dated April 10, 1979. It has a story and three pictures of the Amityville Horror movie, which is being touted as "more shocking than The Exorcist." A caption under a picture of the house in Toms River, N.J. which was used for the film states, "A house in New Jersey was used in the movie, because film crews were afraid of the real house." They go on to reiterate all of those old stories of Jay Anson's about death and mishaps which befell his friends who came in contact with Anson's original manuscript.

What a lot of bunk. This had nothing to do with why the real house was not used. From what I've been able to learn, one of the main reasons was that the Village of Amityville was against the project and would not give their permission for the film to be shot there. James Brolin, who plays George Lutz in the film, has also jumped on the bandwagon—he claims that strange things happened to him while he was filming the movie: he got stuck in an elevator, and he tripped over a cable and hurt his ankle. Very occult indeed. The *Star* also claims that script pages would disappear during the shooting, only to reappear in an altered form.

All I can say is, "here we go again!"

Sunday, April 29, 1979

Ed Lowe is a columnist for *Newsday* who happens to live in Amityville (and also happens to be the son of Chief Ed Lowe of the Amityville Police Department). He wrote a column today about the parade of tourists who continue to travel to Amityville from all over the country, looking for "the spook house" or "the ghost house."

Naturally, residents and policemen alike always direct them to the wrong location. Some people locate the wrong house on their own, and then proceed to gaze in terror, sob, shake, scream, and get "strange vibrations" while actually looking at the wrong building. Mr. Lowe feels that the true horror is that "the American public can be woefully, pathetically feebleminded." A man from Michigan who said that he didn't really believe the nonsense in the book (but was looking for the house anyway) wanted to know, "How could they possibly print the words, 'A True Story' on the cover if the story wasn't true?" I loved Mr. Lowe's comment on this, which is as follows:

> "The idea stunned him, as if there were a natural Law, something on the style of The Law of Averages or that of Gravity, that made it physically impossible for a charlatan to introduce a lie by characterizing it as a truth; a law that would prevent me, for instance, from saying in print, right now, that the man from Michigan disappeared before my very eyes, in a puff of swirling, garlic-scented, multicolored smoke, leaving no trace of himself, his van or his family, except for a small plastic box of rubber faucet washers, which I keep in my kitchen as proof of the event. This happened. I swear it, on my honor as a member in good standing and a past president of the American Society of Neurosurgeons, and I can even produce for public scrutiny the box of rubber washers."

Sunday, July 15, 1979

The promos for the movie have begun to appear in all the major newspapers. "FOR GOD'S SAKE, GET OUT!" The huge block letters scream out at us from the ad. Under this, the title logo from the book, followed by the line, "From the bestseller that made millions believe in the unbelievable." Then, of course, the three stars are listed: James Brolin, Margot Kidder and Rod Steiger. The film is by American International Pictures, who brought us all those great B–grade horror movies of the past decades. I only wish they had stuck with Christopher Lee as Dracula; *that* was more believable.

The Amityville Horror Conspiracy

The movie premieres at two theatres in Manhattan on Friday, July 27th.

Wednesday, July 18, 1979

The Lutzes are at it again. In the July 24th issue of *The Star*, which just came out today, the headline reads, "Amityville Horror Couple: We're Still Haunted. Lie detector tests reveal the truth."

George and Kathy are now claiming that the horrors have followed them to California! They don't mention details other than to say that they have been hounded by "evil spirits" since leaving Amityville. They are in the process of writing three new books: "Unwanted Company," about how the horror has followed them 3,000 miles; "A Force of Magnitude, Amityville Too [sic]," which tries to connect the misfortunes of twenty–five of the Lutzes' friends and associates to the Amityville curse; and "The Amityville Horror Picture Book," with nearly 50 photos of the house, including two which they claim are "spirit photographs."

The Lutzes have also both submitted to lie detector tests which allegedly showed that they were telling the truth about their twenty–eight days of terror. *The Star* quotes Barbara Cromarty's comments on this: "They should have done the lie detector tests three years ago. Now they have the story down pat. I'm far from being an expert, but I understand there's a lot of room for doubt." I agree whole–heartedly with Barbara.

The Cromartys are also now suing American International Pictures for $2 million, claiming that the coming attractions preview (or "trailer" as it is known to the film industry) shows footage of the actual house. They are also basing their suit on the premise that the renewed vandalism expected to be caused by the movie will make the house more difficult to sell. The house is still on the market and in the meantime, the Cromartys have moved out and rented it.

Sunday, July 22, 1979

Five days to countdown. The promo for the A.H. movie has expanded to a full page in the *The New York Times* and the *Daily News*. They have replaced the "Get Out" line with this passage: "On Feb. 5, 1976, the Ten O'Clock News reported that in Amityville, New York, George and Kathleen Lutz and their three children had fled their home in the middle of the night. They claimed an unnatural evil was present and they feared for their lives. This is their story."

Combine this plug for realism with a plug for the book further down ("Read the Bantam Paperback") and you get the distinct impression that this movie is also being promoted as "A True Story." Although they haven't actually used that tag line, they have more than pushed people to believe the movie is true by referring the viewer to the book; and by making the connection between the Lutzes, the 1976 news reports, and the movie. The words, "This is their story" implicitly implies that whatever is in this movie is a reenactment of actual events which happened to the Lutzes.

Today's *Newsday* has two interconnected stories: one about American International Pictures (A.I.P.), which is about to be honored by the Museum of Modern Art, who will begin their five–week tribute and A.I.P. film festival with an early premiere of "The Amityville Horror" on Tuesday; the other story about the A.H. movie itself. The latter includes interviews with Jay Anson and with Elliot Geisinger, the producer of the movie, neither of whom have anything new to say. But the author of the article, movie critic Joseph Gelmis, makes an interesting observation concerning the credibility of the story:

> A number of events and claims in the book have been discredited by investigators, neighbors, two national psychic groups, priests and the village historical society. Possibly the most important disclaimer was made by the Lutzes themselves. At a press conference called by DeFeo's lawyer—who hoped to establish insanity by virtue of psychic influences as his client's defense—the Lutzes denied that objects had moved or other supernatural phenomena occurred. Rather, they implied, it was an intangible feeling of hostile energies in the house that had frightened them.

Good work, Mr. Gelmis! It's about time that a reporter writing about the story has actually done his homework and taken the time to look back in the files at the articles from February of '76. If more of the public had had the opportunity to read these old articles side-by-side with Anson's book, the Lutzes would have seemed more comical than credible.

I was also right about the reason why the A.H. movie was filmed in New Jersey rather than Amityville. Geisinger cites the main reason that the Amityville authorities were not expected to be cooperative. He adds though, that if they had filmed in the house and anything happened to the crew, the producers would feel responsible. If nothing

The Amityville Horror Conspiracy

paranormal happened, "...it might seem to disprove that the house had demonic powers."

They should have filmed in the house.

Wednesday, July 25, 1979

Today's *Newsday* introduces us to Mr. Frank Burch, latest resident of the infamous "horror" house. Mr. Burch is a friend of the Cromartys who has been "house-sitting" for them since they moved out six months ago. The photo of Mr. Burch shows a burly, bearded young man in a Billy Joel T-shirt. The caption reads, "Frank Burch: Sightseer's Nemesis." The article says that Burch has not read the book, is in no rush to see the movie, and feels the whole story was "the biggest duping of the American public of all time."

The Cromartys have, as of last week, abandoned efforts to sell the house. Burch seems to be doing a good job fending off sightseers, but village officials, including Mayor Victor Niemi, are scared to death of the crowds that will form when the movie opens on Friday. They have beefed up security on Ocean Avenue.

Meanwhile, Roxanne and I have been invited to attend a special premiere of the A.H. movie that is being sponsored by WBAB radio in conjunction with A.I.P. tomorrow night on Long Island. The theatre will be filled with listeners who have won a contest to attend the premiere. Roxanne and I will attend with Joel Martin and his family and then I will return to WBAB with Joel to tape a short segment on my reactions to the film.

Thursday, July 26, 1979

I'm glad that today will be busy for me—it will keep me from thinking too much about my son. Today is his eighth birthday but I won't be able to be with him. I'm not scheduled to see the children until I take them away on vacation with me in about two weeks. I miss them a lot, but I'm planning a great trip for them to Bear Mt. State Park and to Great Adventure Amusement Park in New Jersey.

Roxanne and I drive out to WBAB where we meet the Martins and follow their car to a nearby theatre where the premiere is being held. Crowds of excited people swarm through the parking lot of the suburban shopping center. They are the "lucky" ones who have won the right to attend tonight. At the door, each person is presented with souvenirs: a bumper sticker with the logo from the book and movie;

a T-shirt with WBAB printed on the front and the title and picture from the movie printed in bright red on the back; and a copy of the Bantam paperback. This is not the old Bantam edition; it has been given a new cover. The picture of the house is a still from the movie, and the red "devil's tail" descending from the "H" in "Horror" this time points directly to some words in the bottom-center of the cover. These words read, "Now A Major American International Picture."

The words "A True Story" still remain in big black letters on the cover. In my eyes, this movie edition of the book has inexorably linked the two. If one reads a book which is "A True Story" and that book recommends that you see the movie based on that book, then one would naturally assume that the movie is also "A True Story."

We are seated with the Martins in the V.I.P. section, and after a brief introduction, the movie begins. It starts out innocuously enough, with the happy Lutz family purchasing the house. It is amazing how much the New Jersey home looks like the real one. But the film soon progresses from innocuous to silly to preposterous to hilarious. The filmmakers have added some events that were never a part of the book. We now have George becoming possessed and chasing Kathy with an axe. The mysterious "well" which Lutz allegedly saw on a survey map of the backyard in the book, is now an old well which is located *in* the basement and which pours out gobs and gobs of black slime or glop. George falls into this and feels he is being sucked down to the pits of hell.

There are other numerous incidents which have been invented or changed for the movie, but they are almost too ridiculous to mention. A person would have to be more than gullible to believe that this movie was true as portrayed; it is three times more implausible than the book.

That's good. Maybe now more people will realize how ridiculous the story was all along. And that's what I will tell the listeners on WBAB tonight.

By the way, I read an item in Walter Kaner's column in the *Daily News* today that mentioned Jay Anson. He has just received a *million-dollar* advance for his next book, which hasn't even been written yet, based on his tremendous success with *The Amityville Horror*. His next book will be a thriller novel entitled *666*. As far as I'm concerned, it's his *second* "thriller novel."

The Amityville Horror Conspiracy

Friday, July 27, 1979

Today, the official opening day for the A.H. movie, is also ironically a day of major triumph for me! William Weber, the lawyer for Ronald DeFeo, Jr. who originally represented the Lutzes at their '76 press conferences, has confessed his complicity in the Amityville hoax:

I got the shock of my life when I picked up today's *New York Post* and saw this headline on page 5: "Lawyer Claims 'Amityville' book was hokum, not horror." Mr. Weber's story goes something like this: Weber had decided, after DeFeo's trial, to write a *novel* based on the murders in Amityville. The Lutzes told Weber of strange things that were happening in the house (it does not explain how the Lutzes knew Weber in the first place). Weber thought that the Lutzes' story might make a good epilogue to his novel, so he interviewed them. Weber claims that after 41 hours in the Lutzes' company, he decided they weren't telling the truth—but that didn't matter, since his book was a novel anyway. So Weber helped the Lutzes to invent even more "ghost stories" than they had previously told, and the Lutzes agreed to help him with his book. There was even talk of trying to get DeFeo a new trial based on "possession."

In the meantime, however, the Lutzes met Jay Anson and dropped William Weber like a hot potatoe. Weber is now suing the Lutzes for breach of contract for failing to do the book with him. The Lutzes, meanwhile are on a national promotion tour for the A.H. movie and are insisting on T.V. talk shows that all the "horrors" in the book actually took place.

This is a tremendous breakthrough in the case! This man, Weber, has given public testimony to that which I have been saying from the very beginning—that *The Amitville Horror* is and has always been A HOAX! This is the very man who helped to concoct the hoax. Who better than he would know the truth?

There are so many things which the article left out, so many questions I would have asked him had I been the reporter. If only I could talk to him at length... I've got it! What better way to get an in-depth interview from Weber than to have him do the "Joel Martin Show"? Excitedly, I call Joel to tell him about the article and to see if he is interested in getting Weber for an interview. After all, WBAB is only minutes from where Weber lives on Long Island. Joel is intrigued at the idea, and he also congratulates me on the fact that my cry of "hoax" has finally been publicly substantiated. He is optimistic about his chances at getting Weber and will call to let me know whether he was indeed successful when I return from my weekend trip to Washington, D.C.

This new revelation in the Amityville case comes just in time for me to use it for my lecture at the Open University of Washington. I am doing a lecture there tomorrow on the topic of "Ghosts and Other Haunted Stories," which is organized into two parts: Part I will discuss true cases of hauntings, and Part II will tell (as the course description says in the brochure) "the true story of the Amityville Horror (did the media suppress the facts?). He has been in this house and claims, 'I'm going to raise the lid on this case!'" Boy, will I raise the lid now!

Today is also the day for movie reviewers to take their shots at the A.H. movie. Both Kathleen Carroll of the *Daily News*, and Joseph Gelmis of *Newsday* gave the film 2½ stars. Carroll describes the per-formances of Brolin and Kidder as "nicely sympathetic," and that of Rod Steiger as the priest as "overwrought." She is disappointed that the movie never really explains what is wrong with the house and points out that the movie's greatest impact may be to lower real estate values in Amityville.

Mr. Gelmis does a more in-depth review and uses comparisons to the book. He finds it suspicious that the subtitle "A True Story" was omitted from the movie. Gelmis says that a spokesman for the movie distributor says that the Lutzes have seen the movie and have given it their "blessing." Gelmis wonders why the Lutzes would give their blessing to a script which differs so greatly from the "true story" in the book. For example, why would George consent to having himself por-trayed as a would-be axe-murderer in the movie, when this incident never happened in the book? Gelmis also points out that the priest in the movie not only has bleeding palms, but is now also struck blind: Gelmis concludes by calling the movie a "fair-to-middling thriller," and notes that the audience at the sneak preview at the Museum of Modern Art was so worn out by the fast pace of the film that they all applauded when the words "'The Last Day'" appeared on the screen shortly before the finale.

I look forward to my lecture in Washington tomorrow, and also to seeing my friend Ed, with whom I'll be staying. I hope I can calm down enough from today's excitement to get a decent night's sleep. I have to catch an 8:00 a.m. flight in the morning.

The Amityville Horror Conspiracy

Monday, July 30, 1979

The Open University lecture was an overwhelming success. The audience seemed to get caught up in my enthusiasm and excitement about Weber's confession. They were thrilled to be the first ones in the Washington area to hear this bit of news. It seems that the story of Weber's confession was confined to the New York area. What a shame! It's a story that the whole nation should hear. A couple of people came up to me after the lecture to tell me that they really admired the way I stuck to my story of the hoax for all these years. They congratulated me on finally getting substantiation of the hoax from an independant source. It made me feel proud and elated.

I brought home from Washington a review of the A.H. movie from Saturday's *Washington Post*. The reviewer, Gary Arnold, states that the screenplay was adapted from "Jay Anson's unconvincing book, which left one with the overwhelming suspicion that the Lutzes had gone to fantastic lengths to get out of a mortgage." A very perceptive man, this Gary Arnold.

The most exciting news of all is that I just heard from Joel Martin—he will be taping a program with William Weber this Thursday night. Weber seems to feel that it will be beneficial to his court case to get his whole story on the record, and Joel's show is the only place in the media that can give him enough time to do that. The program will be aired on Sunday night, August 5th. Joel will also do interviews with the mayor of Amityville and with the co-producer of the movie and air them following the Weber tapes.

Tuesday, July 31, 1979

Both the *Newsday* and the *New York Post* today are reporting that the Amityville house has been sold for $80,000 to a land developer from Tucson, Arizona. Mrs. Cromarty, however, was quoted as saying she did not know that the sale was imminent. The alleged buyer, Sam Stangl, wants the house because of its reputation for being haunted. He says, "I'd jump up and down and yell whoopee if any of those things happen while I'm in the house." He says he is interested in "adventure" and will live in the house during the few months of the year when he is in New York on business. The rest of the time he plans to rent it out to a psychic research group. Stangl suggests that maybe the Cromartys moved out of the house not because of tourists, but because they were "scared of something." I'm sure the Cromartys will not appreciate that remark.

Wednesday, Aug. 1, 1979

Once again, Amityville resident and *Newsday* columnist Ed Lowe has given us a witty, insider's view of Amityville. Today's column is a brilliant piece of writing with a biting sense of humor. The man is extremely talented and capable of conveying his opinions in a most entertaining manner. This column is called, "Horror Too Dull to Hurt Village."

It opens with three neighbors from Ocean Avenue sitting around a barbecue discussing various ways of eliminating what they call the "AH's" (Amityville Horror fans), who invade their privacy. Cherry-bombs and bees are suggested, but one of the men doesn't think either will be necessary. Why? Because the A.H. movie is such a bomb that the credulity of the story has been destroyed. Mr. Lowe describes the priest as being "Anson's least credible character, outside of Jody the Pig." He notes that the Catholic Church should be appalled by the cowardness and irresponsible behavior of the priest and the nun in the film.

Mr. Lowe's last two sentences bear quotation here: "Had the movie been good, the A. H. believers would have descended on our small, sleepy, old South Shore village in hordes, which was what we expected. But a movie version that highlights and emphasizes the idiocy of the AH book should dissuade some of the marginally gullible saps in the country, so that all we will get, driving up and down Ocean Avenue, stopping traffic, tresspassing on lawns and taking pictures, will be the real, gutter-brained, uneducable, dull-eyed flatheads, the ones who believed the book was a true story in the first place."

But I'm afraid there are more "flatheads" out there than you realize. And they may be incited by tonight's "Merv Griffin Show." The *Daily News* is promoting a special "Merv" show all about the AH movie, with George and Kathy Lutz, James Brolin, Rod Steiger and Don Stroud. I will be teaching my "Introduction to Parapsychology" class tonight at the Forest Hills Adult Center when the program is on, but I can get a T.V. set put in my classroom. I was going to be lecturing tonight on the Amityville Horror anyway, and this will be a good "visual aid" for my class.

Thursday, August 2, 1979

It is late evening and I am burning with curiosity as to how the interview taping between Joel Martin and William Weber has gone. I pick up

The Amityville Horror Conspiracy

the phone and dial the number for WBAB. Joel's wife Chris comes on the line and I can tell immediately from her voice that something is wrong.

"What is it, Chris?" I ask, "Didn't Weber show for the taping?"

"It's not that," she replies, her voice strained, "The taping went fine. But something horrible has happened."

Chris tells me the tragic story. A few minutes before Joel was to do the taping, he received a phone call from his twelve-year-old daughter, who lives in Brooklyn with her mother (Joel's ex-wife). Tracy told her father that, "Mommy is dead." At first Joel didn't believe her, but then the police called on another line to notify Joel of the tragedy. Tracy's mother had been walking to a Carvel Ice-Cream store to buy her daughter ice cream. Less than a block from the store, she was struck and killed by a car. She died instantly.

I am stunned. I have met Tracy many times at WBAB and she is a charming and intelligent young lady. My heart goes out to her.

"But you said the Weber taping went fine," I say to Chris. "How could that be when Joel got the news beforehand? Certainly he was in no shape to do an interview?"

"I think he was in a state of shock," says Chris, "He insisted on going through with the taping and he did an excellent job. I don't think the news had really hit him yet. It's just starting to sink in now."

After talking to Chris a minute longer and then to Joel himself, I offer condolences to them both. I offer to help in any way I can. But I can tell from the pain in Joel's voice that it is a shock he will not get over for a long time to come.

Friday, Aug. 3, 1979

I'm afraid the Amityville residents have a little more to worry about than Ed Lowe anticipated. A full page of good reviews for the movie is reproduced in both *The New York Times* and the *Daily News* today. Phrases like "A real chiller," "well-crafted," and "damnably clever" abound. Obviously, some reviewers like the film. Either that, or they are being well paid to endorse it. One even goes so far as to call the A.H. "The scariest haunted-house movie since 'Psycho." Alfred Hitchcock must be cringing from that comment.

I will be leaving tomorrow to spend the weekend in Suffolk County on Long Island and I plan to listen to the Weber interview which will be aired on Sunday night. I'm glad I had planned to be out there, because I can't pick up WBAB from where I live in Queens.

Sunday, Aug. 5, 1979

An ironic conflict of interests has come up. The A.H. movie is playing at the Smithtown Drive-In. I am going to be taking Roxanne, her three brothers, and her parents to the Drive-In as my guests to see it. Even though Roxanne and I have seen it once already, we can always notice things we missed the first time, and I want to get her family's reactions as Long Island residents.

The only problem is that the William Weber interview will be aired on the Joel Martin Show at the same time the movie is playing. But Roxanne's brothers have a solution: they can take along their portable cassette recorder/radio and tape the program while watching the movie. Then we can all go back to the Salch house and play back the tape of the program.

It should be a fascinating show.

12

The Joel Martin/William Weber Tapes—8/5/79

"At 10:00 on Long Island's Spectrum, an exclusive interview from William Weber, attorney for convicted mass murderer Ronald DeFeo, Jr. exposes the truth behind the Amityville Horror and his unusual role in the story. Is it real or is it a hoax? For the latest chapter of the Amityville Horror, a special two hour report beginning Sunday night at 10:00 with me, Joel Martin here on 102.3 WBAB."

On August 8, William Weber appears on WBAB radio out of Babylon, Long Island. The show is "Spectrum with Joel Martin."

Joel Martin: Attorney William Weber charges that the events depicted in the book and, I assume, the motion picture, "The Amityville Horror," never happened. William Weber should probably know better than anyone should know whether the Amityville Horror was a horror or a hoax, because William Weber was and is the attorney for Ronald DeFeo, Jr. who was convicted of killing his parents, two brothers and two sisters in the mass murder in Amityville in November 1974 in a house on Ocean Avenue, which then became the house depicted in the book and the film "The Amityville Horror."

And we're talking about a book that has sold millions of copies, I think it's into its, what, 13th, maybe 18th printing, not sure, and the film is doing, I understand, very, very well and the book purports to be a true story. William Weber says it is not a true story, and you obviously should know because not only were you associated with the defense in the DeFeo case but also had a connection to the Lutzes, whom the book is about, and the film. I welcome you and I want to thank you very much for taking the time and the opportunity to speak to Long Islanders about a story that is emanating from Long Island and that continues to draw national, if not international, attention.

William Weber: Well, thank you, Joel, thank you for inviting me here tonight.

JM: I don't know where to begin this very complicated story except perhaps to ask you how you first became involved at all with that very infamous house.

WW: Of course. I was initially appointed by the surrogate judge to defend Ronnie DeFeo. We went to trial. Our defense was a defense of what the layman would refer to as mental, as insanity, and after a trial, a lengthy trial, the jury decided that Ronnie DeFeo was not insane, that he in effect was a cold–blooded killer.

I felt that the verdict was very unjust and besides the various avenues of appeal that we had, we wanted to gather some publicity for Ronnie, a commercial venture, and we decided, myself and my associates, and Ronnie DeFeo, that we were going to write a book about the DeFeo story. And starting from that point on, the Lutzes eventually came into the story.

JM: How did you first meet George Lutz, Kathy Lutz, either or both?

WW: They called me. They were interested, supposedly, in giving me information to assist in the defense of Ronnie DeFeo.

JM: So when they called you the trial was still going on?

WW: No, the trial was over.

JM: The trial was over and Ronnie had been convicted.

WW: That's correct.

JM: Sentenced to six life terms.

WW: Yes, that's right.

JM: In theory, at least.

WW: Right.

JM: And this would place it when, 1975?

WW: They contacted me on January 16 of 1976.

JM: 1976?

WW: Yes.

JM: This is well after they were in the house—well, no, about a month after they were in that house, *but during the period.*

WW: It was about two days after they...

JM: They moved out. Now they moved into that house in...1975.

WW: Well, you say moved out, but I don't think at that point they ever intended on moving out. They went out just to gather their thoughts. They wanted to spend a few days at their, at Kathy's mother's house.

JM: But the point is, sir, you did not know the Lutzes before they moved into that house.

WW: No.

JM: You'd never heard of them?

WW: Never.

JM: Because you know one of the neighborhood bits of rumor, and I'm sure you know there were many on Long Island as there continue to be, is that perhaps you, William Weber, attorney, knew George Lutz prior to the time that they moved in so that, in fact, maybe there was some type of reason, some type of thinking about perhaps, you know, devising a defense before and then they move into the house and then they say there were spirits and then you say, see, I told you he was ill; he didn't really kill his parents because he was a cold blooded killer but because these evil spirits got him.

WW: Well, you've given me more credit than I deserve. But, I've heard that rumor...

JM: I'm sure you've heard it—I'm not saying anything new. But the fact is you're saying here categorically that you did not know the Lutzes until that time they approached you.

WW: Absolutely.

JM: One of the things that's very strange about this story, I'm sure you know, is the fact that George and Kathy Lutz, they were fairly obscure people at the time, I mean like all of us, lived their lives of quiet desperation, I'm sure, and didn't have a terrific amount of money. And yet they moved into a house that seemed to be, from all of the reports, even their own admissions in the book, a house which they could ill afford because that's an expensive neighborhood and an expensive house.

WW: Well George had, because of the death of his father, just inherited a land surveying business. So, in his mind he had it up for sale and the windfall that he was gonna get out of that was gonna go towards the living expenses in the house. In addition to that, he was gonna move the land surveying business into the house to save the rental that the William Parry Land Surveying business was paying in Syosset and apply that to the house. So, the finances, he had it pretty well covered.

JM: I see. So that they had some wherewithal, they thought at least, to be able to purchase that house.

WW: That's correct.

JM: But the fact is when they bought that house, which would have been somewhere, what, in mid–75 before they moved in...?

WW: Right.

JM: In other words the murders happened in November of '74, so now we go six months later and maybe it's the spring or the summer of 1973 and these two characters, the Lutzes, decide that they're willing to buy a house where these terrible mass murders were committed.

WW: Right.

JM: In retrospect, since you did not know them before they moved in, what were their feelings about moving into a house where six people had been murdered? Because I know my own feelings, I tell you the truth, I've seen that house and I've been to it—I don't think I'd want to have lived there at that point after those murders, and I have to tell you and my listeners, if they haven't heard me say it before, I was there the night of the killings as a reporter, and I saw one of the bodies and I saw all of the other bodies taken out wrapped, so I understand the horror of the story.

WW: I've spoken to thousands of people in reference to this, and I haven't found one person or family that would be willing to spend a night in that house let alone live in there. And the Lutzes had severe reservations about just that. They were shown the house and Kathy liked it and after she told the real estate woman that she liked it they were then told that it was the DeFeo residence and they had a serious decision to make.

JM: But you mean to say they didn't know that it was the DeFeo house at the time the real estate person showed them that home?

WW: No. I believe them when they say at the time they saw the house they did not know it and I confirmed that with the real estate....

JM: All right. You know why I find that so hard to believe. Because that story made news not only locally, perhaps nationally and internationally, and I don't know anybody who, in November-December of '74 and early '75 and during the period of the murders and the trial, did not know about the DeFeo mass murders, probably the worst in Long Island history.

The Amityville Horror Conspiracy

WW: Well, I'm not saying they didn't know about the mass murders. They just didn't know that the house they were being shown was the DeFeo house.

JM: Was the house where [spoken over W.W.] I see.

WW: But immediately after the real estate lady told them that was the DeFeo residence they knew then where they were.

JM: I see.

WW: But the point was Kathy had then just about fallen in love with what she had seen, so they didn't want to just off the cuff say no, they didn't want the house. They thought about it, they thought seriously about it, and they decided, being intelligent people, that they could overcome whatever thoughts they might have about the DeFeos having been murdered in the house. And since they were getting it at such a tremendous price, they decided to go through with it.

JM: Do you know what they paid?

WW: Well, the listed price is $80,000, but they never paid $80,000.

JM: It was well worth that price in that neighborhood.

WW: Oh, I think it was worth at least $150,000, yes. They didn't have to put up more, well they put up approximately $40,000—

JM: Which was more than they could afford, or not, in your opinion?

WW: I know he couldn't afford it.

JM: All right, so even though he thought he had the money from the land surveying business, you're suggesting that he probably did not have the money.

WW: He was definitely in over his head, especially when, according to his own testimony, the book, etc., and in what he told me, the IRS was after him.

JM: So, you see, the point would very well be taken that perhaps they lived there and got out not because of demons and psychic apparitions but because of—

WW: Financial pressures.

JM: Sure. And the Feds—I don't know if you can compare the IRS agents to demons and psychic apparitions, but close.

WW: I wouldn't compare them to demons at all—white ghosts, maybe.

JM: But it would be, certainly, a good motivation to get out of that house in 28 days.

WW: Well, there was an additional motivation to get out of the house. You have to believe the Lutzes to this extent. During the

28 days that they lived in the house they realized they just could-
n't cope with the memory of what had occurred in there. They
thought they could overcome that but, as the days went by, they
just realized that the memory of the DeFeo killings was too
much for anybody to continue living on a day to day basis in the
same room. It was too much for a husband and wife to sleep in
a bedroom knowing that Mr. and Mrs. DeFeo had been brutally murdered in just about the same area they were lying down.

JM: All right. So they thought they could cope with the emotional
factor of having now moved into a house where these brutal
murders occurred but they found out that, in fact, like most of
us, like the rest of us, they simply couldn't; maybe on a sunny
afternoon it was O.K. but when it was night time and the winds
were howling and it was raining....

WW: That's right. Absolutely.

JM: I get it. They told you this in a conversation?

WW: Yes.

JM: And that you don't doubt?

WW: No, that's exactly the reason why they moved out. That plus the
financial difficulties. They, when they fled, according to them,
you use the word fled, when they left on January 14, they went
to Kathy's mother's house—

JM: Here on the Island?

WW: Yes. To think. To make a decision. Are they going to go back to
the house and live there despite what was happening to them
personally or what were their options? They were there, more
or less, let's say, as a sanctuary for them to gather their thoughts,
to pull back and to see in what direction they were heading.
While they were there a friend of theirs came along and gave
them an idea. The idea was to write a book.

JM: To write a book?

WW: That's right.

JM: About the house?

WW: Yes, about their experiences in the house.

JM: The fact that they were nervous in the house?

WW: No, no. The friend put a few ideas into their heads and they
started that, from that point, from about January 16, embell-
ishing upon their experiences.

The Amityville Horror Conspiracy

JM: I see. So that by the time they called you with the idea they, meaning George and Kathy Lutz, the idea was that they could suggest that perhaps there were evil presences in that house and that might have helped you for the defense?

WW: They didn't call it evil presences....

JM: What did they call it?

WW: They just said that they had some personal experiences in the house that they would like to relate to me because they thought it could help me in the defense of Ronnie DeFeo.

JM: Did they say specifically what would help you in that defense?

WW: Yes, they did.

JM: And what would that be?

WW: Well, this was when I met with them, that the initial conversation was just inviting me over. I ultimately went over to see them. They spoke about dreams that Kathy was having. They spoke about funny feelings, about the change in the relationship between themselves and their children, the children fighting amongst each other when they never had done that before, and that they thought that maybe it was just the house that was no good. I listened to them for a couple of hours and you know I politely told them, I said that the information they were telling me was interesting in one regard but it couldn't help me at all insofar as the DeFeo defense was concerned.

JM: But why did they think it might?

WW: Well, looking back, you know I now know that they wanted me there to gather whatever confidential information I had concerning the DeFeo family and Ronnie DeFeo and then use that information for their own benefit.

JM: I see, so that they really had a more mercenary motive than the altruism they suggested. In other words, they had their own selfish motives in calling you although the excuse simply was to tell you that they wanted to help you in the defense of the DeFeo case.

WW: That's correct.

JM: Even though at that point it would have been defense on appeal because the trial was over.

WW: Right. And their book is full of facts and passages which I told them and which I had received from either Ronnie DeFeo or through my investigation in with asking, asking information of witnesses.

JM: Let me re–identify you, and then I'd be interested in hearing what Ronnie DeFeo suggested that wound up in the book *The Amityville Horror*. For anyone who joined us late, my guest is William Weber. He is a Long Island attorney, a practicing attorney who was the attorney for Ronald DeFeo, Jr., who was convicted of killing his parents, two brothers and two sisters in one of Long Island's worst mass murders ever, November 1974 at Amityville. The house later became, of course, the subject of the bestselling hardcover, the best selling paperback and now the motion picture, "The Amityville Horror."

  And if anyone holds the key to what really happened in that house, if anyone has any question about whether it was true or it was not true, I don't care if it would be Lutz, the man the story was about with his wife, if it was Jay Anson, the author, I don't care who he says he knows, not all of the psychics, not all of the people in the world, it would seem to me that the key to the truthfulness or the dishonesty of this story would be attorney William Weber. Now you said some of the material in the book, Mr. Weber, suggests of course that psychic apparitions were there and then various other evil forces, but some of it actually came from Ronnie DeFeo.

WW: That's correct.

JM: Well how, specifically?

WW: Well specifically, you start at the beginning of the book when the Lutzes say that when they were shown the house by the real estate lady for the first time there was a large sign in front of the house that said "High Hopes." Now that was brought out in the book because it's the foundation of the horror story. To call a house such as that "High Hopes," and the fact is that house was called "High Hopes," but there never was any sign on the front lawn. They never saw a sign. They never knew that the house was called "High Hopes." The reason why they found out is because I showed them a crime scene photograph of an artist's sketch of the house. The sketch was hanging on the wall in the DeFeo residence, and in that sketch there was a sign called "High Hopes."

JM: Because in the book it says on a lamppost at the end of the paved driveway is a small sign bearing the name given the house by a previous owner. It reads "High Hopes." That sign, you say, was never there.

The Amityville Horror Conspiracy

WW: That's right, and if you go to page 8, you know, and we could stay here, I could go through every page all the way up to page 110....

JM: You've got enough notes there, and if people would see that, to make your own book on the story.

WW: That's correct. If you just skip to page 8 there's a quote—

JM: Page 8 in the paperback?

WW: Well, I'm—

JM: You're working from the hardcover.

WW: Yes, I took it from the hardcover.

JM: Fine.

WW: But there's a quote attributed to Ronnie where he says, "It just started. It went so fast I just couldn't stop."

JM: Meaning, of course, the killings.

WW: That's correct. Now that quote was never in any newspaper article, it was never in any trial record or transcript. It was told to them by myself because Ronnie DeFeo said that to his psychiatrist during a private examination.

JM: Now the book also—

WW: I must state to you now that this confidential information was authorized to be released to the Lutzes by Ronnie DeFeo.

JM: All right. You did not know, I should ask parenthetically here, the Lutzes, or rather, the DeFeos. You did not know the DeFeos up until that time you were appointed by the court.

WW: That's correct. Yes.

JM: No knowledge of the DeFeo family whatsoever?

WW: No.

JM: It says here on one of the pages of the paperback that a Channel 5 announcer went on to say that William Weber, the attorney representing Ronald DeFeo, had commissioned a study hoping to prove that some force influenced the behavior of anyone living at 112 Ocean Avenue. "Weber claimed this force may be of natural origin and felt it might be the evidence he needed to win his client a new trial. On camera Weber said he was aware that certain houses could be built or constructed in a certain manner so as to create some source of electrical currents for some rooms based on the physical structure of the house" And it goes on to a lot of—

WW: That's literary license talking. If you look at that quote very carefully, that is not quoting me, it's quoting Steve Bauman as saying, 'Weber said.'

JM: Quoting, yes. Yes. Now I understand..

WW: That's a literary trick, see, because I can't sue them and say you said that about me.

JM: But Steve Bauman might—

WW: And Steve Bauman is suing them.

JM: Yes, I know. He and another Channel 5 reporter, Marvin Scott, I believe.

WW: Right. Now there's a quote that's attributed to Steve Bauman, basically this. It said, the quote is, tragedy had struck nearly every family inhabiting the place as well as an earlier house on the same site. That quote relates to the history of the house.

JM: Which of course is a fine question. What is the history of 112 Ocean Avenue, Amityville?

WW: The history is that there were some tragedies occurring to families who had occupied the house. Not every family, but the quote is information that I gave the Lutzes because that is the only study that I commissioned. I never commissioned the Psychic Research study. I ordered a title policy and in addition to that I went to the Huntington Historical Society.

JM: Hoping to prove what?

WW: I wanted to find out the history of the land.

JM: With the idea being that if you could find that, for example, that it was once an Indian burial ground or a scene of witchcraft or some exorcism that might preclude that a spirit was inhabiting that home?

WW: I didn't know what I was going to find except that in my investigation during the trial I had learned from some of the younger kids there that there was an island across the, right in the middle of the Amityville River, there, and they said that it used to be an Indian burial ground.

JM: Yes, that rumor was around for a long time.

WW: Right.

JM: Yes, I've heard that.

WW: I didn't know what I was going to find by researching the land, but I thought it just would be interesting to go back. And of course I went all the way back to 1657 and found out that the Wyandanch Indians had sold the DeFeo property to a party by the name of Ketcham. And then I traced the history of the conveyances all the way down to the DeFeos.

The Amityville Horror Conspiracy

JM: Now in the book, Lee Lutz, George Lutz, refers to that ground as being at one time an Indian burial ground or some type of haunted ground belonging to the Shinnecocks. His geography stinks because the Shinnecocks were some seventy miles east of the Massapequa and Wyandanch Indians.

WW: Right.

WW: Not only his geography, his research has the same odor, maybe the same odor as what was on the third floor.

JM: Possibly.

WW: But he said that he went to the Amityville Historical Society and did his research.

JM: Now I would be very surprised if you found anything there because Amityville was incorporated long after the Indian—

WW: That's right

JM: —Burial grounds would have been there.

WW: This information is contained in the Huntington Historical Society.

JM: The reason for that I can say parenthetically is because before a certain point of the 19th Century, Babylon, which is really the township Amityville Village is in, was actually a part of Huntington. It was a south Huntington township.

WW: That's correct. Right. So, you know we can go on all night long and—

JM: And pick out discrepancy after discrepancy, but the point is when you did this project, and you say you don't know what you were looking for, you just wanted to know the history of the house, did your homework as a good defense attorney...

WW: No, no. I don't want to mislead you into thinking that this research was done to help Ronnie DeFeo's defense. After the trial, I was working on my own project...

JM: Yes, but this was during or after the—

WW: After the trial.

JM: After the trial but before—

WW: Before I met Lutz.

JM: That's the point. You were doing this on your own because you hoped to write a book about the DeFeo killings. You never did.

WW: That's right.

JM: Why?

WW: Because the Lutzes preempted the field. We've commissioned, we've entered the ventures with several writers and they in turn got their agents on the ball and tried getting us contracts or advances to write a book and we have not been able to succeed simply because, I'm told, there's an unwritten rule in the industry that once the field has been preempted that another "investor's" going to be reluctant to invest in a book.

JM: But at that point when the Lutzes called you and you returned the call and got together with them and you sat down and they told you the story about these terrible 28 days of bad dreams and not being able to sleep and not being able to make love literally, probably, I mean not being able to do anything, waking up in the middle of the night, whatever it is that he did, or could not do, you said, gee that's interesting, pal, but it doesn't help me for my defense. Why, then, did you continue talking to him and under what circumstances did that go on?

WW: Because one of the aspects of my project was, Was Ronnie DeFeo possessed at the time he committed the murders?

JM: I see, so you allowed for the possibility that that might be so.

WW: When they were telling me their story I was thinking ahead and seeing the possibilities of incorporating the Lutzes as an epilogue in the Ronnie DeFeo story.

JM: So that would become an adjunct to that and that possibly if you found some evidence of possession it might have been a decent defense claim, if not in reality, certainly, if you thought Ronnie thought he was possessed, there might be more grounds for an insanity plea. That was a possibility, too?

WW: I don't know if that would have been a possibility. It depends what you mean by possession. Now if you're talking about being possessed by a demon, no, that's not what I'm talking about.

JM: But if Ronnie had believed he was possessed by a demon, if Ronnie had believed that.—

WW: Yes, that would have been a possible—

JM: So, it wouldn't be *unlikely* for a defense attorney, for example to tell his client in private or to suggest to the client, could you have been possessed by a demon; did you believe in demons; do you think you were possessed by evil spirits; or to imply it from the history of the house?

WW: Well, they don't tell them in private. He was asked those questions in front of a psychiatrist.

JM: And how did he answer?

The Amityville Horror Conspiracy

WW: No, there were no demons involved in Ronnie's mind at the time. However, there were suggestions of possession. For instance, Ronnie DeFeo told the psychiatrist that a female with black hands gave him the gun.

JM: Hmm...

WW: He also told the psychiatrist that he never heard the sound of the gun going off, but yet the next day he just had a deafening sound throughout his head. The psychiatrist refers to this clinically as disassociation. The psychiatrist, Danny Schwartz in fact, who incidentally is the same psychiatrist who examined the Son of Sam.

JM: Yes, I was going to say he examined Berkowitz. I recall that.

WW: Right. He said in layman's language it's a form of possession.

JM: Fine. Now it's funny you make that analogy because I recall one of Berkowitz's early claims was that he was possessed by demons and howling dogs, etc. and later on said he had made it up, in fact, in an interview he gave at Attica Prison.

WW: Right. Well, Ronnie never said anything....

JM: I was going to say Ronnie never made such a claim.

WW: No.

JM: All right, so you continued to talk to Lutz and the idea of you and Lutz working together was simply to write a book about the DeFeo case, not a book about the house being haunted when the Lutzes lived there.

WW: The thrust of the book was to be Ronnie DeFeo.

JM: Yes, not necessarily or implicit in that book was to be the details of 28 days of alleged horror that the Lutzes suffered.

WW: Their story was to comprise about one chapter in the entire book.

JM: I mean more as a postscript, an epilogue, perhaps, the house now has gone on to become the residence of and there may be some bad feelings or they're uneasy but this is a reflection of the murders. In other words you never intended to include any psychic phenomena, any talk of spirits or the occult.

WW: That's correct.

JM: Do you have any belief in that subject, Mr. Weber?

WW: Do I?

JM: Yes.

WW: It's funny, but a lot of judges and a lot of learned lawyers have asked me the same question. Now I have done a lot of research about it since meeting the Lutzes.

JM: I believe in a lot of it, and I am not ashamed to say it.

WW: Well, now, I'm not going to bring myself to say that I believe in it. I'll say this, that I can understand their thinking and their philosophy.

JM: Yes.

WW: You know, it was not our generation or the generation past that has come up with this This goes back to the Kabalah, the ancient Jewish history.

JM: Absolutely.

WW: Hebrew history.

JM: The Bible is replete with references to psychic phenomena.

WW: Right.

JM: And the occult.

WW: I had a learned judge once show me a dollar bill and he pointed out all these psychic phenomena that exist in the United States currency.

JM: That's right. The idea of the mysticism of the pyramid on the reverse side of the dollar bill has a history that books have been written about.

WW: Right. So, you ask me if I believe in it. I don't believe in it but I understand it.

JM: O.K. But you couldn't accept the possibility of it existing or happening.

WW: Psychic phenomena?

JM: Yes.

WW: Certain type of psychic phenomena. ESP has scientifically been established.

JM: Yes, it has. Clairvoyance is real.

WW: Right, yes.

JM: What about—

WW: A lion moving itself from the second floor down to the first floor?

JM: I was going to say what about a moving statue, what about a slime on the walls, what about ooze?

WW: Slime in the walls is a very interesting story, because if that doesn't show that the Lutzes are frauds then nothing else does.

JM: William Weber is my guest—attorney for the Ronald DeFeo case, and we're talking about the Amityville Horror.

WW: See, when I was sitting down with the Lutzes explaining or exchanging information and helping them to create the epilogue to the Ronnie DeFeo story, they were shown certain crime photographs, crime scene photographs by me, and many of the crime scene photographs had this blackish, green substance on the doors and on the walls throughout the house. And just looking at the photographs, if one wasn't used to seeing and knowledgeable about that, they would describe it as green slime coming out of the walls and out of key holes.

JM: Hmm.

WW: But anyone knowledgeable with the police investigation would tell you that it's just fingerprint dust, the powder used to obtain fingerprints. That's all it was. Well, looking at that picture, the Lutzes and I dreamed up the story about slime coming out of key holes.

JM: Now when you say you dreamed up, at some point there must have been a rethinking of what the purpose and the design of the book would be. You wouldn't have thought it up to write it in the book about the DeFeo house, would you? At some point you made a move from writing about the DeFeos and the mass murders to writing about a book that dealt with the Lutzes living in that house and being possessed or haunted or whatever.

WW: At an early point we decided to embellish upon the Lutzes' story. We were, there was never any intention to call the Lutzes' story a true story.

JM: That's a very important question.

WW: Never.

J.M.: This was to be fiction.

WW: Well, let's put it this way, you could say something and say the Lutzes claim—

JM: Yes.

WW: But you don't put on the front of the cover "a true story."

JM: The cover of the book, both hardcover and paperback say, *The Amityville Horror: A True Story,* By Jay Anson. Simple as that. The movie does not, and when I spoke to the producer earlier, he, as one of the questions I asked him, he indicated to me they had no intention in the film of ever calling it a true story, and in fact they do not.

WW: Well, they didn't have to.

JM: No, they didn't, at that point, of course.

WW: Because the book, with the publicity—anyone who has read the book is gonna run to see the picture. I don't know why anyone would read the book.

JM: You read the book?

WW: I read it for the first time about three or four nights ago,

JM: And what was your reaction? You'd never read it before? It's been out a couple of years.

WW: I had seen an author's galley of the book and I glanced through it just to see in what areas my name was mentioned.

JM: Ah.

WW: As a protest to Prentice Hall, but that was the only purpose for my ever looking at the book.

JM: The book's a little over two years old. It first came out in hard-cover in the summer of '77.

WW: Right!

JM: Yes, so that you were going to write a story now about the Lutzes' experience in that house. Now you've embellished upon the original thesis or premise of a book which was about the DeFeo mass murders.

WW: Right.

JM: But never as a true story.

WW: Never. It was never to be mentioned as a true story. You know, you talk about Kathy's dreams that are set forth in that book. Now there's a very difficult dream that she recites that to a very large extent, while I wouldn't use the word sacrilegious, but it certainly, it defamed the memory of Mrs. DeFeo.

JM: Yes.

WW: Now only the other day, in court, Mr. Lutz stated that he con-firmed the fact that Mrs. DeFeo had an illicit love relationship with another individual, and, of course, it's mentioned in the book on page 28, no, not 28, I don't have it in front of me, but it's mentioned in the book by Mrs. DeFeo that she had a dream that, I'm sorry, that Kathy mentioned in the book that Mr. DeFeo had a dream that Mrs. DeFeo had a lover.

JM: Yes.

WW: That information was given to them in confidence. It had noth-ing to do with the story whatsoever. We never, I never intended to use it in my book, and it wasn't the truth. It was something that Mr. DeFeo believed, but Mr. DeFeo believed a lot of things that he had no reason to believe. There happened to be an artist painting the various members of the DeFeo house, and he had been in the house during the day for many, many hours, months on end, and Mr. DeFeo believed his wife was carrying on with this individual, and it wasn't true.

JM: I have to take a brief pause. When we come back let's continue and talk more about the Amityville Horror and why you call it outright a hoax, a fraud, hokum, bunk, bull. William Weber, attorney. We're coming right back to talk more about the Amityville Horror.

*   *   *

JM: All right, we're back. And you know I don't like to be melodramatic where that is not necessary, but I want you to know that you're sharing now an hour with the man who has to be the key to more of what the truth is about that incredible house at 112 Ocean Avenue than any man in the world today. Now I know there will be people who say, listen, the energy crisis and inflation and the problems of government and defense are certainly more important than whether there really was ghosts or apparitions or flies or smells or demon pigs in a house in Amityville, Long Island, but the fact is this is not just a little local story, this has become now, internationally, news and if anyone is interested in economy you will probably want to know that this is worth millions and millions of dollars, not only in the sale of the books, hardcover and paperback, but in the receipts of the film and, no doubt, there might even be a sequel—That would not surprise me, I have some suspicion there might be from somebody I spoke to earlier today whose name I choose not to reveal on the air at the moment, but I mean that, too, you'll agree with me is a possibility, and the lawsuits alone could keep a law firm busy forever.

WW: Several law firms.

JM: Maybe several. And a lot of money, in the millions and billions of dollars. And attorney William Weber is a man who has become well known beyond his wildest expectations, I am sure. He was the attorney for Ronald DeFeo, Jr. at the time that DeFeo was charged with the murders of his parents, two brothers and two sisters in November 1974 in the so-called DeFeo mass murder case and in the house that now, of course is the subject of the book and the film *The Amityville Horror*, which William Weber says flat out is a hoax. He just says it didn't happen, no qualifying statement for that, though, nothing.

WW: That's correct. Maybe we should talk a little bit about the Father Mancuso who's in the book.

JM: The priest. Now he plays a prominent role in the book and in the film.

WW: I haven't seen the film.

JM: You did not see the movie.

WW: I just read the book.

JM: Are you going to see the film?

WW: I don't think so. There's no reason to see the film.

JM: All right.

WW: Really, there isn't. But, Father Mancuso was mentioned to us by the Lutzes—

JM: Now that's a pseudonym for a real priest, isn't it?

WW: Yes.

JM: That much we know. There was a priest.

WW: Well, the priest...he has come forward and made himself public. He has put some affidavits in a lawsuit.

JM: Him, too. (in the lawsuits)

WW: Yes. And his real name I have no compunctions about telling you—it's Father Ralph Pecoraro.

JM: He used to be on Long Island but no longer is?

WW: Well, I'm not prepared to say he no longer is. I do know for a fact that the Catholic Church is transporting him from community to community to community around the United States, keeping one step ahead of the process servers.

JM: So, if you see a priest with a large hat who covers his face a lot, that's him.

WW: Probably Father Pecoraro.

JM: I see.

WW: But the, what I want to say about Father Pecoraro is that he was consulted by the Lutzes, not on the day that they moved into that house. He never was there to bless that house. The Lutzes never called him at all for that purpose. The Lutzes contacted Father Pecoraro a day or two after they left to ask his advice as to what they should do. Now if—I'm not going to venture out and say that they just tried to bring him into their commercial venture—I'd give him the credit by saying that they truly sought out his advice.

JM: Because of the emotional problems they were going through.

WW: That's right. This was an upheaval of the family.

The Amityville Horror Conspiracy

JM: Are they Catholic?

WW: Kathy is or was Catholic. In fact, her former marriage had ended in a religious annulment which Father Pecoraro had handled.

JM: Ah, so she did know him.

WW: That's how they know Father Pecoraro.

JM: I see.

WW: They didn't know any local parish priests...

JM: So he was not a priest from Amityville...from that parish.

WW: No, at that time he was assigned to the Rockville Centre Archdiocese.

JM: Headquarters?

WW: Headquarters. With a specialty in counselling and handling annulments.

JM: But not a specialty in haunted houses?

WW: Never. No. No, Father Pecoraro to a great extent has been a victim of the Lutzes as much as the DeFeo family.

JM: So he did go into the house?

WW: No.

JM: Did he ever go into the house?

WW: Never went into that house.

JM: He was called simply for advice about how to handle the situation and being disturbed about living in a house where mass murders had taken place.

WW: Right. And Father Pecoraro told them that they did the right thing by leaving the house for now, that they should consult a psychiatrist and if they didn't receive any satisfaction through the professional help, that he would be glad to sit down with them and discuss this matter with them further.

JM: But the book and the film implied that he had been called to the house to bless it.

WW: Well, they don't imply it. They come out and say it.

JM: (At same time) They say it.

WW: That's one of the many, many—

JM: That's another one—if you're keeping score, that's another one.

WW: Right. They also talk about a local Amityville priest. They don't mention his name, and that's on page 107 of the hardcover book.

JM: For those of you who are singing along, p. 107.

WW: The gist of what's mentioned about that local Amityville priest is that he never had too much faith in Ronnie DeFeo or the DeFeos. I don't really recall exactly what it was, but the fact is that this local Amityville priest was never quoted in any newspapers as the Lutzes say in their book. He was never known to even be on the crime scene, although he was—I found out through my investigation that he was, and I told the Lutzes that the local, this particular local Amityville priest, who asked that his name not be mentioned, and I'd honor that.

JM: Yes.

WW: Because he isn't a part of this project at all, that he never believed that Ronnie was either criminally insane or possessed. That Ronnie was just a bad boy.

JM: Yes. Do you think that the Lutzes knew the DeFeos?

WW: It's funny because there's a story about that from one of the local Amityville boys in *Newsday* that the Lutz boat had been tied up at the DeFeo's boat house. I was never able to substantiate that, but the boy was reliable. He assisted in the actual defense of Ronnie DeFeo. He was as helpful as possible and whatever information he gave me, always, I corroborated. But I was never able to corroborate it.

JM: But if it could be corroborated that the Lutzes had known the DeFeos, we could speculate that perhaps the Lutzes wrote the book to exploit the fact that if they said there were demons, it could have been used to somehow help the defense in the DeFeo case.

WW: In looking back I now know that the Lutzes certainly planned it because in the book they say they had no experience with demonology or psychic phenomena.

JM: Did they?

WW: I have a tape, probably the second or third time I met with them where they spend two hours discussing psychic phenomena, and the gist of that tape shows more expertise about the subject than an individual such as, let's say, Dr. Steve Kaplan, whom you've had on your program, I understand.

JM: Yes.

WW: They're very, very learned and their explanation to me was that in the three or four days that they left the house they took a crash course in psychic phenomena. Nobody could have absorbed the information they had talked about on the tape.

The Amityville Horror Conspiracy

JM: So, flat out, if I ask you do you think the Lutzes knew before they moved into this house what they were going to do once they got out of that house, concerning writing a book about being possessed.

WW: I don't think that they had planned it before they even went in. I think when they found themselves in trouble....

JM: Financially and emotionally.

WW: The thoughts then began to come into their mind as a means of bailing themselves out of the situation.

JM: And then they call you and want to get as much as they can from you about the history of the house and all that they can find out about the DeFeo aspect of that house and you go along with them because you're also writing a book, and you decide to pool your resources and some place along the way you decide not to write the book about the DeFeo killings, or a novel based on the DeFeo killings, you were going to write a novel or...?

WW: Yes, no, it was going to be a true story insofar as Ronnie DeFeo and the defense was concerned and it was going to be a true story insofar as the prosecution was concerned.

JM: Yes, there's nothing immoral about that as far as an attorney writing about a case he's just had.

WW: No, as long as you have a release from your client.

JM: And you would have.

WW: Yes. Of course I have it. We still have it.

JM: From Ronnie DeFeo, Jr.

WW: Right. The third aspect of this story was not going to be a true story. But you have to understand if the title of the book was called Ronnie DeFeo, you weren't going to put a subtitle, "a true story."

JM: Yes, I understand.

WW: In other words we would have just let the reader decide for themselves what really happened that night.

JM: The night of the mass murder. But did the Lutzes suggest to you there might be more money in the deal, and obviously it's silly to write a book the way one would research something in a monastery, for heaven's sake, it's America and you write books the same reason you work on a radio station, you make a living. The same reason anybody, the same reason you're an attorney. I love what I'm doing but I have to eat and I have to pay the bills.

So the reality is that perhaps they told you that there was something in it in terms of financial recompense if you collaborated on writing the book and embellished upon the mass murders by talking in terms of psychic phenomena in that house, not necessarily when Ronnie DeFeo committed the murders but when the Lutzes lived there.

WW: That's true. And now we know that they decided to go along with me in my venture not with the intent of carrying forward their obligations but solely to get whatever information they could out of me to corroborate some suspicions that they had and then to take off on their own with Mr. Anson and create their own story.

JM: All right, but before tha—

WW: To that extent I have to give them a lot of credit because they certainly—

JM: They did it. They pulled it off. They did it well. Better than the Brinks job—I'd be sued for saying that.

WW: Yes, I think you'd better...to not say it.

JM: Then that's all right, I won't say it. Besides, I understand they're in California. They don't listen to me any more. I've talked with Lee Lutz once. He doesn't like the neighborhood. He says he gets nervous when he comes back around here.

WW: Well, he'll come back if he was paid for an interview, I promise you that.

JM: Well, I wasn't going to go that far. I spoke to him privately and then it's more interesting to find out from you what went on behind the scenes. So now you and Lutz are talking about the book but the book is now going to be primarily about their experiences, the Lutzes.

WW: It never was intended for the book to be primarily about the Lutzes.

JM: It wasn't in your mind, it might have been in theirs, but never in your mind?

WW: Never.

JM: Still about DeFeo.

WW: They always were going to be the epilogue to the DeFeo story as far as I was concerned and as far as our writer, Paul Hoffman was concerned.

JM: Yes. So you're talking now and you're writing a book, but in it now you've embellished upon the mass murders and talk about certain ghostly happenings, unearthly happenings.

The Amityville Horror Conspiracy

WW: We never got to write their side of the story. We—Paul Hoffman and I went over their story with them for about 41-42 hours.

JM: O.K.

WW: Paul Hoffman sat down with them in an official interview to get their story. He prepared a general outline.

JM: And later wrote a story himself.

WW: Well, that was an article, not a book.

JM: An article in *Good Housekeeping*.

WW: Yes, right. Yes. That was, the intent of that article was basically to keep the publicity going for our project.

JM: All right. Now at some point, speaking of publicity, and then we'll come back to some of the specifics and what you embellished because you've got a list there that is fascinating beyond belief, in order to keep this story going after the Lutzes moved out of that house, something kept the interest. I recall TV stations coming out to Amityville. I recall Dr. Stephen Kaplan coming out to Amityville. I recall Dr. Stephen Kaplan coming here. He had been the first psychic investigator in the world to be called by Lutz to that house but immediately decided it was a hoax and wanted nothing to do with it apparently.

WW: The Lutzes didn't call Stephen Kaplan at their own doing.

JM: They didn't?

WW: I asked them to call.

JM: But why him?

WW: Well, it's only because he happened to be the closest one available.

JM: Ah. But he was in the phone book.

WW: He was in the phone book. I had known of him from some clients that I had had previously. He's out, I believe, on the north shore someplace.

JM: He was at the time, yes. He's since moved to New York City.

WW: We contacted him. We contacted several other people. Now, you know, contacting and then claiming that these people conducted experiments is two different things.

JM: Which is a fascinating point, because among those who the Lutzes suggest were contacted to verify the psychic phenomena, the apparitions, the unearthly presences in that house, the slime on the walls, the statues moving, Kathy aging, the flies on the windows, and, I don't know, the demon pigs, was a man by the name of Jerry Solfvin from the Psychical Research Center at Durham,

North Carolina, sometimes misidentified as being part of Duke University but in fact it is near and not actually a part of it.

WW: That's correct. And the Lutzes have taken advantage of associating that Institute with Duke University.

JM: They sure have. They did it as recently as a few nights ago when they were on the "Merv Griffin Show" on whatever station runs that in the city. And they suggested that he was in there and they imply in the book, too, that he went in there to investigate. Now I had a tape recording as recently as this afternoon, in private, of an interview with Jerry Solfvin in which he says, "They called me, I took down what they said, I just made a record of the incidents, but that's all I ever did. I did not investigate. I didn't confirm."

WW: No one ever conducted any scientific or psychic experiments in that house. There was a party held and Jerry Solfvin was there. They mentioned the party in the book and talked about all kinds of psychic scientific experiments being conducted in that house.

JM: O.K. They also quote a couple by the name of Ed and Lorraine Warren from Connecticut, who they mentioned again on the "Merv Griffin Show," and who they mention in the book, and who were here as guests, oh, I guess a couple of years ago, and who suggested, in fact, that, my dear, all of this happened. That's what she told me, Lorraine Warren. She believes what the book says is what was. Charming woman.

WW: Yes, she is. I've met her also. Now Lorraine Warren has told me many times all of it happened, but when I start talking to her about what she means by it, that's where we all differ. She's only telling me that her queasiness and her uneasiness which she felt in the house happened. That's the "it" that she's referring to. But she never established or corroborated any of the claims made by the Lutzes in their book.

JM: Well, she said there was a cold spot in the house, a place you went where you got a chill.

WW: Let me tell you, there are more drafts in that house than—

JM: I know.

WW: Than Swiss cheese.

JM: Yes, it's a large enough house that it, it's not well insulated and is poorly ventilated, and it doesn't—

WW: It faces the river....

The Amityville Horror Conspiracy

JM: Yes, it faces right on the harbor there. All right, would you go through, William Weber, attorney for Ronald DeFeo and the man who holds the key to unlock the mystery of the Amityville Horror, whether it is in fact a horror or a hoax, as you suggest. Would you go through some of the things you helped them create? For example, in the film, I can tell you, they make a big deal about all of those flies. Lots of flies, flies everywhere, there are house flies all over the windows.

WW: Well, again, you've got to credit the Lutzes with creative imagination.

JM: Yes. I'll go along with that.

WW: The facts were these. This is what was told by me to the Lutzes, and then you could see how they transposed it to fit their book. I told them how all of the police officers who testified during the trial made it a point to describe the odor and maggots that existed in the third floor bedroom where the body of Dawn DeFeo was discovered. And the reason why I told them that is that we were talking about the credibility of the police officers and I told them that I believed that the police officers had rehearsed their testimony, and one of the reasons why I believed that is that they all made it a point to emphasize the foul odor and the maggots that they found in the third floor room. There was no reason for any of these police officers to mention that except they thought that if they put in some human interest into their testimony that it would be more believable for the jury. So, witness after witness took the stand and just by happenstance mentioned that.

And then I explained to the Lutzes, I said that it was only natural for such a situation to happen 'cause there are more radiators in that room than any of the other rooms so it is a warmer room if the heat is on. Dawn DeFeo was, at the time of her death, was menstruating. The mortal wound she received really was a terrible wound—the bullet entered from the back of her head, came out the front of her face, and it was from a .35 Marlin rifle. You could imagine the damage that was done with it. Suffice it to say that gun could kill an elephant. The body lay in the bed in this warm room for well over 18 hours, so the odor and the maggots that the police say they found would have been a natural phenomena.

JM: Yes.

WW: All right. The Lutzes picked that up and put those flies in every room they thought would benefit them. The odor was put in their minds by this story. In fact, they went ahead and they attempted to find out through, I believe the boy's name is Bobby Kelsky, one of the local Amityville boys who helped clean up the DeFeo house after the bodies were taken out, they tried to ascertain from him whether or not there was any odors in any other rooms, and Kelsky, according to what he told me, just laughed at them.

JM: Yes.

WW: Well, as a result of that they came up with their stories about the odor and the flies.

JM: And that's the way that came about.

WW: Yeah. And coincidentally, the sewing room that they talk about so much in the book, well that's the room that the DeFeo family referred to as the "Bald Eagle Room." It was their television room, and, unfortunately, they did have some troubles living with each other. There was difficulties between the father and the son and Dawn was a freedom–loving girl and, you know, she needed a lot of discipline. The point I'm trying to make is that Bald Eagle Room was Ronnie's sanctuary. I told them that. Incidentally, Ronnie had another sanctuary we can talk about later, the garage, but in the house that was Ronnie's sanctuary and the rest of the family left him alone in there.

JM: Yes.

WW: Well, they converted that Bald Eagle Room into the, they called it Kathy's sewing room. And that's the room where they said nobody was allowed to go into.

JM: But they talk in the book and the film about a secret room, a blood red room, hidden—

WW: There was never a secret room down in that basement. I was down in the basement. I'm sure the Lutzes have been down in the basement. I told them about a secret closet that Ronnie built where his father used to keep money. Ronnie and Bobby Kelsky built the closet underneath the stairway and the only reason why they called it a secret closet was because there were no doorknobs on it. There was a little nail; you would pull the nail to open it. But it really wasn't a secret room, or even a secret closet for that matter. It was referred to as a secret closet whenever Ronnie was told by his father to get money, go to the secret closet, right. The Lutzes were told this by me; they converted that secret closet into a secret room covered with red paint—there never was red paint down in that room.

The Amityville Horror Conspiracy

JM: What about the black gook that was coming out of the toilet bowls? They show that in the film and they talk about it in the book—that when the toilet was flushed, out came, well, it was something in the film like black India ink.

WW: Again, there were—in the crime scene photographs there was black in—not all the toilet bowls—now you've—there's a contradiction on the tapes that I have with the Lutzes. We talked about the first floor and the third floor bathrooms having the black gook. In the book Lutz has expounded on that by saying all the bathrooms had the black gook. The black gook was evidently taken at the crime scene by the police officers who were using the black fingerprint dusting powder. They probably washed their hands off with a towel or something, the towel hit the sides of the bowl and when pictures were taken of the bowl—because I had over 500 colored photographs—every nook and cranny was photographed including the bowls, the Lutzes saw the bowls with the black inside of it. That's the black that Kathy says appeared during their 28 days in that house.

JM: What about the fascinating demon pig with red eyes, Jody, the playmate for the little child?

WW: Well, Jody, that's...I give that credit to the Lutzes 'cause they....

JM: You didn't do that one?

WW: No. I did tell them, though, that Ronnie referred to the next door neighbor, the Irelands' cat, they have a very big cat, as a "pig." He says, he never, well, I'm not going to use the words that Ronnie used....

JM: Was this the Siamese cat who lived next door?

WW: I don't know if it's a Siamese cat.

JM: But he owns a cat.

WW: A big cat.

JM: Yes, I've heard stories about that.

WW: And he said, "That blankety-blank cat reminds me of a pig." And many times this was mentioned to the Lutzes at their houses on tape and Ronnie talked about incidences where he would see the "pig" looking in through the window, in fact once Ronnie told how he threw his shoe and broke the window to get that "pig"—again, referring to the cat.

JM: To the cat.

WW: Well, the Lutzes created Jody, again, in their mind as far as I'm concerned, they were told about a pig in their confidential talks.

JM: Bill Weber, attorney, if I don't ask this question you know somebody will and it would be as good a place as any, I think, to have it answered. What if they had not split from you? At some point the Lutzes decided they had used you, according to your contention, for all they could use you for. They just did not need you or your information any more and why split the loot? They went their own way, found Jay Anson some place to help write that book, and the rest is history, as they say, on the deposit line. What if they would have kept quiet or what if they would have kept you with them and what if they would have said, "Bill, listen, all I have to do is put on this cover, 'true story', stick with me and, you know, we'll see how it goes." In other words, what if you had been part of what was their confederacy to complete this story?

WW: All right. That's a very long question. Let me just say we just met each other tonight.

JM: Yes.

WW: I'm an attorney out here in Suffolk County but I don't have to practice law because I have to feed my family. I also am an Amway distributor, direct distributor, and we make, my wife makes—

JM: They do well.

WW: —Pretty good money at that. And the reason why I mention this is that the last thing I'm gonna do is to try to commercialize and to create a fraud in the same act. There's nothing wrong with anybody making money. I give the Lutzes 100% credit. What I'm against, and violently against over here, is the fact that they've committed a fraud, not only on myself, I'm the small one in the whole wheel, but it's a fraud against the public, and any verdict that we get in court, 'cause were suing them, you know that....

JM: Yeah, I know you're suing, and why are you suing? Are you suing because they didn't cut you in to the profits from this book or because they took material from you?

WW: They took all of the material from me, converted it to their own use under the guise of helping me and Ronnie DeFeo, and they also pre-empted the field, preventing us from getting our book published.

JM: Yes.

WW: So that's the reason, but if I can go back....

JM: But you wouldn't have gone along with them if they had said stick with us.

The Amityville Horror Conspiracy

WW: There is no way, there's no way that I would have ever put my name on a book or associate my name with a book....

JM: About the Lutzes.

WW: Well, the way it's written there.

JM: The way it's written. You would not have associated yourself with this book.

WW: And called it a true story.

JM: Yes. If it had not been a true story, in other...if it had never....

WW: If the words 'true story' were not in their book I don't think I would have had any objections, right, because there is no claim in the body of the book, by the Lutzes, that's a story by Jay Anson. And Jay Anson has all kinds of disclaimers throughout that book. He's protecting himself.

JM: He does it very well. If you speak to Jay Anson and you ask him a question about this he'll tell you, "I'm a reporter. They told me a story, I wrote it down. What do you want from me?"

WW: Don' t give Jay Anson that much credit.

JM: Well, I don't, but that's what Jay Anson would say.

WW: Because a reporter would never have written what he wrote without actually corroborating the story.

JM: That's very true.

WW: I have never met a reporter who never...who ever printed anything or said anything...

J. M: I wouldn't.

WW: ...without corroborating it.

JM: I wouldn't.

WW: There is no corroboration in that book.

JM: There are no witnesses to anything the Lutzes say, in fact.

WW: Well, Mr. Anson says that he interviewed certain police officials in Amityville.

JM: Yes.

WW: If there are any officials that he interviewed, maybe they're the ghosts in this story.

JM: Humph.

WW: Because none of them were interviewed by Jay Anson.

JM: In fact, one of the policemen is suing as well .

WW: That's correct.

JM: One of the Amityville police sergeants.

WW: His name is used throughout the book.

JM: It is in the hardcover and it got changed in the paperback.

WW: Well, because they realized they'd made a mistake.

JM: Yes.

WW: Because they didn't do too well about that particular individual, they even ridiculed the type of police officer he was in a certain way.

JM: It is...it's just an incredible story. One doesn't know where to even end or begin as a matter of fact. The suit is for how much money, sir? Your lawsuit against the Lutzes.

WW: I'm looking, I'm looking....

JM: What is it you hope to gain?

WW: Twenty–four per cent of whatever the Lutzes made, because that was my agreement with them, that I was going to get 24%.

JM: And when did the break happen? That's one question I did not ask yet. When the split came. When did they cut out on you, as they say on my block?

WW: It was around the latter part of March or the early part of April when they came to my house, took the tape, the only tape that I had, and disappeared. But since the court action, the court has directed them to return the tapes to me. So I have copies of them.

JM: Quite frankly, and I know people are thinking this question now, I know they're thinking that Bill Weber is sour-graping, that Bill Weber is simply unhappy that the Lutzes have made this amount of money from something that they were in together, and when the Lutzes realized that they did not need Bill Weber they dumped Bill Weber and now Bill Weber wants what he thinks is his fair share of the take. You know, people are saying that.

WW: I agree with them. What else can I tell you?

JM: Oh, that's all right. But, again, they would go further to suggest that if you were still part of this story you would never have revealed that it was not true, and in fact, many people don't even know that you might have talked about it being a hoax back when the book came out two years ago. Did you ?

WW: Yes. I've been called since the book came out by reporters and writers throughout the country and every time I have ever been asked about this story I've told them the Lutzes are frauds, it's a hoax and I have had nothing to do with them as long as they're calling that book a true story.

JM: Yes.

The Amityville Horror Conspiracy

WW: Every time that there's been any writing or any quote attributed to me that's exactly what I've said. I have never changed my position. Now, you talk about changing positions—only today in the court room I saw a letter written by the Prentice–Hall editor addressed to Jay Anson, and in the letter, and I'm not gonna quote it accurately, I guess, cause I don't have it in front of me, but it tells Anson, "get the story back to the Lutzes and tell them to get their story straight. They'd better do it because we have a tour planned for them." Now I didn't give you the word-for-word quote, but that's in essence what the letter said. And that letter is going to come back to haunt the Lutzes, if no one else.

JM: Would you let me come back after a short break, and if you can hold on just a moment, I'd like to wrap it up with just a few other questions that I think are on people's minds. Attorney Bill Weber will come back to talk more about the latest chapter of the Amityville Horror in just a moment.

* * *

JM: O.K. I've asked Bill Weber to stay just a few more moments and graciously he has consented to do that so that I can perhaps ask a few more of the questions that I think people would want to know about the Amityville Horror which was called in a newspaper headline recently in one of the city papers, "hokum," and Bill Weber says that's what it was, hokum. Not horror. He was the attorney for Ronald DeFeo, Jr. who was convicted of murdering his parents, brothers and sisters and who is now serving life in prison for those crimes. That was in November of 1974. The story, of course, has gone on to become the story of the house as told in the book, *The Amityville Horror* and the film, and Bill Weber says,"It ain't so, Ma, it just ain't so." And as you explained just before, you are suing them for a cut of what you feel rightfully should have been yours. And I just wanted to reiterate because I want to make sure people heard it, you suggest that this is all bull but that you told the world it was bull back when they wrote the book. I don't remember seeing too much written about you at the time, but that could be in your defense, I must say, because it's a lot more interesting to write about stories of houses that are haunted than it is to write about a man who says that house was not haunted.

WW: Yes, there was a writer from *Omni* magazine who spent several months exposing them. I still believe his article has not been published, and it's probably gonna come out in September. But he contacted me well over a year ago concerning this. *The Daily News* in their article exposing the Lutzes has contacted me.

JM: Listen, I interviewed Jim and Barbara Cromarty a year and a half or more ago, perhaps, I don't know, time goes so fast, maybe a couple of years ago, whenever they moved into that house, and I was very surprised when I said I guess you, on the air you must have been interviewed many times, and they said no, this is the first time in depth. And I said, why? And then I realized what I said and they confirmed for me—the Cromartys, the people who lived in the house after the Lutzes moved out, who said the only problems they had were the horrors brought on by tourists and trespassers. And they said, listen, how many people want to interview a couple who say they're living in a house where there are no ghosts or apparitions. And so the Cromartys simply weren't of as much interest as the Lutzes.

WW: Right. I called the Cromartys when they first moved in because there had been a rumor going around, I think you alluded to it before, that I was in cahoots with the Lutzes even before they moved into the house.

JM: Yes, sir.

WW: And I called them, to wish them the best of luck in the house and to assure them that I had absolutely nothing to do with the Lutzes and that I'm completely disassociated from them.

JM: You haven't talked to them in a very long time.

WW: That was the first time I ever spoke to them, and I have never spoken to them since then.

JM: I...they just upped and ran—went to California one day and—

WW: You're talking about the Lutzes.

JM: Yes, the Lutzes vanished on you.

WW: Yes, they did.

JM: And since that time there's been no conversation, no communication except....

WW: Only in the courtroom.

JM: Well, of course, except legally. And the Cromartys—you're not in touch with... ?

WW: No, as I said, I called them to congratulate them, wish them the best of luck.

The Amityville Horror Conspiracy

JM: Yes, at the time.

WW: Right.

JM: Yeah, but not recently?

WW: Never.

JM: And now, of course, there's some speculation about the future of the house and who might buy it and for what purpose.

WW: Yeah. I don't think the Cromartys would sell it to anybody who's gonna make a commercial venture out of the house. I think they have too much respect for the Village of Amityville and too much love for Suffolk County to do that.

JM: Listen. I speak to the mayor of Amityville and he tells me he'd like to see the house moved and I have to tell him honestly, as I did, that if they move the house and it became an empty lot, people would come from all over the country to see the empty piece of ground where the house was, lending even more credence to something about the story because you see what happened and all of the psychic phenomena house disappeared!

WW: In six months time they'd have a 500-foot hole because people would be taking sand and dirt from there.

J.M.   Exactly, exactly. There's no question. There's absolutely no question about that. You had some other incidents that the book and the film purport, the mysterious goings-on, the faces at windows, the invasion of the green slime, the ghosts, the demon-pig, the black toilet bowls, etc., the stigmata on the hands, and, you know, the wherewithal of how they began. Please....

WW: Well, we could talk about the well, the well that the Lutzes talk about. I showed them a survey of the land, of the property, and I told them that these three marks on the back, between the pool and the wall of the house were old wells that were kept by the DeFeos when they had the swimming pool installed— repaired, not installed. They were fascinated about the three wells, only because, you know, why would three wells be on one piece of property? And I didn't have any explanation for that either, but the wells were told to them by me. They were showed the wells on the survey. Of course, in their book he brings one of the wells somewhere into the house, in the basement. You could also talk about the involvement of their children in this story.

JM.   Yes. They misbehave a lot and they have some unusual behavior.

WW: That I believed. I mean, when they initially came to me with that they said that there had been a change in the behavior patterns of their children.

JM: But that would be psychological as opposed to psychic.

WW: That's correct. Right. They also explained that there was a serious change in their personal relationship.

JM: I'm sure.

WW: And you mentioned before the sexual relations between the two of them and many, many other aspects of married life. They just couldn't cope with the memory of the DeFeo murders, living in that house. But, you know, what really hurts is that they'll use their children in the story. For instance, on about page 159 of the hardcovered book they talk about bringing Danny to the Brunswick Hospital Center for emergency treatment because he caught his hand in a window, I believe, or did something to his hand. Well, you know, I also practice negligence law and any time you want to get a hospital report it's very easy. You write a letter and you inquire as to whether or not there's a record. There is no record of any Danny Lutz ever having been treated at the Brunswick Hospital Center.

JM: Now that's important because it...that's very important because in the film they showed the window mysteriously closing on the little boy's hand and they take him to the emergency room of the hospital and you see them leaving and you have to assume if it's Amityville it must be Brunswick.

WW: Well, the book, in the book it says Brunswick Hospital Center.

JM: Yes. And then again, comparing it to the film, they don't show you the name of the hospital but you'd have to assume it was the closest one because the hand was supposedly smashed and then you hear the dialogue between James Brolin and Margot Kidder who are playing Kathy and George Lutz, and they say to each other, gee, it's amazing, none of the bones were broken and yet the window sill smashes down onto the little boy's hand and the blood is spurting everywhere.

WW: They have three wonderful children, really beautiful, well-behaved children, I saw them in Babylon. Now the Lutzes are complaining that because of all this publicity, their children's lives have been adversely affected.

JM: Well, that's as ludicrous as Ronnie DeFeo claiming he's an orphan because of what he did to his family.

The Amityville Horror Conspiracy

WW: That's correct. Absolutely. To put it bluntly. There's no argument with that.

JM: A couple of other things that maybe people would be curious about, Bill Weber. In the film they show a physical resemblance between Ronnie DeFeo, Jr. and Lee Lutz.

WW: They both have beards, and I guess one could conjecture that perhaps they look a little alike, although I fail to see as sharp a resemblance as the film shows. No...Ronnie DeFeo, you know, if I could, would be described as a macho, Italian–looking boy with a dark beard, dark hair. He does have deep, penetrating eyes. As far as his build, it's a, as I said, macho, but it's a very...he has a very good build. George Lutz, first of all, can not be described as a macho-looking Italian. He is of a light, reddish–brown complexion. He has a beard, and to a certain extent he has penetrating eyes. Other than that there is no physical resemblance whatsoever between the two of them.

WW: Absolutely none.

JM: Except for that beard.

WW: Mr. Lutz is probably twice as heavy as Ronnie DeFeo.

JM: Yes.

WW: His body structure is completely opposite to that of Ronnie DeFeo.

JM: In the film they show the clock radio that sits on a table near the bed and it's set at 3:15 A.M. or it's 3:14 and as soon as it comes around 3:15 A.M. on the clock radio, James Brolin, who's playing George Lutz, pops up out of bed and apparently there's some association with 3:15 A.M. and George Lutz waking up every morning in the middle of the night, and you have to assume, or at least I did, perhaps because I was the reporter at the time who more or less fixed an approximate time of death by speaking to neighbors, I was as I told you, one of the first reporters there, and it may have happened somewhere around that period. Now we don't know exactly when it happened.

WW: Right.

JM: Nobody could ever know.

WW: Well, tonight I learned for the first time that you had fixed the time at 3:15, but—

JM: Approximately.

WW: —The papers I had read, the reports, I hadn't seen the time fixed.

JM: It was fixed between 3:00 and 3:30 somewhere.

WW: But that is not what the Lutzes say in the book. Lutz says that the coroner's report fixes the death at 3:15 and that he went and examined the coroner's report. Well, I have all the coroner's reports; Dr. Dan Schwartz, the noted psychiatrist has all of the coroner's reports. Nowhere in there is there any attempt by the coroner to fix the time of death at 3:15. It would be impossible and ludicrous for any expert to attempt to fix a time of death like that. Especially after the bodies were found more than 13, 15 hours after the alleged incident.

JM: That's correct. That's correct. The way it happened with me simply as a reporter on the scene was I was speaking to some of the people in the neighborhood and among the neighbors I spoke to on Ocean Avenue was one woman who said at about that time she heard the wailing of a dog from the DeFeo's home. They did have a dog and she knew it was their dog but the dog was howling and baying and it woke her up and we just conjectured that perhaps at that point the dog realized that something was wrong while one or more of the people were killed. And that was how we conjectured that somewhere perhaps around 3:00 to 3:30 they might have been killed.

WW: The Lutzes attribute that to the coroner's report.

JM: Well, I'm delighted that they attributed it to me but they didn't know; they attributed it to me rather than to the distinguished coroner of Suffolk County. That's fine if that's what they want.

WW: Would you like to apply for that job, by the way?

JM: Which, the coroner's job? No, thank you, no. Absolutely not!

WW: O.K.

JM: One of the things that...well, you had a couple of other items. Please. I had one question. I wanted to make one editorial comment in closing, but please....

WW: All right, will you talk about, they, the Lutzes talk about the Witches' Brew....

JM: But even before the Witches' Brew, if I could stay on that 3:15 for just a moment, you know, one thing that perhaps might make people always have a little bit of doubt in their mind—you talk about things that are strange, unexplained, O.K., maybe unexplained is a better phrase than psychic, I don't know. No noise of any gunshot was heard. Now the dog, it's true, was heard by at least one neighbor. Nobody ever heard the sound of a gunshot.

The Amityville Horror Conspiracy

Now how the heck, as the defense attorney, can you tell me, does one kill six people and not a sound is heard? The family was not drugged. There were no silencers used to the best of our knowledge. Apparently they did not fire at such close range through a pillow according to the reports I read, to conclude—

WW: That's correct.

JM: —That the noise of the gun, the rifle, was muffled. How was it done in total silence? If anything is eerie and psychic, I'll tell you, that is.

WW: Well, you're asking me how it was done?

JM: Yeah, well, I'm asking you.

WW: I don't know. I don't know. The same way every police expert, every ballistics expert....

JM: Nobody has ever figured it out.

WW: Nobody.

JM: Ronnie DeFeo has never told you?

WW: Ronnie has told me repeatedly, time after time, when the right time comes, I'll tell you what happened.

JM: You do speak to Ronnie from time to time.

WW: Yes. I was up to Dannamora just a couple of weeks ago visiting with him.

JM: Yes. Does he have any opinion of all this fuss about the house that was once his home, that's now the Amityville Horror?

WW: Well, again, Ronnie likes to talk in rather explicit language, so, he just...if I used the word "hoax," Ronnie would use a much more explicit word.

JM: think we can read into that, yes. Expletives deleted.

WW: See, he was, he's always advised by me whenever I'm doing something for him. Commercially, he knew the Lutzes and he authorized, as he should, he authorized me to cooperate, and when I told him that the Lutzes fled, he didn't know whether to believe me that they had fled or to just have more hatred for the Lutzes. But now that everything has developed he realizes that we were duped, he included. Incidentally, now you've mentioned that I'm suing. I'm suing also on behalf of Ronnie. The author Paul Hoffman is suing. Bernie Burton and another attorney in Patchogue who was part of the project, he's suing also.

JM: What happens to any monies that Ronnie DeFeo might win in a lawsuit?

WW: Well, as you know, there's a new law that was passed subsequent to the murder.

JM: Because of Berkowitz, the Son of Sam case.

WW: We've inquired of that and we've, well, no one is going to give us a written decision, but it's our opinion that Ronnie DeFeo would not be subject to the terms of that law because his act occurred....

JM: Before....

WW: Prior to the law.

JM: So ex post facto would apply?

WW: That's *no* ex post facto would apply.

JM: Yes, that's what it's....

WW: However, that, you know, could be well changed by the Attorney General. But right now the money that Ronnie has received is really insignificant and you know, it just doesn't pay for anybody to start a law suit over that.

JM: He has not given any interviews at all, has he?

WW: Ronnie?

JM: Yes.

WW: The only interviews Ronnie has given was interviews that I have authorized.

JM: Yes. And is that a possibility? Are you ever willing to allow Ronnie to talk about the case involving him or the events subsequently, his opinions of them?

WW: Yes, if it's gonna help Ronnie in any way, or if it's gonna enhance any commercial project that Ronnie has, will be participating in, we would do them.

JM: Yes.

WW: And, of course, we have to get permission from the authorities. In general they grant that permission. They did even with Berkowitz, as I recall, at Attica after those heinous Son of Sam killings. Yes, they do grant it.

JM: Yes. You were saying about that place called the "Witches' Brew" where Ronnie used to go. Well, actually there is no such place as the Witches' Brew but a place alleged to be the Witches' Brew, a pub in Amityville.

WW: That's correct. At the time the Lutzes were living in that house there was no Witches' Brew bar.

JM: There was no Witches' Brew bar.

The Amityville Horror Conspiracy

WW: That's right. There was a bar there but it was not known as the Witches' Brew. It was called something else if I remember. I don't remember the name that it was called but I do remember that it was owned by an Amityville policeman.

JM: Yes.

WW: And knowing Ronnie and his attitude towards policemen, which was an unfortunate attitude, there was no way that Ronnie was gonna hang out in that particular bar. He did go in on occasion, in fact the days, the day that the bodies were discovered, he ran into that bar to get Bobby Kelsky and his other friends for help.

JM: Yes, I recall that part of the story.

WW: Ronnie hung out in the Chatterbox—

JM: Ah, yes.

WW: —Bar in Amityville. So, the stories that the Lutzes tell about the Witches' Brew are completely false.

JM: Speaking of what the Lutzes say to the American public, which is completely false, attorney William Weber, as we conclude our conversation about the Amityville Horror.... Don't you have to wonder, really, what the heck is wrong with the American public in a sense? I mean, it's nice that you might make money from a lawsuit, and it's terrific that the Lutzes have provided so well for their children. It's nice that so much money has been made in writing the book, and I'm delighted for all of the actors and actresses and the crew who worked on the film because it provides income and it's part of the American economy to write books and make movies.

But, P.T. Barnum, wherever he is in the great beyond, must be laughing himself to pieces—he'd laugh so hard he would die all over again. When he said a sucker is born every moment, or every minute, he really was telling the truth over a hundred years ago. He sure knew the American public. I mean, isn't it incumbent upon us to be able to discriminate between that which is real in the psychic field, or any other field, and that which is, as you suggest, pure out-and-out hokum?

WW: Well, this story isn't so great that the public on its own would have gone out and purchased the millions and millions of copies that they did purchase. This story was a beautifully orchestrated publicity event.

JM: But you had a part of that, too, because didn't you hold press conferences?

WW: That's correct, that's correct.

JM: You kept the story going after the Lutzes were out. You kept interest in it.

WW: Absolutely. Absolutely.

JM: Why?

WW: There's nothing wrong in a beautifully orchestrated publicity event. What's wrong is when the publicity is absolutely and intentionally misleading.

JM: And you don't suggest you did that for a moment?

WW: That I did it?

JM: Yes.

WW: No, because we never misled. When I was doing it, and it really is two events that we're talking about, when I did it there was no intent at that point to mislead the public. We never, I never, called what the Lutzes had experienced a true story.

JM: When did you find out they were going to use that description—"a true story"? When the book came out?

WW: When the book came out. When I saw the artist's, the galley proofs of the book.

JM: Would you be suing them now if the book hadn't done so well? Suppose the book bombed, would you bother suing them for a cut of the action?

WW: If the book bombed...no, there would be no sense in suing them because I would have an empty judgement against them. But if the book bombed, I would be, I feel pretty sure at this point that the DeFeo story would have been picked up by another publisher.

JM: And now it's too late for that?

WW: Yeah, it's too, we've had, at this point, major writers interested in the book but their own publishers, their own agents, have advised them that there's just no way they'll invest the money when someone else has preempted the field.

JM: Yes. Do you know how much money the Lutzes have earned so far from the book, the hardcover, the paperback and the film?

WW: George Lutz has been in court recently. He was asked those questions. He was very, very vague and ambiguous in responding. We have subpoenaed some of the records of Prentice Hall, and to date we can establish that they've gotten approximately $200,000. from Prentice Hall. But that is not a recent accounting. That accounting is about nine months old.

The Amityville Horror Conspiracy

JM: We assume the IRS at some point will come in and they'll find out the truth.

WW: Well, if Lutz is to be believed that the IRS was after him while he was living in Ocean Avenue, there's no reason to believe that they won't come in at this point.

JM: I have a feeling they'll be with him no matter where he goes.

WW: I hope we get our judgement before they come.

JM: Because if they get there first, you're gonna wait.

WW: Then it would be just as if their book had been a flop.

JM: Exactly. Sure. I understand they live well now. They're on the West Coast? And still claim this is true?

WW: Well, their exact whereabouts I'm prohibited by court order from revealing.

JM: But you do know they're in California?

WW: In the articles, I notice you have some articles here, recent articles, where they themselves talk about buying and selling $180,000 homes out there in San Diego and living along the seashore overlooking the water.

JM: They look like they're healthy. They look like they're in good shape, in fact, I have one article here from a thing called the *National Star*. Now, if I'm not mistaken it may be published by the same group that publishes the distinguished Manhattan-based newspaper called the *New York Pest...Post*.

WW: Ha, ha. Yes. An interesting thing about that article if I can interrupt you.

JM: Please.

WW: Kathy—there's a picture in that article showing Kathy taking a polygraph and an individual by the name of Michael Rice administered the polygraph.

JM: Yes. I wanted to ask you about the lie-detector test.

WW: Well, she testified just the other day that it wasn't Michael Rice who gave her the test, but it was a Chris Coogis. So, as far as I'm concerned, this picture that's in the *Star* is a posed picture, misleading, and of course just another attempt to add credibility to their story.

JM: So you don't believe this story in the *National Star* about them having taken a lie-detector test, which the story claims proves they did tell the truth when they said they were haunted by the nightmare of the Amityville house?

WW: I absolutely don't believe it, that's correct.

JM: You will admit, though, that they did understand the American system and the American people very well, I mean you have got to give them credit for understanding how to play the game and win, as we say.

WW: They have all my respect in that regard—all of it.

JM: You know we're from the same wonderful neighborhood in Brooklyn—you know in that neighborhood we would have held a big parade for them, a block party, and celebrated. This is making it.

WW: That's correct.

JM: You can't argue with that.

WW: You remember Bay 50 Street.

JM: I'm sure. I remember all of those streets and I saw that movie about Rocky Graziano years ago. He wins at the end. And they have a motorcade through the streets. See, twenty years ago when I was a kid they would have taken a motorcade, Lee Lutz, and he knew how to play the system.

WW: In this regard, they're king. There's no question about that. They've pulled off a scam, they've made a profit, they haven't violated any law.

JM: No.

WW: They've certainly taken advantage of the memory of certain deceased victims, they've taken advantage of some attorneys, but, let's face it, I'm not gonna become a pauper because they took advantage of me. Win or lose, we'll go on.

JM: But maybe your feelings are a little bit hurt that you didn't get some of the publicity that you might have if they had stayed with you throughout the course of writing this book? I mean we all have egos. There's nothing wrong with saying...

WW: No question about it. I mean I'm an amateur actor, too, you know, but I've learned this. Because I got more publicity out of the DeFeo trial than any attorney could ever hope to get out of any other trial.

JM: Simply because you were court–appointed?

WW: Well, because I was the attorney for DeFeo.

JM: Yes, but the point is you, you got that position as a court–appointed attorney.

WW: Right.

JM: You didn't even solicit the thing is my point.

WW: No, no. And of all the publicity I got, if you were to turn, you know, transpose it in terms of our capital enterprise system, it's nil. So the point is, publicity is good, but it really, unless it's done with a goal in mind of selling a book, of selling a project, the publicity is worthless.

JM: That's true. Which is why after you took over the case and became the attorney of record for Ronald DeFeo you had decided at some point to write a book about the Ronald DeFeo case.

WW: Yes. Right.

JM: Yes. And at some point, also, may have believed, as the *New York Post* article suggests, that in asking for a retrial maybe the Lutzes had something there when they said the house was haunted. At some point you seemed to believe them. Or no?

WW: That aspect of the *Post* article doesn't really quote me. JM: This...this is wrong here? Listen, listen, I don't believe a word they say. The heck with that article—all right!

WW: In fact, the quotes in the *Post* article are not accurate according to the interview I gave to the Associated Press.

JM: You never believed the Lutzes at any point...at any time did you believe any of the suggestions, any psychic phenomena? Or they never really suggested to you there were psychic phenomena?

WW: (at same time) Well, you see?...did I believe...I believed in serious problems in this house.

JM: Yes, but they never suggested to you really in private that there were the kind of things they talked about in the book?

WW: No, no, no, no.

JM: That never happened.

WW: We talked about creating this.

JM: Totally a creation.

WW: Absolutely. Absolutely.

JM: All right. There's really, you know, nothing more you can say except to say that when they go on television now, Bill, they say that it really happened. Simple as that. They say it happened.

WW: Well, in view of the evidence that we have here, some of the facts that I've told you that as you indicated we could go on all night long....

JM: Sure. Yes.

WW: If I were in a debate with them....

JM: Yes, what would happen?

WW: I'd point-by-point, I'm sure that I would come out winning eight out of nine rounds.

JM: And yet in a way, it would be your word against theirs, or not?

WW: Well no, because you see I talk about the Brunswick Hospital, I'll come in with a letter from the Brunswick Hospital saying there was no treatment of any Danny Lutz on such and such a day.

JM: All right. Similarly, wouldn't records show...that's a good point...similarly, wouldn't records show that the police were or were not called in, the Amityville PD, to that house as the movie and the book suggest, when Lee Lutz says he called police there because the doors were flying around, and noises were there.

WW: That's a lie. No. The only time the Amityville police ever came to Lee Lutz is when he went to check a gun with them.

JM: Hmm.... And the stigmata, of course, we covered the fact that the priest's hands bleed and you say that just never happened at all because the priest was never in the house.

WW: Well, I'm not gonna say anything about what happened to the priest. The only thing I know is that the priest told me that he was never at the house and the first time he spoke to the Lutzes about the house was after they fled the house.

JM: Yes. And he was supposed to, as well, have had an automobile accident as a result. Do you know if that happened after leaving the house?

WW: I know nothing about the priest's experience. In fact, if we can find the priest, subpoena him and get him into court, that's the only way we'll ever find out about it.

JM: The one who's called Father Mancuso but is Father Pecoraro.

WW: Pecoraro, right.

JM: And you do not know at this time where he is?

WW: Right now we don't know. We've traced him to Minnesota, we've traced him to California, we've traced him to Texas, and at one time he was back here at his mother's house in Nassau, I believe.

JM: Yes, and did you hear this hot flash about, the rumor about the possibility that the Lutzes may be writing a sequel, a book about the demons which couldn't bear to leave them in Amityville and have surfaced again and are with them in California?

WW: Yes, I heard about it today. (Laughs)

JM: Not from me first, I don't think?

WW: No, no, it was during George Lutz's testimony in court.

JM: Ah. He said that in fact the demons have followed them.

WW: He just told us about the new book that he's writing.

JM: And it will be about what? About exactly that?

The Amityville Horror Conspiracy

WW: Yeah. It's, I think he's calling it, "The Amityville Horror, Part II."

JM: Are you kidding?

JM: No.

WW: I'm not kidding.

JM: That's a very clever title.

WW: Isn't it?

JM: I wonder where he got that from?

WW: I don't know. I'm gonna ask his godfather.

JM: Incredible. But he is gonna write a...that's true, then, a follow–up.

WW: Yes.

JM: And you have nothing to do with that?

WW: Well, he said, though, that it doesn't have any contract or any publisher, that he's just writing the book.

JM: I see. He does not have... I see, so he hasn't yet solicited a publisher. But we can assume he will. Because my understanding is Jay Anson, if one is interested in knowing what happens to the principals in these type of incidents, Jay Anson, sight unseen according to an article in one newspaper column, has a healthy advance for a new book which has not yet even been written, apparently, and movie rights to the tune of some million dollars.

WW: I know nothing about that...

JM: This is what I 've read.

WW: ...but I'll ask Jay Anson when he is subpoenaed....

JM: That's the only time you talk to anybody, when they're on the witness stand.

WW: Yeah. They don't want to talk to me over the phone at this point because they know that the game is up.

JM: Yes. But really all you can do is sue. There is nothing, when you say the game is up, that one could do legally; I mean, they haven't really defrauded anyone, have they?

WW: Well, in the case of Jay Anson, there's a question of whether or not he participated in the fraud with the Lutzes. And in the case of Prentice Hall there's a question of whether or not they knew or, being professionals in their business, ought to have known that a fraud had been perpetrated on us. Because they were advised by us in writing that everything about the Lutzes' experience in that house is a fraud, a hoax and not true. And they did absolutely nothing about it, to correct that title except send a letter to Jay Anson telling him to have the Lutzes get the story straight.

JM: I'm out of time, and I thank you for making your time available because it's been more revealing than perhaps anything I've ever heard about this since this whole business began.

WW: Well, Joel, I want to thank you for inviting me here. Again, like the Cromartys, this is the first official interview I've ever had on the case.

JM: That...I didn't know that! Well, that's interesting. Again, you know, I appreciate your honesty and your time. William Weber, attorney for Ronald DeFeo, Jr., now serving a life term for the mass murders of his family. And William Weber is the man who says that he knows that the story of the Amityville Horror is a hoax because he was there with the Lutzes when many of the incidents in the book and the film were fabricated. We're coming back on WBAB after a short pause, to talk more about the Amityville Horror. My guest will be the co-producer of the motion picture and the mayor of Amityville Village. Stay tuned. We'll be back in just a moment.

13

"For God's Sake, Come In!"

Tuesday, Aug. 7, 1979

It's 7:00 p.m. and I am sitting in the "Green Room" at WNEW T.V. where the program "Midday" is taped. Across from me is Frank Burch, the Cromartys' "house-sitter." We have just been introduced to one another in preparation for doing a show about the Amityville Horror, which will be aired tomorrow. Also in the room is Rick Moran, who will be on the program, too. Each of us, on an independent basis, will be giving our reasons why we feel the A.H. is a hoax. The Lutzes were supposed to be here to represent the opposition, but we have just been told that they have called to cancel because their daughter is ill. We have heard rumors that the Warrens may be coming to take their place, but so far they aren't here.

Frank Burch has us spellbound with stories of the new hoards of trespassers that have been invading Ocean Avenue since the movie opened. Strangely enough, he does not seem in the least upset by his strange lifestyle; he claims to have lost much sleep due to tourists but his eyes are not red or bloodshot. Quite the contrary, Frank has a mischievous twinkle in his eyes as he talks about life in the infamous house. He seems relaxed and somewhat amused by the fact that he has become something of an overnight celebrity because of his current abode.

Frank did not hear the Joel Martin Show on Sunday, but he is quite interested in getting a copy of the tape (it could help the Cromartys in court). I am still reeling myself from that explosive interview. Joel did an incredible job; no one could possibly guess from his performance that he had just received word of a personal tragedy. What a professional. I only wish that his program was heard nationally (or internationally, for that matter) so that everyone could have the chance to hear Mr. Weber's confession.

As we are finishing up our coffee, I look up just in time to see Lorraine Warren come through the door. She is talking animatedly with a young man in a plaid jacket but stops abruptly as she sees me across the room. It is obvious that Lorraine is shocked to see me here. She regains her composure and seats herself on the opposite side of the room, whispering and gesturing to her companion and to the "Midday" staff girl.

A little before showtime, I learn from another staff member that Lorraine has expressed reluctance to appear on the show with me. But she is the only one representing the side that the "horror" is true; Ed is in England on a case so she agreed to fill in for the Lutzes on her own. The young man accompanying her is a representative from A.I.P. (he will not appear on the show but is merely there for moral support.)

"Midday"'s host, Bill Boggs, has improved immensely since the last time the Warrens and I appeared on the show. He is very much in control this time and gives each of us ample time to give our opinions. Lorraine and I are quite cold to each other, but there is no screamfest. She tells Mr. Boggs that she and Ed never said that everything in the book was true; they have just related the horrible things that personally happened to them in the house. This leaves me a bit confused—as I remind Lorraine—weren't she and Ed the ones who debated me on numerous occasions and said that Jay Anson's book was a true story? No, Lorraine insists, they never said the book was true, obviously literary license was used. Maybe the public can tell me if I'm mistaken, but this is the first time I can recall Lorraine saying that they never endorsed the book.

Photo by Rita Allen

Bill Boggs of "Midday" on WNEW-TV introduces Rick Moran, Lorraine Warren and Dr. Stephen Kaplan.

The Amityville Horror Conspiracy

Stephen debates Lorraine.

Lorraine glares at Stephen.

The show is over, but the discussion continues in the "green room" at WNEW.

Photo by Rita Allen

Lorraine leaves quickly after the program but I stay in the lobby for a while talking with Frank Burch. He again expresses interest in hearing the Martin/Weber tapes and in seeing some of the evidence I have collected on the hoax. I express interest in having the opportunity to more closely examine the Amityville house.

"Why don't you and Roxanne come to visit me at the house sometime this month?" Frank invites. "Stay until 3:15 a.m. if you want—that's when all the kooks outside come around and start yelling 'Jodie!' or 'Get out!' You can see first hand what drove the Cromartys out of their own house. Bring the Martins, too; we can all sit around and listen to the Weber tapes."

I agree to call him and set up a time as soon as I contact the Martins. Then I catch a taxi to take me back to Queens, where I can get some rest and prepare to pick up my children tomorrow for our vacation together.

Friday, Aug. 10, 1979

I finally got Brian and Stacy settled in bed for the night. They were overtired from our outing to Bear Mt. State Park, but we all had a great time. Tomorrow we're off to New Jersey where we'll visit friends and then go to Great Adventure Amusement Park on Sunday. But right now I've got a few minutes to relax with the papers before turning in.

And here it is again—Amityville is back in the news, or the *Daily News* to be exact. There's a few paragraphs about a press conference held by the Cromartys in their house. They showed reporters around the house (including a tour of the "red room") and announced that they have taken the house off the market and are moving back in. (I wonder where this will leave Frank Burch?) They also claim that the hoax is being investigated by the Suffolk District Attorney's office. Mrs. Cromarty calls the Amityville story "Long Island's Watergate," a phrase that I have used many times in the past.

I'm tempted to call and talk to Frank Burch now, but I'll wait until next week after the kids have left.

Wednesday, Aug. 15, 1979

An interview that I did on the phone a couple of weeks ago with a writer for the *Midnight Globe* has paid off. I just picked up a copy of the paper dated Aug. 21, and it has a story entitled, "Amityville: Horror or Fantasy?" In the article, I am quoted as saying the story is a hoax, and that it may have been a plan between Lutz and Weber to make money. They mention that I claim to have a witness who can confirm that George Lutz signed a contract for a book even before a psychic researcher was called in.

They also have a brief quote from Lorraine Warren, who says, "No way did that family fabricate the story. Forty-five minutes after Ed entered the house he came under attack by a demon in the base‐ment." A representative of A.I.P. says only that the information they have is contrary to what I say. But the article as a whole seems to lean toward supporting my story. At least the story of Weber's involvement is spreading a little further around the country.

I have called Frank Burch and he has not moved out of the house as yet. The Cromartys are not moving back in right away. Frank again extended his invitation to visit the house, and I have since arranged a mutually agreeable date with Joel and Chris Martin. They will be accompanying Roxanne and I to the house on August 25th.

Thursday, Aug. 23, 1979

A brief Amityville Update: today's *Daily News* informs us that, in spite of horrible reviews, "The Amityville Horror" movie has so far grossed over $35,000,000.

Not bad for a fairy tale.

Saturday, Aug. 25, 1979

We are seated in a semi-circle around the hearth: Frank Burch, myself, Roxanne, Joel and Chris Martin, and a young lady named Patty who works at WBAB with the Martins. Rain drips quietly outside the open windows of the living room as we listen intently to the tapes of William Weber explaining how he helped to invent the "horrors" of Amityville. I can almost picture them now, Lutz and Weber sitting here in this very room, laughing about Evinrude the "pig" cat, and planning how they can all make a few dollars by writing a good horror story.

It has been a quiet night so far, with only an occasional car slow‐ing down outside to get a good look at the "Horror House." Frank thinks maybe the rain is keeping some of them home. "But wait until the bar crowd gets out around 3:00 a.m.," he says. "If you can stick around till then you're bound to see a little more action."

Earlier this evening Frank gave us a tour of the house from top to bottom. We examined all of the bedrooms where the DeFeo mur‐ders had occurred, including the attic room that had belonged to

Ronald. Frank showed us how the moon-shaped windows there still had the original putty that was used to keep the panes of glass in place; if a single one of the odd-shaped panes had been broken and replaced, it would have been quite noticeable.

We looked around the kitchen and dining room and then went outside on the back patio and walked back past the swimming pool to the Amityville River. The night was warm and moist and peaceful. It seemed that the awful memory of the murders had faded from the house and been replaced by the glow of a happy, lived-in home. A few of Frank's young friends have also been living in the house during the Cromarty's absence, and they will all be quite sorry to leave. Even Frank's two young sons have visited their father here and enjoyed playing in the pool and the backyard.

As we walked toward the garage/boathouse to take a look in there, Frank pointed out a large, Siamese cat running past us toward the house next door.

"Hey, you're lucky tonight!" He grinned, "That's Jodie the Pig who just ran by. He loves playing in the boathouse and looking for fish." So we even got to see the famous Evinrude, aka Jodie.

Next we got the grand tour of the basement. Once again, we checked out the "red room" as Frank pointed out the pipes that it gives access to, pipes that run upstairs to the bathrooms and the kitchen.

Now it's past midnight and the Martins and Patty have to be leaving. Roxanne and I will stay at least until three to see if the wackos come out. And come out they do! Frank was right about the bar patrons. At about 2:00 a.m. the street begins to get noisy. Carloads of rowdy teenagers and older delinquents stop and gather on Ocean Avenue outside the house. Our conversation is frequently interrupted by shouts of "Ronnie!" or "Jodie!" or "Get out!... hee, hee, hee, HA, HA, HA!"

"I told you," says Frank. "And this is a quiet night compared to most." The rowdies are periodically chased away by patrolling Amityville Police cars, but new ones show up every few minutes. Some throw small pebbles at the house. "Show us the green slime!" they yell, or "Where's the flies?" Frank tells us how one night he found a young man hanging by his fingertips on the windowsill trying to get a good look inside the house.

I'm glad we stayed to see this because it is such a contrast to the peaceful atmosphere in the house just a few hours ago. And THAT is the true horror of Amityville.

The Amityville Horror Conspiracy

Friday, Aug. 31, 1979

I just finished a program for Connecticut's WTIC radio program with host Brian Dow. He had a three-way telephone hook-up between he, myself and George Lutz.

Yes, that's right, George finally agreed to participate in a radio talk show that I was involved in. It seems that George doesn't like what I've been saying about the case lately and decided to answer me back. In turn I got a chance to interview George in front of thousands of listeners.

When confronted with the fact that the 250-lb. wooden door was still on the house and had never been torn off, George finally admitted, "Well, it wasn't the wooden door that flew off the hinges, it was the screen door." I pointed out to the audience that it is a common occurrence during a Long Island winter to lose a screen door to wind; it happened to me that very same winter, and I didn't even live next to the water like George.

I also pinned George down on the book's claim that Kathy levitated two feet off the bed. "Well," he said, "It wasn't really two feet, that was a bit exaggerated."

"How exaggerated was it, George?" I asked.

"Well, actually she levitated about two inches off the bed," George admitted.

"Two *inches*? Don't you think there's a big difference between two *feet* and two *inches*?" I asked. "For two inches she could have been startled by a nightmare and bounced up from the bed!"

"That's not what happened!" George was getting angry. "I saw her floating. But we can't help it if Anson decided to use literary license and exaggerate the truth."

So George was admitting, at least, that Anson's book was an exaggerated version of the truth. I decided to question him on another issue.

"What about the part of the book where your son's hand was crushed by a window and you rushed him to Brunswick Hospital Center in Amityville—is that just literary license, too?" I asked George.

"No, no, that is true," said George.

"You mean you actually took him to Brunswick Hospital?" I asked.

"Yes," said George.

"George, I happen to know that there is no record of a Danny Lutz ever being treated at the emergency room of Brunswick Hospital on that day or any other day. We can get a hold of the hospital records if necessary. Do you still claim that Danny was treated there?"

"Well, actually we didn't take him to Brunswick, we took him to a doctor." George was beginning to sound nervous.

"So, first you just said you took him to Brunswick, and now you're saying you didn't. Is that correct?"

"What's the big deal where he was treated?" said George. "His hand wasn't broken, so Kathy and I just bandaged it."

"But I thought you just said you took him to a doctor?" I said.

"Are you trying to call me a liar?" George was really annoyed now. "We did take him to a doctor, later, after we had bandaged it at home!"

"But not Brunswick," I said.

"No, not Brunswick, I just told you that," said George.

I stressed to the audience my strong feeling that when an alleged non-fiction book mentions a specific public location like a hospital, and the event never really happened there at all, that is an out-and-out lie. And "literary license"was never meant to be interpreted as "bold-faced lies."

The interview on WTIC was a most important one in that it was the first time that I got to debate George Lutz directly without going through a middle man. And once again, George himself is my best witness to the illegitimacy of this case.

Sunday, Sept. 9, 1979

Last week Roxanne, at my request, had gotten William Weber's office phone number from Joel Martin and called Weber to see if we could set up an appointment to interview him. I have a lot more questions that I would like to ask Mr. Weber about his involvement with the Lutzes. Weber agreed to meet with us and invited us to his home in Dix Hills, L.I., for today.

After following Weber's instructions, Roxanne and I drive up to a pleasant–looking home in an upper-middle class development. I am looking forward to this interview; it will fill in any gaps that might have been left in Weber's story on WBAB due to lack of time. We stroll up the tree-lined walk and ring the front doorbell. Two giggling young girls run to the front door and look out through the screen.

"Yes?" says one of the girls.

"We're here to see Mr. William Weber. He's expecting us." I say. "My name is Dr. Stephen Kaplan."

"My father's not home," says the girl.

"Oh?" I say. "We had an appointment for 2:00 and it's that time now. Did your father say when he'll be back?"

The Amityville Horror Conspiracy

"No." Miss Weber is not exactly talkative, but she's probably been told not to give out any information to strangers.

"Well, maybe he's been delayed. We'll be waiting over there in our car; please let him know we're here when he arrives."

"O.K." she says, and runs back inside to play with her friend.

A half-hour later, Mr. Weber has still not shown up. I go back to the door and ring the bell again. Weber's daughter comes back to the door.

"Excuse me, but didn't your father mention that he was expecting us? Did he tell you to ask us to wait?" I ask.

"I don't know where he went," she replies.

"And he hasn't called home to tell you he'd be late?"

"No."

"Well, we'll wait a little longer," I tell her, "Maybe he got held up in traffic."

The girl gives a shrug of her shoulders and runs back to play.

Another half-hour passes. It is now 3:00 and no sign of Weber. Roxanne and I decide to leave, disgusted. We drove almost 40 miles to get here for nothing and now we have to drive 40 miles back to Queens. Since we only have Weber's office number, we can't even call his home to find out what happened. I'll have Roxanne try to call him at his office tomorrow if we haven't heard from him by then.

Tuesday, Sept. 11, 1979

Weber has never called. Roxanne left messages with his secretary, but they have not been answered. Even if Weber is busy, he could have left a message of apology for us with his secretary. It is most annoying.

But then he must be quite busy. Today's *Newsday* has a story called, "Lutz Family 'Horror' Suit Is Rejected," about the suit between Weber and the Lutzes. The judge has thrown out the Lutzes' $1-million suit against Weber, his partner Burton, and writer Paul Hoffman. Lutz claimed that the trio misrepresented themselves to him and then printed the stories in the *Daily News* and *Good Housekeeping* without their knowledge or consent. The Lutzes claimed that this invaded their privacy, but U.S. District Court Judge Jack B. Weinstein said that since the Lutzes made themselves public figures, and willingly participated in a press conference, that they could not claim invasion of privacy.

Weinstein is allowing to stand Weber, Burton and Hoffman's $2 million countersuit against the Lutzes, although he expressed concern about the ethical conduct of the two lawyers. He indicated that he may refer the matter to the New York State Bar Association, and commented, "There is a very serious ethical question when lawyers become literary agents."

In the course of testifying for this case, George Lutz has made some grave admissions about the book. He says that the book is true, in a general sense, but that certain episodes *were not accurately portrayed* (Italics mine). He conceded the following points:

1: The green slime "was more like Jello."

2: He could not really identify the face he saw in his daughter's window as a pig with red eyes.

3: The drums and horns he heard in the living room were not accompanied by stomping feet (In other words, not a marching band.)

4: The "demon" in the fireplace was really only "something very ugly...etched in the bricks."

5: Last but not least, Lutz stated in court what he had told me on the Brian Dow show; that Kathy only levitated two inches off the bed, not two feet.

It is quite exciting to have the very things I have been trying to prove over the last three–and–a–half years, being validated in U.S. District Court.

Wednesday, Sept. 12, 1979

This is great! *Newsday* has another story about the Lutz/Weber trial entitled "Amityville Book Gets a Bad Review." This article is so hot you need asbestos gloves to handle it!

The opening sentence goes like this: "Brooklyn—A federal judge said yesterday that *The Amityville Horror: A True Story* was *bunk* after a priest testified that he had *never suffered any of the afflictions and illnesses* [italics mine] ascribed to him in the book."

Rev. Ralph J. Pecoraro (alias Frank Mancuso) was ordered by Judge Weinstein to testify by telephone from California, where he is now living. He identified himself as an "ecclesiastical judge" who had annulled Kathy Lutz's first marriage. Pecoraro claims that he went to the house only once—to bless the house—and heard a voice say "Get out." But he also said, and I quote, "the resulting terrors which befell him in the book *never happened* [italics mine]."

He did suggest to the Lutzes that they leave the house, because "even if what was occurring was not paranormal, there certainly was a deleterious effect upon their psyche—their psychological responses were not good, so they should get out." The reason Pecoraro fled to

The Amityville Horror Conspiracy

California was not to avoid demons, but "to avoid annoying telephone calls and other harassment resulting *from the book* [italics mine]."

William Weber also testified yesterday, telling the judge that, during several meetings in 1976, he, Burton, Hoffman and the Lutzes had agreed to collaborate on a *fiction* book about DeFeo and the Amityville house. Lutz, instead, took his story to Prentice Hall, and the rest as they say, is history. Lutz testified to the fact that he and his wife have currently received more than $200,000. from book and movie royalties.

Judge Weinstein, after hearing the testimony of Pecoraro and Weber, made the following statement: "Based on what I have heard, it appears to me that *to a large extent the book is a work of fiction* [italics mine], relying in large part upon the suggestions of Mr. Weber."

Let's sum this up: So far, "*The Amityville Horror: A True Story*" has been called a work of fiction (in whole or in part) by:

1. The Catholic Diocese of Rockville Centre

2. Rev. Pecoraro himself

3. Sgt. Cammaroto and the Amityville Police Dept.

4. Mr. William Weber, the original collaborator

5. U.S. District Court Judge Jack Weinstein

6. To some extent, George Lutz himself.

I'm sure I'm leaving someone out (not to mention myself and other parapsychologists), but these six alone are a pretty impressive group. Could there still be someone out there who could be aware of all this evidence and still believe that the story is true?

But that's one of the problems. Not everyone has access to this information. These are local New York articles. The further away you go from New York the more people believe that the A.H. is true. I have seen this in my travels and in my national and international radio interviews via phone. That's why I feel I must continue to spread this information as far and as wide as I possibly can, because only informed people can make educated conclusions.

Thursday, Sept. 13, 1979

And now the results of the Lutz/Weber trial—an out-of-court settlement was reached yesterday, according to two articles printed today in *Newsday* and the *New York Post.*

The *Post* article is called, "Amityville a horrible fake, says U.S. judge." What a great headline. The Post gives a summary of the trial, repeating Judge Weinstein's comment about the book appearing to be fiction and mentioning that Weber "helped to invent some of the eerie experiences described in Jay Anson's bestseller."

Newsday's headline is gentler: "'Horror' Dispute Ends on a Happy Note." It tells how all parties involved shook hands after reaching an out-of-court settlement in which the Lutzes must reimburse Weber, Burton and Hoffman for their court and legal costs. Both sides refused to discuss any further details of the settlement, but Weber and Burton's attorney, Frederic Black, said that they had sought the settlement because they were afraid that Mr. Weber would end up having to defend himself on questions of his ethical conduct.   It seems the judge had questioned the propriety of Weber negotiating a book deal with the Lutzes while still acting as attorney for Ronald DeFeo. Mr. Black stated, "I did not want to have Mr. Weber defend himself against other matters, even though he had a (publication) release from DeFeo and was doing nothing improper."

Judge Weinstein terminated the case after being informed of the settlement. Lutz told a reporter, "We just want to go back to our real lives. This is something in the past that we want to forget about."

George, if you want so badly to forget the past, how come you're working on three new books about Amityville?

Saturday, Sept. 15, 1979

Joel Martin just called to tell me about a letter he received from the Cromartys' attorney, Michael Zissu. He is requesting a copy of the Martin/ Weber tapes to use in the Cromartys' suit against Lutz and company. So the courts are far from through with the Amityville Horror as yet.

The media is also far from through with it. This week's *People* magazine (dated Sept. 17) has as its cover photo a shot of Margot Kidder (alias Kathy Lutz) screaming in terror as a large, bloody axe looms toward her. Above the photo, large green and white letters say, "The Amityville Horror—Hype, Hoax & Heroine. The movie is mostly baloney, but Margot Kidder is worth shouting about." The article was obviously written before the Weber/Lutz case went to trial; they mention it as an upcoming event.

The article has some interesting quotes from William Weber, e.g., "We created this horror story over many bottles of wine. I told George Lutz that Ronnie DeFeo used to call the neighbor's cat a pig. George was a con artist; he improvised on that and in the book he sees a demon pig through a window."

The Amityville Horror Conspiracy

George Lutz's only reply: "I'm tired of being called a liar. It will be decided in court."

According to this article, the program, "In Search of..." with Leonard Nimoy will present a 30-minute segment *defending* the Amityville Horror this week. I'll certainly have to catch that one to see just how they're going to defend it.

The article also mentions prospective buyer of the house Sam Stangl, but says that his deal to buy the house from the Cromartys has not been closed yet. I get the feeling that the Cromartys may be reconsidering selling the house after all.

The rest of the article is devoted to the life and career of Margot Kidder. But at least they got across the idea that the A.H. may be a hoax. That is a big step forward in terms of informing the public because *People* has a huge circulation.

Next Saturday, I will carry the story of the hoax right into the heart of the Pocono Mountains. I will be lecturing at the Swiftwater Inn for AAPHR, Penny Raffa's group, which is sponsoring a weekend of lectures and workshops there. I love the Poconos, so it will be like combining business with pleasure. I will not, however, attempt to climb any mountains—Moosilauke was the beginning and the end of *that* particular sport.

Sunday, Oct. 7, 1979

It is Roxanne's birthday. I am attending a family party for her at her parents' home on Long Island. We are in good spirits; things have been going quite well for us lately. The Swiftwater lecture was fairly successful; it didn't draw a large crowd but quite a respectable-sized group of interested persons, and the Poconos were beautiful. Afterwards, Penny Raffa discussed with me Ed and Lorraine Warren's recent appearance on the Mike Douglas Show promoting the A.H., and told me that AAPHR had sent a telegram to Mike Douglas because of that program. The telegram suggested to Mr. Douglas that if he wanted to hear the truth about the Amityville Horror, he should contact Dr. Stephen Kaplan in New York.

Well, that telegram evoked a positive response. I was subsequently contacted by the Mike Douglas Show and asked to appear to discuss the A.H.. I suggested to the staff that they also get Mr. Frank Burch on the program to talk about his experiences living in the so-called "horror" house. They liked the idea, and Frank and I are both scheduled to fly to Los Angeles next Sunday, the 14th. We will tape the show on Monday, the 15th, and then fly back home.

On the negative side, that "In Search of..." program about Amityville seemed quite intent on presenting it as a true story. They had on a priest, supposedly Father Pecoraro but silhouetted in black so that his face could not be seen. He talked about the voice that told him to "Get out." The Warrens' experiences were included in the show, and of course, the Lutzes, but there was no one on to suggest that the story might *not* be true.

Today's *Newsday* commented on that "In Search of..." episode. Leonard Nimoy, in the interview, claims that they could not get anyone who represented the opposition to agree to appear on the show. And who did they ask? Ronald DeFeo, Jr., William Weber, and the Cromartys, all of whom allegedly asked "exorbitant fees," and then refused to appear even if their demands were met. Why ask Ronald DeFeo? He wasn't there when the Lutzes' phenomena were occurring, he was already incarcerated at Dannemora. Same thing with the Cromartys; they moved in more than a year after the Lutzes had left. As for William Weber, I'm sure that he would be violating his out-of-court settlement with the Lutzes if he had agreed to appear on the show. (It's a good thing Joel Martin got his confession before that trial!)

But what about me? Haven't I been the one who has publicly represented the opposition from the very beginning? Yet I was never contacted by "In Search of..." If they had done any research whatsoever on the position that the case may be a hoax, they would have had to run into my name among the many articles that have included my findings. Nimoy takes issue with the line from the *People* magazine article which referred to the "In Search of..." show as "a defense of the book or movie," saying "We did the best we could with who would appear." He claims that, "an alternate viewpoint was out of reach." Hey, Leonard, I'm right here in New York, certainly not out of reach of a phone call from L.A., and I've been actively trying to get someone to air my "alternate viewpoint" for years!

It doesn't matter, now, because Mike Douglas will be airing it on his show, anyway. One way or another, the public is beginning to learn the truth that has been suppressed by the media for so long.

Sunday, Oct. 14, 1979

It is noontime and already I'm exhausted. I flew home from Washington, D.C. just an hour ago (having lectured at the Open

The Amityville Horror Conspiracy

University of Washington last night) and I barely have time to re-pack for my flight to L.A. this evening. Frank Burch will be by to pick me up in a few hours to drive to Kennedy Airport. But it is exciting! We are taking the true story of Amityville clear across the country to present it on a national talk-show as respected as the Mike Douglas Show.

In the meantime, I can laugh over my lunch as I read another one of Ed Lowe's columns about Amityville in today's *Newsday*. It is called "Amityville Horror Strikes in Flint." A radio station in Flint, Michigan is conducting a contest—and the prize is to spend Halloween night in Amityville! No, the Cromartys have not agreed to allow the two winners to stay overnight at the "horror" house. They will be spending the night at the only motel in the village—The Colonial Motel (the radio station is calling it The Colonial Hotel to make it sound classier)—and then the Amityville mayor will give them a tour of the village, including a ride past the infamous house. Wow! The disc jockey who came up with this winner is nicknamed "Boogie" (the boogie-man?) and their contest slogan is, "If you're frightened, keep it tightened to AM600, WTAC." The way it works is this: anytime a listener hears a voice on the radio whisper "Get out," they must call the station for a chance to get into the drawing. I am laughing so hard that I'm in danger of losing my lunch.

What's really ironic about the whole thing is that I'll be spending Halloween night in Amityville myself. Roxanne and I have been invited by Frank Burch to attend the Cromartys' third annual Halloween costume party at the "horror" house. Every year the Cromartys have been holding this party to take their minds off of what the drunken sightseers were doing outside, but this is the first time I've been asked to attend. The invitation that I received in the mail was so inventive and clever that it made me bellow with delight. The front of the card reads, in big block letters, "FOR GOD'S SAKE, COME IN!"

Roxanne and I will be checking out the costume-rental shops after I come back from California, in the hope that they will still have something decent available at this late date. We're really looking forward to it.

Friday, Oct. 26, 1979

The Mike Douglas Show went very well, in spite of the limited amount of time that was allotted to my segment. Frank brought along pictures of the house, including one that clearly showed the audience the size of the "red room." We had the pleasure of meeting singer-guitarist José Feliciano; comic-actor Pat Harrington, and former Charlie's

Angel Kate Jackson along with her husband, Andrew Stevens. Mr. Feliciano expressed a belief in the occult, but as I pointed out to him, I also believe in the occult—just not in this particular case. Pat Harrington, after hearing my strong condemnation of the story, commented, "I wish my doctor was as definite in his diagnosis." Kate Jackson was even more beautiful in person than on TV, and quite fascinated with the Amityville story. She and her husband were appearing on the program to promote their TV-movie remake of "Topper," in which they play those mischievous ghosts, George and Marion Kirby.

Nor is this Kate's first time playing a ghost, either. Roxanne had given me a short letter to deliver to Ms. Jackson in her behalf—Roxanne has been a fan of Kate's since she played "Daphne," the ghost on the old horror-soap of the sixties, "Dark Shadows."

It's been quite a hectic month and the excitement is not over yet. There is, of course, the Halloween party in Amityville on the 31st (Roxanne and I will pick up our costumes on Monday—she's going as "Daisy Mae" and I'm going to be "Batman"—appropriate for one who also does vampire research), and tonight I'll be lecturing on the hoax in Norristown, PA at a lecture sponsored by the Visiting Nurse Association. I have been informed that they will be presenting me with a Recognition Award prior to the lecture in honor of my long and successful investigation of the Amityville Horror.

It's wonderful to get this kind of appreciation for doing something that I felt was my duty. I never realized how many people are out there who care about the truth every bit as much as I do.

Wednesday, Oct. 31, 1979

Roxanne and I are in costume and ready for our drive to Amityville. Her "Daisy Mae" outfit is very sexy, a bit like a French maid costume except that the blouse is hot pink with black polka-dots. There's a large bow of the same color pinned in her hair; the rest of the costume consists of a very brief, black satin skirt cut in points, and sheer black stockings. I can see now why she refused to go along with my original idea: that I dress as Sherlock Holmes with Roxanne dressed as Watson. She had told me in no uncertain terms that she did not plan to go to such an exciting party dressed as a man.

My own costume makes me feel slightly self-conscious: navy-blue tights with a red bat sewn on the chest; black satin shorts, boots and gloves; a large black cape; and a black satin hood with bat ears. The

The Amityville Horror Conspiracy

woman at the rental store had explained to me that the costume's colors are purposely made different from the T.V./movie "Batman" in order to avoid infringing on a copyright.

Our first stop is the local gas station, where we get strange looks from the attendant there. Roxanne snickers in amusement as I go for my wallet to pay the man and remember that I had given it to her to hold—I wonder where "Batman" keeps his wallet and keys?—because there are no pockets in my tights. The humor of the situation causes me to smile at Roxanne and crack, "To the Bat-Cave, Robin!" as we pull out of the station and head for Amityville.

Forty-five minutes later, we pull up in front of 112 Ocean Avenue and park in the street. I was a little worried about parking my car here tonight—you see, my license plates read "GHOSTS." Can you imagine seeing a car with "GHOSTS" plates parked in front of the Amityville Horror house on Halloween night? But I was told by Frank Burch that the party-goers have permission to break the usual "No Parking" rules. A security guard comes over to check our invitation and gives us the O.K. Security is tight here tonight, with private guards at the gate and Amityville police patrolling regularly. The Cromartys have also recently installed a strong chain-link fence around the property, so I don't think there'll be any party-crashers tonight.

We are among the first guests to arrive, and the door is answered by a friend of Frank's. A few minutes later, Frank, who has been putting the finishing touches on his costume, comes down the staircase into the foyer. Roxanne and I stare at him in disbelief—the right half of his body is dressed in jeans and a denim jacket, but the left half is clothed in half of a woman's long, gaudy–print evening gown! The female half is also wearing a high-heeled shoe, and that side of the hair has been streaked with blond. But the sight that has *really* riveted our attention is Frank's face—his full, thick, black beard and mustache have been neatly divided down the center; the "female" half is completely clean-shaven!

"How do you like it?" Frank grins at us, that mischievous twinkle in his eyes.

"It's, uh, incredible, Frank," I answer, "but what are you supposed to be, a hermaphrodite?"

"No," says Frank, feigning a hurt look. "You mean you can't tell? I'm George...(he faces the bearded, denim-clad side towards us) and Kathy...(Frank spins around to reveal the gowned side)...Lutz!" Frank then proceeds to act out a scene from the "A.H." movie; his "George" side screaming, "I'm coming apart!" and, "I'm going to kill you, Kathy!" in a gruff and menacing voice; then his "Kathy" side trilling in a high falsetto, "Oh, George, we've got to get out of this house!"

Roxanne and I crack up, our peals of hysterical laughter ringing through the big old house, as Frank's friend answers the door to let in some recent arrivals. The new guests, of course, want to know what's so funny and we insist that Frank do a rerun of his hilarious performance for them.

Before long, the entire first floor of the house is jam-packed with guests. And the costumes! Such a collection of ingenious get-ups has rarely been seen in one place. The bar in the play-room is generously stocked and numerous plates of snacks are circulating.

Roxanne calls my attention to a giant, furry creature who is bending over to get through the front door. It is a great reproduction of "Chewbacca," the Wookiee creature from "Star Wars"; this hulking form has to be almost seven feet tall! Roxanne and I are whispering to each other, trying to figure out how the costume makes the person look so tall.

"Stilts,'" says Rocky, "He's got to be on stilts."

"No," I disagree, "It's a false head, on top of his own. He must be looking out through eye-holes in the body." Roxanne is dubious; she doesn't see any eye-holes and points out that the eyes in the Wookiee's head look quite real and active.

I go over and introduce myself to "Chewy." "Hi!" I say, "I'm Dr. Stephen Kaplan. That's a great costume you've got there. How does it manage to make you look so tall?"

"I *am* this tall," the giant figure replies, to my astonishment. It turns out this young man is an Amityville bartender who just happens to be nearly seven feet tall! He removes his mask for a moment just to assure me he's for real.

Roxanne mingles with the crowd, taking snapshots of all the great costumes. There's a guy who's come as "The Texas Chainsaw Massacre"; the handle protrudes from his chest, the blade from his back, and fake blood covers his arms. There's a couple of Arab sheiks, cowboys, clowns, a devil and angel couple, Renaissance costumes, a surgeon, a female version of the Jolly Green Giant, an alien, a vampire bride and groom, a French maid, Peter Pan, a beekeeper, a construction worker, a family of "coneheads," Julius Caesar, a witch, Raggedy Ann and Andy, a rabbit, and many more. There's one "Miss Piggy," and another very pretty blonde in evening gown and fur stole but wearing pig ears and a pig nose. I think she's an interpretation of Jodie the Pig.

But Roxanne and I agree our favorite costume of all is the couple who came as an electrical plug and an outlet. The young man has his face painted a metallic silver and has a large cardboard "plug" strapped around his body, the prongs covered in aluminum foil. On his head is a white helmet with a yellow light on top and what looks like a vacuum-cleaner hose going from the helmet to the back of the "plug." His attractive lady has a giant "outlet" made of cardboard hung over her shoulders, with her face peeking out from the top hole. The bottom hole has two slots, into which the young man proceeds to insert his "prongs." As he does so, he also kisses the young lady and secretly presses a hidden button which causes the light atop his helmet to blink on and off. Of course, the two are asked to demonstrate this procedure for each new guest that comes and it seems unanimous that had there been a prize for best costumes, it would have gone to this ingenious young couple.

Joel and Chris Martin arrive at the party dressed as "humans," with Joel's daughter Tracy made up like a cat. The Cromarty's lawyer, Michael Zissu, is one of the Arabs. Mr. and Mrs. Cromarty themselves are dressed as "Night" and "Day." Cromarty's uncle, a judge in real life, is dressed in old–fashioned judge's robes and wig. We also have a celebrity at the party—Suzy Chaffee of "Suzy Chapstick" fame—dressed as a roller disco queen.

About halfway through the party, Roxanne and I and the Martins are given the O.K. by Frank Burch to go downstairs to take pictures of the "red room." Since we have previously never been granted permission to take pictures inside the house, we take advantage of this opportunity.

Rocky and I crawl into the cubicle and pose there nearly on our knees as Chris Martin takes the pictures. The red paint on the cement blocks is peeling badly from the dampness, with half of the area showing the white paint that was underneath the red. Red paint chips litter the floor of the area. We also get shots of Tracy and then Joel Martin posing in the "room," and Roxanne finds that it is quite difficult to stand far enough away from the subject to photograph them. The only way you can stand opposite the cubicle far enough away to focus the camera is to scrunch way back against the opposite wall of the closet, which she manages to do after moving a few objects stored there. All of this is done in the most cheerful, party atmosphere; never once does any one of us feel nervous or sense any disturbing presence about the "red room."

Just the opposite. The house overflows with happiness. Not even the tourists and hecklers who are passing by quite often outside now (prevented from getting too close by security) can spoil the mood of celebration and good times inside. Any aura of tragedy that may have been left over from the DeFeo murders has been purged forever by the love that is felt for this house by its owners and their friends. The Lutzes' stories of horror have been exposed for what they are in the media and in Federal Court. This house is not a HORROR. This house is a HOME.

Photo by Roxanne Salch Kaplan

Stephen "Batman" Kaplan with Frank "George-and-Kathy" Burch.

Photo by Roxanne Salch Kaplan

Our host, Barbara Cromarty, as "Night."

The Amityville Horror Conspiracy

Jim Cromarty as "Day."

Our favorite costume: the "Plug" and the "Outlet."

"Batman" Kaplan with "Chewbacca, the Wookiee": He really was THAT TALL!

Stephen with "Jodie the Pig."

"For God's Sake, Come In!

Stephen with Suzy "Chapstick" Chaffee, Frank Burch and Tracy Martin.

The Martin family: Joel and Chris dressed as "humans." Tracy as a cat.

Roxanne points to Stephen, posing in the spot where the famous "moose's head" once hung on the wall. The Warrens claimed to have a picture of the moosehead with the ghost of Padre Pio in the moose's ear.

The Amityville Horror Conspiracy

*Roxanne ("Daisy Mae") and Stephen ("Batman") in the famous "Red Room,"
actually a pipe-well in the back of the closet.
        Even a "demon" would have to be on his knees to have an occult ceremony in here!*

Joel Martin in the "Red Room."

*Roxanne points to the pipe-well that extends in back
of the closet shelves in the so-called "Red Room."*

Epilogue

1994 was the Twentieth Anniversary of the Amityville Horror. About fifteen years have gone by since we first began the arduous process of organizing our notes on this case into an accurate, chronological order. The data we had accumulated was extensive, spanning the years 1976 to the present (plus the additional research we did on the DeFeo murder case which went back to 1974.) Our "diary" of our research ends in Oct. 1979, and the first draft of this manuscript was completed in Oct. 1982. Further revisions and additions were done in the 1990s.

Why then, has it taken so long to publish this book which you now hold in your hands? And why did we persevere for all these years until we finally got it out?

The completion of this project has been a labor of love for Roxanne and I, in more ways than one, despite the fact that it has at times been an extremely painful process. Both of us had followed the progress of the case from the very first day it became a local news item, all the way through its various stages of evolving into a world-renown, modern-day folk tale. Our material had to be organized, rechecked, and verified. Originally I had considered retaining an outsider to put our story into book form, but I soon realized that nobody could convey the intense feeling we had for the project better than Roxanne, who had been there with me through everything.

Much to my delight, Roxanne turned out to be an excellent writer, and since the completion of the first draft of this manuscript in 1982, she has gone on to have several short stories published by (of all people!) Bantam Books. The most recent was a story for *True Tales of the Unknown (Part III)—Beyond Reality*, edited by Sharon Jarvis, in which we attempted to condense some of our Amityville story into a short story called "Hellzapoppin' in Amityville." It was published in August 1991, and it marked the first time that a major publisher made any of our story available to the public. It was a great feeling, but it still left us unsatisfied and frustrated that we couldn't have the whole story told.

The Amityville Horror Conspiracy

During the course of writing this book, Roxanne became Mrs. Stephen Kaplan, and we celebrated our 13th Anniversary this month. She helped me to raise my two older children, who are now grown, and we now have two beautiful little girls of our own: Jennifer and Victoria. They have enriched our lives immeasurably, and we hope to pass on this quest for truth as a legacy to them.

All through the years friends, acquaintances and media contacts have always asked us the same question: Why? Why, Kaplan, do you persist in pursuing this case to expose it as a hoax? I have been told that lying to make money is "the American way"; I have been told that only a fool would pit himself against vast corporations such as Prentice Hall or American International Pictures (aka "Filmways"); I have been told that I should not waste my precious time and energy on something that most people already know is nonsense (an assumption that is not accurate.)

But most of all, I have been told that NO ONE CARES. The public WANTS to be lied to, my contacts tell me, they love to hear a good ghost story whether it's true or not.

It is true that I have not made a single penny of profit from exposing this case, though this was never my purpose to begin with. Yet, the frauds and phonies have collectively made millions. Even people like Hans Holzer, who latched onto the case after-the-fact, have used it for personal gain. Holzer, who originally told me in 1977 that he thought the Amityville Horror case was a lot of nonsense, has since come out with several paperbacks about the "horror" house. The first one purports to be nonfiction, but mixes the facts of the DeFeo murder case in with a lot of garbage about Indian burial grounds and ancient curses that he gleaned from a questionable psychic. His second book fails to even say anywhere on the cover whether it is fiction or nonfiction. It is, in actuality, a novel (and a poor one at that) which places completely fictitious characters in a real setting (the famous house), and relates a totally fictitious plot which is interwoven with oblique references to the real-life DeFeo case and Lutz story. This deliberate attempt to confuse the public is most offensive to me.

In 1982, the Lutzes came out with a book called *The Amityville Horror II*, by John G. Jones, in which they claim that the demons followed them 3,000 miles to California and tormented them from home to home, until an exorcism was performed on George. The "highlights" of this book are:

230

1: When "Jodie the Demon Pig" rides on the wing of the airplane to California (shades of Twilight Zone!), and

2: When Jodie drives a toy car around the Lutzes' new backyard. I kid you not!

In the forward by Mr. Jones, the Lutzes' alleged ordeal in Amityville is summarized as a preface to the new story. On page 14, Jones states, "It was, in every sense, a nightmare. Even today, the Lutzes have trouble deciding what really happened physically, and what occurred *only in their minds* (Italics mine). Dreams, physical attacks, apparitions, and imagination combined, conquered, and eventually shattered outside reality."

This seems to be an out-and-out admission that the Lutzes were out of touch with reality. Yet they go on to create an even more ludicrous story, again with the category of "Nonfiction" printed on this Warner Book.

In 1985, Jones and the Lutzes came out with *Amityville: The Final Chapter*, in which the evil now pursues the whole family around the world. Alas, this was *not* to be the "final chapter." In 1988, Jones and Lutz came out with a fourth book, *Amityville: The Evil Escapes*, in which everyone who purchased furniture from the auction at the Amityville house now had evil happening to them. This time we find Kathy Lutz's name missing from the copyright. We also find a serious contradiction in the classification of the book. The spine of the book reads, "Tudor Non-Fiction," but if you turn to the copyright page, you find this statement: "This is a work of fiction. The characters, names, incidents, places and dialogue are products of the author's imagination, and are not to be construed as real."

Often during my public lectures about Amityville, I pick an audience member to read this contradiction to the crowd. It never fails to get a gasp from the audience—no one can believe the nerve of a publisher to simultaneously claim that the story is both fiction *and* non-fiction.

It was around this same time (that the fourth book came out) that we received a phonecall from a bitter young man claiming to be the son of Kathy Lutz (George's step-son)—one of the boys who had lived in Amityville with George and Kathy during those infamous 18—28 days of terror. The caller said that he was willing to tell *his* side of how the Lutzes fabricated the story, but that he expected some financial remuneration. Young "Lutz" said that he needed the money

The Amityville Horror Conspiracy

for his mother Kathy, who he claimed was very ill and financially destitute, having been abused and then abandoned by George who allegedly ran off with all the profits from the books. When asked how he felt about the hoax, the young man would only say that he was tired of being used by George and that he wanted to get back at him and help his mother at the same time.

Roxanne and I of course expressed interest in talking with him, but when we told him that we could not afford to pay for the information, we never heard from the "Lutz boy" again.

Ed and Lorraine Warren also went on to profit from the hoax with numerous books, TV appearances and high-profile "demon" cases, including one case in which they supported a murderer who said, "the devil-made-me-do-it." When asked about the legitimacy of the Warrens, I like to hold up a newspaper article I have kept which shows Ed Warren exorcising a levitating, demonic Cabbage Patch doll!

Many books, too numerous to mention, have taken to referring to Amityville as though it were the "landmark case" for haunted houses. "More Terrifying than the Amityville Horror!" these covers proclaim, usually in bright red letters and sometimes even with demonic tails on the letters. One thing that really upsets me, as a teacher, is when I see the Amityville Horror story retold in children's *textbooks* and *workbooks*, such as the chapter, "House of Terror" in *Great Mysteries*, by Henry Billings and Melissa Stone, published by Steck-Vaughn, an educational publishing company. While they do throw in a line of disclaimer ("No one knows what really happened."), the inference that the kids make from the story is that it is a true historical occurrence. I have complained to these textbook publishers numerous times but they always cite their disclaimers as an excuse for pushing this trash on unsuspecting, naive children.

Hollywood is not to be outdone by the publishers. There have been at least seven movies with "Amityville" in the title, spanning the years 1979—1993. In "Amityville 3-D" (1983), also known as "Amityville: the Demon," there is a character, Dr. Elliot West of "the Institute for Psychic Research, State University, Long Island," who looks suspiciously like yours truly and who doesn't believe that there are demons in the Amityville house. (One of my organizations was listed in the Yellow Pages as "Psychic Research Institute.") Late in the movie this character is dragged down "into the pits of Hell," which is located in a well down in the basement, by a slimy, bug-eyed demon! My wife and my son were the only two people in the movie theater who were laughing so hard during this horrific scene that their 3-D glasses were falling off! The other patrons in the theater failed to see the humor and stared at my family as if we were nuts!

If you're wondering why the original author, Jay Anson, was not involved in the sequels, then you never heard the tragic news that Mr. Anson passed away in March of 1980. He died of a heart attack, the last of many he had suffered since pre–Amityville fame. Mr. Anson never got a chance to enjoy the millions he made from the "AH" and from his successful novel, *666*.

Mr. William Weber, to our knowledge, never gave another public interview about his part in the creation of the hoax after the one included in this book. That "Joel Martin Show" was taped shortly before Weber and the Lutzes settled out of court, with the stipulation that Weber no longer discuss the case in public.

Jim and Barbara Cromarty also settled out of court with the Lutzes and the publishers in their invasion of privacy suit, reportedly for almost a half a million dollars. This settlement prevented the Cromartys from discussing the case in public as well. They kept the house for a while longer, but eventually sold it after the tragic death of Barbara's oldest son to an undisclosed illness. I believe the sad memories along with the constant harassment from the tourists became just too much for them to take. We recently learned—from our plumber Dennis, of all people—that the Amityville house is now owned by relatives of the plumber's wife, and that they are very happy there and have experienced no strange phenomena. The tourist problem seems to have lessened, perhaps because of better fences and tighter security, but people still steal pieces of the picket fence.

A frightening thought—Ronald DeFeo, Jr. could be out on parole as early as the year 2000. He is said to have gotten married while in prison, and even fathered a child during conjugal visits. He has never revealed his motive for the murders, but he has publicly denounced the "horror" stories as recently as a few years ago when he was back on Long Island to ask for an appeal in court. Last year, 1994, marked the 20th anniversary of the murders.

People continue to ask me why I pursue this case. What has Stephen Kaplan gained from all this? Certainly not money. If I am for-

The Amityville Horror Conspiracy

tunate enough to receive any royalties at all from this book, it will mark the first time I have made a financial profit from the Amityville case. I have at times received small fees for lecturing on the hoax, but that amount was negligible compared to what I expended to research the case. But I never did it for money. I did it because I sincerely believe that the public has the right to know the truth about parapsychology.

How are you, the reader, to know the difference between the charlatans and the legitimate researchers if we in the field don't clean up our own field? Let's suppose for the moment that one of you out there has been experiencing an actual parapsychological phenomenon in your own home. Perhaps it is poltergeist activity; objects are moving about on their own and you are frightened and confused. Where do you turn? Assuming that you are able to find out the name of a psychic researcher in your area, how do you determine the legitimacy of this individual? A person does not have to be licensed to call themselves a parapsychologist.

Well, you could try to research your own problem by going to your local library. There you would be directed to the nonfiction, "occult" section where you would most likely find books on: the history of psychic research, telling you about J.B. Rhine's ESP experiments developed in the 1930's; lurid stories about witchcraft and Satanism; amusing anecdotes about haunted houses; and hordes of astrology books. A very limited selection, to say the least. And perhaps from this limited selection, you would choose *The Amityville Horror: A True Story* to compare to your own phenomenon.

This is deplorable. The idea of the "AH" being used as a standard casebook for haunting is totally abhorrent to me, but this is what has happened over the years. New cases are referred to by the media as "More Terrifying than the A.H." or "The NEW Amityville Horror Case."

So back to the perpetual question: WHOM DID IT REALLY HURT? So what if the Lutzes stretched the truth, or even lied? Business is business, and no one got hurt, right? WRONG! The field of parapsychology was hurt. All of the honest, decent researchers in the field were hurt. And this, in turn, hurts you, the public, because the quality of service available to you is lowered.

Who else was hurt by this story? Let's go back for a moment to Mr. Hans Holzer who wrote the book *Murder in Amityville* which was in turn the basis for the movie *Amityville II: The Possession*, a so-called "prequel" to *The Amityville Horror*. This story features a family called "Montelli," a thinly disguised DeFeo family. After experiencing strange phenomena in the house, Mr. Montelli proceeds to beat his wife and kids. "Sonny" (alias Ronald, Jr.) becomes possessed; he has incest with his sister (another vicious rumor that was spread about Ronald and his sister, Dawn), and finally kills his whole family with a shotgun. The priest in this story, against the wishes of his superiors, knocks out a police sergeant with his gun, runs off with "Sonny," the mass-murderer and attempts to exorcise him. At the house evil Indian spirits pour out of the "secret room" (this time a large, foul-smelling, insect-infested, tunnellike opening) and blood flows everywhere.

Roxanne and I once met the father and brother of the real Mrs. DeFeo after a lecture I gave on the hoax, and we know that their family is hurt terribly every time their dead relatives are defamed in this way. At the time we met, the two men thanked me for my efforts to expose the hoax, and expressed their anger and sorrow at the disrespect for their deceased family's memories. Hasn't this family been through enough? Must the media predators continue to spew out progressively more offensive versions of the tragic murders? Where is the justice when this family must suffer through lurid versions of their personal tragedy just so a few people can make a buck? Although legally you cannot slander or libel a dead person (i.e.: you can make up anything you want about them because they can't sue), it is morally as low as you can go to defame a family that is no longer around to defend themselves.

What about the Roman Catholic Church? Why do they remain silent unless forced into court, as Father Pecoraro was? Don't they object to images such as a priest hitting a policeman over the head with a gun and running off with a murderer? Their "ostrich" mentality has always been a major source of disappointment to me—a public denial of the Amityville case by the Church early on might have prevented it from going as far as it has.

Roxanne and I continue to believe that there are people out there, like yourself perhaps, who do still care about the truth. This manuscript has been rejected by so many publishers that we could wallpaper our home with rejection slips; they all find it fascinating but believe the public will not care to read about an "unhaunted house."

Still we have never given up in all these years, and were inspired by letters such as this one:

The Amityville Horror Conspiracy

Charles J. Coveleski
Hamburg, PA

Stephen & Roxanne Kaplan
Parapsychology Institute of America
Elmhurst, NY 11373

Dear Dr. Kaplan,

    Upon reading the chapter "Hellzapoppin' in Amityville" from the book *True Tales of the Unknown: Vol. III*, I first heard that the Amityville Horror story is a fraud. After reading your facts on how the Lutzes faked the series of events at 112 Ocean Ave., and your assessment of the house, I am thoroughly confused. The story in *True Tales: Vol. III* described the party you and your wife attended at the house with the new owners. I couldn't believe what I read in the media and from this book could be so very different.

    To further upset me, I recently bought a book entitled: *Amityville, The Nightmare Continues* by Robin Karl. This book leads the reader to believe that no one has lived in the house since the Lutzes moved out. That statement alone proved to me the total insincerity of this book. Please help me straighten these ideas out. I love to read about the unexplained (and explained). If you could, please help me get the full story of the Amityville "phenomenon."

    I have three questions I wish you to answer:

—Is the Amityville Story true?

—Does anyone occupy 112 Ocean Ave.?

—Has anything else unusual been reported about 112 Ocean Ave.?

    To conclude, I would just like to thank you for your time and to say that I really wish I could read your manuscript, *The Amityville Horror Hoax*. Please do not give up trying to get it published. You have one sale already!

Sincerely,

Charles J. Coveleski

We will not allow the truth to be buried and forgotten by time. Unless people in our field speak up, parapsychology will continually be misused by phonies trying to make money off of other people's misfortunes. We deplore those in our field who would use "devil-made-me-do-it" excuses to defend murderers, or take advantage of people experiencing legitimate psychic phenomena. We have been called dreamers, or even Don Quixotes for this attitude, but still we continue to fight the windmills—especially *The Amityville Horror* which has become, like Frankenstein's monster, a creation that will not die.

Though I have received some accolades for exposing the hoax (1980 Albert Einstein Award, 1982 Parapsychology Hall of Fame Award, etc.), my original goal to stop all the hoaxsters from making money has been a failure. The Amityville legend continues to grow all over the world, where the name of this sleepy Long Island town is now synonymous with the word "Horror." I'm sure the legend will outlive me by far.

The haunting of Amityville lies more in the falsehoods that were fabricated by the hoaxsters than in any ghosts. The irony is, I know that some cases of ghosts and haunting are real; I have experienced them first-hand. There is no need for fabrication, hallucinations, touched-up photographs or apostles of lies—the truth is, haunted houses do exist. But what was conjured up by the Lutzes, Anson, Weber, Holzer and others should only be classified as science fiction, or in some cases, merely *trash*.

There are those who felt we did not have a ghost of a chance to publish this book. To them, this long overdue volume is proof that it can and has been done. Our deepest thanks to everyone who has helped us to keep the faith over the long years, and a special thank you to all of you out there who still believe that TRUTH is the American way.

Dr. Stephen Kaplan
Roxanne Salch Kaplan
Queens, NY
February 1995

If you wish to write to the Kaplans at the Parapsychology Institute of America (P.I.A.), please send a stamped, self addressed envelope to:

P.I.A.
P.O. Box 252
Elmhurst, NY 11373

In Memoriam

On Friday, June 9th, shortly before this book went to press, my husband, Dr. Stephen Kaplan, passed away of a sudden heart attack. Although he was being treated for congestive heart failure, he had lately improved tremendously with medication and we both felt he was on the road to recovery. He was still working full time as a teacher for the New York City Board of Education and, in fact, finished a full day of work on the day of his death. He came home to his usual routine: changed clothes, checked his phone messages, watched some TV, then lay down to take a nap from which he never awoke.

Stephen's death comes as a shock to me and to our children, as well as to hundreds of close friends and family members who attended the services. I am sure there are thousands of his "fans" worldwide, who will miss him as well. The radio airwaves will never be the same on Halloween again, and hundreds of TV talk shows will be lacking their most unique guest. Stephen's close friend, Joel Martin, said to me that in losing Stephen, "We're not just losing a man, we're losing a force of nature."

Stephen spent the last week of his life excitedly making the final preparations for this book. After all these years, we were finally going to see our story published, and he was elated. He felt *The Amityville Horror Conspiracy* was his life's work, and next to family, it was the most important thing in the world to him. Among the notes I found on his desk was an idea for publicity for the book that referred to it as "H.I.S.—Honesty, Integrity, and Scholarship." These words that Stephen intended for our book can also be used to sum up his life, for he lived for those three ideals. If you have enjoyed reading our story, then you have already given Stephen the greatest tribute possible. Please spread his message to all your friends.

Stephen, the children and I know you are watching over us still. We love you and will miss you always. We will never forget the lessons of love you gave us.

—Roxanne Salch Kaplan
June 1995

Biography: Dr. Stephen Kaplan

Dr. Stephen Kaplan was born September 19, 1940 in the Bronx, New York City, N.Y. He graduated from the City College of New York with a Bachelor's degree in Sociology and a Master's degree in Communication Skills. He then earned a second Master's degree in Interdisciplinary Studies at the State University of N.Y. at Stony Brook, where he also received the Chi Epsilon Delta award as an instructor of parapsychology and occult sciences.

He has been a teacher in the New York City school system for over a quarter of a century, as well as an instructor of parapsychology in their Adult Education programs.

Dr. Kaplan has devoted many years to research of strange phenomena and their causes. In 1971 he founded the Parapsychology Institute of America and later that year, the Vampire Research Center. He is considered the "Father of Vampirology," and has been recognized around the world for his unique studies.

A true non–traditionalist, Dr. Kaplan obtained his Ph.D. in Sociology from Pacific College, a "university without walls," in 1977, after writing a thesis on the sociological implications of parapsychology.

Dr. Kaplan has been a guest on over 2,000 radio and TV programs, and has been interviewed by as many newspapers, magazines and journals. He is listed in *Who's Who in the World* (1991—1992), and *Who's Who in America* (1992—1993), and has been the recipient of numerous awards. Dr. Kaplan has also lectured at various colleges and public libraries across the United States and Canada, and has been a consultant to off–Broadway plays, movies and television programs.

Biography: Roxanne Salch Kaplan

Roxanne Salch Kaplan was born on October 7, 1953 in the Bronx, New York City, N.Y. She moved at the age of 4, with her family, to the suburban town of Centereach, in Suffolk County, Long Island, and lived there until her early twenties. Since that time she has been a resident of Queens, New York.

Roxanne began working with the Parapsychology Institute of America and the Vampire Research Center as a researcher and corresponding secretary in the early seventies. Since 1977, she has been the associate director of both organizations, as well as acting as travel coordinator for Dr. Stephen Kaplan's many personal appearances. Ms. Kaplan has also been a contributing author to the following books: *In Pursuit of Premature Gods and Contemporary Vampires* by Dr. Stephen Kaplan; *Vampires Are* by Dr. Stephen Kaplan as told to Carole Kane; and the *True Tales of the Unknown* series, Volumes I, II, and III, edited by Sharon Jarvis (published by Bantam Books).

Ms. Kaplan received an Associate in Science degree in Business Administration from Queensborough Community College in 1979; she continues to sing with the Queensborough Chorus and has performed with them at the nationally televised Liberty Weekend Closing Ceremonies, and with the Brooklyn Philharmonic Orcnesura at the World Stage Concert at Carnegie Hall. She is currently working toward a BA degree at Queens College, CUNY.

Roxanne and Stephen Kaplan were married in February 1982 at the historic Caroline Church in Setauket, Long Island. They reside in Queens with their two beautiful daughters.